# DEATH SENTENCE

## SHERYL BROWNE

Safkhet Publishing

First published in 2015 by Safkhet Select, Wilhelmshaven, Germany
Safkhet Select is an imprint of Safkhet Publishing
www.safkhetpublishing.com

Text Copyright 2015 by Sheryl Browne
Design Copyright 2015 Safkhet Publishing

Sheryl Browne asserts the moral right to be identified as the author of this work
under the Copyright, Designs and Patents Act 1988.

ISBN 978-3-945651-06-3

All characters and events in this publication,
other than those clearly in the public domain, are fictitious
and any resemblance to real persons, living or dead, is purely coincidental.

All rights reserved. No part of this publication may be reproduced,
stored in or introduced into a retrieval system, or transmitted, in any form or by any
means, including but not limited to electronic, mechanical, photocopying or recording,
without the prior written permission of the publisher.

Printed and bound by Lightning Source International

Typeset in Crimson and Zombie Control with Adobe InDesign

Find out more about Sheryl on www.sherylbrowne.com
and meet her on Facebook at
https://www.facebook.com/SherylBrowne.Author

Sheryl Browne           *author*
Kim Maya Sutton         *managing editor*
Rebecca Wojturska       *proofreader*
William Banks Sutton    *copy editor*

 The colophon of Safkhet is a representation of the ancient Egyptian goddess of wisdom
and knowledge, who is credited with inventing writing.
Safkhet Publishing is named after her because the founders met in Egypt.

For my family for supporting me
and all those who read and share their love of books
~ thank you!

# DEDICATION

I owe a huge debt of gratitude to Safkhet Publishing, who not only commissioned me to write my first book, having read and loved my writing, but opened an imprint for three further novels. Despite my determination, I was at a point then where I wondered whether continuing to pursue my dream was sheer self-indulgent madness. Safkhet believed in me, giving me huge impetus to keep writing. My first book, Recipes for Disaster – Sexilicious Romantic Comedy Combined with Fab, Fun Recipes – was published in 2012 and shortlisted for the Festival of Romance Innovation in Romantic Fiction award. Since then, I've just kept writing. My writing has of course grown as I've explored new genres. I wasn't sure Safkhet would take The Edge of Sanity, but … they loved it. I'm hoping their faith was well placed as the book does seem to be getting some excellent reviews, one fabulous such review recently on Best Selling Crime Thrillers where the book sits proudly alongside such hugely talented authors as, Harlan Coben, Lee Child, Patricia Cornwell. To my absolute delight, the book also recently featured as a Crime Thriller Hound Book of the Week, who said, "Sheryl Browne really delivers with her first thriller, a powerful and emotional read". Needless to say, I am thrilled.

I am now doubly thrilled to be bringing you my next book, Death Sentence, the title of which was suggested by a chief constable, who was also kind enough to offer me some advice around forensics and police procedural. I can't name him in case he arrests me! However, he knows who he is and I'd like to offer him my heartfelt thanks. Thank you, too, to all the awesome professional book bloggers and readers who have been kind enough to read my books and post reviews.

I am humbled. Writing is who I am. I wouldn't be here without you.

# CHAPTER ONE

Rebecca looked up from her laptop as Matthew dashed into the kitchen, looking as deprived of sleep as when he'd fallen into bed late last night. Noting the dark shadows under his eyes, the perpetual worry that seemed etched into his brow, Rebecca really wished he wouldn't push himself so hard, as if he alone could make the streets safe. But then, throwing himself into his work was his way of coping with his demons, Rebecca knew.

'Have you had any more thoughts about Ashley?' she asked, as he grabbed a coffee. Now probably wasn't a good time; Matthew had already received an urgent call from his detective sergeant, but they had to make their decision soon. It wouldn't be easy. They were both aware of what a profoundly life-changing commitment it would be, the emotional implications of taking on a child who was a stranger to them, despite the family ties. Ashley was older than Lily would have been, but the wounds of their daughter's loss were still painfully raw.

Matthew took a sip of his coffee. 'Some,' he said, glancing uncertainly at her, his velvet brown eyes a kaleidoscope of emotion, his grief, which was always palpable, but which he worked hard at hiding. His frustration at not being able to save Ashley's mother, which was ridiculous when it was obvious his sister was hell-bent on self-destruction.

Rebecca understood his hesitation. It was a huge decision for both of them. In her mind though, at thirteen years old, if his niece was going to survive her dysfunctional childhood and learn to cope with life, in care was not where she needed to be.

'You know I'm OK with it, don't you?' she reminded him, gently.

Matthew glanced at her again, that same curious expression Rebecca so often saw in his eyes. As if he couldn't quite grasp why she hadn't fallen apart after Lily and the subsequent miscarriage. God knew, there were times when Rebecca had felt close. So many times, when her mind played over that fateful second Lily's hand had slipped from her own; when she would hear the impact, dull, metallic, final. In the bleak, listless weeks that followed the accident, she'd simply ceased wanting to be. Black, empty nothingness was what she'd felt, what she'd craved. Not even wanting Matthew to comfort her, she'd just wanted to curl up on her own in the dark where life couldn't touch her. She hadn't let go though. She'd held on, by her fingernails it had seemed sometimes, because eventually she'd realised that the baby growing inside her would need her. For Matthew, too, who had eventually reached his own lowest ebb, broke down and wept in her arms. Only once though. He cried until Rebeca had thought his heart would break, but, after that night, when they'd lain together limbs entwined, grieving the loss of Lily and the baby that had given them new hope, it was as if Matthew had shut part of himself away. The part that was emotionally vulnerable.

Knowing that, knowing him, a man who drove himself to work harder when he was hurting, a man determined to fix the hurts of the world when he could never hope to, Rebecca had stayed strong. Aware that Matthew might be the one to fall, somehow, she'd survived. And now, she suspected, but didn't say for fear of swaying him unfairly, she would stay strong still, this time for Ashley, who clearly desperately needed someone to simply just love her. Rebecca could do that, she was sure.

Watching her studying him, seeing the determination in her eyes, Matthew despaired of himself, his own inability to be as positive as she was. How many women, he wondered, having gone through what Becky had, would still be standing, let alone considering taking on a child she hardly knew: his niece, not hers. A child abandoned by her own mother, who preferred the company of the bottle. Matthew sighed inwardly, still not able to understand how his sister could have turned her back on her own daughter. He wanted to take Ashley. At least, he thought he did. Who else was there, if not him? The truth was, though, he was scared. Scared for himself— how could he not see Lily every time his eyes fell on another young girl wandering around the house? More scared, though, for Becky. Could she cope? Truly? Seeing another child in Lily's place?

Instantly assaulted by the flashback he tried constantly to block out, Matthew closed his eyes, seeing with absolute clarity the quiet pleading in Lily's. She'd been silently begging him, her daddy, to fix things, as he'd cradled her in his arms. He hadn't been able to fix it. Matthew swallowed back the pain and anger that burned steadily inside him. He *should* have been there, at home, on time, not pouring over some case that would probably never be solved. They might never have taken that route to the cinema, might never have left the house at that time, if he'd been back, as he should have been. Instead, even knowing deep down in his gut that that bastard Patrick Sullivan might make good his threats, he'd been late.

*How?* He asked himself, as he did at least a thousand times a day. How could any God in heaven be so cruel as to snatch away the life of a child in front of her mother's eyes? Rebecca had never known about Sullivan. Imagining that someone had deliberately ploughed a car into her innocent daughter ... Matthew wasn't sure that wouldn't destroy her, no matter how hard she fought to stay strong. And then, with no evidence against Sullivan, Matthew had decided to keep the information from her. As far as Rebecca knew it was a hit-and-run, assailant unknown. Matthew knew though—and he'd made himself a promise the day he'd watched his daughter's life slip away—one way or another Sullivan was going to pay.

Tugging in a tight breath, Matthew buried the memory, which was the only way he knew how to cope with it, then smiled as Rebecca, ever intuitive of his mood, walked across to him. 'Did I ever tell you how much I love you, Detective Adams?' she said, hooking her arms around his neck and gazing knowingly up at him.

'Frequently.' Mathew swallowed. She did tell him, often, but he wasn't sure how she could. Why she was still with a man who hadn't been there when she'd needed him and then emotionally missing for months thereafter?

'So? What about Ashley?' she urged him.

Still, Matthew was hesitant. But then, what kind of a future would the girl have if they didn't take her? Chances were, coming out of care, she'd end up following in her mother's footsteps, abusing alcohol, homeless, spending her nights on canal embankments, in subways, freezing cold half the time and not even knowing or caring where. Her days begging funds to fuel her addiction ... No, he couldn't let that happen. Then there was Becky. She must feel so lonely, rattling around this place on her own. Finally moving into the barn conversion, renovated with a family in mind, only to lose their children, had been the cruellest twist of all. He'd thought he'd been doing the right thing investing some of his father's insurance pay-out in a property outside the city, yet close enough to ensure all amenities. It had been a mistake. The place was too isolated, half of it still a building site since the builders had gone bust, no neighbours— nor was there likely to be any in the foreseeable future, which could only exacerbate Becky's isolation.

'I'll make some calls today.' He finally made a decision and prayed it was the right one.

Rebecca blinked, surprised.

'Really?' she asked, her wide aquamarine eyes peppered with that same haunting vulnerability Matthew had seen when they'd lost Lily, when she'd miscarried the baby she'd so desperately wanted.

'As soon as I've attended this call-out, I promise.' Was it possible she really did want this? That in some God-moves-in-mysterious-ways way that it might help fill the void in their lives? Matthew hoped so. Hoped that they were sufficiently prepared to deal with the baggage that would surely come with a teenager starved of natural parental affection.

'Unless you get side-tracked, of course,' she said, giving him a reproachful look.

As she had every right to, because he did get side-tracked, often. Not this time he wouldn't. 'I'll make the calls,' Matthew assured her, notching her chin up with his forefinger and locking his gaze firmly on hers.

Raising her eyebrows, Rebecca smiled amusedly. 'Ooh, masterful,' she teased.

'I'll ring you as soon as I know anything.' Matthew circled her waist, drawing her closer. 'And if it's masterful you want, I think I can manage that too.'

'Oh, yes?' Rebecca held his gaze. 'Does this mean I'm on a promise, Detective Inspector?'

'Definitely.' Matthew's mouth curved into a smile. If there was anything to thank God for, he supposed it was that, after months of living in their own private hell, lying side by side yet poles apart in the bedroom—mainly because of the ghosts that relentlessly came to haunt him, the guilt—they'd at last found each other again.

'You need to go.' Rebecca stood on tiptoes, her infinitely kissable, pillow-soft lips brushing his, leaving Matthew wondering if he couldn't delay another five minutes, ten possibly? Closing his eyes, he leaned in to her kiss and …… cursed as his phone beeped again in his pocket.

'Damn.'

'Sorry, I, er …' Shrugging apologetically, he reached for it.

'Duty calls, I know.' Rebecca sighed pseudo-despairingly and rolled her eyes. 'Go,' she urged him, 'before I'm tempted to drag you upstairs and handcuff you to the headboard.'

'Now there's a thought.' Giving her a mischievous wink, Matthew planted a kiss on her forehead.

'You will remember to ring me, though, won't you?' Rebecca asked, reaching to straighten his askew tie.

'Scout's honour,' Matthew assured her as he checked his message. 'If we're both still good with it, we could make an appointment to see her at the care home. How does that sound?'

'Like I might definitely be making good my promise with the handcuffs,' Rebecca assured him, messing up his tie again, as she tugged him towards her to press a rather firmer kiss on his lips.

'You're a manipulator, Mrs Adams.' Matthew gave her a mock scowl, wishing to God he had been able to be there for her, been able to give all of himself. Matthew wasn't sure he'd ever forgive himself for that. Post-Traumatic Stress Disorder, the psychiatrist had labelled it. Selfish is what Matthew called it.

'I know.' Rebecca trailed a finger down his lapel. 'And don't you just love it, Detective Inspector?'

'Depends on what you have in mind.' Matthew smiled, glancing again at his beeping phone. His heart sank fast as he read the message from his DS, who'd now arrived at a possible murder crime scene. A young female, apparently. Possibly a known informant. Matthew's gut clenched in cold apprehension.

'Later,' he said, making sure to keep his smile in place as he turned to head through the open lounge to the front door.

'Have a good day; keep safe.' Rebecca followed him. 'Have you got your inhaler?' she asked, checking up on him, as she always did. Matthew hated the thing, but he tried not to mind. A radiographer by profession and a worrier by nature, she was bound to remind him, he supposed.

'Yes, I've got my inhaler.' He pulled open the front door and patted his jacket pocket, indicating it was where it should be. 'See you later.'

'I'll be here. Love... —'... *you*, Rebecca finished, as the door closed behind him.

Rebecca felt it immediately. It was almost palpable, the deafening silence of a house without children. A beautiful house, three-quarters of a mile from the village school, a couple of miles from High Wycombe and access to the motorway, tastefully decorated with rescued pieces and white walls, it was perfect; and empty.

Her bare feet sounded loud on the natural wood floor as she padded across the lounge, debating what she should do before she went to work. She had too much time on her hands. That was the trouble. Time she didn't particularly want to fill with housework. Perhaps she should consider going full time at the hospital? They could certainly use her with one radiographer off on maternity leave. But then, she'd need to be part-time to make space in her life now for Ashley.

Swallowing, Rebecca hugged her arms about herself and walked across to her laptop. Selecting her photo album, she found the up-to-date photo they'd requested the care home to send them. Please, *please* let it work out, she prayed, looking back at the young girl looking yearningly out at her. She wasn't Lily. Nothing could ever replace their little girl in their hearts. Sometimes, when she was alone, Rebecca was sure she could hear her laughing. Or worse, crying. Heartbreakingly, sometimes she could hear her singing and gyrating along to some X Factor girl band pop song. Matthew had suggested they move, but Rebecca wasn't ready to, not yet. She wanted to be reminded, to hold the memories. She also wanted to hold onto the feel of her— something she wasn't quite sure Matthew would understand—the smell of Lily, that special smell that bonds mother and child together, and which seemed to permeate every pore of the house,.

Ashley had never had that bond as far as Rebecca knew. She was alone, on her own in a world she was ill-equipped to ever function in. She was also family. With her ebony hair, brushed to a silken sheen, and almond-shaped eyes the colour of rich cognac, she could almost be Matthew's child. She was beautiful. Fragile, yet from the set of her jaw, strong, Rebecca sensed. Heaviness settled in her chest, and she found herself physically hurting for the girl, who must feel so alone. Poor thing, thirteen years old and already she'd been abandoned, abused and neglected, starved of affection, how heart-breaking was that?

More so for Matthew, who'd tried so hard to help his sister, searching for her in places that most people wouldn't feel safe. He'd persuaded her home twice, securing places for her in rehab. Twice she'd left again, her craving for alcohol stronger than her craving to see her daughter grow.

Still, he searched for her, trailing from London to Birmingham after her, though he, above most people, knew in his heart she could only be helped if she wanted to help herself. He was a good man, a man hurting. Rebecca wished he'd share that hurt more with her instead of channelling it into his work. She swallowed back another tight lump in her throat. Then almost shot out of her skin as Matthew, who'd obviously realised there was something he'd forgotten before driving off, shouted, 'Ditto, always,' through the letterbox.

\*\*\*\*

Matthew pulled in a terse breath, as he climbed out of his car. 'Is it Brianna?' he asked his detective sergeant, who walked towards him from the short alley that led from the back of the Thai Restaurant.

'No official ID yet, but ... ,' DS Steve Ingram hesitated. 'It looks like it, yes.'

'*Fuck!* Matthew grated, knowing what *no official ID* meant.

'Right.' He blew out a sigh and steeled himself to walk back with Steve to see for himself.

*Brianna Phillips?* Matthew couldn't believe it. He'd only spoken to her yesterday. Scared witless, refusing to say why, she'd come to him and asked him outright if he could offer her protection in exchange for certain information. Videos, she'd hinted, directed by Patrick scum-of-the-earth Sullivan, Matthew was willing to bet. He'd been out of prison, what, six months? And he was as free as a bird to do what he liked, to whoever he liked, pedalling his crap, coercing underage kids to star in those videos. For what he'd done to Lily, the bastard should have been banged up forever. Or, better still, met an excruciatingly painful demise while he was in there.

*Parasitic scum.* Matthew's jaw tensed, his lungs tightened, as he tried, and failed, to still the images that played over and over, his child, her eyes silently pleading, the light in them finally fading, his world disintegrating. Before then, the goading look on Sullivan's face when he'd paid him an official visit in prison. Sullivan's brother under investigation, running the show while he was locked up, Sullivan hadn't liked it.

'How's that pretty young wife of yours, DI Adams? Pregnant again, isn't she?' he'd enquired idly, blowing smoke circles into the air like he hadn't a care in the world. 'Congratulations, Adams. Didn't think you had it in you.'

Matthew swallowed back the bile in his throat, picturing how Sullivan had casually stubbed out his cigarette and leaned forwards.

'Give her my regards, won't you?' he'd said, his eyes as black as molasses and swimming with pure evil. 'I would do it myself, but I'm a bit busy ... banged up ... in here.'

It *had* been a threat. Matthew had been sure of it. A threat the murdering psychopath had eventually attempted to have carried out. And Matthew had been able to do nothing about it. The bastard was out now though, wasn't he, no bars to provide him an alibi. *Not for long, Sullivan. Not for long.* If it was the last thing he did, Matthew aimed to make sure Sullivan was taken off the streets, by whatever means.

*Dammit.* He should have done something more when Brianna had come to him. There was no way he'd been able to make promises, offer her a safe house, but he should have done something, found her some kind of accommodation, stayed on it, before it came to this. Matthew swallowed again, hard.

'Visual ID not possible then?' he asked, tugging his collar loose.

'Afraid not.' Steve shot him a wary glance. He didn't offer details. He didn't need to. He knew Matthew would be filling in the blanks. Matthew was, graphically. Closing his eyes, he counted silently. At five, he managed to get a tenuous grip on his emotions.

'Timing?' he asked, feeling the abject sense of failure he always did when one of these girls turned up drugged and beaten, raped, or worse.

'Not sure yet. Last night at a guess,' Steve offered. 'The body wasn't discovered until they opened up shop and, er ...' he stopped and gauged Matthew cautiously again.

'Put the trash out?' Matthew finished sardonically.

Steve puffed out a breath and nodded slowly. 'Pathologist and scene of crime officers are present,' he went on, professionally following protocol, outwardly calm. Not detached though. Matthew eyed his colleague—a rugby-playing brute of a bloke— and noted the faint odour of vomit sympathetically. New to the squad, Steve was what, twenty-eight? Keen. *Corruptible?* Matthew wondered. The man was about to get married. He'd met his fiancée, a stunning girl, and judging by the love-struck look on Steve's face when he'd introduced her, she was enough to keep him content at night even fantasising about her. Matthew guessed Steve wouldn't be looking elsewhere. It was an iron-willed man or woman who didn't succumb in some way to the seedy world of sex and drugs, though, sometimes getting sucked in, sometimes getting psychologically screwed. Detachment was a requisite part of the job if you wanted to sleep nights. Matthew only wished he could attain it.

Sighing, he braced himself as he headed around to the back of the restaurant. It was her. Matthew noted the bleeding heart tattoo on the girl's upper arm immediately. Gulping back the sour taste in his mouth, he took in the lifeless, broken body of the teenager in a succession of sordid, stomach-churning snapshots. Face down, her head twisted to one side, she was almost unrecognisable. Her eyes swollen like two overripe plums. Her nose and lips split. Right arm, fractured, judging by the impossible angle. One shoe missing. Clothes ... in brutal disarray. Matthew glanced away.

Nodding a greeting at one of the SOCOs taking requisite photos of the surrounding area, he noticed a fat bluebottle buzzing over the nondescript grey bin the girl was sprawled in front of. His stomach turning over and a distinct wheeze in his chest, Matthew tried hard not to breathe in the pungent stench of rotting oriental food and dead flesh.

'I take it this is our crime scene?' He turned back to the pathologist, who was busy making an external examination of the body.

'Judging by lividity,' the pathologist indicated the dark purple discoloration on the underside of the girl's torso, 'I'd say, yes.'

Matthew nodded. 'Do we have a time?' he asked, nurturing a faint hope that there might have been witnesses.

'From the body temperature and degree of rigor mortis, I'd say post mortem interval is about eight hours.'

'Cause of death?' He glanced at the deceased girl's eyes, now grey, opaque and empty, trying to remember what colour they were.

'Asphyxiation, ligature.'

After suffering what kind of humiliation and terror, Matthew wondered, nausea sweeping over him.

'Can we rush this one through, Nicky?' He shrugged hopefully, knowing she was probably backed up.

The woman studied him for a second, and then, 'I'll do my best,' she offered. Obviously, she'd picked up on the hint of desperation Matthew had heard in his own voice.

Matthew nodded his thanks, outwardly trying for composed, inwardly, broiling with hot, impotent anger.

'Anything under the fingernails?' he asked, praying there might be something they could go on.

'Looks like they're clean,' she said, going back to her painstaking evidence collecting. 'Very clean.' She glanced meaningfully at him again. 'The autopsy might yield something, but I wouldn't count on it.'

'No, nor would I.' Matthew smiled bitterly, pinching the bridge of his nose with his thumb and forefinger. God really would have to be in his heaven, wouldn't he, he thought cynically, for there to be enough DNA present to give him the bastard on a plate. Clearly, the assailant had cleaned up after himself. Clearly also, he'd known he wouldn't be interrupted, meaning his minions had been on lookout or, possibly, doing his cleaning for him.

The pathologist paused in her bag-sealing and vialing and sat back on her haunches. 'Matthew,' she asked, 'are you okay?'

Matthew's gaze flicked back to her face. Nicky had been the pathologist in attendance after Lily, ergo was one of the few people who would guess that Matthew was very much not okay; that this kind of crap got to him, more and more every day.

'Yep, never better.' He smiled tightly, glossing it over, because it was simply the only way he could get through it. 'Ring me, will you, Nicky?'

Nicky nodded and went back to her task as he turned away.

'Sir?' his DS followed him, as Matthew headed back to his car, his stride purposeful, belying the sinking helplessness he felt inside.

'Matthew?' Steve called again. 'Shall I stick around?' Oversee the preliminary examination until removal of the body, he meant, always keen to follow rules and do things exactly by the book.

Sometimes, though, when murdering scumbags walked around scot-free, flouting the law, Matthew couldn't help thinking that rules were made to be broken.

'Do that.' He nodded despondently over his shoulder. 'And keep me posted, particularly as to the whereabouts of the missing shoe.'

Dragging a hand over his neck, Matthew pondered as he walked, tried to get his head around someone as devoid of feeling as Sullivan calmly checking he'd left no evidence. But then, the bastard has always been meticulous, making sure to cover himself when he'd decided he needed to teach people a lesson. Concocting alibis if ever one of his girls found courage enough to point the finger at him, alibis mostly provided by other young girls too terrified not to lie for him. Even the piece of scum's wife lied for him, obviously preferring to turn a blind eye than give up the luxurious lifestyle her husband's businesses afforded her.

*Vermin!* Matthew's fist hit the brick wall without process of forethought. His chest heaving, he counted silently in an attempt to control his fury, studied his stinging knuckles as globules of rich, red, fresh blood popped through the wounded flesh. *Focus*, he warned himself, groping ineffectually for some kind of detachment, trying hard to still the almost overwhelming desire to go directly to the 'respectable' Surrey home of the shit-dealing, pimping bastard who'd prostituted that young girl, abused her, used her, raped her probably, and—as sure as the sun rose in the east—murdered her. Patrick Sullivan. Pat to his friends, Pit-bull to those who crossed him, the man would never let go a grievance.

Matthew wasn't about to either.

# CHAPTER TWO

Rebecca was searching for a file in ultrasound when she heard her co-workers *oohing* and *cooing*, and cries of, 'Oh, isn't he adorable!'

*Melanie popped in from her maternity leave,* Rebecca guessed, *brought her brand new baby to show off to everyone.* Keen to get a glimpse too, painful though it would undoubtedly be, Rebecca retrieved the file she'd been searching for and headed back around reception.

'Becks!' Melanie beamed, coming towards her, her precious bundle in her arms.

'Mel! How're you doing? You look absolutely fabulous.' Forcing back the familiar sadness that washed over her whenever she saw a woman radiating that special kind of happiness only a new mum could, Rebecca smiled back and pulled Melanie into a hug. 'Ooh, I've missed you.'

'Me too. And the gossip,' Mel said. 'Intelligent conversation's a bit difficult with someone who doesn't do much more than gurgle. Mind you, he makes up for it with his gorgeousness, don't you, little man, hmm?' She held her bundle up for inspection.

'Oh, he's a heartbreaker, aren't you, sweetie?' Rebecca looked him over approvingly. He was too. Reaching to brush his baby-soft cheek with the back of her hand, Rebecca's heart physically ached with longing as she gazed down at him. He was perfect. With his softly curled eyelashes and adorable cupid lips, he really was beautiful. Laughing, she reached for a tiny flailing hand, as he stretched and yawned, his baby-blue eyes clear with the innocence of childhood. *A fragile new soul,* Rebecca thought awestruck, *untouched, untroubled, untarnished by life.*

*It's Matthew's job to try to make sure they were never tarnished by some of the sordidness out there,* Rebecca reminded herself, and tried not to mind that he still hadn't rung her. The nature of his job meant he worked long, unpredictable hours. She'd known that when she'd gone out with him. She'd married him anyway, because she'd loved him, utterly, all of the man who was so obviously caring of other people, as frustrating as he might occasionally be, more so since Lily. Now, when he was involved in a case, he was literally immersed in it, to the exclusion of everything else. He did try to make up for his workaholic tendencies lately, though: booking restaurant tables, bringing her flowers, delivering them personally on special occasions. Rebecca smiled inwardly, recalling how he'd turned up with arms full of red roses for their anniversary, right here in radiography. He'd got the wrong day. Melanie had enlightened him as to the reason for Rebecca's bemused expression. Hugely embarrassed, he'd simply shrugged and smiled what Mel called his killer shy smile. Matthew had always had a ready smile. Still he tried, but the underlying sadness was always there now, etched deep into his eyes.

'Talking of heartbreakers,' Mel cut through Rebecca's thoughts, 'how's that gorgeous husband of yours?'

'He's fine,' Rebecca answered, though it was obvious to anyone who knew him that Matthew still carried his guilt over Lily's death around like a stone in his heart. As if his being there by her side that evening could have prevented the accident.

Mel raised her eyebrows. 'Really?'

'Really.' Rebecca smiled. She knew her friend was fishing out of caring not nosiness. Mel had been there for her when she'd gone into too-premature labour and lost little Mia. The much-needed friend who'd held her hand until Matthew had made it to the hospital.

'No gossip to share there, I suppose?' Mel probed hopefully.

*Wondering whether I have any news in the baby-making department,* Rebecca guessed. 'No, nothing to report,' she said and mentally crossed her fingers. Mel would be furious with her, but, for fear of jinxing things, Rebecca wasn't ready to share her news yet.

Mel knitted her brow sympathetically. 'But you are trying?'

'Frequently.' Rebecca assured her, thought in truth, they hadn't been until recently. They'd held each other, woken sometimes in the same position they'd fallen asleep in, Matthew's arms wrapped tightly around her. Making love though hadn't come naturally, as it had always done previously, each of them feeling that somehow it was a betrayal of their grief, of their children.

'You'd better go and sort your little man out.' Pushing her sad thoughts aside in light of Mel's obvious joy, she nodded at the baby, who was getting a bit fractious and about to make his presence known.

Mel rolled her eyes. 'He needs a feed. He's just like his dad, permanently ravenous.'

She gathered him to her. 'Are you going to take his niece in, Becks?' she asked the question she'd obviously been burning to, as Rebecca walked with her towards the exit.

'I think so,' Rebecca answered cautiously, the decision still having not yet been finalised. 'Matthew seems uncertain. I'm not sure he's convinced I can cope, but I'd like to, yes.'

'You should.' Nestling her baby in one arm, Mel turned to wrap her free arm around Rebecca and squeezed her into a hug.

'Seeing how you were with Lily...,' she paused awkwardly. 'Well, if ever little man needed a foster mum, you'd be my first choice. You were both such great parents, Becks. It breaks my heart, it really does.'

Rebecca's breath hitched in her chest. 'Don't tempt me. I might steal him.' Her smile now a little forced, she gave Mel a hard hug back and then planted a kiss on the little man's peachy cheek.

Waving Mel off, Rebecca kept her smile fixed in place, and then headed quickly for the loo, where she quietly gave in to the tears which tended to sneak up on her unexpectedly, tears for Lily, her lost baby, for herself. This time though, she realised, she was crying for Matthew, who really had been a great parent, if only she could make him believe that he was.

※※※※

Brianna's mother broke down as they left. Pausing on the drive of the house, a middle-class, unspectacular house, home to the child her parents had given birth to, nurtured, obviously cared for, until the age of sixteen, a child now lying stone-cold dead on a mortuary slab, Matthew heard her heaving sobs as the front door closed.

It was the realisation that she'd be lying there alone that got to the father, caused him to excuse himself from the lounge, to try—and fail—to supress his own grief when the kitchen door closed behind him. Matthew had guessed what was going through the man's mind. He could never hold her, comfort her, talk to her, he could never, ever make things all right for his little girl ever again: take back the argument, unsay the heated words that caused her to leave. They'd both been expecting the worst, Matthew knew. Most parents of runaways lived with that fear eating away at them day and night, day after tortuous day. They wouldn't have processed the finality of it yet. God help them when they did. It would haunt them for the rest of their lives.

Sighing, Matthew ran a hand wearily over his neck.

'No news is better than *that* news,' he told Steve, pulling his ringing mobile from his pocket as they walked back to the car.

'Adams?' he answered distractedly, and then, realising it was Becky, squeezed his eyes closed. *Hell!*

'Becky, hi. No, I didn't. Sorry, I got caught up in something and I ... I forgot. Sorry.'

13

Veering away from the driver's side, he fished his car-keys from his pocket and tossed them to Steve, indicating he should take the wheel while Matthew took his call.

'Oh, Matthew!' Rebecca sounded disappointed.

'Sorry,' Matthew repeated, climbing in the passenger side. 'Something needed my full attention. A young girl …' He stopped, kneading his temple with his free hand. Rebecca would be sympathetic when he shared as much as he could. She always was. She didn't need the gory detail, though. She didn't need to feel the parents' heartbreak, which she undoubtedly would.

Rebecca didn't answer immediately. Matthew heard her long intake of breath, and then, 'Bad, I take it?' she probed gently.

'On a scale of one to ten, eleven,' Matthew admitted, grateful for one thing in the shit-fest his life had become after Lily. That God had seen fit to spare Becky. She'd rescued him in the weeks after the funeral: literally prised the booze from his hand, led him upstairs, and just lay with him, her warm body up close, her limbs like a soft blanket around him. He hadn't shed a tear until then. The tears had come that night though. *Christ* and some. He'd sobbed his heart out, right there in her arms. Without Becky, he might well have gone the same route he had when his father had decided life was no longer worth living: haunting the pubs, staying as long as he could after hours, stumbling home, falling unconscious into merciful oblivion, until the harsh light of reality jolted him sober. He wasn't sure he'd know how to be without her. He wouldn't want to be. He loved her. So much his heart physically ached at the thought of having almost lost her.

'I'm on my way back to the office now,' he said, grateful, yet again, that Becky seemed to be steering him to where he needed to be emotionally. 'I promise I'll ring you back within the hour.'

'*Hmm?*' Rebecca didn't sound convinced.

'If I don't, I'll give in gracefully to what you suggested earlier,' Matthew offered, glancing warily at Steve, lest he get the gist.

'You're earmarked for the handcuffs anyway,' Rebecca replied smartly. 'And, as things stand, I can't promise to be gentle with you.'

Matthew laughed. 'Um, you might want to rethink that one, Becky.'

'One hour,' Rebecca replied, a mock-warning edge to her voice. 'I'll be waiting.'

Matthew nodded sombrely. 'Yes ma'am.'

'Goodbye, DI Adams.'

'Goodbye, Mrs Adams.'

'Oh, and, by the way, I love you,' Rebecca said quickly, 'though God knows why.'

'Ditto,' Matthew said quietly, 'but without the God knows why bit.'

Smiling, genuinely, despite the events of the day, Matthew pocketed his mobile, glancing again at Steve, as he did. 'Repeat any of this and you're demoted, Detective Sergeant,' he imparted, noting the smirk playing at his colleague's mouth.

'Yes, boss.' Steve straightened his face. 'Fancy anything,' he asked, as they drove by Eddie's Expresso Bar. 'Mocha? Latte? Leather whip to go with the handcuffs?' He nodded at the sex shop next door.

\*\*\*\*

True to his word, Matthew made the relevant calls, reporting back to Becky that, subject to a successful introductory meeting and the usual protocol, they'd got the green light. There was something else he needed to do though, before seeing Ashley, who—dragged from bedsit to squat halfway around the country—was so young when he last saw her, probably wouldn't even remember him. He needed to try to find Kristen again. Try to find out whether his sister was capable of remembering she had a daughter.

After driving the hour and a half to Birmingham—the last place he'd found her sleeping rough—Matthew tried her usual patch first, the corner of a landing on the grease-stained steps leading from the bus station to a city shopping centre. Kristen wasn't there. Another statistic had claimed her space, curled up in his sleeping bag, his well-cared for dog curled up beside him inviting more sympathy than he did.

'Spare some change, mate?' the guy asked, as Matthew approached him. His look wasn't hopeful, more resigned. Bland almost, any vitality he might have had in his eyes dulled; by booze, Matthew guessed, noting the several empty cider cans to his side.

Matthew offered him a short smile. 'I'm looking for someone,' he said.

The guy recoiled in an instant, shuffling further into his corner, assuming he was the law, as Matthew guessed he would. 'My sister,' he elaborated, drawing Kristen's photo from his inside pocket.

The guy looked warily up at him and then down to the photo Matthew held out in front of him. Perusing it for a second, he dragged his hand under his nose and shook his head. Matthew had guessed he would do that, too. If he had seen her, he probably wouldn't recall.

15

Chances were, if she'd shared a shop doorway with him, he wouldn't remember. The photo was of a fresh-faced, seventeen-year-old. Not Kristen. Not who she was now.

Sighing, Matthew nodded his thanks and reached into his pocket again, this time for money, though it went against the grain. Might be the guy would buy food, might be he'd spend his take for the day on booze. The dog would get fed, though. Matthew was certain of that. He bent down, patted the animal, and moved on to his next port of call. One of many he'd make, and possibly come up empty-handed. He had to try, though. Had to be sure in his mind that, in bringing Ashley into his home, he was doing the right thing. Because, once she was there, once she was settled, Matthew was damn sure he wouldn't let her go back.

An hour later, he got lucky. Calling into a charity-run initiative helping rough sleepers, he learned that Kristen had taken advantage of their drop in service, giving her access to such basic needs as food, shelter, showers, sleeping bags. She hadn't taken advantage of any of the alcohol recovery or mental health services, but at least she was taking care of herself in some shape or form. That was a far more preferable scenario to one of many Matthew had hardly dared envisage. Asking around, he eventually found himself on the canal towpath, checking likely places: benches located within walking distance of supermarkets, the long flight of locks leading into the city, the bridges that provided sparse protection from the elements.

Kristen was huddled under one of them, her back to the wall, her knees drawn up, a one-litre bottle of cider nestled between them. Her hair cropped short, Matthew hadn't recognised her immediately. But for the sound of her voice, the animated hand gestures as she'd talked to the bleary-eyed guy to her side, putting the world to some sort of alcohol-obscured rights, he might have walked past her.

The guy noticed him first as he paused. 'All right, mate?' He nodded him a greeting, took a slug from his bottle, ran a hand over his mouth, and turned his unfocussed attention back to Kristen.

Kristen noticed him then, as Matthew loitered, wondering why he'd bothered, what he'd hoped to achieve. 'Matt?' she said, closing one eye and squinting at him. 'Hey, it's Matt.' Establishing through her haze that it was actually him, she elbowed the man to her side, then attempted to push herself to her feet. One foot scraping the gravel and sprawling out in front of her, she failed, landing heavily back on her backside. 'What're you doing here?' she drawled, her face, drawn and unhealthily pale, forming into a smile. A smile that would fade in an instant, if he went anywhere near the bottle she was now clutching proprietorially to her chest.

'Kristen.' Offering her a tight smile back, Matthew glanced at the guy, who'd leaned his head against the wall and appeared to be drifting off, and then back to her. 'How're you doing?'

'Good,' she said, her smile widening briefly, before she remembered she wasn't doing so good, and that Matthew knew it.

'I came about Ashley,' Matthew got to the point. Further enquiries around the subject of her health and lifestyle would only lead to argument. He'd been down this road. It never led anywhere but back here.

As if on cue, Kristen took a drink, a long one, then looked away. She didn't speak. Didn't even ask how Ashley was. *Unbelievable.* Frustrated, Matthew ran his hand over his neck. *How had this happened?* He asked himself for the millionth time, and for the millionth time, he came to the same conclusion: there was no answer. No absolute reason why Kristen's over-indulgence of alcohol should lead to addiction, other than a genetic propensity possibly? Their father had drunk, more when he was struggling with a case, some sick bastard not brought to justice who should have been. Kristen had overindulged as a teenager, as did most kids. She'd carried on indulging as a student. When their father had hit the bottle big time after his suspension, Kristen had seemed determined to do the same. When their father decided to quit on life, rather than quit his habit, Kristen had taken off, shacking up with some deadbeat workshy tosser. The only interest they'd had in common was smoking dope and drinking themselves into oblivion. Kristen had thwarted all attempts to make her see the guy was a loser. Thwarted all attempts at contact eventually, trailing around from bedsit to bedsit, leaving no forwarding addresses, not returning his calls.

Too wrapped up in working through his own feelings around their father's suicide, Matthew hadn't been aware of Kristen's downward slide into alcoholism. With Becky's support, he'd managed to clean up his act. Kristen never had. Mathew was scared for her, furious with her for not even seeming to want to try but, aware of his own failings, he couldn't wholly condemn her. His heart ached for her as he watched her prop the bottle back between her knees and wrap her arms about herself, probably cold through to the bone. The lined parka coat he'd given her was nowhere in evidence, he noted, no doubt that had been traded in for a fix.

Guessing there was no point enquiring as to its whereabouts, Matthew braced himself to say what he'd come to. 'Becky and I have decided to have Ashley come and live with us, assuming you don't have any objections, that is?' He delivered his news and waited hopefully for a reaction.

Well, his assumptions had obviously been right. Matthew felt a wave of despair wash over him. There was no reaction. Nothing. A flicker of guilt in her eyes maybe, a shrug of indifference, and then, 'Perfect! Rebecca to the rescue again,' Kirsten sneered sarcastically.

Matthew held his tongue, watched as Kirsten took another mood-altering slug of booze. Even if she'd paused for thought about all that Becky had gone through, she wouldn't feel for her. It was a fact that alcohol seemed to numb your awareness of anyone's pain but your own. Matthew was all too aware of that.

'I just thought you should know.' He shrugged and waited again. Then, still getting nothing back, he reached into his jacket pocket for the cigarettes he'd bought her, walked across and bent to place them in front of her.

Kristen wouldn't meet his eyes.

*C'est la-vie.* Matthew sighed inwardly, straightened up and turned to go. He couldn't do anything here.

'Do you have any money?' Kristen called after him.

Matthew stopped. Should he relent and help fuel her habit, or just keep walking?

'I need food,' Kristen added, the one sure-fire way to make him relent.

Matthew sighed. The liquid variety, invariably, he thought, turning back.

'It's all I have.' He offered her the twenty pound note he'd had ready in his pocket. 'Get something hot, Kristen, will you, even if it's only a bag of chips. And go to the drop in centre tonight, yes? They're expecting you.'

Kristen nodded, still not looking at him as she took the money and stuffed it in her own pocket.

'I'll catch you around.' Matthew shrugged and turned again to walk away.

'I couldn't handle her!' Kristen called, causing Matthew's step to falter. 'I tried! I needed help, Matthew!'

Matthew kept walking. He'd tried to help. It had made no difference.

'You're just like him!' Kristen continued, shouting behind him. 'Too concerned about everyone else, complete bloody strangers, to see when your own family is falling apart!'

Anger welling inside him, Matthew whirled around. 'That's crap, Kristen. I tried to help you. You know I did.'

Kristen laughed disparagingly. 'Oh, yes, you did your duty, Matthew, just like Dad. Exactly like him. You got me dry and then hung me back out. It wasn't enough! I needed someone to be there. I needed someone to care. I couldn't do it on my own!'

Dangerously close to a cutting retort, Matthew stopped and searched his conscience. The truth was, while dealing with his own problems, he probably hadn't been there emotionally. Though he'd tried to do everything he could practically. She was right about the old man. He'd also done practically everything he could bringing them up. Their father's career, though, had become his obsession after losing their mother. Five years younger than Matthew, just eleven when she'd died, Kristen had missed her, needed her mother's guidance during that crucial period of her life, but... couldn't she see that that's exactly what Ashley needed?

'She's your daughter, Kristen,' he tried. He wished he could make her see. Make her find the will to fight the addiction. No one could do that for her.

'I know that!' Kristen glared at him. 'I gave birth to her!'

Matthew glanced skywards, debated, and turned away. He wasn't going this route: the blame route. When she'd fallen pregnant, he'd thought he'd done all he could in the absence of the baby's missing father. Maybe it wasn't enough. Maybe nothing he did would ever be enough. He couldn't do this though. Not here. Not now.

'She's... different,' Kristen said, stopping him again in his tracks.

Yet again, Matthew turned back. 'Different how?'

'Different,' Kristen repeated. 'She has needs.'

'Special needs?' Matthew furrowed his brow. This was the first he'd heard of it.

Kristen looked confused, uncertain. 'Not special, no. Just ... different.'

Well, given her upbringing she was bound to be that, wasn't she? Different to all the other kids around her, her peers. Matthew had been there, bullied relentlessly, his family circumstances and his asthma making him 'different'. Glancing again at Kristen, whose attention was back on her bottle, Matthew shook his head and turned to go. She was making no sense, nor would she, no surprise there. No doubt he would find out what Ashley's needs were from the care home. He'd cross that bridge then.

'She's better off without me!' Kristen shouted after him. 'You know she is, Matthew.'

19

# CHAPTER THREE

Ashley was listening to music on her phone when they came. Sitting cross-legged on the lawn, well-away from the noisy brats in the play area, she could sense them watching her through the patio doors, her uncle and aunt, supposed to be. *Long lost uncle and aunt*, Ashley thought cynically. She didn't even remember them.

*They won't take us.* Emily was right beside her, as always. Ashley tried to ignore her, plucking a daisy instead and splicing the stem with her thumbnail.

*The mom might. She's smiling.* Emily continued to relay events, even though Ashley feigned disinterest. *The dad's frowning, though. No, they won't take us.*

Ashley shrugged and selected another daisy. Closing one eye, she threaded one stem through the other, like soft green cotton through the eye of a needle. 'You don't know. You can't read minds,' she said and reached to pick another daisy.

*I can read faishes,* Emily lisped huffily. *And his is not a happy face.*

Ashley didn't care. Even if they did take her and she got to move in with them, they wouldn't keep her for long. She'd rather not go than have them end up looking at her the way the other couple had, like she was a weirdo. Ashley had tried to tell people about Emily, but no one believed her. After a while, she'd stopped trying, because of the looks. Those and the endless questions the doctor kept asking her: Was she lonely? Did she feel shy, fearful, upset or angry? Did she ever hear voices? People talking to her who weren't there? *Well, that's just plain stupid,* Ashley had once pointed out. How could people talk to her if they weren't even there? That hadn't gone down too well.

She hadn't admitted it, but she did get angry when the other kids picked on her. She hadn't meant for Kaitlyn to fall off the top of the slide that time, but Kaitlyn kept banging on, calling her a *derbrain*, like it was really original, saying she'd blab on her for talking to herself. On and on she'd gone. Ashley had only meant to shut her up. It worked, she supposed. She hadn't done it since.

Reaching for another daisy, Ashley glanced towards a group of kids whooping and screaming as they played tag. She was lonely sometimes, too, something else she didn't admit. She liked playing with the little ones, though. Miss Cummings, the care home manager, seemed pleased that the younger kids liked her, and the doctor didn't seem to worry about her so much since Ashley had told him she didn't hear voices and absolutely never saw things that weren't there.

Would they take her, she wondered idly. Probably not. Ashley didn't want to go anywhere anyway just to come back again. How was that supposed to *not* make her feel upset?

*I bet they don't even come out and shee us.* Emily sighed dramatically. Ashley shrugged again. 'Not bothered.'

*Ooh, you are, too!* Emily's eyes swivelled towards her. *You want a proper mum and dad, just like I do.*

'No I don't.' Ashley spliced another stem.

Emily, though, wouldn't leave it. *Liar,* she said, folding her arms in that know-it-all way she had.

'Am not,' Ashley countered. 'It's OK here.'

*Liar, liar, pants on fire.* Emily persisted, annoyingly.

'I am *not.*' Ashley glanced at her through her curtain of hair. 'It's not that bad. We get to use the computers, watch TV and ...' Ashley stopped and shrank back as one of the kids shot past, snatching at her daisy chain, as he went.

*Get tormented by boys. Nasty horrible ones.* Emily picked up, her eyes sweeping contemptuously over the boy, as he skidded into a turn to face them.

'Loopy Ashley did a poo,' Jack, an idiot fat-cheeked bully, sang, hilariously, smirking as he jogged backwards. 'How many dollops did she do-oo?'

'Piss off,' Ashley mumbled, her cheeks heating up.

'If you go down to the woods today you're in for a big surprise,' the boy sang crassly on. 'If you go down to the woods today, you'd better hide your eyes. Coz Ashley Adams is going there too. She'll be pushing a pram and shaggin' a man ...'

Ashley glared at him. 'Go a-*way.*'

'... and talking to her invisible sister.'

*Uh, oh.* Emily's eyes, Ashley noticed, had narrowed to icy slits, which definitely meant trouble. She looked from Emily to Jack, whose eyes by comparison were growing wider, huge, like great bulbous orbs in his stupid face.

'What the fu ... ?' he started, but the words died on his lips.

'Oh, shit.' Ashley winced, as his feet slid from under him and Jack flailed backwards.

*Serves him right.* Emily nodded, satisfied, as Jack's head hit the path with a sickening crack.

'Crap. We are *so* going to be in trouble.' Hearing the patio doors fly open, Ashley glanced warily up, to see the man who was supposed to be her uncle running towards them.

He reached Jack, who was now bellowing like a stuck pig, dropped to his knees, and quickly checked him over.

'Come on, you're all right,' he assured him. 'Nothing damaged but your pride. What's your name, hey?'

*He'll take him, not us.* Emily stated, matter-of-factly. *He's asked him his name, so ...*

'J ... J ... Jack,' Jack hiccupped a reply.

'Well, Jack, that wasn't a very nice thing to do, was it? Calling other people spiteful names?' The man scooped Jack up into his arms and headed back towards the office.

*Miss Cummings has just offered to carry Jack, but the man shook his head.* Emily kept up her running commentary. *I expect he thought he'd be too heavy for her. He's a nice man. Shame he's going to take Jack home instead of us, isn't it?*

*I don't care,* Ashley said silently. Squeezing her eyes closed, she tried hard to shut Emily out, and Jack, who was snottily declaring, 'She pushed me!'

*Oh, yes you do.* Emily selected a wisp of her hair, smoothed it through her fingers, and then popped it in her mouth. *He's taking him inside now.*

Matthew manoeuvred Jack through the patio doors the care home Manager held open for them.

'This way is probably the quickest route to the sick room.' She headed across the office to the door adjoining the hall. 'We'll take him straight up, if you don't mind?'

'No problem,' Matthew said, offering Jack a reassuring smile as he followed her, though he was obviously a bully and a liar. Feeling a touch guilty, condemning the boy, who'd probably had a rough start in life, he carried him up to the sick room. Then, double-checking his injuries weren't as life-threatening as his sobs might have conveyed, he left him in the care of Miss Cummings to go back down to the office, where Rebecca waited.

She was still watching Ashley, obviously quite taken, Matthew guessed, going back into the room.

'Is he all right?' Rebecca glanced at him from where she stood at the window.

'He'll have a headache, I'm guessing, but he'll live,' Matthew assured her, walking across to join her.

Rebecca wrapped her arms about herself. Matthew noticed she was shivering despite the unusual warmth of the spring evening. Nervous, he guessed, wondering whether things would work out.

'Penny for them?' he asked, wrapping his own arms around her and pulling her close.

Rebecca breathed out a sigh and relaxed into him. 'She's lonely,' she said, nodding towards Ashley.

Matthew brushed his cheek softly against hers, as he observed Ashley over Rebecca's shoulder. 'She obviously has difficulty making friends.'

Rebecca twisted to glance up at him. 'Can you blame her, if the other children are that horrible to her? That little bully was absolutely vile.'

'No,' Matthew contemplated. He'd done exactly the same as a kid, withdrawn on the receiving end of bullying. Picturing the snarling youth who'd repeatedly put the boot in—Sullivan was a vicious bastard even then—Matthew drew in a short breath. He'd had his first asthma attack around the time the bullying started. And hadn't Sullivan mercilessly used that to his advantage? Matthew had been breathless, defenceless, bewildered, hopelessly trying to work out why Sullivan and his brainless minions had wanted to make his life a living hell. He was wiser now, aware of how a coward's mind worked. They honed in on their victims, people who were weaker, different, showing off their prowess to shore up their own pathetic self-image. The victim's already negative self-image is validated, their self-esteem dwindles further, the child withdraws ... Is that what Kristen meant by different, he wondered?

Rebecca leaned closer into him. 'She's probably just shy. I was at her age. A lot of children are.'

'Yes, but ...' Again Matthew was hesitant, for Becky's sake. For Ashley's too. Yes, they were aware of the huge commitment taking on a child would be. How could they not be? Were they really qualified to offer Ashley all the help she might need, though? 'What if she has real socialisation problems, Becky? What then?'

Rebecca turned to face him. 'Then we help her. Isn't that what this is all about?'

Matthew nodded. 'I suppose. I'd hate to see her spend the rest of her childhood in care, but ... are you sure, Becky? It's asking an awful lot of you. She's not your responsibility, after all.'

Rebecca thought about it. 'No,' she conceded, 'but then aren't responsibilities supposed to be shared in a marriage? Let's at least get to know her. That's what the introductory period is for, isn't it?'

Matthew debated. By the nature of his work, the lion's share of the responsibility he couldn't help thinking, would fall on Becky. 'But what if it doesn't work out, Becks? If we can't be the kind of parents a vulnerable teenage girl needs?'

'Then we'll be faced with the same problems all parents have,' Rebecca pointed out. 'Unlike all parents though, at least we'll have access to expert help if we need it.'

Matthew looked her over, amazed, not for the first time, by her optimism. How he ever got lucky enough to meet a woman he loved so completely, a woman who evidently still loved him, despite all that had happened and his too many flaws, he would never know. 'You're a pretty special person, Mrs Adams,' he said huskily, 'do you know that?'

'Course I am.' Rebecca laughed, stood on tiptoe and planted a kiss on his nose.

Matthew's mouth curved into a smile. Unable to resist, he pulled her closer and kissed her, possibly more thoroughly than he should, given where they were. They were healing, Matthew couldn't help but offer up a small prayer of gratitude for that. They would never be whole again, but they were finding a way forward together, rather than isolated in grief. Knowing he'd reached a place where he couldn't see any way forward, Matthew considered it a small miracle, that miracle being Becky, whose loss had been greater than anyone should have to bear. Maybe taking Ashley was meant to be, after all.

'Shall we?' he asked, softly.

'Yes, let's.' Rebecca nodded determinedly and turned back to the window. 'Do I look okay?' she asked him, smoothed her top down over her jeans and checked her hair: fabulous, wild, auburn hair streaked gold, which she normally wore tumbling down her back, but which she'd now wrestled into a top-knot. Her serious look Becky called it, as if he would ever not take her seriously.

'You look fantastic,' Matthew assured her, giving her shoulders a squeeze, before reaching past her for the door.

'Flatterer.' Rebecca smiled, then, bracing herself, she stepped out into the grounds. 'Let's do this,' she said quietly, clasping Matthew's hand as they walked towards Ashley.

Yep, he was definitely a lucky man. Matthew squeezed her small hand in his.

'Hey there. Ashley, isn't it?' Rebecca called, as they neared her. 'How are you doing?'

She offered her a reassuring smile as the girl glanced guardedly up.

'OK.' Ashley shrugged and glanced back down.

Rebecca hesitated, and then tried again. 'That's pretty.' She indicated the trail of daisies Ashley was stringing together, at which the girl dropped her gaze further. Concerned, Rebecca glanced at Matthew. She didn't want to push her or crowd her, but she so wanted this to go well.

She was wondering what on earth to say next when Matthew took a step forward.

'It's a daisy chain. Isn't that right, Ashley?'

The girl's eyes flicked interestedly towards his.

'Might have been a bit longer if that little sod hadn't snatched it. I'm Matthew,' he went on quickly, as Ashley's mouth twitched into the tiniest of smiles. 'Do you remember me, Ashley?'

The girl shook her head, looking back and forth between them uncertainly.

'Your mum's brother,' Matthew clarified, looking briefly troubled at the mention of his sister, but hiding it well. 'And this gorgeous lady here is my wife, Becky.'

Rebecca shook her head, and then demonstratively rolled her eyes. 'He's very good at flattery, Ashley, especially when he wants something. Watch out for that.'

Matthew splayed his hands. 'Would I lie?' He looked between Rebecca and Ashley, his expression now a picture of innocence.

Ashley's smile widened and Rebecca felt elated and saddened all at once. Matthew was a natural with children. She watched him, as he crouched down to Ashley's level, talking quietly to her, his expression unintimidating, his body-language calm and relaxed. He was generally calm, thinking things through before he reacted. There were times, especially after losing Lily, when he was tense and distracted, definitely moody. He always apologised, though, assuring her his moodiness was nothing to do with her. He had his weaknesses, a tendency in the past to reach for alcohol in his darkest moments, but he was a good man. A caring man. It was there now, Rebecca could see it, the intensity in his eyes, the compassion, as he studied this girl who looked so utterly lost.

Matthew caught her watching him and smiled uncertainly. Rebecca offered him an encouraging smile back and nodded him on. Taking a breath, Matthew turned his attention back to Ashley.

'Rebecca and I have something to ask you, Ashley. You don't have to answer now, if you don't want to. And if you want to talk it over with Miss Cummings first, that's fine, but we wondered if you'd like to come and stay with us?'

Ashley's gaze dropped immediately back down.

Glancing again at Rebecca, Matthew paused, and then went on carefully. 'Maybe stay always, if we all get along and you like it there.'

Rebecca closed her eyes, pride flooding through her. She loved this man, absolutely. She so wished he could learn to love himself a little more. That he could trust that she did love him, that he could tell her properly that he loved her. She knew he did, in her heart.

His eyes—where lately so many shadows danced—didn't lie. Rebecca could see his love for her there. She felt it when they'd found each other again, when they'd made love, tentatively at first, and then more passionately, tasting each other, touching each other to the very core. She hadn't asked him why he couldn't speak the words he once so easily did, but her counsellor had confirmed what she'd feared, that Matthew might be frightened of saying it out loud, perhaps because he'd lost too many people he'd loved. Or perhaps because he didn't think he was worthy of being loved.

Matthew waited a second, and then, 'What do you think, Ashley?'

Ashley didn't look up.

'Ashley?' Matthew hesitated, and then reached out to gently brush her hair from her face. 'Hey, it's okay,' he said softly, noting the slow tears plopping down her cheeks. 'You don't have to do anything, or say anything you don't want to.'

Ashley nodded and sniffled, and eventually looked at him.

'I thought you liked Jack,' she said, her voice so small it broke Rebecca's heart. 'I thought you'd take him. I...'

Matthew swallowed visibly, as she trailed off. 'What, and leave a beautiful girl like you sitting here all alone?'

Dragging a hand under her nose, Ashley blinked at him.

'Not a chance. My wife would kill me.' Matthew got to his feet, offered Ashley his hand and gave her a mischievous wink.

Ashley cocked her head to one side, and then, amazingly, she laughed, only fleetingly, but it was definitely a laugh. Cautiously she searched Matthew's face and then, her eyes less guarded, she reached out, took Matthew's hand, got to her feet, and that was it. The deal was struck. Matthew would never turn back now. It simply wasn't in his nature to let that girl down, let anyone down. Rebecca knew it. And that, along with the fact that he wasn't half bad-looking, was the main reason she loved him: because he had a heart of pure gold.

'He cooks too,' she whispered one of his other attributes in Ashley's ear, as they headed towards the office.

Ashley looked at her interestedly. 'What? Proper food?'

'Yup. Takes the lid off the box and everything,' Rebecca assured her.

'I heard that,' Matthew said, wearing his serious face, which actually wasn't that scary.

'*And* he can find the oven. Hasn't quite learned how to turn it on yet, but...'

'Typical.' Matthew rolled his eyes skywards. 'They're ganging up on me already.'

# CHAPTER FOUR

'Anything?' Matthew asked, praying that the scrapings from the underside of Brianna's fingernails might have produced something, blood not belonging to the victim, a particle of skin. Anything.

Glancing apologetically over her mask, Nicky shook her head.

Matthew blew out a frustrated sigh, anger mounting inside him. *How?* Surely there had to be something?

'Nothing on the clothes?' he asked, hoping there might be something there, a hair, a fibre of clothing, body fluids.

'Nothing substantial,' the pathologist sighed in turn, probably as frustrated as he felt.

'Was she's sexually assaulted?' Matthew asked, a taut band of tension tightening between his temples.

'There's not much in the way of defensive wounding, but—'

'Because she was probably too shit-scared to defend herself,' Matthew cut in furiously.

Nicky's eyes flicked worriedly to his. 'She did have sexual intercourse,' she went on, as Matthew tugged agitatedly as his shirt collar. 'There's also evidence of bruising so, at this stage I would say there's a high probability of rape, yes.'

Matthew nodded slowly. Counting silently in an attempt to quell his temper, he fixed his gaze on a skeletal guide on the opposite wall. 'No body fluids, I take it?'

'Nothing,' Nicky confirmed what he'd already guessed.

Matthew closed his eyes, and swallowed hard. '*Bastard,*' he uttered. 'Is the cause of death confirmed?' he asked, his jaw clenching.

'Definitely asphyxiation.' Nicky indicated the dark brown ligature marks around the girl's neck. 'With a tie probably.'

'No DNA there then either?' Matthew sighed. He wondered why he'd bothered harbouring the hope that that there might have be a sample of skin left behind.

'Sorry.' Nicky shrugged, as if that too were a foregone conclusion. *Unbelievable.* Matthew shook his head incredulously. He was beginning to wonder if Sullivan hadn't worn the same protective clothing the SOCOs wore. If it was Sullivan, which Matthew's every instinct was screaming at him it was. If he hadn't attended to business while his minions kept lookout, he'd have had one of them do it for him. And they had *nothing* to go on? Matthew struggled to comprehend it. Not even a footprint? The SOCOs were still on it, meticulously combing the area for signs of trace evidence, but short of coming up with a conveniently discarded spliff end with Sullivan's prints and saliva on it, they had absolutely nil.

'Time of death?' despondently, he asked for confirmation there, too. As if it would make any difference. Sullivan would have a cast-iron alibi whatever time it was.

'Judging by rigor and postmortem hypostasis,' Nicky glanced at her notes, 'almost certainly two a.m. or thereabouts.'

Sighing again, heavily, Matthew nodded his thanks and left Nicky to finish her job, while he went off to establish Sullivan's whereabouts at two a.m. No doubt he'll have been tucked up in bed with his wife, which, of course, his wife would confirm, claiming she went to the bathroom at precisely one minute past two, noticing the time on the digital alarm clock, as she did. God, he could use a drink. Checking his watch, Matthew decided that, however soothing to the nerves it might be, a double brandy at four o'clock in the afternoon wasn't such a good idea. How, he considered, as he made his way to his car, did people like Sullivan ever sleep with their conscience?

※※※※

Patrick Sullivan pressed his hand to the back of the girl's neck, holding her down. Finishing the business he'd come to attend to, he released her, sorted himself out, and zipped up.

'See how easy it is, Natalie?' he enquired, almost pleasantly.

Choking back a sob, Natalie got shakily to her feet, wiped her hand under her nose and tugged her skirt down, attempting to make herself decent.

She'd be hard pushed to do that. Patrick noted the ladder up the back of the hold-up stockings she was wearing and her scuffed heels, which did nothing for him. Did the girl not realise they were supposed to be an adornment to her legs, a turn-on? How were they going to do that when they looked as if they belonged in the bloody charity shop? Sighing despairingly, he headed to the bathroom.

'You have rent to pay, sweetheart,' he called back, checking his nose for stray hairs as he washed his hands. 'Now get your act together and get your arse out there.'

'But Patrick...' the girl implored tearfully.

Patrick's sigh was agitated now. Shaking his hands dry, he came back into the lounge area of the apartment.

'But what?' he asked impatiently.

Natalie blinked at him beseechingly. 'I still don't feel well, Pat. I ...' Noting his uncompromising expression, she trailed off, biting worriedly down on her bottom lip.

'Mr Sullivan,' Patrick corrected her stonily.

Shrinking back, Natalie nodded hurriedly and glanced down.

'You've had an abortion,' Patrick informed her impassively. 'Not given birth to bleeding triplets. And that was weeks ago. Now sort yourself out.'

The girl nodded again, not too keen, Patrick noted.

He was getting seriously annoyed now, wasting valuable time when he had more pressing things to attend to at the club, the guy whose drugs consignment had gone astray, for one, which was enough aggro for one day.

'Are you hearing me, Natalie?' He walked across to her and clutched her face in his hand, his fingers digging hard into her cheeks.

Patrick noted Natalie's puckered-up mouth, as she attempted a more fervent nod, and curled a lip. Like a bloody sow's arse, he thought wearily. How old was she now? Nineteen? Twenty, he made the calculation, and already well on the way to being past it.

'Tonight, Natalie,' he said. Then, loosening his hold, he turned away to retrieve his cashmere overcoat, which he'd folded carefully over the back of the sofa.

'And smarten yourself up. That's my reputation on the line out there. Don't ever forget it.'

Looking her derisorily up and down, he fed his arm leisurely into his coat, pulled it on, and sauntered across to the mirror to check his reflection. Not bad, Patrick, my old son, he assured himself, admiring his dark good looks as he straightened his tie and smoothed down his hair, which was still all his own. *Thank God*, he thought, checking his shirt cuffs were aligned correctly with his coat sleeves. He'd been dreading starting to lose it at thirty like his old man had. Patrick worked hard at maintaining his image, but he drew the line at wearing a bleeding falsie. The old man looked like a twat. One of these days, Patrick would take great pleasure in telling him that.

'*Comprendre?*' he asked, turning back to Natalie to fix her with an icy glare.

Natalie nodded again, more readily this time.

'Good.' Patrick dragged his gaze away and headed for the door, reasonably satisfied.

He'd already given her three week's grace and still she wasn't back on the job. She'd been taking liberties, thinking she was special because he'd moved her into one of his more upmarket pads. Well, she wasn't. None of them were.

'Don't treat me like an idiot, Natalie,' he warned her, glancing over his shoulder.

'I won't.' She smiled tremulously. 'Pat ...' she said, as he reached for the door. 'Mr Sullivan,' she corrected herself quickly, 'do you think you could, you know, let me have something?'

Patrick stopped in his tracks and turned to stare at her, now truly dumbfounded. She really was taking the proverbial, wasn't she?

Natalie chewed doggedly on a nail. 'Just to keep me going.'

Shaking his head disdainfully, Patrick looked down to pluck a microscopic piece of fluff from his lapel.

'I'll make it up, Pat, I swear.'

Patrick looked back up, his eyes narrowed as he studied her, wondering how she actually had the gall to ask him for drugs. For *free*? When she'd been sitting on her arse watching telly instead of working? He was astounded. He really was.

Natalie gulped back hard, she'd clearly noted the look.

'I've been sick, Pat, honest, I have, but I'll be back on my game tonight, honest I will. You'll get your money, I swear.'

Patrick massaged his neck, the mother of all migraines threatening. *I should shove her out now*, he thought, attempting to keep a lid on the fury bubbling inside him. *Move her to one of the shithole bedsits reserved for drug-addled tarts on their way down. That'd teach her a lesson.*

'Are you having a laugh, Natalie?' he asked quietly, then lifted his right hand and circled the palm of it slowly with the thumb of his left.

'No!' she refuted, panic fleeting across her features as her eyes shot from his face to his hands and back. 'I wouldn't, Mr Sullivan. You know I wouldn't. You've been good to me.' She hesitated, swallowing again, as Patrick studied her mutely. 'I lost my confidence, that's all. I'm good now. I'll make it up, Pat. You know I will.'

She stopped and waited, her expression telling him she knew this could go either way.

Nah, he'd leave her be, for now, Patrick decided, in a rare moment of extreme generosity. She was good when she was on her game, brought in a tidy wad normally. One more chance he'd give her. Just one, no one could call him heartless, after all. Slowly, he reached into his inside pocket.

Natalie closed her eyes, wilting with relief when Patrick drew out the contents.

'Here,' he said, holding out a twist of crack cocaine. 'That's top stuff, Natalie,' he said, as the girl took a tentative step towards him.

'Thanks, Pat.' She smiled and reached greedily for her fix.

'My pleasure.' Patrick caught hold of her wrist, as she made a grab for the package, and yanked her towards him. 'Make sure you deliver, Natalie, do you hear me,' he pushed his face up close to hers, 'unless you want Mummy and Daddy to know how you pay your rent.'

'I will!' Natalie locked panic-struck eyes on his. 'I promise. *Ouch! Pat...*' She squirmed in his grasp '... you're hurting.'

'You'd better, Natalie,' he snarled, twisting her wrist cruelly. 'Or you won't be sitting pretty. Trust me, you take liberties one more time and you won't even be breathing.'

With which Patrick shoved her away hard. 'I'll be back tomorrow. *You'd* better have something for me, Natalie. I'm warning you.'

Tossing his offering at her, Patrick eyeballed her meaningfully, and then turned to stroll to the door, leaving the girl sprawled on the floor.

*Is it worth the bloody effort,* he asked himself, reached back into his pocket for his nail file as he waited for the lift, and then worked to free a speck of dirt from under his index nail. All this stress, he could do without on top of a shedload of heroin gone missing, all thanks to Detective Inspector determined-to-get-him-banged-up-again Adams.

Rolling his shoulders, Patrick attempted to loosen his knotted muscles. He had a score to settle with Adams, big time. As for the tarts: ungrateful, the lot of them. He worked his backside off for them. Made sure they had decent digs. Nicely furnished apartments, most of them, where they could do what they want, entertain their clients in style. He watched their backs, beat the crap out of anyone who slapped them around. And did they appreciate it? No. Nothing but grief, thinking they could pull a fast one. Taking the odd day's sicky, he'd tolerate, occasionally, depending on reasons why. Taking the proverbial he wouldn't, end of.

And then they had the cheek to threaten him, *Patrick Sullivan*, with telling tales to the police? Detective Inspector bloody Adams, of all people, the spineless little shit, nursing a grudge that went way back. Patrick pressed his forefingers to his temple, his migraine now well on the way to being a full blown one as his mind shot back fifteen years, his old man knocking the living daylights out of him because he'd kicked Adams around a few times. Not because he gave a damn about Adams, as far as the great Michael Sullivan, big shot bullying bastard and drugs kingpin was concerned, the copper's son could have been found floating face-down in the canal. No, what irked his old man was that Patrick had been dumb-fuck enough to cause the filth to come sniffing around.

He'd called him dumb-fuck a lot, hammered it home with each blow. Patrick was a complete eejit, a disappointment since the day he'd been born, he'd reminded him. Unlike Adams, of course, the straight A grade perfect copper's son, whose old man bristled with pathetic pride. Every parents' evening, Adams' old man was there, patting his goody-two-shoes son on the back, puffing up his chest. The only time Patrick's old man's chest puffed up was with pure violent rage, the only physical contact with his fists. Attempting to quell the humiliation, which washed over him afresh every time Adams popped up to remind him of his past, Patrick re-straightened his tie, and tugged down his shirt cuffs.

No one dared call him stupid nowadays. Not even the old man, since it had occurred to him that Patrick was big enough to take him on. No one treated Patrick with disrespect. Not anymore. He pocketed his file, rolled his shoulders again, and stepped into the lift. His head was going to explode soon and spill his brains, he would swear. He could do without his upcoming meeting with Tony Hayes, a big bruiser and a bad loser, who definitely didn't piss about when it came to calling in his debts. If he was going to keep his legs intact, Patrick needed to buy some more time. Find out which clever bastard had diverted the drugs supply to line their own thieving pockets when Adams had managed to put customs under surveillance, meaning the drugs drop was off. He'd have to meet Hayes, he supposed. Standing the man up wasn't an option, if he wanted to be able to actually stand up ever again. After that, he needed to get home. Wash the grime off. Do a few lengths of his heated pool and relax. Never mix business with pleasure was Patrick's motto. His home was sacrosanct, away from all this.

****

Dripping wet, which didn't help his mood much, Patrick shrugged out of his overcoat as he came into the foyer of *Seventh Heaven*. 'Is he here?' he asked warily, handing the coat to one of his bouncers.

'Watching the show.'

The bouncer knew who he meant—Tony Hayes commanding respect wherever he went— and nodded towards the main lounge area. The man was built, his dinner jacket straining across his bodybuilder chest, but his expression was one of trepidation nevertheless.

Swallowing throatily, Patrick tried not to break out in a too obvious sweat.

'Right.' He nodded, feeling an unpleasant queasiness gut-level. Knowing there was no avoiding the meet, though, and preferring it to be on his own turf, Patrick realigned his cuffs, braced himself, and went on through towards Hayes and his two henchmen, who were perched on stools at a table one of the pole-dancer's was performing on.

Patrick looked across approvingly as the girl writhed and gyrated, as if making love to her pole, finally squatting to give Hayes an abundant eyeful. Thank God some of them knew what the punters wanted. Considerably relieved that the man had been adequately entertained while he waited, Patrick walked across to him, attempting to keep his stride purposeful, despite his distinctly shaky legs.

'Tony.' He fixed his smile in place and extended a hand. 'How's business?'

Ignoring the hand Patrick offered him, Hayes, a short, stocky, heavy-jowled man, gave him a cursory glance, and then turned his attention back to the girl.

'Nice,' he observed, looking her appreciatively over.

Patrick did likewise, more than happy to distract Hayes from business with pleasure. She wasn't bad, he had to admit: lithe and tanned, blonde hair down to her bum. The ankle bracelets were a nice touch. He took in the sequined ankle bands she was wearing along with her black sequined thong. It was the stilettos that did if for Patrick though: six inch heels on long shapely legs. You could keep the rest as far as Patrick was concerned.

Rewarding the girl with two crisp twenty pound notes, folded and appropriately placed, Hayes reached for his whisky and took a leisurely sip.

'I like what you've done with the place.' He glanced around, taking in the vintage plum coloured walls, rich mahogany woodwork and gilt-edged mirrors, *French, nineteenth century, Louis XVI style*, which had set Patrick back a bob or two. But then, needs must if you wanted to attract the right clientele. The place looked like a sleaze-pit in his old man's day. Even Patrick couldn't blame the town council for trying to shut them down.

'Another drink, Tony?' Patrick offered. Desperate to keep him sweet, he nodded at a passing waitress, indicating the man's glass needed topping up. Hayes was here for information, but Patrick was guessing it wasn't the name of his interior decorator he came for.

Hayes, though, didn't want another drink, it seemed. Placing his hand over his glass as the waitress attempted to pour, he pushed himself away from the table and got to his feet, the two heavies at his side immediately shadowing him. 'I have a prior engagement,' he said, turning to face Patrick.

Standing a good few inches taller than Patrick's five-eight, both of his henchmen looked like pro wrestlers who would enjoy taking him apart, limb from limb. Patrick gulped back a knot in his throat, and hoped the perspiration popping out on his forehead wasn't too obvious.

'You have news for me, I hope?' Hayes' tone was impassive, his expression bland, belying the ruthless bastard he was underneath.

Patrick felt perspiration now wetting his armpits.

'I'm working on it, Tony,' he assured him shakily. 'I have an idea who was involved and I—'

'Ideas don't pay the bills, Patrick, do they?' Hayes interrupted flatly. 'I'll give you another week,' he said, and smiled, the look in his arctic blue eyes deceptively amiable.

His throat suddenly too parched to speak, Patrick gulped again, hard.

'After that, we start seizing goods to recoup our losses,' Hayes casually examined his well-manicured nails, before looking pointedly back at him, 'starting with your balls.'

Sickening apprehension immediately squeezed his pelvis in that particular area, and Patrick searched for a way to stall but came up with nothing.

'I, er, think I might need a little more time than a week, Tony,' he tried, wishing he'd taken the conversation through to the office, where his humiliation wouldn't be witnessed. 'I've got people on it as we speak, but—'

'Seven days, Sullivan.' Hayes stepped past him, his two heavies moving simultaneously with him, both of whom would think nothing of taking Patrick outside and biting his ears off by way of subtle indication of what might come next.

'I don't care how you do it,' Hayes imparted, over his shoulder. 'Burn your poxy club to the ground if you have to and claim on the insurance. I don't give a toss. If you want to keep hold of any part of your tackle, sort it.'

With which Hayes headed towards the exit, cueing his henchmen to follow.

*Neanderthals,* Patrick thought bitterly, swiping a trail of sweat from his cheek with the back of his hand. Then he drew his shoulders up, lest anyone notice he was rattled, and headed for the bar. He needed a drink. He needed several.

'Gin,' he snapped, indicating the barman to get his arse over to him pronto. 'Make it a large one.'

'Ice and a slice, Mr Sullivan?' the barman enquired pleasantly.

'No, I do not want ice and a fucking slice! Do I look gay, or what!?' Patrick glared at the kid, a university grad. *God help the state of the country.* Patrick eyed the two-fingers of gin he was offered despairingly. The idiot wasn't even capable of serving up a decent drink.

'I said *large*,' he seethed, slamming the glass back down and turning to walk around the bar. '*Christ Al-bloody-mighty*, do I have to do *everything* my ...'

Patrick stopped as he heard a distinct sneer from a table just behind him. *Oh, for ...* His jaw set in a grimace, Patrick eyed the ceiling. Just what he needed. His old man, obviously having decided to stumble in, had witnessed proceedings and was clearly about to revel in his humiliation.

'Patrick.' His father raised his glass, as Patrick turned to face him. 'Well done, me boy. Couldn't have done better meself. Hayes will be quaking in his designer loafers, so he will.' Taking a drink, his father wiped a hand over his mouth and looked back to Patrick, that same derogatory look in his eye Patrick had suffered since he was knee-high.

'You'd better make that your last.' Patrick attempted some degree of civility for the sake of paying customers.

'My last, my ever-lovin' shon, will be when *I've* finished drinking.' His father slurred, one eye closed and the other unfocused, as he pointed his now empty glass in Patrick's direction. 'Meanwhile, it would pay you to concentrate on keeping your balls, yer fucking eejit.'

'You've had enough,' Patrick warned him, seething quietly inside.

'Lucy!' Ignoring him, his father clicked his fingers and waved his empty bottle, indicating that one of the dancers should bring him another.

*And serve it whilst sitting in his lap, no doubt.* Patrick curled a lip, repulsed, as he watched his alcohol-soaked old man openly leering at the girl, who sashayed across willingly enough, bottle in hand and a smile glued to her face. The look in her eyes as she glanced at Patrick, though, told her she didn't want Michael Sullivan's sweaty wet paws all over her and his whisky-laden breath in her face. The girls were all much the same to Patrick, dressed in uniform sequined thongs, he couldn't be arsed to differentiate one from the other, unless they had exceptional ankles, but even he could sympathise.

'Come here, my little temptress.' His old man slapped his knee, and then reached a hand around the girl, squeezing her backside demonstratively. 'Dance for me, darlin',' he growled. 'Shove those tempting ripe breasts in me face and let me die a happy man.'

Patrick watched on, wishing the old bastard *would* die as he yanked the girl close and buried his face in her cleavage, his hairpiece skewing on his bald head as he did. The drunken old sod was a complete embarrassment. Fury bubbling inside him, Patrick turned back to the bar to down his gin in one.

He was about to start on another when a crash behind him signalled his old man was on his way out back, stumbling over stools, as per, and cursing liberally as he went.

Walking back towards Patrick, adjusting her bra-top and looking somewhere between grim and flustered, Lucy eyed him worriedly. 'He wants me to take him another bottle. Should I?' she asked.

Obviously, the mighty Michael Sullivan intended to make use of the office with Lucy after he'd made use of the urinal, as if he was capable of successfully doing either. Reviled, as he watched his father stumble through to the corridor, Patrick had a lightbulb moment. 'No,' he said thoughtfully. 'I'll do it.'

Gesturing the girl to put her abundant assets to better use elsewhere, Patrick went around the bar and selected a *Jameson* original Irish whiskey. His father normally only ever drank *Gold Reserve*, but Patrick had a feeling he wouldn't be savouring the taste of it tonight.

# CHAPTER FIVE

'So, you followed in your father's footsteps then?' Steve asked, making idle conversation, as they waited outside Sullivan's residence, set in its own private grounds, complete with tennis courts and swimming pool. If there were any justice, the pool man would over-chlorinate it and Sullivan would choke to death. Matthew amused himself with the thought. Then again, that wouldn't be a painful enough way for an evil runt the likes of Sullivan to go.

'Something like that,' Matthew shrugged an answer and reached for his coffee, which was lukewarm, and really wasn't satiating his thirst for something stronger. 'I doubt I'll make DCI anytime soon though.'

'You don't fancy another pip on your epaulette then?'

'Maybe. Sometime.' Matthew shrugged again and took a drink from his cup. Assuming he wasn't up on a charge himself, that was. The need to get Sullivan off the streets was so all-consuming sometimes he was sorely tempted to look at alternatives to the legal way.

'Still on the force, is he, the old man?' Obviously aware of his father's ranking, Steve pursued the conversation, though Matthew would much rather he didn't.

'Nope,' he replied shortly.

'Retired, then, is he? Got a decent pension, I imagine. I suppose it's worth—'

'Dead,' Matthew cut him short.

Steve shifted uncomfortably. 'Oh, sorry, mate,' he offered his condolences embarrassedly. 'I didn't realise.'

Matthew smiled and nodded shortly, hopefully indicating subject closed. The fact that his father had started down that alternative route, also determined to get certain vermin off the streets, and then taken his own life—his only viable alternative to disgrace as he saw it, wasn't a subject Matthew wanted to discuss.

Sipping his coffee, Steve fell silent for a while, mercifully, and then, 'So, what's Sullivan's story?'

Matthew tugged in a breath. 'Oh, he definitely followed in his old man's footsteps,' he supplied, with a sneer of derision. 'Michael Sullivan,' he went on, crushing his empty coffee cup, as he recalled how the man's unpunished activities had eaten away at his own father like cancer, 'local bigshot and drug king-pin, expects his sons to worship the ground he walks on.'

'And do they?' Steve asked, attempting to profile Patrick Sullivan, Matthew guessed.

'I seriously doubt it.' He laughed scornfully. 'They towed the line when they were younger, no choice but to, Michael Sullivan isn't averse to teaching people a lesson if they cross him.'

'Blimey,' Steve shook his head, 'you'll have me feeling sorry for him in a minute.'

'I wouldn't waste any sympathy on Patrick Sullivan. He gave as good as he got, mostly kicking the crap out of anyone who wasn't in a position to fight back.'

Mostly him, Matthew didn't add, checked his watch instead, and wondered where Sullivan was. Wasn't he overdue his stress-relieving swim in his heated swimming pool? The thought stuck in Matthew's craw.

'Did his old man ever get done?' Steve was obviously keen to collect details.

'Never. He's retired now. Ran his cartel out of *Seventh Heaven*, before handing the reins over to his pimping little prodigies: a legit business on the face of it,' Matthew filled him in. 'Behind the scenes: drug-dealing, lap-dancers offering services under the table, supplying girls to punters who liked them young.'

He paused, swallowing back the bile in his throat as Brianna's broken body flashed graphically through his mind.

'He ran the whole operation with an iron fist, one he didn't hesitate to use if anyone dared disrespect him—anyone including his sons and his wife.'

She'd often walked around with bruised eyes and split lips, Matthew had noticed even back then, and was the only person in the Sullivan family he'd ever had an ounce of sympathy for.

'Definitely like father like son, then.' Steve swilled his coffee back and crumpled his cup. 'Talking of whom ...' He nodded through the windscreen as a black BMW cruised into view.

****

Patrick took a long tout on his spliff as he drove, hoping to wind down before he reached home. Proceedings at *Seventh Heaven* hadn't improved his mood. He could still hardly believe that, after dropping his father off at a nice leafy secluded spot on the river bank, he'd gone back to the club for a wash and brush up, only to find one of his staff on the take. Should have taken the thieving little shit out back and chopped his fingers off. Patrick's mouth curved into a smile, as he recalled how his brother had once done just that. He'd been generous, left the guy with nine fingers, and then made him flush his own pinkie down the toilet. The idiot should have known better than to shave drugs off a stash and think he could get away with it. His brother had sorted him. Reliable Joe had been. Patrick tightened his grip on the wheel, incensed afresh at the way his brother had been shot down like a dog. Some novice on the drugs squad might have gotten trigger-happy, but Patrick had no doubt that Adams had had a part to play in it. The man had been a thorn in Patrick's side all his life.

Then he'd learned two girls had gone off sick. Obviously piss-taking was catching. Shaking his head, Patrick took another terse draw on his joint. To make matters worse, the new girl he'd taken on turned out to have about as much sexual allure as cold tapioca. Apparently dance-school trained, but new to the doing it naked bit, Patrick had guessed she was probably nervous and had magnanimously given her another chance to come back for a private session. Dancing in front of an actual audience with nothing but a few sequins covering her bits and bleeding brainless oafs leering at her couldn't have been easy.

Nice bits though. What was her name? Jamie Collins. That was it. Patrick pictured the girl in his mind's eye. She was getting on a bit at twenty-six, but definitely tasty. She reminded him of Rachel, had that innocent look about her. Rachel had been the first girl he'd fancied; fancied as in getting to know, rather than shag. He'd have liked to have spent more time with her, Patrick reminisced as he neared his house. No chance of that, though, was there, with his old man on him like a Rottweiler. Patrick understood, to a degree, why the old man had had to put him right on a few things. He was acting like a dumb-fuck, he'd pointed out, forcefully: letting his balls rule his brain and getting emotionally involved with one of the toms.

'*Jesus Christ*, you'll be passing freebies to any slag with a sob story at this rate!' he'd ranted on, his eyes bulging, meaning he was seriously aggravated. Patrick had learned to read the signs.

'Did you really imagine the girl was in love with you?' He'd splayed his hands incredulously, one of which was bruised, again, thanks to his having had to knock some sense into Patrick. She was interested in the drugs, not him, the smell of money, not his fucking aftershave. And how long did he think it would take her to point the finger if she was offered the right incentive down at the station?

Shit-for-brains, he'd have the filth all over them. Again!

Yes, Patrick had understood, to a degree, why the old man had needed to keep him in line in his youth. It had toughened him up. Patrick would give the old bastard that. He understood now why he'd had to keep his girls in line, too. Give any one of them an inch and they'd take a mile. What Patrick had never held with, though, was his father laying into his mother whenever the mood took him. If a man wanted treating with respect in his home, then he should treat his woman with respect. Never hit a woman without cause or provocation was another adage Patrick lived by, which is why he got seriously annoyed when they provoked him. His home was his castle and...

'*Oh, man.*' Patrick groaned as he neared his castle, to find Adams parked slap bang in front of his electronic gates. Just what he needed after the day he'd had. Opening his window, he hurriedly blew out a line of smoke and tossed his half-smoked spliff out after it.

Watching as Adams climbed out and made his way to his driver's side door, Patrick took in the length and breadth of him. Tall and reasonably well-toned, he wasn't quite the scrawny kid who hadn't got the balls to stand up to him anymore. Hadn't got the balls now either, Patrick reassured himself there too, recalling how he'd goaded Adams, mercilessly, on numerous occasions. Bound by the law, the sap had just stood there and taken it. Even when the poor sod had been grieving the loss of his kid, Patrick had wound him up, reminding him he had a cast-iron alibi when she'd had her tragic accident. He'd been right there, he'd pointed out, as Adams had glared at him across the table: in prison, dealing, trading heroin for phone cards, food, tobacco. The copper's cheek had twitched. His expression might have been murderous, but he hadn't moved a muscle. Personally, Patrick would have been tempted to reach across the table and throttle him, but not Adams. Nah, goody-little-two shoes Adams, just hadn't got the bottle.

'Patrick.' Matthew nodded as he neared his car, his little lapdog sidekick behind him.

'Well, well, DI Adams,' Patrick smiled flatly. 'To what do I owe the pleasure? *Again?*'

Matthew looked him over, working to keep his expression impassive. 'As if you didn't know,' he said, after a pause.

'I don't actually.' Sullivan shrugged languidly. 'Why don't you enlighten me, *Detective?*'

Matthew's jaw tensed. Pushing his hands into his pockets, he resisted the urge to clock the bastard one there and then. 'Brianna,' he said calmly.

Sullivan furrowed his brow. 'Who?' He looked back at Matthew, his expression one of feigned innocence.

He was baiting him, Matthew knew, challenging him to lose it. And so help him, sometime, sometime soon, he just might.

'Brianna,' he repeated tersely. 'One of your girls.' *You despicable piece of shit.*

'My girls?' Sullivan pondered demonstrably. 'Brianna? *Brianna?* Ah, Brianna, cute little thing, bit mouthy, as women tend to be. So, what's she done now? Got caught in possession again, I suppose.' He sighed and shook his head, pseudo-despairingly.

Trying to quell the explosion in his, Matthew leaned in closer. 'Got her face beat to a pulp and her windpipe crushed, you bastard.' He locked furious eyes on Sullivan's. 'Where were you?'

His expression hardening to a challenge, Sullivan held his gaze. 'Where was I when?'

'You know very fucking well when. Last night. Two a.m.'

Sullivan glanced away, casually flicking a speck of ash from his lapels.

Matthew made a supreme effort then, not to reach in and drag him through the window.

Unruffled, Sullivan turned his gaze back to him. 'Home,' he said, with another casual shrug. 'It was my daughter's eighteenth. Where else would I be?'

Matthew sucked in a breath and straightened up. 'And your daughter can corroborate this, can she?'

'My wife can, yes. You don't get to harass my daughter, Adams, no way.' Sullivan's gaze switched from mocking to threatening. Matthew had seen that look before.

Eyeing him unemotionally, he stepped away from the car. 'Out,' he ordered.

Sullivan blinked, surprised. 'Yerwhat?'

'Drug search,' Matthew informed him impassively.

Sullivan laughed. 'Drugs?' He stared at him incredulously.

'Drugs.' Matthew nodded shortly. 'I can smell them, Sullivan. Out.'

'Oh, for ...' Sullivan shook his head. 'You're scraping the barrel, Adams. And you know it. They're for personal use.' He reached wearily for his door. 'You won't find anything more. And, if you *are* planning on finding anything, you might want to have a rethink. Unless you're not too bothered about getting your partner kicked off the force, that is?' Sullivan nodded to where Steve loitered uncertainly behind Matthew. 'Probably better not to take a leaf out of your old man's book and stitch me up, don't y'think?'

Obviously knowing he'd got the upper hand, Sullivan climbed out, giving Matthew a supercilious smirk as he did.

He was right. Matthew knew it. His stomach churned at the very closeness of the man, as he squeezed past him to the car, no choice but to with Sullivan allowing him little space. He'd wanted an excuse, any excuse to haul him in. He couldn't involve Steve though. Dammit, he hadn't been thinking.

Sullivan waited while they searched, Steve giving Matthew quizzical glances, as they did. There was nothing, of course, as if Sullivan would be likely to have a stash of heroin stuffed in his boot. Matthew sighed, exasperated. He must have left his brains at home this morning.

'Oh, dear, come up empty-handed, have we?' Smoking a legit cigarette, Sullivan blew a fat cloud of smoke over Matthew, as he emerged from the car. 'Maybe you should give up being a copper and do something more fruitful with your life, Adams. I'm looking for a chauffeur if you're interested. Pays well. Nice steady work, much less frustrating.'

His temper dangerously near spiking, Matthew counted silently. At seven his anger subsided some.

'Inside.' He nodded towards the house, a sprawling Grade II listed building. Testament to how fruitful this lowlife's money-making endeavors were.

'If you insist, Detective Inspector.' Sullivan sauntered back to his car. 'Just so you know, though,' he said, as he climbed in, 'you're barking up the wrong tree, sunshine. Whatever happened to Brianna was nothing to do with me.'

Suppressing a sigh of utter contempt, Matthew looked Sullivan over distastefully and headed back to his own car to follow him up the long pebbled drive.

Minutes later, he sighed inwardly again, as the third Mrs. Sullivan climbed out of the indoor heated pool, blonde, tanned and healthy in a microdot bikini, to fawn all over the man. Bought and paid for, Matthew thought, as she reeled off Sullivan's alibi for him.

'He was here,' she said, looking as innocent as a newborn baby, 'dancin' wiv Taylor, weren't you, babe?' She moved across to where Sullivan was watching Matthew with wry amusement. 'And then we went to bed. He's a lovely little mover, aren't you, hun?'

Oozing innuendo, the woman fluttered her eyelashes coyly and draped herself around Sullivan's neck.

'Yeah.' Sullivan's amusement turned fast to irritation, as he realised she was dripping water all over him. 'Watch the coat, sweetheart.'

His smile was now more a grimace, as he eased her away from his cashmere.

*How long before the doting husband routine wore off,* Matthew wondered, and Sullivan reverted to form, giving her the odd slap for some imagined misdemeanor.

'And what time would that have been, Mrs Sullivan?' he asked futilely.

'What, when we went to bed, you mean? Bout two-thirty,' the woman said. 'I noticed the time cos I was keeping an ear out for Taylor. You know what kids can be like.'

'No, he doesn't.' Sullivan looked at Matthew, his eyes full of calculated malice. 'Doesn't have any kids, do you, *Detective?*'

His heart twisting violently in his chest, Matthew looked away. *Count,* he commanded himself, swallowing back the hatred that threatened to choke him. *Ignore the bastard.* Taking a shallow breath, attempting to stave off the imminent wheeze in his chest, he caught Steve's eye, who clearly noted something was wrong, and moved towards him.

'Oh, that's a shame,' the woman said, as Matthew shook his head, indicating Steve should stay. 'Patrick dotes on his daughter, don't you, Pat? We're working on having a baby of our own,' she imparted. 'Didn't go to sleep until dawn, did we, babe?'

Looking suggestively up at Sullivan, she reached to trail a long fingernail down his torso, while Matthew suppressed an urge not to shove the excuse for a human being in the pool and hold him under.

'That's right, sweetheart. Taylor can't wait to have a little sister or brother to play with.' Sullivan locked goading eyes with Matthew. 'Happy?'

*Not until I see you banged up for life or six feet under.* Matthew's gaze didn't flinch. 'I'll be back,' he warned him evenly.

'Ooh, move over, Arnie. I'm shaking in my boots.' Sullivan blinked girlishly.

'One day, Sullivan,' Matthew promised. 'One day.'

'Yeah, right, maybe when you grow a pair, Adams. Meanwhile—' Adjusting his collar and cuffs, Sullivan nodded towards the annexe doors they'd entered by. 'Don't have an asthma attack on the way out, will you? Oh, and give me a ring sometime, about that chauffeuring job. I'm thinking you might need one soon. Not going to go down well with your superiors, is it, you wasting valuable police resources, harassing innocent people?'

*Sub-species,* Matthew thought. Then, the tightness in his chest warning him of just such an attack, he turned away before he did

43

something that would be worth serving time for.

'I guess that gives him his alibi.' Steve sounded as despondent as Matthew felt, as they descended the steps from the annexe.

Matthew swallowed back his repulsion. 'As usual.'

'I didn't know you had asthma, boss,' Steve commented, as they headed for the car. He was trying to sound casual, only mildly interested, but Matthew guessed he was actually wondering how bad it was. As in, could it cause a problem on the job? If so, how was it he was doing the job?

'I don't,' Matthew said shortly. That was, he didn't. Supposedly outgrowing his childhood asthma, he hadn't had an attack in years. Not until Lily...

'Oh, right. He was trying to be witty then, was he?' Steve nodded back towards the house.

'Presumably.' Attempting to avert the conversation, Matthew glanced across the grounds, and there was Taylor, Sullivan's daughter, leading a horse from the arena back to the stables. *Birthday present*, Matthew wondered. Possibly. The girl wanted for nothing. Everything a teenager could wish for bestowed upon her by her caring father. Yet he pumps girls her age full of drugs, forces them into prostitution, beats them to death.

His anger white hot, slow-burning, Matthew looked back towards the annexe. Sullivan was watching him from the doors, a satisfied smirk all over his face and casually... *cleaning his fingernails.* Matthew's heart stopped, as he noted the metal file he was using, and then kicked back hard.

※※※※

'Fetch us a drink, will ya, babe.' Chelsea said as the coppers drove off. 'I need to towel meself off before me boobs freeze.'

'Silly cow,' Patrick muttered behind her. 'Get it yourself.'

Taken-aback, Chelsea blinked and turned back towards him. 'What's your problem?' she asked. Planting her hands on her hips, she looked him over, feeling mightily miffed. Hadn't she just bigged him up, spouted a load of rubbish about him being the world's greatest lover, when the truth was, he was only ever interested if she was dressed up like some cheap trollop in stilettos. Chelsea was almost at the stage of telling him to take her sodding shoes to bed with him and be done with. What *had* he been up to anyway? Clearly something if the law had come sniffing around.

'*You're* my problem. What did you have to go and do that for?' Patrick shot her a moody glance then dropped his gaze back to his overcoat, brushing at his lapels as if they were crawling with fleas.

'Do what?' Chelsea was truly astonished, and damned if she knew what she was supposed to have done now.

Patrick looked angrily back up. 'You've got chlorine all over the coat, you silly tart.'

'Don't be so stupid, Pat. There ain't nothing there but a bit of water. Honestly, you're dead neurotic, you are sometimes.' Chelsea rolled her eyes and padded back towards him, dabbing at the lapel herself as she inspected it at close quarters. Very close quarters. She couldn't see a thing without her glasses.

Which is possibly why she didn't see Patrick's expression darken to pure thunder. 'What did you call me?' he fumed, catching hold of her wrist.

Chelsea snatched her gaze from his coat to his face, 'Nothing.' Her eyes grew wide as they searched his. 'I only said you—'

'Shut your mouth!' Patrick cupped her face with his free hand, his fingers digging deep into her cheeks. 'Do not *ever* call me stupid, understand? *Ever!* Got it?'

'Yes! I wasn't. I won't!' Chelsea panicked, as he shoved his face up close to hers. Now she could see: the blue-grey vein jutting in his temple, the terrifying look in his eyes. 'Patrick,' she whimpered, 'you're hurting me.'

'Silly bloody tart, walking around like a trollop,' Patrick ranted furiously on, a bubble of spit forming at the corner of his mouth, 'in front of Adams, for fuck's sake. What? Fancy him, do you? Reckon the copper could give you good seeing to, is that it?'

'No!' Desperate to get away from him and whatever foul mood he was in, Chelsea tried to prise his fingers away.

'Patrick, stop it! You're scaring me.'

But Patrick only increased the pressure. 'If I ever see you simpering over him again, I'll do more than scare you, Chelsea. I'll cut your brainless little head off. Got it?'

Chelsea swallowed, attempting a nod.

'I didn't hear you!' Patrick bellowed.

'Yes!' Chelsea screamed, and felt a warm trickle on the inside of her leg as her bladder gave way.

'Trollops, the lot of you. Go and cover yourself up!' Patrick muttered, disgusted, and shoved her away, hard.

Chelsea's first thought, as her legs slipped from under her, was that she was flailing backwards towards the deep end. Her second thought, around her lack of skills in the water, was cut blindingly short, as her head smacked violently against the tiles.

# CHAPTER SIX

Approaching his house, Matthew immediately noticed there were no lights at the windows. Knowing Rebecca should be home and trying to quash the paranoia that had been his constant companion since the accident, he stepped on the accelerator, bumped the car over the building site that passed for a drive, and screeched to an abrupt halt.

Apprehension overriding any police training to err on the side of caution, he threw himself out of the car, rammed his key into the lock, and thrust the front door wide.

'Becky!'

'Here,' Rebecca said from the sofa, which backed towards the door, sounding perfectly relaxed.

*Thank Christ.* His heartbeat returning to somewhere near normal Matthew started breathing again.

'What's up, guys?' Closing the front door and trying to sound casual, he walked around the sofa, to find the two ladies now in his life each end of it, feet tucked up, a popcorn bowl between them, and the TV paused.

'Film night,' Rebecca reminded him, around a mouthful of popcorn. 'We started without you.'

'Ah, right.' Mathew winced inwardly, realising he'd forgotten. 'Sorry.' He ran a hand wearily over his neck. 'I—'

'Got detained?' Rebecca gave him a despairing glance. She was smiling though, in that way she did that told him he was a hopeless case but that she might just forgive him if he grovelled sufficiently.

'Sorry,' Matthew mouthed again. His eyes flicked towards Ashley then, who, while not totally at ease yet and still hiding behind her hair if she got nervous or embarrassed, certainly seemed at home tonight. *That's good*, Matthew smiled quietly. It would take time before she was fully comfortable around them, he was aware of that. Aware also that, as his child protection and safeguard training dictated, he should be careful of not invading her space, emotional or physical. It might make things a little awkward sometimes, but support was what she needed, a caring environment. With patience, they'd get there eventually, hopefully.

'So what are we watching?' he asked, giving his wife an appreciative glance, who, with her fiery auburn hair splayed about her shoulders and wearing one of his shirts over her leggings, looked frustratingly tempting.

'*Taken*, One and Two,' Ashley supplied. Then, one hand groping for popcorn, she pointed the remote and pressed play. 'Liam Neeson,' she added, dropping the popcorn into her mouth.

'Great.' Matthew nodded tolerantly. He wasn't so sure he was as big a Neeson fan as the ladies appeared to be, though.

'Have you eaten?' he asked, over the action on the screen.

'No,' was the reply twofold. 'We're starving,' Rebecca informed him, as both girls dipped simultaneously into the popcorn bowl.

'So I see.' Smiling wryly Matthew headed for the kitchen. 'So, what do you fancy? I could grab something out of the freezer, if you—'

'Pizza,' Rebecca interjected decisively.

'Pizza's good,' Ashley concurred, now having sampled his dubious skills in the culinary department.

'No takers for home cuisine then?' Matthew asked, turning back.

'Uh, uh,' was the definitive answer.

'A lesser mortal might be hurt, you know?' Matthew did his best to look wounded. 'A man's ego is a very fragile ...'

'*Shhhhh*.'

'Right.' Matthew eyed the ceiling. 'Double pepperoni with extra mozzarella?' he enquired after his and Rebecca's usual preference.

Ashley paused the film again. 'Erm?'

Matthew glanced curiously at her. 'It that okay with you, Ashley?'

Ashley shrugged. And then, there she went again, dropping her gaze, the hair flopping over her face.

'Ashley?'

Ashley shrugged, not over-enthusiastically. 'Yeah, it's fine.'

But clearly not that fine. Matthew read the body language.

'How about vegetable feast with garlic bread?' he offered, guessing teenager plus food might possibly equal fad.

Ashley looked up to beam him a smile. 'Cool.' She nodded happily.

Definitely progress, Matthew decided. She should smile more often. Obviously she didn't realise it, but she was extremely pretty. Hopefully, with a little persuasion, she'd come out of her shell and be the confident young woman she should be, instead of cowering at the hands of some sadistic bully.

Instantly reminded of Sullivan, like the man didn't dog his thoughts every minute of every day, the images of Lily didn't haunt his every waking night, Matthew vowed to do something, whatever it took, to stop him preying on vulnerable young people. People like Ashley, who would stand no chance in his evil clutches.

Right then, determined to help her enjoy some family time, Matthew headed for the front door, thinking it would probably be quicker to collect the pizza than have it delivered. 'Back in ten,' he called behind him. Then, realising all eyes were glued to the screen, he shook his head and let himself out quietly.

Ashley waited for the front door to close, then, 'He's all right, isn't he?' she commented, glancing sideways at Rebecca.

Rebecca glanced enquiringly back at her.

'Well, obviously I think so.' She nodded, thinking Ashley might be seeking reassurance. Thanks to being dragged from address to address by her mother, Ashley didn't know Matthew well, but she liked him. That was plain to see. With her family background, though, Rebecca supposed she might find it difficult to easily trust people.

Ashley nodded thoughtfully in turn. 'A bit like Liam,' she said.

Puzzled, Rebecca blinked at the screen where Liam the action-hero was busy scaling roofs to rescue his wife. 'Well, he is tall, I suppose,' she conceded. 'I'm not sure he looks a lot like him, though.'

'No, I didn't mean in looks. I meant he's, um, considerate,' Ashley clarified, unfurling her legs, planting her feet on the floor, and tucking her hands under her thighs. 'He kind of weighs things up, thinks things through. You know?'

Rebecca thought about it. 'Yes. Yes, he does. It's his job I think, plus...' she glanced hesitantly at Ashley again, wondering how much she should confide. A little, she decided, on a need–to–know basis '... he's had some heartbreak in his life,' she explained carefully. 'I think that makes him more sensitive to people's feelings.'

Ashley turned to fix her gaze on Rebecca's, her huge, rich cognac eyes awash with such uncertainty Rebecca's heart slipped a little inside her.

'Do you love him?' she asked bluntly.

Rebecca smiled. 'I do, absolutely. He's a good man, Ashley.'

She reached to give her shoulders a reassuring squeeze. 'You'll be safe here, I promise.'

Ashley nodded again, looking a little less troubled.

'I'll get us a drink while we're waiting for pizza,' Rebecca suggested, getting to her feet. 'Coke?'

'Please,' Ashley said. 'Rebecca,' she stopped her before she got to the kitchen door, 'can I ask you something else?'

Rebecca turned back. 'Ask away,' she said. 'We don't keep secrets.'

'How come you don't have any children of your own?'

Rebecca's heart stopped then, literally skipping a beat inside her.

'We did have,' she said, and breathed. 'A little girl. Her name was Lily.' Rebecca waited for the familiar feeling of grief to wash over her. 'She would have been eight now. We lost her in a car accident.'

Sadness like a lead-weight in her chest, Rebecca waited, hoping she hadn't told her too bluntly, too soon. Wouldn't not telling her now she'd asked be tantamount to lying though?

'She died?' Ashley looked so stricken Rebecca had to work at holding back the tears. She simply nodded. She couldn't trust herself to speak just then.

'That's terrible.' Ashley's eyes filled up. 'Do you miss her?'

'Every minute of every day,' Rebecca answered honestly. 'I still carry her, though. In here.' Mustering up a smile, she pressed a hand to her heart.

Ashley nodded slowly. 'I do that,' she said quietly. 'A friend,' she added quickly, as Rebecca glanced at her quizzically. 'I lost her, too, but I feel her sometimes. You know, like you said, inside.'

Looking her over, shocked, Rebecca swallowed hard. God, what must this poor child have been through in her short life?

'Are you going to have another baby?' Ashley asked, stopping Rebecca as she took a step back towards her.

Oh. Caught off-guard, Rebecca's cheeks flushed at that. 'Yes.' She smiled, a touch embarrassed. 'Well, we're trying.'

Ashley nodded, again. Clearly she was also one to weigh things up. 'Sorry about your little girl,' she offered, after a pause. 'That must have been really shitty.'

*Ahem.* 'It was,' Rebecca agreed, 'for Matthew too. I'll go and get that coke.' Feeling very close to tears now, Rebecca turned back to the kitchen. She wasn't sure she'd done the right thing, but maybe confiding in Ashley was no bad thing. It might be a way of breaking down a few barriers, getting Ashley to share a little more, too. 'By the way, you can call me Becky, you know,' she called from the kitchen. 'All my friends and family do.'

'Okay,' Ashley called back, and then attempted to shush Emily, who was practically bursting with excitement.

*I told you. I told you,* she said, jigging around the room and clapping her hands. *They like us.*

Me, Ashley thought determinedly. They like me. You're … not … here.

*Duh.* Glancing down, Emily swept her hands over the outline of her body. *I am, actually.*

Aware of Rebecca in the next room, and desperate to be seen as normal, doing what normal kids did, Ashley tried to ignore her.

*He is nice, isn't he?* Emily sighed dreamily. *Really handsthome.*
'Shut up, Emily,' Ashley scowled.
*She probably won't let him keep us though. Not now they're having a baby.*
'They're not,' Ashley snapped, irritated, because that, in fact, had been the first thought that had flashed through her mind.
*Yeth, they are. She just said so. They won't want us if they have a brand new baby of their own, will they?*
'Emily,' Ashley hissed, 'will you please shut the fuck up!'
'Ashley?' Rebecca came back into the room, tray in hand and her brow knitted confusedly. 'Who were you talking ... Oh, my *GOD!* The tray hit the floor with a resounding crash, as something thudded violently against the patio doors.
'Becky!' Ashley launched herself at her, as the apparition splatted heavily against the windows again. 'What *is* it?!' she screamed.
Oh God. Oh God. 'I'm not sure.' Rebecca's panic escalated as the creature bashed at the glass, frantically flapping and clawing. And then, it stopped, as suddenly as it had started. Everything was still again, so quiet, Rebecca was sure she could hear her heart beating.
Staring petrified at the large picture windows, she saw nothing beyond them now but the impenetrable ink-dark of the night. She hugged Ashley tight.
'A b... bird,' she stuttered, gulping back her own terror. 'It's just a bird, Ashley. It's all right.'
The hairs standing on the back of her neck, Rebecca almost cried with relief, as she realised that that must be what it was. A poor bird lost its way. Damn workmen. Three times she'd asked them to fix that patio light before they'd gone bust. Matthew would need to bump it up his To-Do-list quickish.
'Come on,' she said, giving Ashley another reassuring hug, 'let's draw the blinds, put the fire on, and tuck up together on the sofa until Matthew comes back.' *Who would be duly despatched again, to check for dead bodies,* she didn't feel it prudent to add.

※※※

'So how did it go last night?' Matthew asked Steve, who was yawning widely as he climbed into the car the next morning.
'Huh?' Steve scratched his head, clearly the worse for wear.
'The wedding rehearsal,' Matthew reminded him. 'I thought you were checking out the church, making sure the vicar didn't think you were too much of a sinner?'

'Oh, yeah,' Steve nodded, 'good. I managed not to mess up. Lindsey was well-pleased.'

Matthew smiled, noting the slight flush to Steve's cheeks and the crumpled appearance, which possibly meant the man had dressed in a hurry.

'I take it you two celebrated afterwards?'

Steve looked a touch bashful. 'Yeah, we did a bit.'

'A lot, judging by the state of you.' Matthew started the engine. 'I hope you're up to the job, Detective Sergeant, if you'll forgive the pun?'

'Course I am.' Steve nodded piously. 'A good strong cup of caffeine and I'll be good as new. Haven't got any of those strong mints you keep in here, have you?'

'No,' Matthew said quickly. Unfortunately, not quickly enough. Before he had a chance to stop him, Steve opened the glove compartment, and Matthew's heart dropped like a stone.

Obviously astounded, Steve didn't say anything for a second. He just stared at the thirty wraps of heroin therein, and then, 'You're not serious?' He turned his stunned gaze towards Matthew.

Averting his gaze, in favour of pulling out of the car park, Matthew didn't answer. Largely, because he had no clue how to.

'Where'd you get it?' Steve asked tersely, clearly thinking he might have obtained it from the police store, which would definitely impact on him.

'Friends in the wrong places.' Matthew kept his eyes on the windscreen. The less Steve knew about his illegal drug purchasing activities, the better.

'Have you got those addresses I asked you to dig out?' he asked, making a weak attempt to change the subject.

'Yes.' Steve slammed the glove compartment shut. 'Sir.'

Contempt on a scale of one to ten, that was way off it. Matthew knew it was no less than he deserved.

'I don't bloody believe this.' Steve laughed incredulously. 'So what are you planning to do with it, if you don't mind my asking? I mean, I'm only your partner, after all.'

Matthew sighed inside. Involving Steve was the last thing he'd wanted. He wanted Sullivan, though, so much he could taste it.

'Crush a parasite,' he grated, his anger exacerbated by the fact that, having seen the stuff, Steve now obviously *was* involved. Why hadn't he thought to put it under the damn seat, for Pete's sake?

'Sullivan?' Steve deduced.

'One and the same.' Matthew nodded tightly.

51

Steve shook his head despairingly. 'So you're going to fit him up, just like the man said?'

Matthew hesitated. 'Call it plan B.'

Steve said nothing, which spoke volumes.

Matthew glanced warily at him. 'You didn't see it. If anyone asks, you have no idea. Whatever happens, I'll back you.'

'Oh, well, that makes me feel a whole lot better. I'm about to get married, for God's sake!'

'I know. Steve, I ... *Bloody Hell!* Narrowly avoiding cutting someone up at the roundabout, Matthew swerved and braked hard. 'Watch where you're going, can't you! Prat,' he growled at the driver, unfairly.

'Or killed,' Steve muttered. 'Definitely sacked.'

'Steve, just forget you saw it, okay?' Matthew could hear the hint of desperation in his own voice. 'This has nothing to do with you. I—'

'Or banged up,' Steve went on over him. 'That's it then, isn't it? I can kiss goodbye to my career, can't I? Ask me it's *you* who's the prat.'

'Look, Steve...' Frustrated, Matthew ran a hand through his hair. 'I'm not going to do anything that might incriminate you. Just forget we had the conversation and—'

'Right.' Steve's expression was scathing. 'Look the other way, you mean?'

'Yes.' Matthew kneaded his forehead. 'No.' He sighed, knowing that, whatever he said, he was digging a bigger hole and dropping Steve squarely in it. 'I'm not asking you to do that, Steve. I—'

'That's *exactly* what you're asking me to do, mate, and you know it!' Steve shouted furiously. 'I think it's about time you shared, don't you?!'

Matthew eyed him quizzically.

'You and Sullivan, you two obviously have a history, one that runs much deeper than you're letting on. I think you need to fill me in, don't you, *sir?*'

Matthew heard the derisory edge to the salutation and really couldn't blame him. 'It's ... difficult.' He shrugged evasively.

'Difficult how?' Matthew could feel Steve's eyes drilling into him.

'Complicated,' Matthew amended, searching for a way to divert the conversation.

Steve wasn't about to be diverted, though. 'Personal?'

Matthew dragged a hand over his neck. 'Some.'

'You're not giving me a lot of waggle room, here, Matt. I'm mean, it's either turn a blind eye or go to the DCI. One of us is going to be stuffed and I'm not going to—'

'*Dammit!*' Matthew slammed the heel of his hand against the steering wheel. 'He killed my daughter! Okay! Now, for Christ's sake, can you just drop it?!'

'What?' Steve turned to him astounded.

Feeling a definite wheeze in his chest, Matthew tried to breathe through it. 'Lily,' he clarified, guessing there was no way now that Steve would, or could, drop it, 'She was with Becky. They …' he faltered.

'How?' Steve asked, clearly winded.

'Hit and run.' Matthew tightened his white-knuckled grip on the wheel. 'No witnesses, no substantial evidence. Sullivan was doing time. He set it up, though. As sure as God made fucking little green apples, it was him.'

Steve furrowed his brow. 'But you had nothing to go on?'

Matthew laughed sardonically. 'Nothing but good old intuition, as they say.'

Steve exhaled heavily. 'Blimey.'

'So, is it personal?' Matthew shrugged ambiguously, his gut clenching as his mind played over the graphic images of that Godforsaken day. 'Some people would probably say so. The thing is, though, whatever his method, drugs, guns, knives, cars, his fists, he'd do the same to someone else's daughter, wife, sister. We both know it. And he'll just keep right on doing it, until someone stops him.'

Steve nodded slowly. 'No disrespect, sir,' he said, 'but don't you think that someone should be someone other than you? That you should maybe step away from it?'

'Walk away, you mean?' Matthew glanced at him. 'The way I see it, that would mean personal getting in the way of putting that bastard away.'

Matthew drove on, as Steve fell silent, obviously contemplating his best course of action.

'So,' he said gruffly, after a moment, 'what's the plan, assuming you don't actually want to stitch him up?'

Matthew felt a huge surge of relief flooding through him. Steve had obviously decided not to go to the DC, at least not yet.

'We pay his girls a visit, all of them. Talk to them. Hope they can give us some kind of lead regarding his drug activities, distributers, couriers, drop points. Something around what happened to Brianna. We might get lucky.'

Which wasn't likely, Matthew was well aware. He'd been this route before: customs under surveillance, eyes on Sullivan and the suppliers. Sullivan had got wind of it somehow. Result: no result. Finally, the drugs squad had got one of their own on the inside, but she'd need time to gain the cretin's trust, gather enough concrete information to warrant going that same route again. Meanwhile, if Sullivan got even a sniff of it, that would be it, game over. The chances of any one of his girls giving him anything to work with were slim to nil, but Matthew had to at least try.

'And if we don't get lucky?'

'DS Collins is undercover,' Matthew reminded him. 'She might get something. That's not going to happen anytime soon, though, is it? I need a way of bringing him in now.'

Steve's gaze strayed to the dash. 'Plan B,' he said, his expression uncertain at best.

# CHAPTER SEVEN

Sighing, Matthew considered his next port of call. All he'd got for his efforts so far approaching girls on the streets was his cash supply depleted and sore feet. The girls they'd paid a visit to at their various places of abode hadn't offered anything either, other than to confirm what Matthew already knew, that Sullivan did indeed fill his father's shoes admirably. Each and every one of those girls had been terrified of what might happen if Sullivan found out the law had been sniffing around.

'Do you always part with money for no information?' Steve gave him a curious glance, as they entered another apartment building, this one more upmarket than the rest.

Matthew shrugged. 'Not always.' He flashed his ID at the concierge, who glanced perfunctorily at it, before turning his gaze back to whatever he was watching on his PC. Matthew suspected the guy wouldn't be on Sullivan's payroll very long.

'Right.' Steve rolled his eyes, stepping into the lift beside him. 'Must have missed the one you didn't bung. You've been giving twenties away like they were going out of fashion.'

'It might buy us a future favour.' Matthew shrugged again, as if it was no big deal. 'It might also buy a few of the girls five minutes out of the rain.'

'Yeah, right.' Steve shook his jacket lapels free of water. 'Like they're going to use it to go and buy a Starbucks? Do us a favour.'

'Do I detect a touch of cynicism, DS Ingram?' Matthew asked, leading the way out of the lift. The man was right, though. Chances were the majority of the girls would take a short walk across the road to their dealers and be back doing business five minutes later.

'I was trying not to be cynical.' Steve followed him moodily. 'Even after that shit with the girl behind the Thai restaurant. But then, I opened my boss's glove compartment...'

Acknowledging the jibe with a contrite nod, Matthew hit the doorbell of the apartment he'd paused in front of. The man had every right. He'd spent a considerable amount of time pondering what Matthew had told him. Probably debating whether he'd developed some kind of fixation, waging a personal vendetta on a known criminal based on nothing but fresh air.

'So what's this?' Steve glanced around the tastefully decorated landing. 'Bit fancy for a working girl, isn't it?'

'High class,' Matthew supplied, 'upmarket clientele, by appointment only.'

'Oh, right. Out of my league then?' Steve creased his brow thoughtfully. 'Joking, boss,' he added, as Matthew shot him a warning glance. 'Lindsey's plenty enough for me, given she doesn't dump me if this little lot goes belly up.'

Matthew sighed, reaching for the doorbell again, as the door squeaked open a few inches.

'What do *you* want?' The girl's tone wasn't exactly welcoming. Obviously she'd already established who it was through the peephole.

*Christ.* Catching sight of her face, Matthew winced inwardly. 'Walked into another cupboard door, Natalie?' he asked, taking in her split lip and bruised cheek. 'Or was it a lamppost this time?'

'Fell over the dog,' Natalie said tartly, unhitching the chain and pulling the door open. 'You'd better come in, but you'd better not let Pat know you've been here,' she warned him, heading into the lounge.

'No.' Matthew followed her, indicating Steve to do the same. 'Wouldn't want you falling over any more dogs you haven't got, would we, Nat?'

Natalie shrugged, unperturbed, reached for her cigarettes on the coffee table and turned to face him.

'So, whose handiwork was it, Natalie?' Matthew asked, noticing the bruises also adorning her forearm as she lit up. 'A punter? Or did the lovely Pat feel the need to have a forceful word?'

Natalie drew in a lungful of smoke. 'What do you want, Detective Adams? I don't have all day. Time is money, y'know.'

'Yeah, I know. Have to make sure Pat lives in the style to which he's become accustomed, hey, Natalie?'

Shrugging again, Natalie blew out a cloud of smoke. 'I do all right.'

'Yep, looking good, Natalie.' Smiling ironically, Matthew kneaded his forehead. 'Brianna's not looking too good, unfortunately,' he glanced back at her, 'as you can probably imagine.'

Natalie took another tight draw and turned away.

'I don't know nothing about Brianna.' She stubbed out her cigarette, snatched up her make-up bag, and headed for the mirror.

'No,' Matthew watched her, as she attempted damage limitation to her face, 'not many people do know much about her, suddenly. Strange that, when she'd been in Pat's employ for, what, two, three years?'

Natalie's gaze flicked to Matthew's, as she applied foundation to her cheek.

'Gets her face beaten to a pulp, raped, strangled to death, and people are hard-pushed to remember even her name. Bit sad that, don't you think, Nat?'

Natalie dropped her gaze, her eyes now fixed on the make-up bag she was ferretting through.

'She had a life, Natalie. Dreams, ambitions, parents worried sick about her. Just like you.' Matthew continued to watch, as she extracted her lipstick, making an 'O' with her mouth before applying it. Her hand was shaking, he noted. 'And now she's dead,' he paused, studying her carefully.

'Obliterated,' he went on quietly, as Natalie dropped her lipstick back in her bag and resumed searching through her make-up.

'And it's like she never fucking well *existed!*'

'God!' Natalie dropped the bag as Matthew raised his voice, the contents spewing across the floor. '*What?*' she cried, whirling around. 'What do you want me to say, Matthew? I can't tell you anything!'

'Can't or won't?' Matthew fixed his gaze hard on hers.

Natalie pulled her silk dressing gown tight. 'I can't! You *know* I can't. Look what he did to her. If *I* say anything …' Realising she'd said too much right there and then, Natalie stopped, her eyes wide, and petrified.

'What *who* did to who, Natalie?' Matthew pressed her, hoping, praying … if only she'd just name names.

Natalie glanced hurriedly down. 'I can't, Matthew,' she said shakily. 'You've been good to me, and I'm grateful, but … I just can't.'

Matthew closed his eyes. That was it. He'd had his chance, and he'd blown it. Wearily, he dragged a hand across his neck. 'Can you at least tell me why?'

Natalie shook her head and swiped at a tear on her cheek.

'Right. Okay.' Matthew exhaled, long and hard, and then bent to retrieve her lipstick from the floor. 'Keep painting the smile on, Natalie.' He handed it to her. 'You know where I am.'

Natalie nodded, her gaze still fixed to her feet.

Gesturing Steve, who'd been watching and learning—what a soul-destroying, completely hopeless job it was, Matthew headed for the door.

'She talked to you!' Natalie blurted tearfully behind them. 'She was on the take, and then she talked to you and …'

****

'Pull him.' Matthew instructed, nodding at Sullivan's car driving directly in front of them.

Steve glanced at him askance. 'For what?'

'Breathing,' Matthew suggested, 'which should be an offence against humanity where vermin like him are concerned.'

Natalie had confirmed what he already knew. Matthew's gut twisted afresh. He should go to the DCI. Follow protocol and do it by the book. The chances of the girl making a statement, though, were nil. He had corroboration of sorts but, even with Steve as a witness, without a statement, Sullivan named therein, it amounted to nothing. No, as far as Matthew was concerned, until he had indisputable evidence, the book was out of the window.

'Right.' Steve nodded. 'Can't see that sticking somehow, boss.'

'Rear lights,' Matthew said, as they continued to follow Sullivan, who was obviously aware of being tailed, and cruising towards his house is if he hadn't a care in the world. Baiting him. Always bloody baiting him.

*Scumbag.* Matthew kneaded his temples. Sullivan would be secured behind a very different automated gate if Matthew had his way, permanently. All he needed to do was to pull him in and get him banged up long enough to get him stripped of his personal effects. God willing, he could do it without having to falsify evidence.

'Er, his rear lights are not out,' Steve pointed out, flicking the blues and twos nevertheless.

'Not yet, no.' Matthew's jaw clenched, as the BMW convertible the son of a bitch had obviously worked his fingers to the bone for, slowed to a stop, Sullivan no doubt sitting cockily at the wheel, that smug can't-touch-me look all over his face. Well, Matthew had got news for him. Climbing out of the passenger side, he nodded Steve on, indicating he should have the pleasure of informing Sullivan why he'd been stopped.

Glancing questioningly at Matthew, Steve did as bid. He waited while Sullivan took his time lowering his window, and then, 'Excuse me sir,' he said politely, 'do you realise your rear lights are out?'

'Aw, for fuck's sake,' Sullivan groaned wearily. 'Are you having a laugh, or what?' Thrusting his door wide, he climbed out and walked around to check for himself.

'Nope.' Matthew smiled tightly, joining Sullivan at the back of the car. 'Your lights are out,' he reiterated, kicking one in with the heel of his shoe. 'Both of them.' He made short work of the second light.

Sullivan's response was to stare, dumbfounded for a second, and then laugh out loud. 'Oh, deary me, a girly tantrum. We are desperate, aren't we, Adams? What you going to do now? Write me a ticket?'

Matthew didn't react. 'Move away from the vehicle, please sir,' he requested courteously instead.

Sullivan cocked his head to one side. 'Why?' His look was now one of discernible irritation.

Matthew moved towards him, no attempt this time to hide the anger broiling inside him. 'Because I'd quite like to kick *your* lights out,' he grated, getting some small satisfaction from the flicker of fear he saw in the man's eyes.

Sullivan soon collected himself, squinting at him curiously. 'What are you up to, Adams?'

Matthew held his gaze. 'Just a routine search.'

Sullivan balked. 'Oh, man, you have to be joking. You sad bastard, Adams, you can't keep pulling me over and searching my property without my consent.'

Matthew shrugged indifferently and turned towards the driver's side. 'I think you'll find I can, Sullivan, given grounds for reasonable suspicion.'

'*Reasonable suspicion?*' Sullivan spluttered and made to follow him. Unfortunately, he found himself blocked by Steve's intimidating bulk. 'You're fitting me up, you bastard!'

Matthew ignored him, in favour of climbing into the driver's seat of the BMW. His mouth was dry, his hands shaking, as he retrieved the wraps from his pocket. Was he really going to do this?

'You haven't got a snowball in hell's chance of getting away with this, Adams!' Sullivan shouted around Steve. 'I'll walk. You *know* I will. And *you'll* be stuffed. You won't even get a job as a bloody security guard! Do you hear me?'

'I don't think he's in a listening mood, Patrick,' Steve offered, squaring up to him. 'I'd button it, if I were you.'

'What bloody grounds for suspicion?' Sullivan attempted to push past him.

'Back up,' Steve warned him.

'*He* is legally obliged to tell me what his grounds for suspicion are.' Sullivan jabbed a finger in Matthew's direction. '*And* what he's searching for. I know my rights! You hear me, Adams? Do this and you're finished!'

Matthew pressed the heel of his hand against his forehead, trying to still the images, his daughter's blood seeping towards him, staining the road crimson and soaking into his clothes, the ugly fat fly, which seemed to be buzzing around in his head. He was losing it. He swallowed hard. Sullivan was right. He had no hope of making this stick. Was he really willing to risk screwing Steve's career up, along with his own? What the *hell* had he been thinking? He hadn't been, clearly. Matthew felt the tension slacken a little, as another option occurred. He needed that nail file. The tie might be useful too, which Sullivan was overly fond of straightening. He didn't need to drag Sullivan in to get it, though, did he?

Re-pocketing the drugs, Matthew climbed out of the car. 'Patrick Sullivan,' he said, pulling out his ID card as he walked towards him. 'Detective Inspector Matthew Adams,' he introduced himself, as per protocol during a public search. 'Following a tip off, I have reasonable grounds to believe that you are carrying drugs for purposes of supplying.'

'I don't bloody believe this. You are, aren't you?' Sullivan looked utterly astonished. 'You're going to fit me up?'

'I'm therefore informing you that I intend to carry out a body search.'

'Piss off, Adams.' Sullivan moved towards his car.

'Failure to give consent will result in you being detained for twenty four hours for questioning without formal arrest. Your call, Sullivan.'

Sullivan stopped and turned back. Cocking his head to one side, he appraised Matthew for a second, and then, 'Good film you were watching last night, was it?' he asked.

Fear tightened Matthew's stomach like a slipknot. 'What?'

'*Taken*,' Sullivan went on, narrowing his eyes, weighing Matthew's reaction. 'I thought it was pretty good myself. *Taken Two* wasn't up to much, but ...'

Blind fury sweeping through him, Matthew was on him, slamming his fist so hard into the man's face, he heard bone and sinew crack. '*Bastard!*' he spat, wiping a hand across his mouth, as Sullivan sank to his knees. Matthew wasn't finished with him yet though. Not by a long chalk. He took a step towards him.

'Whoa!' Steve caught hold of Matthew from behind. 'Enough!' he shouted, attempting to pull him off. 'Matthew, leave it!'

But Matthew wasn't hearing him. Surging forward, he grabbed hold of Sullivan, heaving him to his feet by his cashmere-fucking-lapels and dragging him towards him. 'Do *not* go near my wife again,' he seethed. 'If you do I *will* kill you.'

'She's quite tasty,' Sullivan said quietly, thin globules of blood trickling from his mouth, his eyes, black pools of pure evil. 'Girl's tasty too.'

'Bastard!' White-hot rage exploding inside him, Matthew slammed him hard backwards into the car, and then followed through, landing a low blow to his stomach. His temper nowhere near abated, he watched Sullivan crumple, and then kicked him like the fetid animal he was.

'That's enough!' Steve was on Matthew's back, his muscle-bound arms wrapped hard around him.

'Get him off me!' Sullivan screamed, shielding his head from further assault, his voice high-pitched and hysterical. 'Fucking madman, get him off!'

Locking his hold tight, Steve hauled Matthew away. 'Leave it!' he growled, close to his ear. 'He's not worth it.'

Matthew closed his eyes. His chest wheezing, his head reeling, he tried to draw air into his lungs, to think, but the only thought in his head was that he wanted to kill Sullivan, to stop him, to shut him up, once and for all. Counting, desperately trying to control his rage, he looked back to Sullivan. He couldn't quite believe it when Sullivan's mouth twisted into a smirk. Even through the blood smeared across his face, the man's expression was unmistakeable: triumphant.

# CHAPTER EIGHT

Detective Chief Inspector Davies leaned back in his chair. Placing his hands under his chin, he regarded Matthew with quiet despair. 'You do know he's filed charges?' he asked him.
Matthew shook his head. 'It's bullshit. He's trying to get my card marked, that's all. The man's a complete—'
'*Bullshit?*' The DCI's chair hit the wall behind him as he shot to his feet. 'He's at the hospital, Adams!' He balled his fists on his desk and eyeballed him furiously. 'You've probably broken his jaw and the best you can come up with is *it's bullshit?*'
Guessing he was pissed, with good reason, Matthew glanced down. 'It was provoked, sir.' Running a thumb over his own bruised fist, he attempted to explain. 'I—'
'So *you* say!' Davies barked over him. 'Have you taken leave of your senses, DI Adams? Have you been drinking? What?'
'No,' Matthew assured him adamantly. He guessed his drinking would always come up, the months after Lily's death, when he'd been too permanently hung-over to make a right judgement call. He really wished Davies hadn't brought it up in front of Steve, though.
'Because if you are, Adams, I don't need to tell you what the consequences—'
'He threatened my wife!' Matthew's gaze snapped back up. 'He's been following me, for Christ's sake, watching my house! What the *hell* would *you* have done?'
He'd been right *outside* his house, waited until he'd left and Rebecca and Ashley alone inside and then made sure they were petrified out of their wits. There had been a bird. Matthew hadn't been able to work out how it had flown anywhere, maggot riddled and obviously dead. He'd thought a cat maybe? It had been Sullivan, Matthew now realised, his blood running cold.
'I'd have gone through the proper channels, Adams, thereby securing the chance of a formal investigation,' DCI Davies replied tersely. 'DS Ingram,' he turned to Steve, 'I assume you can corroborate these threats?'
Steve shifted awkwardly in his seat. 'I, erm...' He glanced worriedly at Matthew.
'Well?' Davies urged him impatiently.
Steve's shoulders slumped. 'No, sir,' he said, his gaze now anywhere but on Matthew. 'I was too far away to hear the whole conversation.'

DCI Davies sighed heavily and turned to walk towards his window. 'It's a bit of a mess, isn't it, Adams?' he commented, gazing out.

'Yes, sir.' Matthew tried for contrite, though any remorse he was feeling was that he hadn't broken Sullivan's neck. At least then he would be sure Rebecca was safe.

'You do realise you've jeopardised the undercover operation?' Davies asked, as casually as if he were asking about the weather.

*What?* Matthew stared incredulously at his back. 'You're joking?'

'Unfortunately not.' DCI Davies clasped his hands behind him and continued to gaze out of the window, as if he hadn't just delivered a bombshell, announced that the only other plan to nail Sullivan hadn't just been taken off the table. 'We're going to have to pull back, at least until we've cleared this mess up. I think you've marked your own card, Adams.'

Davies turned back, eyeing Matthew meaningfully. 'Not going to be very popular with your colleagues for a while, are you?'

'Bloody hell.' Steve glanced disbelievingly from the DCI to Matthew.

'Bloody hell, indeed.' Davies smiled shortly. 'Thank you, DS Ingram. You can leave now.'

DCI Davies waited while Steve did as bid, casting now very worried glances in Matthew's direction as he went.

'As for you,' Davies turned back to Matthew, 'I think you should take some gardening leave.'

'Uh, uh.' Matthew shook his head. No way was he going to be out of the loop, not knowing what that bastard Sullivan was up to, not now.

'It wasn't a suggestion, DI Adams, it was an order. And, off the record, if you are hitting the bottle again, don't. Okay?'

'What?' Matthew laughed incredulously. Now he had to be joking. They were going to take Sullivan's word over his? Believe there was no provocation? Assume he was back on the booze? *Jesus Christ.* Matthew tried to rein in his tempter.

'Look, John,' he said shakily, 'cut me some slack, will you? I lost it. I know I did. But you *know* me. You also know Sullivan. You must know he pushed me.'

'To the limit probably, but sorry, Matthew, no can do. It shouldn't have happened. Look ...' glancing at him sympathetically, DCI Davies walked around to perch himself on the edge of the desk, '... I know you think Sullivan had something to do with ... the accident ...'

*'Think?'* Matthew balked, astonished. 'He as good as told me. He

tried to warn me off. For God's sake, John?'

'As *good* as told you,' DCI Davies repeated, his meaning implicit. 'There was no evidence against him, Matthew, no witnesses to put him at the scene. The man had an alibi,' he reminded him, as if Matthew needed reminding. 'Take some leave,' he offered, more quietly. 'Spend some time with Rebecca.'

Matthew nodded tightly. 'Right,' he said, swallowing back his disgust and getting to his feet. 'Is that it?'

DCI Davies nodded reluctantly. 'For now.'

'Cheers.' Matthew grated, and turned to slam out of the office. 'Thanks for nothing,' he muttered, striding to his own desk and grabbing his jacket from the back of his chair.

'So?' Steve, who'd been quietly watching him, asked warily.

'So what?' Matthew headed for the door.

'So, what happened?'

'Exactly what Sullivan wanted to happen, Steve!' Matthew rounded on him angrily. 'I'm stuffed. Out! On gardening leave. Pending a psych evaluation, and then on permanent leave probably. Why they *hell* didn't you cover my back?'

Steve scanned his face, his expression unimpressed. 'That's exactly what I did, sir,' he said, his tone flat. 'If not for me it wouldn't be assault you'd be up on a charge for. It would be manslaughter, or worse. I couldn't verify something I didn't hear, though. Maybe I should have lied in there, I don't know. Should I?'

Matthew dropped his gaze. 'No,' he conceded, with a despairing sigh. 'I, er ... Sorry.' He shrugged apologetically. 'I'd better go.'

'Haven't you forgotten something?' Steve reminded him, as Matthew turned back to the door. 'A certain something obtained from friends in wrong places?'

*Hell,* the heroin. Matthew realised he was about to leave with it still in his desk drawer. In which case, it might well have been discovered and then he really would be stuffed.

'You'll find it's over here,' Steve said, as Matthew headed back. 'I thought it might be safer where I could keep an eye on it.'

Guessing he owed Steve more than a half-arsed apology, Matthew nodded gratefully and walked around to the drawer Steve had opened.

'I'll keep you up to speed.' Steve extended his hand, once Matthew had retrieved his illegal goods.

'Cheers,' Matthew shook it, feeling like a total shit for having let the man down, and then worse, as DS Collins came into the office.

'Nice going, sir,' she said, casting him a scathing glance, as she

64

marched past. She was still wearing her sequins under her coat, Matthew noted, and obviously also not overly impressed with him.

****

'Matthew?' Rebecca called, as she came into the kitchen.

'Here.' Matthew looked up from where he sat at the table, nursing a substantial whisky, the bottle parked to one side, Rebecca noted, with some trepidation.

'Twelve?' she asked about his day, which had obviously been a rough one.

Matthew laughed sardonically. 'Way off the scale.'

Rebecca walked over to him. 'It's three a.m.,' she pointed out, gently.

'I know. I'm sorry. I just ...' Heaving out a sigh, Matthew trailed off.

'I take it you can't sleep?' Rebecca ventured. The fact that he'd tossed and turned when he had finally come to bed after mooching about outside for a good hour had given her a subtle indication.

Matthew shrugged. 'Brain's too active. Sorry,' he repeated. 'You're cold.' He looked her over, concerned, as Rebecca rubbed her goose-pimpled arms.

'My foot-warmer deserted me.' She smiled, studying his face. God, he looked so tired. What on earth was it that was worrying him?

'Come here.' Matthew extended and arm and pulled her towards him. 'I'll warm you up.'

Smiling, Rebecca settled into his lap and snuggled into him. 'Not after half a bottle of whisky you won't.'

'Er, no, probably not,' Matthew conceded, with a small smile.

'Do you want to share?' Rebecca glanced up at him.

Matthew drew in a breath and shook his head. 'Just work stuff. Something I have to try to figure out. Nothing to worry about.'

Rebecca didn't push him. She knew better than to do that. Matthew would never share anything he thought might be too upsetting, as if she were made of cut glass. She couldn't help but love him for trying to protect her, but she really did despair of him keeping his emotions bottled up.

Matthew squeezed her closer. 'Sorry,' he said again and planted a soft kiss on the top of her head. 'How's Ashley?' he asked, after a pause.

'Good. Fast asleep with her earphones still plugged in.' Rebecca debated, then, 'She talks to herself, have you noticed?'

'Sorry?' Matthew's mind was obviously elsewhere.

'Ashley, I've heard her. The thing is, it's not to herself exactly, more as if she's talking to someone else.'

'Oh.' Matthew furrowed his brow. 'So, what do you think? An imaginary friend possibly?'

Rebecca hesitated. 'I think it's a real friend. Or at least it was. Someone she might possibly be grieving the loss of.'

'Really?' Matthew contemplated. 'They never mentioned anything at the care home. Do you think it's a problem?'

'No. Not really. I'll mention it to the counsellor, but I think it might just be her way of expressing her emotions. It's just...' Rebecca looked up at him. 'She broke a statue. The porcelain Japanese lady in the lounge, you know the one. It's no big deal, but...'

'But?' Matthew urged her.

'I heard her talking, just before I heard the crash. I was in here. She kept telling whoever it was to stop it. She sounded quite distressed, and ...' Again, Rebecca hesitated, not wanting to add to Matthew's problems. But then, he should know, she supposed '... when I went in, the statue was broken, the scatter cushions were ... Well, scattered everywhere. The magazines on the coffee table, too. She said she saw a mouse, but I'm not convinced.'

Matthew's frown deepened.

'She might just be testing us,' Rebecca suggested.

'Testing you.' Matthew glanced apologetically at her. 'I'm sorry, Becks. I should have been here earlier. I—'

'Got detained, I gathered. You don't have to keep apologising, Matthew. I know the nature of your work means unpredictable hours. I also know it takes a lot out of you. Come on, come to bed.' Slipping off his lap, she threaded an arm through his and urged him up. 'Lie with me, even if you can't sleep.'

'Now there's an offer a man can't refuse.' Matthew smiled and got unsteadily to his feet.

'Unless he's incapable,' Rebecca reminded him. She tried not to read too much into his sitting up drinking. Obviously, he did have some things he needed to think through. Not that he'd be doing much sensible thinking with however many whiskies under his belt. Hopefully, the news she had to tell him would cheer him up a bit. She wouldn't tell him yet, though, not while he'd got so much on his mind. 'I've booked a day off tomorrow,' she said instead, chatting as they walked towards the stairs. 'I thought Ashley and I would go shopping.'

Mathew stopped dead. 'Shopping?' He sounded alarmed.

'Yes?' Rebecca turned to face him, puzzled. 'You know that thing we do when we need to buy things. Ashley needs some stuff. Don't worry, we won't break the bank.'

Matthew ran a hand over his neck, another telling indicator of his stress levels. 'Do you think that's a good idea?'

'Yes.' Rebecca eyed him curiously. It wasn't like Matthew to vet her shopping habits. 'She doesn't even have a decent phone. I thought it might be nice if she had some of the normal things a teenager should have. Plus her wardrobe needs a bit of a makeover. Do you not think it's a good idea then?'

'No. Yes. I, er…' Matthew appeared confused, indecisive, definitely not himself, possibly due to alcohol consumption. 'It's a great idea.' He smiled, finally. 'In fact, I'll come with you.'

Now Rebecca was definitely worried. Matthew tried, but shopping was not on top of his list of fun things to do. 'You? Shopping? On a work day?'

'I have some leave,' Matthew said quickly. 'Annual leave I need to take, so…' He shrugged, trying for nonchalant, but still he looked as confused as Rebecca felt.

She needed to get him to bed, she decided. He was exhausted. Whatever he was worrying about would still be there in the morning.

'You hate shopping,' she reminded him. 'In any case, I thought it would be a perfect opportunity to do a bit of girl-talk, which I'm thinking you would also probably hate. Come on.'

Taking hold of his hand, she gave him a tug onwards, at which Matthew winced.

'Matthew?' Rebecca glanced down at the hand he was now attempting to retract. 'What on earth have you done?'

'Car door,' Matthew was quick to answer again. 'We were out on a shout. Steve got a bit keen. I'll come shopping with you,' he repeated, holding her gaze, searching her eyes. Rebecca detected a hint of desperation in his.

'Okay,' she relented, growing more concerned as she glanced again at his bruised knuckles and then back to his face. 'But you get to pay for lunch,' she warned him, attempting to lead him upstairs, 'and no complaining in the lingerie department.'

'Do I ever?' Matthew said, sounding relieved, more like himself.

Still Rebecca was concerned. It was true he didn't mind the lingerie-shopping bit, he was actually quite good at selecting it, but shopping generally wasn't something he would volunteer for. She needed to talk to him properly, get to the root of what was troubling him. Tomorrow would be soon enough, though, when he'd had a chance to catch up on his sleep.

※※※※

Matthew was still dead to the world when Rebecca went back up to check on him the next morning. Even sleeping, he looked troubled. No wonder when he'd woken at least three times in the night, clearly haunted by some recurring nightmare. Was he feverish, coming down with something? There was an awful bug going around at the hospital. Looking him over, she noted his sweat-dampened torso, half in and half out of the duvet he'd wrestled with. He was obviously exhausted. Trooping round the shops was probably the last thing he needed. She'd leave him, she decided. The rest would do him good.

Padding back out, she closed the door carefully behind her and headed along the landing to Ashley's room.

'Ready?' She poked hear head around the door, and then pressed a finger to her lips when Ashley looked up from the clothes she was searching through. 'Matthew's still sleeping.'

Ashley nodded. 'Two minutes,' she said and went back to her clothes-strewn bed.

*Not so far off normal teenager then?* Rebecca smiled, reminding herself mess was good, as she headed downstairs.

She found a pen and wrote Matthew a quick note: *Sorry, you've been outvoted. Stay and catch up on your beauty sleep. Back around five. Catch you later. xxxx P.S. Haute cuisine not necessary. I'll bring some ready meals in. P.P.S. Love you loads.*

Adding a few more kisses for luck, Rebecca looked up as Ashley appeared.

'Do I look okay?' she asked, peering uncertainly from under her curtain of hair.

'Lovely,' Rebecca assured her. She took in the trainers, which had seen better days, the black leggings and faded grey tee. 'I think we could improve on the trainers, though,' she suggested diplomatically. 'What do you think?'

'Cool.' Ashley brightened and dragged her hair from her face.

She was definitely pretty, Rebecca decided. Exceptionally pretty.

'How about me? Will I pass?' She indicated her own attire: her oversize cable-knit sweater over a loose fitting shirt-dress.

'Yeah, good,' Ashley offered. 'Like the boots.'

Rebecca glanced down at her trusty Lolita ankle boots, red in colour, and quite trendy for someone who must appear ancient in Ashley's eyes. More importantly, they were made for walking in, thank goodness. Feeling distinctly wobbly herself earlier, Rebecca might have been struggling to keep the pace otherwise.

'Come on then, let's hit the shops, before Matthew wakes up and decides to tag along.'

She plucked up her bag and car keys, hooked arms with Ashley and the two headed for the door. Rebecca was actually looking forward to this. She hadn't had a good girly shop in ages.

# CHAPTER NINE

Realising the shrill cry piercing his brain wasn't part of his nightmare, Matthew bolted upright. Sweat saturating his forehead and pooling at the base of his neck, he disentangled himself from the duvet and stumbled out of bed.
*Dammit.* Where *was* the bloody thing? Glancing around the room for his ringing mobile, he tried to shake his head free of black crows picking over dead carcasses, and his gut feeling that something was very wrong. Searching through his clothes, he finally located the phone in his jacket pocket and jabbed urgently at the answer button. 'Adams?'
'He's filed,' Steve announced, without ceremony. 'Came in with his solicitor in tow. I thought you should know.'
'Right.' Matthew sucked in a tight breath. 'What am I looking at?'
Steve hesitated. 'Section 18 Assault,' he then delivered the bad news solemnly.
*GBH with intent*, Matthew mentally translated, which meant, if it stuck, it would be prosecuted in the Crown Court, ergo, he was stuffed, totally.
'You'll need to come in and make a statement,' Steve reminded him, after another uncomfortable pause.
Matthew closed his eyes and swallowed hard.
'Matt?'
'Yes!' Matthew answered shortly, 'I gathered. I'll get showered and be right there.'
Which meant his intended search of the house would have to wait. Whatever Davies chose to believe, Sullivan *had* been here. The man had been crawling around his property, spying on his wife, like some sick animal hunting its prey. Leaving nothing to chance, Matthew had intended to take the place apart, search it inch by inch. Listening devices and hidden cameras weren't unfeasible. Anything was possible where Sullivan was concerned.
'Not sure it will help much, but I did mention I heard you telling him to stay away from your wife,' Steve offered. 'Like I say, not sure it will do any good, but ...'
'Okay.' Matthew nodded, grateful that Steve, at least, didn't seem to be casting him as the villain. 'Thanks, Steve.'
'Least I could do,' Steve said, awkwardly.
'Has he left?' Matthew asked, trying to focus on the here and now,

rather than the waking nightmare his life was about to become.

'Sullivan, is he still on the premises?'

'Left about an hour ago. I tried to call you, but you weren't answering.'

Meaning Sullivan was now free to do what he liked to whoever he liked and no one could touch him. It had been a clever plan, Matthew had to concede. Sullivan had obviously considered it worth taking a beating to make sure Matthew's hands were tied. He'd turned the tables: stitched *him* up. One provocation too far was all it had needed. Sullivan had known it.

'I'll be there shortly,' he said, hanging up. He'd have to talk to Rebecca, Matthew realised, grabbing his trousers and tugging them on. He'd hoped not to. At least not yet, some small part of him hoping this wasn't happening. That his colleagues would take his word over a piece of lowlife scum; that his wife might even be offered protection.

*Hah!* Fat chance. Matthew laughed cynically, angrily stuffing an arm into his shirt. They'd claimed to believe his theory that Sullivan had something to do with Lily's death, but without proof, there could be no prosecution. This time, Davies had made it blatantly obvious he thought Matthew had been making up fairy stories, taking an opportunity to seek some form of retribution. And this time, it was him being prosecuted.

In which case, this time, he *would* make sure Sullivan got what was coming. And if he had to go above the law, so be it. His jaw tight-set, his emotions spiralling, Matthew headed for the landing.

'Becky?' He headed down the stairs and across the empty lounge to the kitchen. Finding that empty too, he went back upstairs to check out Ashley's room, even knowing she wouldn't be there.

Nothing. *Shit!* Matthew turned full circle, dragged his hand through his hair in frustration, and then went to the bedroom window to check on Rebecca's car. Gone, he registered, turning to race back down to the kitchen. Panic knotting his insides, he scanned the working surfaces, trying to unscramble his brain and remember what the hell Rebecca had said. And there it was, a note propped against the kettle. Matthew squeezed his eyes shut tight, his heart sinking fast. *Shopping.* Sullivan was walking around scot-free, following her possibly, and she'd gone shopping.

'*Christ.*' Matthew ran to the front door, grabbed up his car keys from the console, and then stopped. But *where* had she gone shopping? Talk about bloody incompetence! Cold apprehension snaking its way down his spine, Matthew pulled his phone from his pocket. Why hadn't he been listening properly? Why hadn't he remembered? What in God's name had he been doing drinking? He needed to stay alert. He needed to be protecting his wife, and he'd downed half a bottle of whisky? What the *hell* was the matter with him?!

Trying to slow his breathing, his rapid-fire thoughts skipping all other possibilities to arrive at worst case scenario, he selected Rebecca's number, and his heart plummeted to the pit of his stomach.

'Becky, can you ring me as soon as you get this?' An audible wheeze in his chest, his throat tight with emotion, Matthew spoke as calmly as he could to her voicemail. 'It's urgent.'

xxxx

'So, which is it to be? iPhone or Samsung?' Rebecca asked after Ashley's choice of new phone and tried not to worry too much about the damage to her bank account. The delight on Ashley's face was worth every penny.

'Um?' Ashley squeezed her eyes closed. 'Samsung,' she finally plumped for. 'Then I can transfer all my stuff from my old phone.'

'Sure?' Rebecca smiled indulgently. They'd only been in the shop almost an hour. Not time enough, surely, to make such a momentous decision?

'Sure.' Ashley nodded happily and went off to browse, while Rebecca sorted out the contract and payment.

Pleased with their progress, Rebecca watched Ashley, as the assistant filled in the paperwork. She looked better already, new chunky ankle boots on her feet, rather than her tatty old trainers, a bit of a restyle to her hair. Ashley hadn't wanted too much taken off, just a reshape around her face. That was definitely a right decision. There were women who would kill for hair that was naturally silken smooth. Aware her own strawberry frizz was in need of a trim, Rebecca made a mental note to book an appointment for next time she was in town and went to collect her charge, before Ashley tapped her way through every PC keyboard in the shop.

'So where next?' Rebecca asked, hooking arms with her as they walked.

'*New Look*,' Ashley decided. Clearly she was revelling in being let loose in the shops. Rebecca guessed that, in the normal scheme of things, giving teenagers free rein in the shopping centre wasn't generally a great idea, but Ashley had never had a normal scheme of things, as far as Rebecca knew. And a little over-indulgence seemed to be doing a hell of a lot more good than it did harm. The megawatt smile Ashley had beamed her when she'd sanctioned the boots, was pure gold in terms of reward. The little gold locket she'd also bought her wasn't massively expensive, but the look on Ashley's face, one of genuine delight, had been priceless.

'New Look it is. And then coffee,' Rebecca decided. 'My old bones can't keep up with you.'

'You're not old,' Ashley gave her a reassuring glance over her shoulder as she made a beeline for teenage heaven. 'Just more mature.'

'Yes, cheers, Ashley. I think.' Rebecca rolled her eyes and then scooted to keep up with her.

*New Look* purchases in hand, leggings and cropped sweaters for Ashley, another oversized sweater for Rebecca, they collected up their caramel lattes and Belgian chocolate teacakes and parked themselves at *Costa Coffee*.

'So where else do you want to try for your slim leg trousers?' Ashley asked, and then attempted to lick latte from the end of her nose.

'Not sure.' Rebecca did likewise.

Ashley cocked her head to one side, laughing at Rebecca as she failed miserably. 'You missed,' she said.

'Yup.' Rebecca used the back of her hand instead.

Still laughing, Ashley followed suit—and Rebecca thought that now might be a good time to have a chat with her. As they'd already touched on the subject and, on the basis she would have to share her news with Ashley anyway, it was probably better sooner, rather than later. 'Can I ask you something, Ashley?' she started hesitantly.

Ashley's guard went up immediately. 'Suppose.' She shrugged and proceeded to pick chocolate off her teacake.

'Do you like living with us? With Matthew and me?'

Ashley glanced back at her. Rebecca expected another non-committal shrug. What she got was a pleasant surprise.

'Yes,' Ashley said, straight off, and then knitted her brow. 'Why?'

'Do you think you'd like to stay?' Rebecca pushed on.

'Huh-huh.' Ashley's expression was apprehensive.

'We'd like you to, too.' Rebecca smiled reassuringly. 'But I do have something to discuss with you. Not something bad,' she added quickly, noting Ashley's immediately downcast eyes, the way her hand withdrew from her cake, as if she'd suddenly lost her appetite.

Rebecca took a huge breath, then, 'I need a friend,' she announced.

Ashley's gaze flicked cautiously back to Rebecca's face.

'Matthew's my friend, of course, and I love him dearly, but

...' Rebecca paused, wondering how she could put this without appearing to be slating Matthew. 'Well, he's a man,' she opted for, 'and I need someone I can talk girl stuff with. Could you be my friend, Ashley, do you think?'

Ashley tipped her head to one side, her brow creased thoughtfully. 'I am your friend,' she said, now looking confused.

'Good.' Rebecca didn't have to feign relief. 'Because I have a secret I need to share. It's just between you and me, I don't want Matthew to know yet, but...' she took another breath '... I'm pregnant.'

Rebecca swallowed and waited.

'Oh.' Ashley's almond-shaped eyes widened. 'Shit,' she said bluntly. 'I bet that's a bit scary. After what happened before, I mean.'

'Yes, yes it is.' Rebecca nodded, amazed. She hadn't really known what reaction to expect, resentment possibly, signs of insecurity, indifference.

Ashley actually seemed interested. 'Can I ask you something?'

'Ask away.' Rebecca smiled, ready to reassure her if she asked whether they would still want her to stay, which she expected she might. The pregnancy might not go full-term. Things might not work out with Ashley long-term, but Rebecca wanted her to know that another child, God willing, was something she'd factored in anyway.

'How do you know you'll love it?' Ashley asked, catching Rebecca off guard.

Rebecca considered, guessing this was something to do with Ashley's own unloved past. 'I think it's instinctive, or at least it should be,' she answered honestly, sensing that that was what Ashley needed.

'Yeah.' Ashley's rich cognac eyes turned a shade darker. 'My mum obviously wasn't very instinctive.'

Aware this was sensitive ground, Rebecca trod carefully. 'Sometimes something goes wrong,' she offered gently. 'For some reason, mother and baby don't bond.'

'She was probably too drunk,' Ashley said startlingly, and then, 'Do your parents love you?' she asked.

'Yes.' Rebecca nodded, as Ashley held her gaze, probably trying to work out what would make a person lovable. 'Yes, they do.'

'You're obviously worth loving,' Ashley smiled, a smile so sad it was heart-breaking.

Rebecca reached across the table, taking hold of the hand Ashley wasn't picking at her teacake with. 'And so are you,' she assured her.

Ashley shrugged again, then, 'Do you have any sisters or brothers?' she asked, neatly changing the subject.

'One: a brother. He lives in Cambridge. You'll probably meet him at Christmas, but beware, he can be a real pain sometimes.'

'Aren't boys always,' Ashley commented drolly.

'Um?' Rebecca was contemplating her answer when Ashley confided something that took her completely by surprise.

'I had a sister,' she said, plucking a little of her cake as she spoke. 'She was a real pain, too.' Popping the cake in her mouth, she chewed and glanced around. 'I still think she's here sometimes.'

A *sister?* But ... Matthew had never mentioned a sister. Did he even know? Astounded, Rebecca gauged Ashley carefully. 'Is that who you talk to, Ashley?'

There was that shrug again. 'Sometimes.'

Rebecca was about to probe a little deeper when Ashley emitted an audible sigh and flopped back in her seat. 'Must be nice to be normal,' she said, longingly.

Seeing her obvious self-doubt, Rebecca swallowed back a lump in her throat. 'Sometimes people perceived as normal are just better at papering over the cracks, Ashley,' she pointed out, softly. 'No one is normal. We all have our faults. The thing to do is not blame yourself for other people's shortcomings. They just weigh you down in the end, fill you full of doubt and stifle who you are, you know?'

Ashley frowned. 'I think so.' She nodded, slowly.

Rebecca hoped so. Dearly hoped she wouldn't go through the rest of her life thinking her mother's faults were because of her. 'So, now we've put the world to rights,' she checked her watch, 'we'd better go and see if Matthew's recovered from his hangover while we've been spending his money. Are you going to eat the rest of that teacake, or donate it to a worthy cause?'

At which, Ashley grinned and stuffed it in her mouth. 'You shouldn't eat for two,' she mumbled, between chomps. 'You'll get fat.'

'Thank you.' Rebecca grabbed up her bags. 'You're doing my confidence the world of good.'

'Just offering you a bit of friendly advice.' Ashley smiled cheekily, as she squeezed out of her seat, which was as near normal teenager as she could be, for now.

'Don't forget your phone.' Checking the table as they left, Rebecca picked up the old phone Ashley had left behind.

'Could you put it in your bag?' Ashley asked, busy with her new phone.

Along with her earphones, her new *Miss Selfridge* dangly earrings for safekeeping, and her half-drunk bottle of coke. Rebecca rolled her eyes and made a mental note to put *bigger handbag* on her next shopping trip.

'Does Matthew drink much?' Ashley asked, as they walked back to the car. Her eyes were on her phone but her antennae were on red alert, Rebecca imagined.

'No,' she assured her adamantly. 'Only ever occasionally, and usually when he's struggling with some upsetting case at work. He's a good man, Ashley, trust me on that, even-tempered, fair, and good fun, if you can ever get his mind *off* his work, that is.'

# CHAPTER TEN

'So, you're telling me that you can take men off the job to escort Sullivan to the hospital, as if he's lost the use of his legs, but you can't allocate protection for a woman he's threatened?' Matthew tried to get his head around it.

Sighing, DCI Davies propped his elbows on his desk and kneaded his forehead. 'We have a duty of care, Matthew. The man—'

'Duty of care?' Matthew stared at him astounded. 'What about a *duty of care* to one of our own, John? For God's sake, we're talking about my wife!'

'Look, Matthew,' DCI Davies looked back at him, his expression somewhere between sympathy and exasperation, 'don't you think you might be getting a little paranoid here?'

'*Paranoid?*' Matthew shook his head, incredulous. 'He told me what *film* we were watching. Are you saying that was just a wild guess?'

Davies drew in a breath. 'Not according to Sullivan he didn't.'

'Ah, I see. Well that must be right then. Obviously, I must have misheard.'

'That's the point here, though, Matthew, isn't it, who heard what and who didn't? DS Ingram was standing two yards away from you. His account of what was said, or not, does *not* tally with yours. Either way, I see no evidence of actual threats.'

Matthew noted the *don't-challenge-my-temper* look on the man's face and felt a mixture of sheer disbelief and creeping hopelessness.

'Right.' He drew in a terse breath. 'So what you're actually saying is that you don't believe me.'

'I didn't say that, Matthew. I said—'

'I heard.' Matthew turned away.

'I'll try,' Davies said, behind him. 'If you're really concerned, I'll try and get someone out to your house tomorrow, but I can't prom—'

'Forget it,' Matthew tossed over his shoulder.

'I said, I'd try,' Davies called after him, as Matthew banged furiously out of his office.

'Not fucking good enough, *sir*,' Matthew shouted back. *Stuff it*, he thought, not giving a damn about possible charges of insubordination, or the loaded hush that fell over the outer office as he stormed through it, the most notable pause in conversation being that between Steve and DS Collins.

'Looks like someone's determined to balls up his career,' she commented, as Matthew neared Steve's desk.

'Leave it, Sally.' Steve shot her a warning glance. 'Cut him some slack, hey?'

'As long as he's not dragging everyone else down the slippery slope with him.' DS Collins swept majorly unimpressed eyes over Mathew and headed back to her own desk.

'He's not being very helpful, I take it?' Steve nodded towards the DCI's office as he stood to walk to the door with Matthew.

'Not a lot, no.' Selecting Rebecca's number, Matthew pressed his phone to his ear. *'Dammit,'* he muttered, as Rebecca's voicemail picked up for the umpteenth time. 'Becky, will you *please* pick up?' He left yet another message. 'I need you to call me.'

'Problem?' Steve asked.

'No, 'course not,' Matthew grated sardonically and selected his home number. 'Sullivan's made threats to my wife. She's on the missing list. Me, I'm just being the tiniest bit paranoid on account of the fact that the bastard killed my daughter! No problem, Steve. Should there be?'

Steve glanced away uncomfortably, then, 'Can I have a word?' he asked, over a silence now so profound a paperclip could be heard dropping.

Matthew held up his hand, indicating Steve should wait while he made his call. 'Becky, it's me. Can you pick up?' Pulling a frustrated breath when she didn't, he went on, 'Becky, if you get this, can you please ring me urgently. If not... I'm on my way back. See you soon.'

Matthew prayed to God he would see her soon, that he was being paranoid, at least on this. 'I need to go, Steve. I'll catch up with you later.'

'I'll walk with you. One second.' Steve turned to grab his jacket from the back of his chair and follow Matthew out.

'Well?' Matthew's stride was brisk, his attention span nil.

'I'll help you out. I'm taking some sick leave,' Steve announced, 'as of now. Least I can do.'

That got his attention. Matthew glanced curiously sideways at him. 'Have you cleared it?'

'Not yet, no. I'll let Davies know and then I'll come and keep watch on the house.'

'If it's not too late to do any damn good,' Matthew growled, then, 'Sorry, Steve.' He closed his eyes, feeling some sense of relief. 'Are you sure about this? It won't do you any favours.'

Steve shrugged. 'They can bollock me, but they can't sack me.

'There's something else,' he said, as Matthew swung out of the doors at the back of the station.

'What?' Matthew didn't pause, but headed swiftly for his car.

Keeping pace with him, Steve ferretted in his pocket. 'This.' Waiting until Matthew had climbed behind the wheel, he presented him with a plastic evidence bag.

Matthew looked at it, noted the contents, and then looked back to Steve, astonished.

'I, erm, volunteered to assist the officer assigned to make sure duty of care was carried out,' Steve explained. 'Sullivan had to take his coat off and that, er …'

Matthew eyed Steve narrowly. 'Fell out of his pocket?'

'Something like that.' Steve glanced at him sheepishly. 'I know it won't be admissible, given how it was obtained, but, well, I saw him using it when we paid him a visit, clocked you'd seen it and … I figured we had nothing to lose.'

Matthew thought about it. It wouldn't be admissible. No way on God's green earth would it be. It might also be too contaminated to collect any DNA from, but …

'I thought if forensics managed to come up with anything we could … I dunno … convince the DC to ask for a search warrant? Maybe get lucky and get hold of the tie? Something anyway,' Steve trailed off, assessing Matthew worriedly.

'You could get kicked off the force, you know?' Matthew warned him.

Something Steve had obviously considered. He nodded. 'I'm not sure I want to stay on it, to be honest, boss. Lindsey's got this idea about us running a dog kennel together. She's trained, got her dog counselling certificate and everything. We're both into them, dogs, I mean, and … Well, to be honest, I'm struggling to sleep nights, you know?'

Matthew did know. Oh, how he knew.

'I wondered …' Steve hesitated, scratching his forehead with is thumb. 'It's just a hunch, as they say, but …'

'I need to go, Steve.' Matthew started the engine.

'The shoe,' Steve said quickly. 'Brianna's missing shoe. It wasn't found. I wondered whether it might be worth trying to link it to similar cases, maybe find an MO? I dunno, I'm probably just fishing in the dark, but—'

'Do it,' Matthew said, wondering why he hadn't already actioned that himself. 'Before you go off sick. And get that to Nicky.' He handed the bag back. 'We'll discuss the pros and cons later.'

Pulling his car door shut, Matthew skidded into reverse. 'I owe you one,' he shouted through his window, as he careered towards the car park exit.

'Two.' Steve shouted back. 'I'll see you at your place a.s.a.p.'

※※※

'So what do you fancy?' Rebecca asked after Ashley's preference for dinner as she signalled to turn into their road. 'Lasagne or ... *Shit!* she cursed, as something thudded metallically into the back of her.

'I think I'll pass on the shit,' Ashley said, fending off the dash, as Rebecca slammed on the brakes.

'What the hell is that idiot *doing?*' Rebecca glanced angrily through her rear view mirror at the idiot behind them. 'Are you all right?' She turned anxiously towards Ashley.

Ashley mustered up a smile. 'Yep,' she assured her. 'All in one piece.'

'Right, I think I'll give *him* my considered advice on his driving skills.' Rebecca heaved her door open and climbed out huffily, only to meet the driver who'd just rammed them coming in the other direction.

'God, I am *so* sorry,' he said immediately. 'Damn sat nav's got me going around in circles. I wasn't paying attention. Are you hurt?'

Rebecca's bluster depleted a little. 'No, but we could have been. Seriously. You really should keep your eyes on the road.'

'I can't apologise enough,' the man said. 'I'll pay for any damage, of course. If you let me have your details, I'll get on to my insurance straightaway.'

'I don't think I have my documents with me.' Rebecca frowned and turned back towards the car.

'Not to worry.' He reached inside his overcoat and extracted a pen and notebook. 'We'll just swap names and phone numbers. And vehicle registrations, obviously,' he said, as Rebecca turned back, eyeing him dubiously.

*She doesn't like him,* Emily, ever-present, when Ashley wished she would just go-away, observed. *I don't. He's got a funny face.*

'Right,' Rebecca nodded, 'okay. It's Rebecca Adams.' She watched while he wrote it down. '01—'

'Oh, wow! I thought it was!' The man's eyes widened interestedly as he looked back at her. 'Matthew has your photo on his desk,' he explained, in answer to Rebecca's puzzled expression.

By which, Rebecca seemed somewhat reassured, Ashley noted. Emily was right though. He was funny-looking, smarmy, and he looked like he was sucking on a gobstopper.

'DS Sullivan.' The man extended his hand. 'Matthew's my boss. I've just dropped him off, actually. He's got one on him, I'm afraid.' He sighed melodramatically and glanced skywards.

Now Rebecca looked doubly confused. 'Matthew?'

'You know how he is,' the man went on chummily.

*He's a troublemaker,* Emily said. *He's got slitty eyes. I don't like him.*

'Shush.' Ashley was trying to listen.

'Obsessed with his work,' the man elaborated, with a sigh. 'Wants all the t's crossed and i's dotted, every criminal brought to justice. He's like a one-man crusade sometimes.'

'Well, yes,' Rebecca nodded thoughtfully, 'he does take his job seriously, but I can't say I blame him, given the line of ...'

'No, no, I don't either,' the man said quickly. 'We all stand in awe of him. He's like a dog with a bone, refuses to let go once he's got his teeth into a case, particularly if it's some young girl, who's been ...' he trailed off, glancing pointedly towards Ashley. 'Well you probably know what I mean better than I do. It's understandable he'd lose it sometimes.'

'Lose it?' Rebecca blinked at him, astonished.

'My fault. I cocked up, again.' The man glanced embarrassedly down. 'Let a piece of crucial evidence slip through my fingers, lost us a big case. The boss was well-annoyed, as you can imagine.' He furrowed his brow, pressing a hand to his chin gingerly and wincing demonstrably as he did.

Rebecca was now staring at the man, looking utterly confounded.

'You mean,' her gaze strayed to the obvious swelling on his face, 'Matthew did that?'

'Like I say, my fault,' the man smiled benevolently and winced again. 'I'd better let you go. Sorry to deliver the old man back in such a bad mood. Don't worry about the details.' He waved his notebook as he turned back to his car. 'I know where you are.'

※※※※

'Where the *hell* have you been?' Matthew demanded, immediately when Rebecca and Ashley came through the front door.

'Shopping.' Rebecca glanced warily at him, and then beyond him, bewildered, as she noticed the lounge in complete disarray: cushions tossed arbitrarily from sofas, cupboards pulled away from walls. The console table next to the front door had been moved, too, drawers open, the contents spewing out. The items that were normally on top of it were strewn on the floor, and the wall-mounted phone socket appeared to have been unscrewed and left dangling.

*What on earth?* Rebecca shook her head, confused. 'Matthew, what's wrong?' She looked back at him, panic rising in her chest.

'Why wasn't your bloody phone on?' Avoiding the question, Matthew seemed almost to be challenging her, as he came towards her.

A feeling of uneasiness washing over her, Rebecca deposited her bags on the floor and urged Ashley on past her. 'I left it in the car. I … Matthew, what's going on?'

'I said I'd come with you!' Matthew glared at her angrily. 'Why the bloody hell didn't you wake me, Rebecca?'

He'd called her Rebecca. He never did that, ever. She scanned his face, growing more and more anxious. His eyes had darkened, she noticed, flint-edged and hard, his pupils were so large there was barely any chocolate-brown there at all. He was furious, palpably. *With her? But why?* Rebecca blinked back the tears pricking at the back of her own eyes.

'I thought you could use the sleep,' she answered uncertainly. 'You looked exhausted and I didn't want to disturb—'

'I've left you a thousand messages, Becky!' Matthew raised his voice, causing her to flinch. 'Didn't it occur to *you* to ring *me?*'

'No!' Rebecca held his gaze, though her stomach knotted queasily inside her. 'Why would it? I said we were going shopping. I left you a note! I didn't realise I had to ask your permission or check in every five minutes!'

Matthew closed his eyes, looking momentarily as stunned as she felt.

'You don't. I—' He paused, pinching the bridge of his nose hard between his thumb and forefinger. 'I'm sorry. I was—'

'What's this all about, Matthew?' Rebecca cut in, disoriented and desperately worried. She'd never seen him like this before, ever. Had he been drinking again? In the day? He'd been in a very dark place once, drinking to anaesthetise himself. Rebecca was aware of that and why. But he'd stopped. For the sake of their relationship and his job, he'd cut down considerably. Or so he'd said. And now this.

'I just need to know where you are, that's all,' he said shortly.

His tone was less aggressive, but still intimidating. Rebecca felt a hard kernel of anger unfurling inside her. 'Don't do this, Matthew,' she warned him. 'Just don't.'

Looking him over disappointedly, Rebecca left it there. She needed explanations, and she needed them now, but out of earshot of Ashley, who'd undoubtedly already witnessed enough upset and anger in her life.

'We'll talk in the kitchen.' She glanced up the stairs to make sure that Ashley wasn't loitering on the landing and then moved past him. 'I'm going to make some tea, assuming *that's* all right with you, of course.'

'Becky ...' Sighing heavily, Matthew turned to follow her. 'Look, I'm sorry. I didn't mean to lose my temper. There are some things I need to explain. I—'

'No?' Rebecca turned back, wondering how it suddenly seemed that she didn't know Matthew at all. 'I don't suppose you meant to lose your temper with your colleague either?'

'What?' Matthew narrowed his eyes quizzically. 'Which colleague?'

'The one who just dropped you off, who then, incidentally, ran into the back of my car. And no wonder. To his credit the man actually stood up for you, though I have no idea—'

'What man?' Matthew stepped quickly towards her, his expression now thunderous. 'Becky, what fucking *man?*' he shouted.

'DS Sullivan!' Rebecca shouted back tearfully.

'*Jesus Christ.*' Matthew paled, visibly. 'You spoke to him?'

'Of course I spoke to him! He ran into the back of my car!'

Matthew took another step towards her, catching hold of her arm. 'What did he say?'

Rebecca felt herself starting to shake, inside and out. 'I gave him my details,' she stammered, fear clutching at the pit of her stomach. 'He talked about you. He—' she stopped, noting the look now in Matthew's eyes, one of pure unbridled hatred. 'Matthew, stop! You're frightening me.'

'When?' Matthew demanded furiously.

'Just now.' Rebecca caught a sob in her throat. 'I told you.'

'We need to talk,' Matthew grated, loosening his grip on her arm to fumble for his phone.

Rebecca watched in disbelief. It was true. All that man had said was true. This Matthew wasn't the Matthew she knew. Rebecca swallowed hard, watching him pace, the agitation in his body language, as he searched for a number. His knuckles were bruised. She noticed them again, a sick feeling of trepidation washing over her. Cautiously, she stepped past him, her mind running through all sorts of reasons why he should be like this. Was he having some kind of a breakdown? She needed to get help, call someone, Steve possibly? Her brother? Her gaze strayed to the dangling landline socket, and her heart sank. Her mobile, she realised, was still in the car. Glancing again at Matthew, who was busy with his call, Rebecca took her chance. Her car keys still in her hand, she flew to the front door and yanked it open.

'Becky!' Matthew whirled around, pursuing her as she fled. Rebecca could almost feel him on her. Panic surging her forwards, she pulled open the car door, threw herself inside and dropped the locks fast.

'Becky! For God's sake!' Matthew tugged at the door handle, slamming the flat of his free hand against the driver's side window.

'Becky, don't!' he shouted, as she shoved the key in the lock and started the engine. 'Listen to me. *Please.* I'm begging you.'

She needed to ring someone. She needed to do it now. Closing her eyes briefly, her heart thundering inside her, Rebecca pulled away.

Matthew gave chase, as she plunged her foot down on the accelerator. The car rattling as it dipped and lurched over deep tyre-tracks and divots, Rebecca pressed her foot harder down and gripped the steering wheel tight.

'*Becky!* Matthew called, losing ground, as she forced the car on. 'Becky!'

God, no... Matthew ground to a halt, his head reeling as he watched the car disappear into the distance. What the hell had he done?

His chest tightening, he turned to run back to the house. 'Ashley!' Coming through the front door, he scrambled through the rubbish he'd dumped on the floor in search of his own car keys. 'Ash...' *Shit!* Matthew straightened up to find her standing right behind him.

'Why did you do that?!' Ashley's screamed. 'We had a lovely day and you had to go and spoil it!' Her arms were rigid at her side, her eyes wild. 'Why did you *do* it?'

Matthew's heart flipped over, as the front door slammed shut behind him. Trying to still his escalating panic, he turned his attention to Ashley.

'Ashley, I know what it looked like. I know it seemed like I was angry. I was. I am, but *not* with Becky *or* with you. She's in danger and I'm scared for her, Ashley. I don't have time to explain right now. I have to go and look for her. Do you understand?'

Her expression a little less hostile, Ashley nodded uncertainly.

'Will you help me? Will you stay here in case she comes back?'

Another small nod, the fury he'd seen sparking in her eyes beginning to wane.

'The phone's working.' He indicated the socket he'd unscrewed while he'd been searching for any kind of device that might somehow have been planted. 'Stay by it.'

Placing his hands on her shoulders, he locked his gaze on hers and prayed she'd realise the importance. 'Ring me if she does come back. Ring me if you're worried about anything. Slide the bolt on the door while I'm gone, and don't answer it to anyone. *Anyone*, Ashley,' he reiterated forcefully. 'After what you just witnessed, I know your instinct is not to trust me, but I need you to, for Becky's sake. Can you do that?'

Ashley's nod was more fervent, this time.

'Okay, good.' Matthew turned back to the front door. 'Make sure to lock it.' He glanced meaningfully at her again, before racing to his car.

# CHAPTER ELEVEN

'Typical copper, thinking he's above the law.' Patrick shook his head disgustedly, as he watched Matthew drive past the lane he'd parked discreetly in while he waited. 'He's way over the speed limit, look at him. You'd think he'd have learned his lesson, wouldn't you? I mean, there are only so many kids you can put in the ground, before you get a light-bulb moment and realise it might be a good idea to stop bending the rules, don't y'think?'

The lady didn't answer. That was okay. Patrick didn't really expect her to.

'Did you know he's bent?' he asked, putting the finishing touches to the spliff he'd been rolling. 'As bent as a nine bob note, my old man used to say, bless him. Well, actually, no, don't bother with the blessing bit. He was a vicious bastard. He was another one who needed teaching a lesson. I shot him up with dodgy heroin, yesterday, actually. Funny old day.'

Patrick lit up his joint and paused to reflect.

'Course, I had to make sure he was pissed as a fart first,' he said, and took a deep tote, 'which wasn't difficult. He liked a drink, the old man did. Needed something to relax him,' he went on, exhaling thoughtfully. 'It's hard work, see, running a drugs cartel, as he liked to call it. Then there's the tarts, always trying to pull a fast one, pocketing money to pay for their habits, which is a definite no-no. That's what I do, by the way. Not the prostitution bit, obviously.' Patrick had a little chuckle at his wit. 'No, *I'm* the top-dog now. Very stressful it is, too. Profitable, but stressful. Course, the old man had the added stress of having to beat some sense into his dumb-fuck son every five minutes.'

Patrick paused again, remembering the look in his father's eyes, somewhere between terror and dawning realisation that it was payback time, before he'd twitched one last time and then tripped off into oblivion. Not a nice way to go, but needs must. It was the only way he was going to go quietly. Selfish bastard might have made sure his insurance premiums were paid up though.

'Anyway, where was I? Oh, yes, Matthew, our goody-two-shoes detective. His halo's a bit tarnished, sweetheart, but I don't suppose he told you that, did he? He fits people up, does DI Adams: falsifies evidence.'

Taking another long tote on his spliff, Patrick held it a while and then blew it out nice and slow. 'And when that doesn't go according to plan, he gets a bit pissed. He did this,' Patrick lifted his bruised chin to the rear view mirror and poked a finger at it. 'But I told you that earlier, didn't I? Not nice, is it, marring a man's good looks, just because he knows he can get away with it, particularly a man who's recently bereaved.'

Taking another leisurely draw, Patrick's mind drifted back poolside. She really was a careless cow, that Chelsea, dripping chlorine all over his cashmere coat, giving the copper come-hither eyes right under his nose, and then she goes and cracks her skull open, as if he hadn't got enough to worry about. Like soft clouds they were, he recalled, the drops of blood that plopped into the water, rolling and swirling, before finally dispersing. Patrick had idly wondered, as he'd watched, what blood to water ratio would be needed to turn the whole pool red.

'Course, he didn't know that, I suppose,' he offered magnanimously. 'My wife's departure was very ... sudden. Not that it would have made much difference. He's had it in for me for a long time, has our delightful DI Adams, determined to make my life a misery one way or another.'

Still not much of a reaction from the back, Patrick noted. *Ah, well, maybe later.*

'They fitted my brother up, him and his bent oppos. That was just before your darling daughter met her unfortunate demise. Then they shot him down like a dog. Don't suppose he mentioned that over Sunday breakfast on the patio, either, did he, sweetheart?

'Did he mention he likes prostitutes?' Patrick twizzled his neck in hopes of a response. There wasn't much of one. Mind you, she would be a bit hard-pushed to talk, he conceded.

'Natalie's one of his favourites.' He turned back to the windscreen. 'Pretty girl, aged about nineteen. Or should I say, she *was* pretty?' Thinking that was a nice intriguing touch, Patrick let it hang.

'I don't like people who cross me, see, Mrs Adams, or take things that are mine. Your husband has something that belongs to me. I get it back, along with due recompense for a very tricky work-related situation he's caused me, he gets you back, in some shape or form. Fair exchange is no robbery, after all, is it? Let's just hope he's not too dense to see the good sense in that, hey?'

'Right, we'd better get off. Don't want your old man coming back and finding us in flagrante, do we? Now then, what do you think, shall we stop off at your house and pick up your lovely niece en route? Don't want her getting lonely, while hubby's off out on his white charger, do we?'

****

She would have been safe. He could have kept her safe. *Should* have! Mathew slammed his fist against the steering wheel. Instead, he'd probably delivered her right into the bastard's hands. Killing the engine, Matthew swallowed back the sick taste in his throat and reached for his inhaler. Taking two short puffs, he waited for the damn stupid wheezing to abate, and then climbed heavily out of his car.

Where might she have gone? Melanie's? He should probably contact her first and then ring round her other friends. He tried to think; to quash the mounting panic threatening to suffocate him and formulate a plan of action. Might she have gone to her brother's? Her parents, he wondered, attempting logical thought, before his mind slipped into... complete fucking insanity. He was thinking like a copper, following routine procedure. This wasn't routine. This was his wife! And his friends on the force had turned their backs on him. Where the *hell* was she?

His emotion in danger of spilling over, Matthew stopped before he reached the front door. Attempting to compose himself before speaking to Ashley, he turned away, and his gaze fell on a lone wood-pigeon settling on the crumbling roof of the half-renovated barn opposite. The bird had lost its mate. For months, two plump pigeons had settled on the crest of that roof, cooing and canoodling contentedly. And now that lone bird was lost.

Matthew felt lost. He had no clue what to do. None. Did he call it in? She wouldn't even qualify as a missing person yet. Matthew felt nausea claw at him again as that thought landed icily in the pit of his stomach. And if she was officially missing: taken by that piece of scum, what then? If she was still alive... he clamped his mind down hard on the possibility she might not be, then the bastard wanted something. In which case, he would make contact, make demands. Matthew knew the protocol. The first instruction would be not to involve the police, an instruction that Matthew would advise anyone in a kidnap situation to ignore, until now. Whatever sick, twisted game Sullivan was playing, there would be no rules, no criminal profile that would fit. Even as a kid, Matthew had Sullivan down as a sociopath, a product of physical and emotional abuse. He didn't tick just that box, though, committing only haphazard, spontaneous crimes fuelled by fits of rage. He was also cool, calm, and meticulous, a highly organised psychopathic killer, viewing his victims as objects to be tormented and violated for his own warped amusement, and leaving few clues behind. Sullivan had obviously had eyes on him for a long time, watching his and Becky's every move. He'd known what film they'd been watching. Matthew felt fresh bile rise in his throat. He knew about... *Ashley!*

Dread propelling him, Matthew turned to race back to the front door.

'Ashley!' he shouted, aware he'd told her not to open it, that he'd probably scared her half-witless. 'Ashley, it's me, Matthew. Can you open the ... *Shit!* Dropping his keys as he fumbled them into the lock, Matthew stooped to retrieve them, straightened up, and closed his eyes with relief, as he heard the bolt on the front door slide back.

'Ashley?' He stepped in as the front door opened and glanced quickly around. There was no sight of her downstairs. 'Ashley?'

'Here.' Ashley's voice was small and tremulous.

Matthew's head snapped up. She was on the landing? Vaguely aware that the opening door and her location meant the geography didn't add up, Matthew dismissed it in favour of breathing again. 'Are you okay?' he asked, his guard still up, his eyes searching the landing beyond her.

Ashley walked towards the stairs. Stopping at the top, she nodded apprehensively, stepped down three steps, and then lowered herself to sit.

'Are you sure?' Matthew noted the hair over her face, the hands tucked under her thighs, closed body language that meant she was anything but.

Ashley nodded again, a small, but determined nod. 'You didn't find her, did you?'

Matthew debated. He could lie, but doing that wouldn't make her vigilant, which he needed her to be.

'No,' he said hoarsely. 'Can I join you?' He indicated the stairs.

Ashley hesitated for second, and then nodded and shuffled across to allow him space.

Wearily, Matthew climbed the stairs and sank down heavily next to her. Where did he start? How did he explain his behaviour? That the terror that had gripped him the minute he'd realised Rebecca had gone out simply wouldn't let go of him? He'd known, absolutely, with every fibre of his being, that Sullivan had been targeting her.

How do you explain that to a teenager? And then go on to tell her, God help them, that the ice-cold fear slicing through his gut told him he'd found her.

Praying he was doing the right thing, Matthew took a breath. 'I'm sorry about earlier,' he started, knowing that, if he was going to ensure Ashley's safety, he needed her to do everything he asked of her. To which end, she needed to be able to trust him. 'I acted like I did because I was worried, Ashley. Rebecca's ...' he faltered, gulping back his heart, which seemed to be working its way up his oesophagus.

'It's something to do with that man, isn't it, the one who ran into the back of us?' Ashley picked up.

Matthew looked at her, still unsure how much he should disclose.

'I know it is,' Ashley met his gaze, 'so you might as well tell me.'

Taken aback by her intuitiveness, Matthew searched her eyes and read what was there: fear, definitely that, uncertainty, but also a quiet defiance, he noted, as if daring him to lie to her.

'Yes.' He nodded, at length. 'I ... think she might be in trouble.' He dragged his hands up over his face. 'But I don't want you to worry, Ashley. We'll get some people on it, the best.' He paused again, knowing that that was exactly what he couldn't do yet, and feeling utterly impotent.

'Are they looking for her now?' Ashley studied him carefully.

'Not yet, no,' Matthew answered honestly. 'The thing is ...' He hesitated, choosing his words carefully.

'You don't know whether she's missing yet,' Ashley supplied, leaving Matthew grateful and also slightly in awe of her obvious maturity.

'No. I don't.' Again, he answered honestly, on the basis he had no more than his instinct screaming at him to go on.

Ashley nodded slowly, and then, 'Becky's strong,' she offered, as if trying to reassure him in some way.

Matthew swallowed. 'I know.' He tugged in a breath, fighting back the tears that were too damn near the surface, as he recalled how Becky had pulled herself up after the loss of Lily, the miscarriage. She'd been determined to support him, despite his inadequacies as a husband: holding him up, keeping him strong when he'd felt like crumbling. And when she'd needed him ... He hadn't been there. *Dear God ...*

'She's all right, Matthew,' Ashley said, as he heaved out a shaky sigh. 'She's scared, but she's all right.'

Perplexed at that statement, Matthew glanced from the hand

Ashley had placed hesitantly on his arm to her face. Her expression was earnest, her wide brandy-coloured eyes seeming to have taken on a luminescent quality. She seemed to be willing him to believe that she was alright. Because she needed him to? Matthew found himself transfixed by her penetrating gaze, and then felt his heart thud against his ribcage, as his mobile rang, loud against the silence.

Scrambling to his feet, Matthew yanked it out of his pocket. The number was unrecognisable, he quickly noted. Sullivan, he guessed, who would have all bases covered: unregistered phones at his disposal.

'Adams?' he answered, over a terse intake of breath.

Nothing the other end. Matthew descended the stairs and waited.

'I take it you don't need me to warn you not to contact your friends down at the station?' Sullivan enquired casually, after an agonising pause.

'Where is she?' Matthew's jaw tensed as he fought to supress the rage surging through every vein in his body. It wouldn't help to lose it now. He had to stay calm; until he was alone with the bastard, then he would do what he should have done on the blackest day of his life, kill the excuse for a human being and take great pleasure in doing it slowly.

'Your partner,' Sullivan paused, prolonging the agony, whilst he took a draw on whatever shit he was smoking, Matthew guessed, his gut twisting, 'put him off the scent, Adams. As far as he, or anyone else, is concerned, everything on the home-front is gravy. Got it?'

'If you touch her, Sullivan,' Matthew couldn't keep the anger from his voice, 'so help me—'

'Tut, tut, temper, Detective Inspector. You don't want to rile me now,' Sullivan retorted smoothly, '*do* you?'

The last was said with implicit meaning.

'*Bastard.*' Matthew raked a hand furiously through his hair.

'Correct,' Sullivan replied flatly. 'Not sure my old man would be too pleased to hear you slighting his good name, though. Come to think of it, I'm not either. So keep it zipped.'

Matthew clenched his teeth, hard. 'What do you want, Sullivan?'

'All in good time, Adams. I'll call back. I have someone else pressing to attend to. Looks like the little lady's struggling to breathe. Make sure you pick up pronto if you don't want her to keep struggling.'

'You fucking *animal!* Realising Sullivan had ended the call, Matthew slammed his fist hard into the nearest wall.

'Matthew! Don't!' Ashley scrambled down the stairs. 'You'll hurt yourself.'

Matthew gulped back the hard knot in his throat and attempted to focus on the slim hand that had caught hold of his wrist.

'She's all right!' Ashley said it again, as Matthew's thoughts crashed through his mind like a runaway train.

'She *is*,' Ashley repeated, tearfully but insistently, because she needed to believe it? Matthew needed to believe it. God help him, he needed her to be.

Nodding, Matthew tried to reel in his emotions. 'Okay.' He closed his eyes and attempted to reassure her. 'I'm okay. I—'

*Shit!* His gaze shot to the door as the doorbell rang. Recognising his DS's silhouette through the opaque glass, he glanced guardedly at Ashley, then gestured her behind him and reached to open it.

'I came as soon as I could,' Steve said, turning from his perusal of the road to Matthew. 'Bloody hell,' he knitted his brow, 'you look like death. Is everything OK?'

'Yes,' Matthew said quickly. 'Fine.' Running a hand shakily over his neck, he forced a smile. 'I, er, think I might be coming down with something. A bug, probably.'

'Just what you need.' Steve shook his head and took a step inside. 'I had a word with Nicky,' he started, and stopped, as his gaze fell on Ashley.

Obviously taking Matthew's cue, Ashley managed a smile. 'Hi.'

'All right?' Steve smiled easily back.

'Yeah, good,' Ashley assured him. 'Just on my way up to listen to some music.' Exchanging meaningful looks with Matthew, she turned to head back up the stairs.

'Use your earphones, Ashley,' Matthew called after her, trying desperately for normal.

'I know, I know. It does your head in.' Sighing demonstrably, Ashley took his cue there, too, thank God.

Steve waited diplomatically, until she'd disappeared around the stair rail, then, 'I've been going through the files regarding that case we discussed,' he said. 'Looks like we might have a link. Nothing concrete yet, but...'

'Great.' Matthew did his best to look relieved. 'You'll keep me up to speed, yes?'

'Will do,' Steve promised. 'I've got a bit more digging around to do, but I'll fill you in as and when. So, where do you want me? Out front, presumably.'

'Crap.' Matthew banged the heel of his hand demonstrably against his forehead. 'I meant to ring you. Sorry, Steve. Brain's gone AWOL, I swear. Rebecca's safe.' He smiled reassuringly, though saying his wife's name almost crucified him. 'She's spending some time with her mother. Ashley has a dental appointment and then I'm driving her up there, too, so ...'

*You don't have an appointment!* Emily picked up, as Ashley eavesdropped on the landing. *He's telling fibs.*

*Obviously.* Answering silently, Ashley rolled her eyes. *He's trying to keep Becky safe, dimwit.* Leaning her head back against the wall, Ashley caught the tear that rolled down her cheek with the back of her hand. She liked Matthew. A lot. She liked Becky, too. Not just because she'd bought her stuff, but because she'd talked to her, like an adult, rather than some freak. Part of her couldn't help wishing Becky away though, when she'd said she was having a baby. No matter Becky's assurances she wouldn't, Ashley couldn't help thinking that she would be sent back to the care home. That she'd be in the way. Hadn't she always? She'd been a bit pissed about it on the drive home. She was Matthew's family, after all, she'd reasoned. If anyone had a right to stay, didn't she? And now this had happened.

*Ith's not your fault.* Emily assured her, looking back from where she was peering through the rails on the landing at proceedings down in the hall. *Ith's that man's. I told you I didn't like him.*

Ashley thought it probably was her fault, though. As if somehow her wishing Becky away had made it happen.

*She is all right, you know.* Emily wriggled around to face her.

*But how do you know? You can't see her.* Ashley wasn't sure she believed her.

*No, but I can feel her.* Emily shuffled across to sit next to Ashley. *Here.* She reached to press a hand to Ashley's heart. *You can, too, if you concentrate hard.*

# CHAPTER TWELVE

Matthew snatched up his mobile when it rang. 'Adams?' he answered tersely, thinking it might be Sullivan.

'Have you left yet?' Steve asked.

Matthew blew out the breath he hadn't realised he'd been holding in. 'About to,' he said, wishing he'd checked the caller number. Sullivan was about to play him like a fiddle, Matthew guessed. One wrong move and he could do … He didn't dare contemplate what. And anything might count as a wrong move in Sullivan's warped mind, even finding his phone engaged.

'Haven't got time to swing by the hospital, have you?' Steve's tone was sombre.

*Hospital?* Matthew felt a pang of apprehension prickle his spine. Why would Steve want him down at the hospital when he was supposed to be on gardening leave?

'It's Natalie,' Steve supplied.

'Natalie?' *Oh God, no.* Matthew tightened his grip on the phone. 'What happened?' he asked, as if he needed to.

'I might be wrong,' Steve said, 'but I'm guessing the same someone who wasn't happy with Brianna talking to you wasn't too happy with Natalie talking to you either.'

****

'It's just for a while,' Matthew attempted to reassure Ashley as he pulled into the hospital car park. 'I promise to keep in touch and let you know what's happening.'

Ashley glanced sullenly back at him, clearly not thrilled at the prospect of going back to the care home, which was where she should be now, if only the manager had been there. Matthew wasn't prepared to drop her without assurances she would be watched at all times.

'I could lock myself in.' She made a last ditch effort to be allowed to stay with him. 'I wouldn't answer the door to anyone, or the phone. And I wouldn't be any trouble.'

'Ashley—' Matthew parked up and checked his mobile for the fiftieth time. Why hadn't that bastard rung back? 'It's just not possible. You know it's not.'

'Right, fine. Whatever.' Ashley puffed out a sigh and sat huffily back in her seat.

Looking like she should. Matthew felt for her. Like a truculent teenager not thrilled at not getting her own way. 'It's not that I don't want you there, Ashley. I—'

'Yes it is.'

'What?' Matthew did a double-take, sure he'd heard her speak, equally sure that she hadn't.

'Nothing.' Ashley shrugged. 'I could help,' she tried again, turning huge, hopeful eyes on him. 'I could cook meals and stuff. You have to eat. And I could, you know, just be there, in case Becky...' she trailed off uncertainly.

'Ashley...' Matthew hesitated, not sure how to put it but exactly how it was. 'She won't be coming back unless I do everything the ... person ... who's holding her wants me to do. I'm sorry,' he added quickly, as Ashley immediately retreated into herself in that defensive way she did.

Matthew debated and decided the truth, however distasteful, might be better than her assuming she wasn't wanted, though following him everywhere but the bathroom, she actually was getting in the way. He needed to think, to be alert. He couldn't do that with Ashley to worry about.

'There are things he might demand regarding you, Ashley,' he said, then paused and waited, hoping she really was as mature as she'd seemed.

Ashley fell quiet.

'Do you understand, Ashley?'

Nodding, at length, she peered up at him from under her curtain of hair.

'As much as I want you around, Ashley, and God knows I could use the company, I'm just not prepared to take that risk.' Matthew made sure to hold her gaze. 'He needs to know you're out of the frame and, for now, the care home is the safest place for you.'

Ashley's eyes flicked uncertainly down and then back to him.

'Besides, Becky would kill me if I let anything happen to you,' Matthew attempted a little levity, but almost choked on the words. 'Come on.' Reaching across, he gave her shoulders a squeeze. 'We'll get through this. We just have to trust each other.'

'Okay,' Ashley's voice was small. 'But you have to promise me you'll let me know what's happening. I'll go mental in there if you don't.'

'I will. I promise.' Matthew mustered up a smile. 'Right, while we're in there,' he nodded towards the hospital, 'I'll need you to stick right by my side. Right by it, Ashley. No loo calls, unless I'm waiting outside. No wandering off. Okay?'

Ashley rolled her eyes and reached for her door. 'You'll be telling me not to talk to strangers in a minute. I'm, like, almost fourteen? I can look after myself, y'know?'

Somehow, Matthew didn't doubt that she could, despite the bullying incident they'd witnessed when they'd first met her at the care home. The pain in his chest was physical this time, as he recalled Becky's face that day, the determination in her eyes. She'd made up her mind to try to be a mother to Ashley. *Christ*, what kind of twisted fate was it that would allow a woman who'd managed to smile in the face of adversity, who'd lifted his spirits from the very pit of despair, someone who cared so much, to suffer so much?

His emotion threatening to spill over, Matthew swallowed hard and tried to compose himself as they headed for the hospital entrance.

'Like the boots, by the way,' he said, attempting some semblance of normality as they walked.

'Becky bought them.' Ashley's eyes were fixed downwards.

Matthew felt the knot in his chest tighten. 'I gathered,' he said quietly.

'She's all right.' Ashley turned her gaze towards him, unwavering certainty still in her eyes. 'I can feel it.'

Matthew nodded, trying to humour her, though what he actually felt like doing was dropping to his knees right there in the car park and sobbing his heart out.

※※※

'Sugar?' Patrick enquired politely.

She shook her head, her eyes huge over the duct tape. Pupils like saucers, Patrick glanced back at her interestedly, as he stirred the tea. He couldn't tell if her eyes were blue or green. Somewhere in between, he decided, carrying the tea over. The colour the sea should be instead of shitty brown. She was pretty. He could see what Adams saw in her. She was wasted on him, classy bird like her. You could always tell a bit of class by the shoes.

Personally, he preferred stilettos on a good pair of legs, but the ankle boots with the dress, and a fair expanse of flesh in between, were definitely sexy.

Placing the cup, one of his best *Harrods William Edwards* fine china, on the occasional table next the sofa, he smiled, and then came to stand in front of her. Yes, very tasty, he thought. Not bad at all. Appraising her leisurely, he considered, and then leaned in to trace his index finger the length of her thigh.

She flinched at that. Well, she would, he supposed.

'Sorry,' he apologised, holding her gaze, his eyes level with hers. Blue, he decided on the colour. They reminded him of his mother's. His mother had that same look about her sometimes, he recalled, wide-eyed and petrified; tiptoeing around, trying to avoid the wrath of his father. 'I wasn't copping a feel, sweetheart,' he assured her, though he probably actually was. 'Don't panic, your virtue is safe ... for now. I was just admiring. I have a bit of a thing for legs, you see. Women's legs, obviously.'

Glancing down, he clutched her thigh lightly, his gaze flicking alternately to her face, assessing her reaction, and then back to her thigh, as he traced the outline of her taut muscle: down over the knee, then further down, gliding slowly over the smooth jut of her shinbone.

'I prefer them in stilettos, I must admit,' he said, his gaze finding hers again, as he squatted to wrap his hand around her ankle.

'Have you ever noticed how stilettos give women shapelier legs?' he asked conversationally, as he slid his palm back up her inner calf.

'Like sculpted porcelain.' He stopped, cupping her calf muscle. 'Do you know why that is?'

He looked expectantly up at her.

As if he genuinely thought she might be interested. Repulsed, Rebecca recoiled inwardly.

'It's because women who walk in high heels exercise their inner and outer calf muscles more evenly than women who wear flat shoes.' He chatted absurdly on, as if he were discussing something as emotive as the weather. 'I read about it. Can't think where.'

His gaze was back on her thighs. Rebecca swallowed, fearing she was going to be sick, and then she would die, surely, choking on her own vomit. *Oh, dear God, please help me.* She squeezed her eyes closed and gulped back hard.

'Women who wear flat shoes exercise their inner calf muscles more, see. Makes them bulk, obviously.' He turned his attention to her other leg.

'Can't abide fat calves, or fat thighs. Yours are not bad. Nice and toned,' he said, working his way upwards again.

Rebecca tried to keep breathing, short shallow breaths, attempting to filter out the sickly sweet smell of his aftershave, which was exacerbating her churning nausea.

'Did you know wearing high heels can improve your sex life?' He locked eyes swimming with innuendo on hers, causing her stomach to curdle.

'You look surprised, but it's true. It's been scientifically proven that the muscles are more relaxed when women wear high heels. Makes sense they'd be relaxed during sex then, don't y'think. Are yours?' He cocked his head to one side. 'Does hubby do it for you, Rebecca? Does he make you come, hey?'

Rebecca looked away, desperately trying to hold back her tears.

He reached her inner thigh, the clammy soft palm of his hand coming to rest there. Rebecca tried not to react, to supress the moan that was climbing her throat. Her hands still tied behind her, she'd stand no chance of fighting him off, though she would die trying. From the look in his flat grey eyes— deep-rooted, dark evil—she was sure that was exactly what the vile bastard wanted.

'I thought we might test it out. See how relaxed you can be. What do you think?'

He waited.

Her heart thrumming rapidly inside her, Rebecca prayed silently, hoping against hope that he might have some shred of humanity.

'Later, though,' he said, standing abruptly, 'when hubby's here to see. Wouldn't want him to miss out on all the fun, would we?'

Rebecca's gaze shot back to his face.

He smirked, an ugly distorted smirk, the bruising and swelling to his jaw adding to his grotesqueness.

'I see I have your attention,' he said, sliding his hands casually into his trouser pockets. 'In case you're wondering, which obviously you would be, I'm banking on him riding to your rescue, sweetheart. The thing with Matthew Adams is he just doesn't know when to give up, see? Persistent bugger, he is, a constant thorn in my side, trying to outwit me, trip me up, either that or fit me up, tosser. Dead irritating, he is. Even as a kid, he refused to back down. Got me into some serious grief with my old man, I can tell you.'

Shaking his head, he turned to walk over to the full length mirror adorning the wall, where he paused. His back to her, as he adjusted his tie and smoothed down his hair, Rebecca took the opportunity to glance hurriedly around, trying to imagine where she might be. In some luxury apartment that much was clear from the plush furnishings, but it could be any apartment anywhere. In London still, she guessed, but the blindfold he'd forced her to wear on the journey had ensured she had no idea where. She looked him over, taking in his designer clothes and well-groomed appearance, as he went through some obscene, self-obsessed ritual: adjusting his tie, yet again, checking his shirt collar, the cuffs. Even his fingernails were manicured and spotless. Rebecca couldn't help but notice those as he'd pawed her. He seemed to be in no need of money. What *did* he want then? She tried to make sense of it, to assimilate, to think of anything she might use to dissuade this obviously sick individual from whatever sadistic action he seemed intent on.

Snapping her gaze away as he turned suddenly back to face her, she tried to stay calm. If she were to panic, to react, God only knew what that might drive him to do.

'Oh, dear, you haven't drunk your tea,' he observed, strolling back towards her. 'But then, I suppose you'd find it a bit difficult with tape stuck all over your pretty little face, wouldn't you? Brace yourself, sweetheart. This might hurt a bit.'

****

'Don't move, Ashley.' Matthew fixed his gaze hard on hers. 'Stay right there, where I can see you, OK?'

The querulous look was back, he noted. 'Matthew, I've got the message.' She sighed. 'I'm not a six-year-old.'

'I know,' Matthew conceded. If he wanted her to act like an adult, he supposed he should be treating her like one. 'Just—'

'Don't move. Yes, I've got it.' Ashley rolled her eyes, adjusted her earphones and turned her attention back to her phone.

'I'll be on the other side of that door. If anyone approaches you, you come straight in, pronto.'

'I will,' Ashley assured him.

Still Matthew was hesitant. Checking the hospital corridor, he'd established the nurses' station was only yards away, but even having extracted promises, he doubted the two nurses on duty and up to their eyes would be able to watch her every second. Not knowing what to expect, what condition Natalie might be in, Matthew would rather Ashley didn't go in with him, though.

'Matthew, go.' Ashley eyeballed him exasperatedly as he prevaricated. 'The sooner you're in, the sooner we can leave, yes?'

Such was the infallible logic of teenagers. Relieved that she seemed to be acting as near to normal as possible, Matthew nodded and turned to the side room, trepidation mounting inside him as to what he would find on the other side of that door.

Steve opened it, as he reached for the handle. 'All right, boss?' He looked him over worriedly.

'I think we can dispense with the "boss" bit, Steve.' Matthew's smile was strained.

Steve nodded and then inclined his head, indicating the bed behind him.

'She's just come round.' His expression was grim, at best.

Matthew glanced past him. 'Has she said anything?'

'Nothing.' Steve shrugged despondently. 'But then, the state she's in ...'

Guessing what that meant, Matthew braced himself. 'Keep an eye on Ashley, will you?' he asked, nodding towards the viewing window in the door.

His heart sank as he approached the bed. Her face was deathly pale against the white of the sheets, her eyes and lips swollen, her cheek—probably broken.

'What did you walk into this time, Natalie?' he asked her softly. 'An articulated lorry?'

Natalie turned her head slightly towards him, wincing as she did.

'Don't try to move,' Matthew urged her. Then, seating himself carefully on the edge of the bed, he took hold of the hand that wasn't stuffed full of tubes. 'Was it him, Nat?'

Natalie didn't answer, but the slow tears that trickled from the corner of her eyes told Matthew all he needed to know. He couldn't promise her he would pull him in. That wasn't going to happen. If it was the last thing he did, Matthew intended to make sure Sullivan never had the benefit of a solicitor or bars to protect him ever again, but ... 'He'll get what's coming to him, Natalie,' he promised her instead, his voice cracking. 'I give you my word.'

Natalie nodded, a small nod, leaving Matthew hoping she'd got some small comfort from knowing that he meant it. And he did. As God was his witness, Matthew intended to make good his promise.

'Try to get some sleep.' He gave her hand a gentle squeeze. 'I'll drop by later. See how you're doing.'

Steve eyed him questioningly as he walked back towards him.

Wondering how this was going to play out, Matthew guessed, motioning him outside.

'Take a statement as soon as she's ready to give one,' he said, for protocol's sake, once they were in the corridor.

'Will do.' Steve furrowed his brow thoughtfully. 'Er, Matthew,' he hesitated, 'can I just ask, because ... Well, if there's anything I need to know ...'

Matthew glanced at Steve curiously.

'Are you and Natalie, erm ...' Looking uncomfortable, Steve nodded towards the side room door '... you know?'

Getting the gist, Matthew stared at him, incredulous. 'No, Steve, categorically not,' he assured him. 'I offer an ear, that's all. It helps to be a friend sometimes, rather than a copper. It's about trust, Steve.

There's a line though. You'll learn.'

Steve nodded slowly. 'Right,' he said. 'Not sure Lindsey's going to be very impressed if I go around befriending pro ...' Glancing over to where Ashley was slouched against the wall, Steve caught himself '... working girls.'

'No.' Matthew smiled half-heartedly. 'Comes with the job, though, Steve. Just keep your wits about you. Look, I've got to go.' He glanced at his phone again. Still no call. What sadistic game was Sullivan playing? Matthew's throat tightened. What he'd done to Natalie was a warning, a message the piece of scum knew he'd be sure to get. Matthew had no doubt about that.

'Nothing on the nail-file yet,' Steve filled him in as to where they were at with forensics. 'Nicky's backed up, but she said she'd do her best.'

'Right.' Matthew nodded distractedly.

'There's something else though,' Steve went on. 'Natalie's shoe was missing.'

'And?' Matthew eyed him curiously, and then glanced at Ashley, who was now trying to get his attention. 'One minute,' he mouthed in her direction.

'That link I was telling you about, there's another case: similar MO to Brianna. A couple of years ago,' Steve supplied cryptically, clearly mindful of the teenager in their midst. 'I'll fill you in later.'

Matthew nodded, his heart plummeting further as he realised the implication. Another case meant what had happened to Brianna had definitely been planned and executed, which meant, with or without evidence, that Sullivan fell into the category serial killer. Matthew felt the meagre contents of his stomach turn over.

'Keep me posted,' he said tightly, turning to escort Ashley along the corridor and as far away from all this as possible.

'We'll have to go later,' Ashley said, as they exited the hospital.

Matthew wasn't listening. He was trying to get his head around what was happening, hopelessly trying to get into Sullivan's mindset. What did he want with Becky? In exchange for what? A fresh wave of panic clutched at his stomach as he acknowledged that an exchange might not be Sullivan's game plan. Was it purely personal, he wondered? Was it him he wanted? If so, why not just have chosen his moment and taken him out. A single shot would have done it, or a well-aimed car, the bastard. The dead of night, a quiet street: that was more Sullivan's style, until now. None of this made sense. Suddenly Sullivan seemed as unpredictable as he'd once been predictable. As if something had tipped him over the edge, making him careless of the consequences of his actions. And that thought frightened Matthew more than anything.

'To the care home,' Ashley went on, her step faltering as she glanced up at him. 'We can't go now. You have something else you need to—'

Matthew marched her on. 'We're going now, Ashley. No arguments.' Reaching the car, he opened the passenger side door first and all but bundled her inside.

'But we can't!' Ashley insisted, as he headed around to his own door.

'It's not open for negotiation, Ashley.' Matthew climbed in, started the engine and pulled fast out of the car park. 'We're going straight there. I'll catch up with you as soon as—'

'No!' Ashley screamed it. 'We can't!'

'*Shit!* What the...?' Matthew's arm went out instinctively, stopping Ashley lurching forwards as the car simultaneously screeched to an abrupt halt.

'You need to go to Rebecca!' Scraping her hair from her face, Ashley turned to him. 'You have to go!' she repeated, her expression desperate, her voice frantic.

Matthew swallowed back his own desperation, looking astounded from Ashley, who was clearly disturbed, to the dead lights on the dashboard.

'She has my phone,' Ashley continued nonsensically, as Matthew tried to comprehend what the hell had just happened. 'Becky, she has my old phone!' Ashley pulled the hand nearest to her from the steering wheel, demanding his attention, as Matthew turned the key in the ignition and got no response.

Not even a flicker, *Goddammit!* He tried the ignition again, and then delved frantically under the dash for the release to the bonnet.

'You're not listening to me.' Ashley refused to let go of his other arm, as he reached for the door, trying to figure out where to start assessing what had gone wrong mechanically, wondering where his breakdown card was. *Christ*, he didn't need this. Not now.

'Ashley, for God's *sake!* he yelled, as she tugged.

'It has a 'Find my Phone' app on it!' Ashley yelled back, tears springing from her eyes.

Matthew stopped dead. 'What?' He stared at her thunderstruck.

'Becky has it in her bag and I think I've located it.' Ashley blinked at him over the sleeve she was dragging under her nose.

# CHAPTER THIRTEEN

Matthew watched Ashley carefully as he waited for Steve to come back on the phone, noting the curtain of hair over her face, her retreat from anything she might find threatening. What the hell had just happened with the car, he couldn't fathom; his gaze strayed from Ashley to the now illuminated dash, which had pinged into life as mysteriously as it had died the second she had his full-on attention. That was nuts. He was losing it, going out of his mind, must be. Condemning his imagination, which was running all sorts of riots, Matthew turned his attention back to Ashley. 'Okay?' he asked her.

Ashley nodded fervently.

'Sure?' Matthew pressed her, remorse that he'd snapped at her, adding to his already overwhelming guilt.

Ashley glanced up at him at last. 'Yeah, I'm good.' She shrugged awkwardly. 'Sorry I yelled.'

'Me too.' Matthew offered her a smile and then sat to attention, as Steve came back on, finally.

'It's a rental property,' he gave Matthew the information he'd asked him for, 'on application to PL Property Consultants, Mayfair. Penthouse suite, apparently. Nice pad, if you've got the odd few million lying around. Currently unoccupied from the looks.'

'Do we know who owns it?' Matthew asked.

'Not listed. I can find out, but I'll need to do a bit more digging; client confidentiality and all that crap.'

'Great, thanks. Can you send me the spec?' Matthew asked. He wasn't sure how he was going to handle it yet, but knowing what the layout of the apartment was would be a definite plus.

'Blimey, I didn't realise a DI's salary was that good,' Steve replied wittily. 'Maybe I'll stay on the force after all.'

'I wish.' Matthew sighed, playing along in order not to alert Steve to what was going on unless he had to.

'Spec's on its way.'

'Cheers, Steve. One more thing, can you log onto a mobile account for me?'

'Can do. Whose?'

'Hold on, I've got the number here.' Matthew reeled off the number Ashley had given him. 'I might need you to help me pinpoint the location of the phone.'

'Right, I'm on it.' Steve paused. 'So, are you going to tell me what this is all about?'

Matthew took a breath. 'Just a proverbial hunch. I'll let you know if it comes to anything.'

'Right.' Steve paused again. 'And would this hunch have anything to do with Sullivan?' he asked warily. 'Cos, if you're flying solo, mate, I just thought I'd remind you you're already in it, up to your neck.'

Matthew hesitated. Giving Sullivan even a hint of police involvement might make the difference between getting Becky back safely and not getting her back at all. He forced his mind not to dwell on that thought. Steve's help, though, he might just need. Even so, to have him sniffing around before he'd even established any dialogue with Sullivan …

'No,' he erred on the side of caution. 'I'm just doing someone a favour. Missing person, not much police action, you know.'

'So you were just being paranoid about the man then, like the DC said? And now Becky's at her parents your mind's at rest, yes?'

Matthew heard the incredulity in Steve's voice. 'For now,' he answered guardedly.

'Right,' Steve didn't sound convinced. 'Well, I'm here if you need me. Just so you know.'

※※※※

'Remember, you stay in the car,' Matthew instructed Ashley, his tone, he hoped, brooking no argument. 'Drop the locks, keep your phone at the ready, and don't do anything that might attract attention. Okay?'

Ashley nodded determinedly. 'I will,' she promised. 'Matthew,' she caught his arm again as he reached for his door, 'be careful, yes?'

Matthew nodded, guessing she was imagining all sorts of scenarios. 'I'll be back before you know it,' he assured her and climbed out, and then bent to peer back in at her. 'Meanwhile, you … ?'

'Drop the locks, I know.' There was no demonstrative roll of the eyes this time, just another adamant nod.

'Good girl.' Matthew closed the door and headed towards the main road, glancing back as he walked to make sure his car wasn't conspicuous.

Locating the place hadn't been too much of a problem: right slap bang in the middle of Mayfair, making it high profile, which Matthew couldn't fathom. Getting past the twenty-four hour a day concierge might prove more problematical, he realised. Showing his ID wasn't viable, not without a warrant to back it up. The guy wouldn't let him up without notifying the tenant anyway, presumably. *Dammit.* Matthew toyed with the idea of tripping the fire alarm. There'd be one in the underground car park, he guessed, but that would be accessible to tenants only. In any case, it would alert everyone in the building, including Sullivan, which he definitely didn't want.

So what then? Frustrated, Matthew loitered on the pavement outside the building, guessing he wasn't about to get a break: that the security guard might decide on a conveniently timed call of nature anytime soon, and then pulled out his mobile.

'One more favour,' he said, when Steve picked up.

'Good job I love you, isn't it?' Steve quipped. 'Go on then.'

'I need a name of someone currently living in the building. Anyone will do.'

'OK, give me a minute.'

Matthew waited while Steve pulled up the details. 'Abrahams,' he came back on. 'Sixth floor, apartment number ...'

'Excellent. Cheers, Steve.' Matthew ended the call, leaving Steve mid-sentence and googled four local pizza parlours. Calling each of them, he ordered a good selection, gave Ashley a quick call to reassure her, then waited and prayed.

*Thank you, Lord.* Matthew blew out a sigh of relief as two pizza delivery guys arrived in close succession, followed two minutes later by a third. It was now or never, he guessed, offering up another prayer as he sailed through the doors, the security guard being somewhat distracted.

'I've told you, there's no one here by any of those names.' The guy splayed his arms in despair, as he addressed the disgruntled deliverymen. 'You must have the wrong building.'

Shaking his head as one of the men insisted he hadn't, the guy sighed, picked up his phone, then, 'Oh, for ...' banged it down again, as the fourth pizza bearer appeared.

'Abrahams, sixth floor.' Matthew grabbed his chance, pointing his thumb towards the lift as he passed hurriedly by behind them.

'Yeah, yeah.' The guy waved Matthew on, now looking considerably frustrated, as he plucked up his phone again.

His mouth dry, sweat tickling his forehead, Matthew willed the lift to arrive. Sighing with relief when it did, he stepped in and tried to look inconspicuous until the doors slid closed. So far so good, he thought, hitting the button for penthouse level, and wondering what the hell he was going to do next. Ringing the doorbell was hardly an option. He couldn't loiter too long outside either, drawing attention, eventually drawing Sullivan's attention. Assuming he was here. Assuming Becky was.

Steeling himself, as the lift doors swished open, Matthew immediately scanned the small lobby leading directly to the apartment. Something wasn't right. His every instinct was screaming at him that something wasn't right, but he had no idea what.

*Damn.* Sullivan would know he was here now. Matthew noted the wall-mounted CCTV camera, as he approached the front door, only to stop in his tracks when he realised the door was open a fraction. Matthew's stomach tightened. It was an invitation to go in, obviously. Some kind of trap, he assumed, waiting for him to walk right into, and he had no choice but to. His heart-rate kicking up, a pulse pounding in the base of his neck, he extended a hand, pushed the door wide, and walked inside.

He should have come armed. His jaw tightened, as he noted the opulent décor, red leather in abundance, black walls, gilt-edged mirrors. Shot the bastard the first chance he got, preferably in the gut, and then enjoyed watching him squirm. Quickly establishing all exits to the room, every hair seeming to prickle over the surface of his skin, Matthew turned for the kitchen. More black, marble and steel, a tea cup on the working surface, he registered, contents half-drunk, the kettle: cold. No sign of life. Mathew listened, hearing only the ominous tick of the wall clock, loud against the silence.

Bedroom, he instructed himself, foreboding at what he might find there ratcheting his fear to a whole new level. His limbs heavy, his heartbeat now sluggish, Matthew located the main bedroom. Faltering for a split-second, his hand visibly shaking, he pressed down the handle and took a tentative step inside. Wall-to-wall mirrors, he noted. Triple bed. Upholstery: black and grey silk. In the middle of the bed; placed strategically centre-duvet...

Matthew's heart stopped dead.

One single shoe, red leather, suede panels, zip front, Lolita ankle boots: bought for Becky's birthday. His stomach lurched, Matthew turned instinctively for the en-suite, where he was violently sick.

*Where was she? Dear God ... Please don't do this.* Glancing at the ceiling, sweat saturating his shirt, Matthew swallowed back the acrid taste burning the back of his throat, rammed on the taps, and threw cold water over his face. *Please don't,* he prayed harder, to a god he didn't much believe in, clutched the sink for support, and squeezed his eyes closed. Still they came, staccato images, seared into his mind: Lily, life extinct, eyes vacant. Becky...

*No!* Emitting a guttural moan, which ricocheted distortedly off the tiled walls around him, Matthew panted out short, heavy breaths, tried to still the walls which seemed to be closing in on him, to stave off the imminent asthma attack, and then froze, as his mobile rang in his pocket. *Sullivan?* Matthew groped for it and pressed it shakily to his ear. He didn't speak. Couldn't.

'Cat got your tongue?' Sullivan enquired, causing the walls to shift in another inch. 'Or do you need a minute, Adams, is that it? Take your time.' His tone grew sickeningly more gloating by the second. 'Slow breaths, Matthew, just like you did when you were a shit-scared, snivelling little kid.'

'Where is she?' Matthew's voice was hoarse. Silently, he cursed his pathetic weakness.

'Do they know about your asthma, your friends down at the station?' Sullivan ignored the question. 'I don't suppose they do, do they? I'm thinking you'd be relegated to a desk job, if they did. Stress-induced, isn't it, Adams? You feeling a bit anxious, hey?'

'Where the fuck *is she?*' Matthew yelled, slamming his fist against the over-sink mirror.

'Tut, tut, temper, DI Adams,' Sullivan continued to goad, as Matthew struggled to pull air past the audible wheeze in his chest. 'Aren't you coppers supposed to remain detached at all times, even on the grisliest of cases? I must say, I do wonder how you—'

'You *bastard!*'

'We've established that, Matthew. We also established the fact that I'm not overly fond of you calling me one,' Sullivan's voice took on a menacing tone. 'Don't do it.'

Matthew turned to press his forehead against the cool of the wall tiles. 'What do you want?' he asked, turned again, leaned his back against the wall, trying to do the simplest thing of all, and just breathe.

'I take it you found my little memento?' Sullivan asked casually.

Matthew closed his eyes, desperate not to hear what might come next, desperate to know.

'If it helps, she did take it off willingly.'

Matthew's chest heaved. His stomach turned over.

Sullivan went quiet for a second, and then, 'She's in one piece, Adams,' he announced, causing Matthew to slide to his haunches. 'And if you don't want the next memento to be, shall we say, more personal, you'd better be ready to do exactly what I say *and* make sure it happens, *comprendre?*'

'Not hearing you, Adams,' Sullivan prompted him when Matthew didn't answer.

Matthew shook his head. The man was completely insane. 'Just ...' he faltered, fighting to forestall the inevitable cough that always accompanied the attacks '... tell me what you want.'

'Well, now let me see?' Sullivan said leisurely. 'Several things,' he went on, at length. 'Your money, for one.'

The rest of his father's insurance pay-out, Matthew wasn't surprised.

'I think you owe me that much, don't you?' Sullivan continued, as if he actually expected an answer. 'Your little charade at customs cost me, Adams. Cost me dear. And, let's face it, it's not like you'll be needing it for your daughter's school fees or anything, is it?'

'You fucking animal.' Bile rose in Matthew's throat.

Sullivan went quiet for a second, and then, 'Next, you call off your over-keen partner.'

'What?' Matthew tried to keep up with him.

'Ingram, he's digging around, trying to come up with something that he can make add up to more than fuck all. Tell him to drop it.'

Alarm bells rang in Matthew's head. *How the hell ... ?'*

'He also has something that belongs to me. Stole it, to be precise, not very cleverly, if you don't mind me pointing out. I want it back. I want it back pronto, Detective Inspector Adams, otherwise you'll go to bed every night hearing your wife scream. And, trust me, she will be. I'll call you back. Two hours. Your progress report better be good.'

'Wait!' Matthew scrambled to his feet. 'I need proof.' He stopped again, feeling the infuriating cough tickling its way up his windpipe. 'I need to know she's safe.'

'She is. For now.'

'Not good enough.' Matthew's voice was gruff, his breathing laboured. 'I need to speak to her.'

'Not possible,' Sullivan said bluntly.

Matthew's jaw clenched. 'Then no dice,' he said, his heart squeezing inside him.

'Oh, very droll,' Sullivan sneered. 'You just going to pop off back home and leave her to her fate, are you? I don't think so, Adams.'

Matthew didn't answer, knowing that Sullivan knew full well he would do nothing that might endanger her.

'She's not here, is she,' Sullivan stated matter-of-factly. 'She's all tucked up somewhere nice and cosy. There's no reception there, otherwise I'd be happy to oblige, obviously. Not.'

'No reception? Why?' Matthew asked, terror gripping him as he imagined what kind of place would have no mobile reception.

'Because it's got thick walls,' Sullivan informed him dryly. 'Don't worry, Adams. She's not entombed in a coffin ... yet. I'll ask her something. Something personal only she will know,' he went on, as Matthew felt the walls shift another inch. 'And hurry it up. I have other things I need to be doing.'

Sweat tickling his eyelashes, Matthew frantically tried to think, groping for anything that bastard might not guess at or already know, somehow.

'She has nice legs, your wife,' Patrick commented idly. 'Shame about the scar on her left thigh, but still, they're not bad. Nice and toned...'

Matthew gulped back another wave of nausea. 'Our baby,' he said quickly. 'Ask her ...' he stopped, trying and failing to ward off a cough '... the name of our second child.'

'How very touching. Makes me want to weep, it really does,' Sullivan drawled mockingly. 'I'll call back. Makes sure you pick up pronto. Mess me about, Adams, and she's dead, end of. Got it? Oh, and do something about that cough, yeah? It's seriously pissing me off.'

His head screaming, his chest rasping with the effort of trying to breathe, Matthew dropped the phone to his side as the call ended. *Bastard,* he thought, fumbling in his pocket, finding his inhaler, trying to take the requisite breath in, and out, in readiness to suck the medication out of the inhaler.

'Damn, stupid ... *fucking* thing! *Jesus Christ!'* He could not do this!

White hot rage coursing through him, fury at his inadequacy, Matthew hurled the inhaler hard across the room.

'Why?' he implored, as the canister separated from the chamber and clattered to the floor. *Why?* Dragging his hands over his face, Matthew dropped again to his haunches. He tried to fight it, to think: what did he do next? *How?*

He was beaten, Matthew knew he was, by the asthma, but *not* by Sullivan. Never by Sullivan. Walls for support, Matthew pulled himself to his feet and walked across the bathroom to retrieve the medication that would allow him to breathe. Rebecca needed him. She needed him to be rational, to be calm and functioning. He would find her. And while he did have breath in his body, he would find Sullivan and destroy the bastard like the vermin he was.

## CHAPTER FOURTEEN

He hadn't found her. Ashley's heart sank, as she watched Matthew walk back towards the car. He looked exhausted, his face pale and drawn, like a man defeated: lost and lonely. Ashley knew how that felt.

*It might be better if he doesn't find her,* Emily commented.

Ashley tried to ignore her, wishing to God she could cut her sister's thoughts in her head.

*Matthew would keep us even if he was on his own. He's nice,* Emily went on, despite Ashley's determination not to hear her.

*So is Becky,* she replied silently.

*Yeth, but she's having a baby. A brand new one. She won't want us under her feet, will she? She'll be tired and moody and nasty.*

Ashley closed her eyes. *Be quiet!* She fumed, her mind immediately hurtling back to their last cold, dank flat. Where the curtains were always drawn and things crunched underfoot when she walked. An involuntary shudder shook through her as she remembered the cockroach. She'd hit it with the pan, at least five times, before it cracked. And then her mother had woken up. And Emily had cried and her mother had screamed at her, always pissed off with her, losing her temper if she got under her feet. Always losing it.

Ashley scrunched her eyes tighter, wishing she could blot out the memory: Her mother screeching at her, her hair demented and her eyes wild. "Why can't you be *normal*?" she'd spat out the words. "Why can't you help out with Emily, You're driving me mad!"

Once she'd stopped screaming, she'd taken her pills. Ashley recalled how her mother used to wash them down with the water, which didn't taste like water and which Ashley knew full well wasn't water. When she'd stirred again, finally, she'd put her song on. It was always the same one. And, as usual, her mum sang along, as she mascaraed her eyes and slicked on her lippy, like an angry red slash for a mouth. And then she'd taken Emily and gone out. 'Back soon,' she'd said, banging the front door shut behind her.

She never did come back though.

'Ashley?' Matthew pulled the driver's door open and sank into the seat beside her. 'Everything all right?'

Ashley nodded quickly. 'Huh, huh,' she said, wiping her nose on her coat sleeve, something else her mother would have gone mental at her for. 'Just thinking.'

Sighing expansively, Matthew nodded, pushed his key into the ignition, placed his hands on the steering wheel and then paused, almost as if he'd forgotten what he was doing.

Ashley watched him for a second, noting the tight set of his jaw, his long eyelashes closing over his eyes. He had nice eyes, caring eyes. Haunted eyes, Ashley had noticed, since Becky had gone. 'Are you all right?' she asked, scared for him, scared for herself.

'What?' Matthew answered distractedly.

'You didn't find her, did you?' Ashley tried to supress the seed of doubt that Emily had planted in her head: that if Becky did come back and have her baby, then *she'd* be in the way, just like she'd always been.

Matthew hesitated, then, 'No,' he said and took a deep breath.

'So what now?' Ashley wondered if he was ever going to breathe out.

Matthew thought about it, then, 'I'm taking you back,' he said, starting the engine. 'And then I need to go to the station.'

Ashley felt a surge of panic rise inside her. She didn't want to go back, not to the home, not to the flat. She couldn't!

'But I don't want to, Matthew,' she implored him. 'I want to stay—'

'I'm taking you back, Ashley. Now! No arguments.' Matthew checked his rear view and reversed sharply.

'*No!* I don't *want* to!' Ashley screamed ... and the car died. Right there, in front of his eyes, the dashboard went dark and the car stopped.

'You *have* to be kidding.' Matthew pulled his hands from the wheel as if it might electrocute him. 'Did you do that?' He turned his stunned gaze on Ashley, hearing the incredulity in his own voice, and wondering if he really was going out of his mind.

'No,' Ashley refuted tearfully. 'I didn't do *anything!* I don't want to go back there, Matthew. You can't make me. I'm not a kid. You can't—'

'Stop!' Bewildered, his mind reeling, his panic escalating, Matthew shouted, 'For God's sake! Just stop!'

Matthew breathed in and out steadily, trying to control his breathing, his temper.

'You're going back,' he repeated, more quietly. 'You can't stay with me. It's not safe. End of subject.'

'I'll stay right by your side, just like you said,' Ashley kept on, sounding as desperate as Matthew felt.

'You can't,' he said adamantly, trying to stay calm, to hold on to rational thought.

'I could stay in the house.' Ashley twisted in her seat to face him. 'Or go to a child-minder, or—'

'We don't have a child-minder, Ashley. You have to go—'

'Anywhere then,' Ashley countered. 'A friend, a relative, I don't care. I *can't* go back there.'

Matthew pressed his thumb and forefinger hard against his forehead, trying to stave off the hopeless exhaustion. 'Ashley—'

'I won't be any safer there than I am here. They're always picking on me and shoving me around. I spend most of the time outside on my own anyway. I don't see why I have to be there to do that. I could stay here in the car if you have to go somewhere. I wouldn't budge, I promise. Matthew, please?'

Matthew's shoulders sank, his resolve waning as he remembered her doing just that, sitting alone in the grounds, a sitting target, if Sullivan's depraved mind went off in that direction. Would anyone even notice if she went missing?

'I won't stay.' Ashley faced front again, slamming herself back in her seat. 'I'll run away,' she announced. Her tone was resolute, her arms folded.

*Great!* Sighing inwardly, Matthew congratulated himself on his sensitive handling of the situation. 'Ashley, please don't make this more difficult for me. I don't have a choice. I have to—'

'I will!' Ashley shouted over him. 'I *hate* it there. I won't stay.'

Wearily, Matthew shook his head. 'You can stay somewhere tonight. At a friend's. We'll talk about it more tomorrow,' he said, and was only mildly surprised when the dashboard pinged back to life.

Matthew glanced sideways at her as they set off. She hadn't said anything, yes or no, but he really did have no choice here. She must realise that.

'About the bullying, by the way,' he said, hoping that when he did drop her off, she'd realise it was because he did care, 'I know how you feel.'

Ashley glanced curiously at him, struggling to understand how, at five eleven and reasonably toned, he could ever have been a victim, Matthew guessed. Most people did, which is why he chose not to share it.

'Yep,' he dredged up a semblance of a smile, for Ashley's sake. 'I might look as if I can hold my own, but I've been there, too. They're cowards, Ashley. Bullies pick on people to shore up their ego in front of their friends, that's all. It's their problem, not yours.'

Ashley shrugged. 'I know. Still makes them vicious bastards though.'

That it did, Matthew conceded. And if he was going to rid the world of one of those vicious bastards, he had to get Ashley to a safe place and find Sullivan. His chest tightened at the thought of what that animal might be doing right now. What might be going through Becky's mind. *Please God, make he hasn't touched her.* Terror slicing through him, as his mind supplied a graphic illustration of what Sullivan was capable of, Matthew tightened his grip on the wheel.

****

'Come on, don't piss about,' Patrick snapped irritably and attempted to pull the stubborn cow out of the back of the van. The coast was clear. That part of his plan had worked out nicely. The last thing he needed now, though, was to be spotted by some animal loving dog-walker poking their nose in.

Reminded of Adams's derogatory reference to him as an animal, Patrick's irritation intensified. The sad little copper was going to be sorry about that, very sorry indeed, particularly when he'd had time to contemplate the consequences of his insults.

'I said, move it! Now!' Clutching the woman's ankles, he dragged her out of the van, only to end up with her landing in a heap at his feet.

*Women.* He sighed exasperatedly as he heaved her up. Obviously she couldn't get up on her own with her hands tied behind her, but she was getting right on his nerves. Patrick wasn't happy about that. He was beginning to wonder whether to just finish her off and be done with. He'd got Adams exactly where he wanted him. He'd taken the bait, and Patrick was reasonably sure he'd follow instructions hereafter in hopes of finding his pretty little wife in the same condition he'd lost her. Careless that, DI Adams, Patrick mentally addressed him. Very, considering how careless you were with your kid.

Blimey, she'd got some spirit. He'd give her that. He smiled bemusedly as she persisted in trying to pull away from him, pointlessly, considering her petite stature compared to his honed physique, of which Patrick was proud. He'd worked hard, toning himself up with relentless work-outs at the gym. Image was all, as far as Patrick was concerned, which is why he never dressed in anything but designer, making sure he looked the part, should any insignificant piss-ant think about messing with … *Crap.* Glancing down, he lost the smile fast when he saw the state of his mud-caked alligator leather loafers.

*Marvellous.* Four-hundred-and-fifty quid those cost. She was trying his patience, she really was.

'Stand the fuck up, can't you?' He snarled, as she continued to squirm, which obviously meant she was going to end up with bruises all over her pretty porcelain skin. What was it with these bloody women? Patrick tightened his grip on her arms. Could they never obey a simple instruction?

'Aw, for fu—' Gritting his teeth, a migraine definitely threatening, Patrick glanced down again, to where the silly bint was attempting to kick him. Not sensible with no shoes on, he decided, particularly as she'd now gone and splattered mud all over his *Armani Collezioni* Velvet texture trousers.

That was it. Patrick was officially annoyed. He'd acted like a complete gentleman, hardly touched her, offered her tea in his best *Harrods* bone China, and she shows him no respect whatsoever. No choice but to, Patrick pulled his fist back and punched her. That should stop her shenanigans.

'Silly bitch,' he muttered. 'Now, do as you're told, before I get seriously angry.' Letting go of one of her arms as she wilted, he yanked her along by the other.

Reaching the dilapidated property, he ferretted in his pocket for the key to the door, pushed it home and shoved the door open. The place was a shithole, but it would have to do. Snatching her in a hurry, Patrick hadn't had much time to think it through, other than to consider what Adams' first ports of call might be. Dead predictable coppers were. They'd be all over his home turf like flies over dog turd. The plus was, it would definitely be the last place Adams would think of looking.

'Move.' He pushed the woman before him. 'Inside.'

Staggering forwards, Rebecca stifled a moan as her bare toes stubbed on something. She wouldn't show any signs of weakness, she'd already decided, feed the animal's need to show off his pathetic prowess. She *wouldn't!* The absolute bastard. If only her hands were free, she'd poke her thumbs in his flat evil eyes and watch them pop. Gulping back the bile in her parched throat, Rebecca continued to walk forwards, until he barked, 'Stop! You'll do yourself an injury, stumbling around in the dark, stupid cow. Stay there.'

Rebecca waited, heard the hinges creak on the door, as he closed it, and then opened it again and slammed it shut. Where was she, she wondered, trying to recall any of the journey which might give her some kind of clue. It smelled of mildew, damp moss, leather, and old hay. In the countryside somewhere, presumably, but it could be any building anywhere. She'd lost track of time, blindfolded in the back of the van, lost all sense of direction as he'd driven for what seemed like hours, careering around corners, careless of his cargo.

Careless of anything or anyone, she realised, her chest physically constricting with fear. He had no feelings, none that were normal, talking to her about women's legs, muscles and orgasms, his disgusting clammy hands on her flesh, the look in his vile eyes, like that of a persecutor pulling the legs off a spider. What did he want? It could only be money, but why pick on Matthew, a police officer?

Rebecca's thoughts were cut short, as he came towards her. She could feel him, smell him. Her skin crawled and her stomach heaved with repulsion.

'I'm going to take this off,' he said, jabbing a finger into the side of her head. 'When I do, you do as I say, nice and slow and nice and calm. *No* girly tantrums. Got it?'

Desperate to see, to breathe properly, Rebecca nodded.

'Good.' He hooked a finger under the silk pillow slip he'd tied around her head and yanked it off.

'Just so you know,' he said, his face close to hers, a pungent mixture of stale whisky, cigarette smoke, and sickly sweet aftershave assaulting her senses before she had time to focus, 'there's nowhere to run and nowhere to hide.'

He waited while her eyes adjusted to the light, smiled pleasantly, and then waved his arm around, like an estate agent showing off a property. It was empty, dusty and derelict, crumbling brickwork, boards at the windows, Rebecca noted, her heart sinking. Original beams supported the roof, ropes and chains hanging from a cross-beam.

Her heart lurched into her mouth. Rebecca quickly averted her gaze, lest she draw his attention to what possible use he might make of it. The front door looked like the original, stout wooden and heavy. He'd placed the key on the inside of the lock, she registered, which meant it could be locked from both sides. Her gaze strayed to the hefty iron bolts, top and bottom.

'Nowhere to go,' he repeated, obviously following every movement of her eyes. 'All exits are well-secured.' He bent to flick at the mud spatters on his trousers, tsking as he did, and then looked back at her, with a scowl.

'The door is solid wood, by the way, so if you were imagining you might claw your way out with your fingernails, think again. Your hands will be, shall we say, otherwise engaged, in any case.'

Cold terror gripped Rebecca's stomach, as she followed his gaze back to the cross-beam.

'But that's for later. Let's get you comfortable for a while first, shall we?' He smiled again, an almost paternal smile. Rebecca felt the hairs rise on her flesh.

'Get the old circulation going and do something about those feet. Can't have you walking around barefoot and hurting yourself, can we?' he chatted jovially away, unbelievably.

Rebecca stared at him, waiting, wondering. Was he really oblivious to the broken brickwork and debris he'd just force-marched her over?

'Sorry about that.' He nodded at her face, obviously referring to the swelling Rebecca could feel forming under her eye, red-hot, throbbing right down to her cheekbone. 'But you did ask for it, didn't you?'

He looked at her, as if expecting a reply.

Rebecca glanced down and back, her throat constricting, as she looked back at him. Even without tape on her face, was he really expecting an answer?

'I asked you a question,' he said quietly. 'Bit rude not to answer, sweetheart, don't y'think?'

Dear God, he was. Rebecca swallowed, and nodded, barely.

'That's better,' he said, apparently satisfied. 'Course, you would've struggled to answer a bit, I suppose.' He cocked his head to one side, surveying her thoughtfully. 'Here, let's take this off,' he said, at length. 'Then we'll get you some water. How does that sound?'

Rebecca's overwhelming urge was to knee him hard in the groin. She nodded again instead, playing along. No choice but to. No choice. *Oh, dear God, please, please help me.*

Carefully, his eyes almost crossed as he concentrated on his task, he reached to peel a corner of the duct tape away from her face, then ripped it away fast.

'*Ouch*,' he said, as Rebecca winced, and then, 'Needs must.' He shrugged, and smiled. 'I'm going to untie your hands now, so you can get the feeling back. I've got to retie them anyway, so it's not a problem,' he chuntered inanely on, as if he was being noble. As if he was concerned she thought she might be inconveniencing him in some way.

Swaying on her feet, Rebecca attempted to still the nausea rising inside her, as he moved around behind her, his hands touching hers, as he worked to untie her.

'Don't try anything silly now, will you, sweetheart?' he said, leaning close to her ear as he loosened the knots, 'because, if you do, DI Adams is going to struggle to identify the body. Got it?'

Gulping back hard, Rebecca nodded, and prayed she wouldn't vomit, as he came back to stand in front of her.

'Better?' he asked, as the blood rushed to her hands like a thousand burning needles.

Rebecca stared at him, horrified. He was smiling again, looking at her as if he might be indulging a child. He was completely insane. The smidgeon of hope that he might let her go faded. She stood no chance. Absolutely none. She was going to die, here, in this cold, lonely place. And her baby? Her hand straying instinctively to the soft round of her tummy, Rebecca closed her eyes, forced back the tears that welled up inside her, and then snapped them wide open as she felt the flat of his hand close over hers.

'You don't have something you'd like to share, do you, Mrs Adams?' he asked, amusement now dancing in his cruel, grey eyes. 'A happy upcoming event possibly?'

'No!' Rebecca croaked, too quickly. Much too quickly.

He raised his eyebrows.

Rebecca dropped her gaze. 'No,' she repeated, shaking her head vehemently.

'Right,' he said, and paused.

Her heart twisting with a new kind of terror, Rebecca looked warily back at him.

'Shame.' He smirked. 'We could have occupied ourselves thinking up baby names while we wait for your white knight to ride to your rescue. Not to worry, we'll just have to think of something else to occupy us, won't we?'

He lowered his gaze, his loathsome eyes eating her up as they trailed over her.

'Nice tits,' he commented appreciatively. 'Adams likes them like that, does he? Firm and fulsome.'

Rebecca gagged, as he reached out, cupped one of her breasts and squeezed hard.

'I'll get you some water,' he said suddenly, pulling his hand away. 'You look a bit pale. Don't move,' he instructed and took a step to his side. 'It will be worse for you if you do.'

Her mind racing, her whole body shaking, Rebecca glanced towards him as he crouched to ferret in a large canvas bag, nestled against one of the side walls.

'You know, if you ever did want to share, I'm a good listener,' he offered, as he pulled a bottle of water from the bag. 'My daughter's always confiding in me. Mind you, some of it would make your hair curl, I swear. Kids nowadays ...'

He tutted and rambled on, making conversation. *Making conversation!* Rebecca felt her head swim. Desperately, she looked from him to the door, and then, her pulse racing, her heart thrumming wildly against her ribcage, she took the only chance she might have, and flew towards it.

It was hopeless. She knew it was, but... She *had* to try. A petrified sob escaping her throat, she twisted the key, her other hand swiping at the top bolt... and then he was on her, grabbing her hair, yanking her head back, dragging her back through the dust and the dirt, forcing her round to face him.

'Did I say *don't?*' he roared, a globule of spit at his mouth, his face so close to hers she could see a blue-grey vein pulsing at his temple.

'*Did I?*' His eyes bulged with rage, as he pushed his face closer.

'Stupid bitch!' he spat. Then, bringing his hand back, he landed a searing blow to her face and shoved her away hard.

'You just don't learn, do you?' Wiping his hand over his mouth, he loomed over where Rebecca lay sprawled on the floor.

'Next time my aim will be lower.' His gaze moved meaningfully to her midriff. 'Now... do... not... *move!*

'Oh God...' Rebecca sobbed, realising the enormity of her mistake. Now, he would take no chances. She should have waited. She should have talked to him, tried to reason ... There was no reason. No reasoning. None. 'Why are you doing this? What do you *want?*'

'Your husband,' he said calmly. Then, yanking the key from the door, he turned back to his bag. 'Now, come on, let's get you up and dressed properly, hey? You'll want to be looking your best when he sees you, won't you?'

As he turned back to her, Rebecca's horrified gaze dropped from his ludicrously smiling face to his hands, in which he held a pair of blood-red stilettos.

# CHAPTER FIFTEEN

'Taylor?' Patrick tapped on his daughter's bedroom door. Getting no answer, he knocked again and poked his head inside. 'Hi, sweetheart, how you doing?' he asked, glancing to where she was sitting cross-legged on her bed, her earphones in and her eyes glued to her phone. Patrick might have guessed. Kids nowadays, they spent their whole lives plugged into some gadget or other. Couldn't be healthy, he thought, shaking his head as he walked across to her. 'Hello, earth to Taylor.'

Taylor glanced up at him from under her eyelashes.

Bleedin' long eyelashes, Patrick thought. 'You wearing falsies?' He narrowed his eyes suspiciously.

'Yerwhat?' Taylor gave him a look. That look. The one that told him she thought her old man was past it and out of touch.

Well, he wasn't. Patrick was very much in touch with what eighteen year old girls got up to. And he wasn't having any of it. Taylor was destined for better than hanging out on street corners with delinquent tossers. Patrick's mind drifted briefly to the teenagers he was happy to see hanging out on street corners, but he dismissed the irony of it. Privately educated, Taylor was destined for better things. She was going to uni to get a proper degree. None of those mumbo-jumbo ten-a-penny business studies or creative crap ones either. The Royal Veterinary College, University of London, was where Taylor was going, to get her foundation in veterinary nursing, he reminded himself proudly. Then quashed a surge of anger as he remembered he wouldn't be seeing much of her, all thanks to Adams, at least not until he'd got himself sorted and settled in his villa. And then it would depend on Taylor wanting to spend her holidays in Spain. She'd have a new life beckoning here, after all, new mates. *Yes, she would*, Patrick told himself. Loved her old man, his clever little girl.

Course, she could have gone for veterinary medicine if she'd stop fannying about with her girlfriends and put her mind to it, he also reminded himself.

'The eyelashes.' Patrick jabbed a finger towards his own eyes.

'Oh, those.' Taylor turned her attention back to her phone. 'They're all the rage. Do you like them?'

'No, I do not like them,' Patrick informed her, shoving his hands in his pockets, as he studied her. She was growing up too fast. Much too fast for his liking. Boys sniffing around, after whatever they could get. Well, no one was going to break his little girl's heart, not unless they fancied a broken neck.

'They look like tarantula legs,' he said, a shudder running through him as he visualised actual spider legs. He hated the bloody things. 'Get 'em off. And the lipstick while you're at it.'

'*Dad!* Taylor looked back at him, wide-eyed and clearly peeved. 'It's Elizabeth Arden's, Rustic Red!'

'I don't care if it's Queen Elizabeth's pure gold. Wipe it off. You look like a tart. If you have to cake your face in crap, wear something lighter, pink or peach or something.'

'Oh, for God's sake,' Taylor rolled her eyes, twanged her earphones out and shuffled off the bed. 'You are *so* outdated, Dad, you're practically prehistoric.'

'And the falsies,' Patrick reminded her, as she stomped past him towards her en-suite. 'Take 'em off.'

Taylor turned back. 'I can't. They're attached. See?' With which she plucked at her eyelashes, pulling her lid away from her eyeball. 'I have to get them done at the salon, unless you want me to blind myself trying.'

'All right, all right,' Patrick relented. In truth, if she'd batted her eyelashes, false or not, he'd have given in anyway. 'They can stay, for now. The lipstick goes though. It doesn't suit you.'

'God, honestly, you'd think I was about two,' Taylor muttered huffily and turned to flounce onwards.

Patrick couldn't help wishing she was still two. There were a lot of perverts out there, ready to take advantage of an innocent young girl. He sighed, forgetting the minor fact that he was one of them.

'So how's Saffron?' he asked after the horse that had cost him an arm and a leg.

'Yeah, good.' Taylor sounded more cheerful, as she splashed water in the en-suite. 'She's doing really well in the arena. I got her up to a canter the other day.'

'Yeah, well, you be careful. Horses can be temperamental, you know.'

'*Dad,*' Taylor came back to the bedroom, dabbing at her face with a towel, 'I have had a bazillion riding lessons? I do know what I'm doing.'

Patrick smiled, pleased to see his girl looking less like she did actually hang about on street corners. 'I know, sweetheart,' he said. 'You're a natural with animals. Beautiful and talented, that's my Taylor.'

He wrapped an arm around her, giving her shoulders a squeeze, as she padded back across the room.

'I'm glad you're progressing with her. We might have to get Saffron stabled for a while, though,' he said, broaching the subject he'd actually come up to talk to her about.

'Why?' Taylor's eyes grew wide again, as she plopped down on the bed, this time with ready indignation.

Patrick glanced down, rearranging his face to suitably grieving. 'Chelsea's left,' he explained, shrugging sadly. 'Taken off with some prat.'

Taylor looked disbelieving for a second, then, 'Good,' she said, tucking her feet up.

'That's not very nice, is it?' Patrick was surprised, genuinely. He'd known Chelsea and Taylor weren't exactly best friends, but still, he wasn't used to his baby being bitchy.

'I tell you she's buggered off and you say "good"?'

'Well, let's face it, Dad, she was loads younger than you, and if ever there was a tart...'

Patrick considered, for all of two seconds. 'Yeah, you're probably right.' He sighed stoically.

'You should get someone your own age, Dad,' Taylor suggested. 'I mean, it is a bit embarrassing, you running around with fake-bake babes all the while. You should find someone genuine who really loves you. You know, for who you are, not for your money.'

'Yeah, maybe.' Patrick pondered demonstrably. *Not*, he thought. He couldn't abide all that soppy stuff, doe-eyed women telling him they loved him, thinking they were offering him some prized possession if they opened their legs. And he certainly didn't want some flabby fat cow his own age. Firm and toned was Patrick's preferred choice. His thoughts drifted to the rather tasty Mrs Adams, who actually wasn't that young, but who'd obviously looked after herself. Nice ankles, good bone structure: high cheekbones, which were always a sign of natural beauty. Shame he'd had to bruise them. Her eyes were something else, huge, like bloody great headlights in her head. She'd looked like a petrified gazelle when he'd left her. Worried, obviously, that she'd riled him. And so she should be.

'Did you argue?' Taylor interrupted Patrick's contemplation of whether, and how, he should punish the woman. He really would prefer to save the good stuff until Adams turned up for the show.

'Some,' he admitted. They'd argued on average at least once a day lately. Taylor wasn't likely to believe that they hadn't.

Taylor's gaze flitted to the bruises adorning his chin. 'Did she do that?'

'What?' Patrick gawked. 'Do us a favour, Taylor. If she had, I'd have floored her.' He had floored her, in actuality, but Taylor didn't need to hear details. 'I told you, I went into the back of someone, cracked my chin on the steering wheel. Painful, it was, too.'

Patrick's hand strayed to his face, his thoughts back to Adams and the many ways he'd been considering giving the jumped up little detective his due payback.

'So, why does Saffron have to be stabled?' Taylor's tone was back to defiant.

'I have to go away. Business,' Patrick said, with an apologetic shrug. 'I've had a word with your aunt Suzie in Brum. She said you could stay—'

'Uh-uh, no way.' Taylor shot off the bed, ready to throw a major moody. 'She's totally common. And her house is the absolute pits. Can't I just stay—'

'No, Taylor.' Patrick eyeballed her adamantly. 'There's no way I'm going to leave an eighteen year old girl in this rambling great house on her own.' In fact, there was no way he was leaving his daughter anywhere in the vicinity until he'd cleared his debt with Tony Hayes. Some people would sink to any level to make their point, and Hayes was one of them, ruthless bastard.

'I could get Hannah to stay,' Taylor tried, as he headed for the door. 'We could—'

'No, Taylor! Not this time.' Patrick's word was final.

'That is *sooo* unfair!' Taylor shouted after him, as he headed back along the galleried landing. Patrick pressed his forefingers against his temples, a misty aura drifting into his vision warning him of another impending migraine. He hated upsetting his daughter. This was Adams' fault. All of it.

Patrick stormed onwards and then stopped, and paled. If that was one of Taylor's false eyelashes, he thought, squinting down at the cream Axminster carpet, it was a bloody big one. Petrified, Patrick stood frozen to the spot, perspiration breaking out on his forehead. His fight or flight instinct told him to run, but there was nowhere to run except back the way he'd come. And then the little bastard would scurry off, its hunched legs gambolling over each other as it scarpered under one of the beds to reappear God knew when and where; probably when he was sleeping.

His heart palpitating, Patrick ran his tongue over his dry lips and then jumped back a step, as it moved. 'Fuck! Taylor! Here, now!'

It was watching him, Patrick would swear it was, ready to come at him like greased lightning. 'Taylor!'

'What!?' Taylor said moodily behind him. 'I'm busy.'

'Spider.' Swallowing, Patrick nodded towards his worst nightmare.

'Oh, for God's sake, Dad?' Taylor stomped up behind him.

'Shit, it's moving.' Patrick almost dove over the stair rail as she squeezed past him.

'It's not going to hurt you.' Taylor sighed and rolled her eyes, and then bent to pick the thing up. Patrick almost had a heart attack there and then, as she did.

'It's more frightened than you are.'

'I'm not frightened.' Patrick pulled himself indignantly up. 'I just didn't want to flatten it and make a mess on the carpet.'

Cupping her other hand over it, knowing better than to show it to him, Taylor laughed, possibly the only woman in the world who could get away with it. 'Yeah, right. You should see your face, Dad. You've gone a pale shade of white.'

'That's because I have a migraine,' Patrick pointed out and tried to look marginally less terrified. 'Put it well away from the house,' he reminded her, as she went downstairs with it. The ugly little fucker would only come back in if she didn't.

His heart rate returning to somewhere near normal, Patrick glanced worriedly around, lest there were any other spiders lurking. He couldn't stand them. Even the word gave him the heebie-jeebies. That was his old man's fault. What kind of father locks his kid in his bedroom with a house-spider as big as the house and then taunts him through the door? Patrick could still hear his drunken drawling.

'Cissy', he'd called him, humiliating him. Always humiliating him. No one calls *him* a cissy. Deserved all he got, evil old sod.

Course, he might have seen the thing lurking on the landing just now sooner if not for the migraine, which was undoubtedly down to the stress Adams had caused him. The man had a lot to answer for, Patrick seethed inwardly. And answer he would.

※※※※

'Yep, wassup?' Steve answered his phone, over a wide yawn.

'Sorry, did I wake you?' Matthew turned to give Ashley a reassuring nod, as he let himself out of Melanie's front door. Ashley wasn't too thrilled at being dumped there, but she'd accepted it was better than the alternative.

'Nah,' Steve assured him. 'I'm still up, dedication to duty and all that. I'm just going through that case I mentioned. It's almost identical: little in the way of evidence to go on, one shoe missing. The crime scene was somewhere near Oxford. Hold on, I'll pull up the details.'

'No, no need,' Matthew said quickly.

'Oh, right.' Steve sounded surprised. 'So why the call? I assume it's urgent at this time of night?'

Climbing into his car, Matthew took a breath. 'I need you to drop it, Steve,' he said, no other way to say it than how it was.

Steve made a glugging sound, as if choking on a beer. 'Scuse me?'

'Your investigations, I need you to put them on ice.' Matthew waited, guessing Steve wouldn't be very impressed.

Steve hesitated, and then, 'Would you like to run that by me again, boss, cos I'm not sure I'm following.'

Matthew massaged his forehead. 'Steve ... Look, I need you to trust me on this. I want you to drop it, no questions.'

'No questions?' Matthew could hear the incredulity in Steve's voice. 'You are joking?'

'I've never been more serious in my life,' Matthew assured him.

'But there's a clear link, for Pete's sake. We place Sullivan in the area, start checking out his alibis, and—'

'Not happening, Steve,' Matthew stated forcefully. 'Just leave it. OK?'

'Right.' He could almost feel the man's frustration in the ensuing short silence. 'You'll bring me up to speed, I assume, at some point?'

'As soon as I can,' Matthew promised, wishing he actually could. He'd never felt so alone in his life.

'Right,' Steve said again, his brusque tone indicating he thought it was far from right. 'I'll catch up with you then?'

'Will do. Steve ...' he said quickly, before Steve had the chance to end the call, which he probably was about to do pronto. 'There's something else I need you to do.'

'Oh, yes?' Steve's tone was now wary.

'The nail file, can you pull it?'

The silence was thunderous this time.

'I can't explain right now, Steve,' Matthew offered weakly, 'I just need you to—'

'Trust you?' Steve cut in tersely.

Matthew nodded, hoping to God he could trust Steve. 'Yes,' he said, in the absence of anything more reassuring to say.

'I'll do my best,' Steve said, clearly guessing no other information would be forthcoming. 'Anything else? Wouldn't like me to go and offer to clean Sullivan's pool out, would you, since we're treating him so kindly?'

'Drown the bastard in it, more like,' Matthew grated. 'Steve, I have to go. Call me, will you, as soon as you have it?'

'Yeah, whatever.' Steve sighed heavily, as Matthew hung up. 'Shall I go and buy a few wraps of H and hand them over to Sullivan with our compliments, while I'm at it?' he muttered angrily to himself.

Shaking his head, he leaned back in his chair, staring thoughtfully at his PC screen for a while, and then clicking over the images of the Oxford crime scene again. It might as well be the same case. The MO's identical and Matthew says it's a no-go? Right out of the blue? Uh-uh. It didn't add up. And now he wants him to pull something that, while not admissible as evidence, might definitely pin the bastard to the crime? DI Adams was definitely in some kind of trouble. Deep shit by the sounds of it. Steve wasn't sure what was going down but, while he would do what was asked of him, he wasn't about to sit around contemplating his navel while Matthew drowned in it.

It didn't take Steve long to find Rebecca's parents number. Reminding himself to be careful not to put the wind up anyone, he rang it, pretending he was an old friend and, bingo: no Rebecca currently visiting. After a nice little chat, her mum offered Steve Matthew's home number and said to remind Becky to ring her. She hadn't spoken to her in a while.

# CHAPTER SIXTEEN

His heart skipping a beat, Matthew immediately picked up the call on his hands-free.

'You know you can be dead irritating sometimes, don't you, Adams?' Sullivan muttered.

'Where is she?' Matthew worked to keep his tone even.

'Not very polite, either, are you? I believe I asked first.'

Disbelieving, Matthew shook his head. 'What?'

'I asked you whether you knew how irritating you were?' Sullivan repeated, taking his time. Knowing he could, because he knew he'd got Matthew exactly where he wanted him, dancing to his tune. And Matthew would, because there were simply no other options. If he got Sullivan hauled in somehow, there was no guarantee he'd reveal where Becky was. If he enlisted a few heavies of his own and beat the piece of scum to a pulp ... Oh, how Matthew wanted to do that ... the chances were Sullivan would do all he could to make sure she was never found.

'Well?' Sullivan waited.

Impotent anger broiling inside him, Matthew clutched the phone hard to his ear.

'Yes,' he supplied what the bastard wanted to hear.

'Yes what?'

Matthew drew in a tight breath. 'Yes, I know how irritating I am.' He almost choked on the words.

'Always were,' Sullivan rambled perversely on, 'thinking you were something special cos your old man was a copper. Turned out he was a bit of a failure, though, didn't it, Adams? Bent as a nine bob note, as my dear old dad would say.'

Matthew gripped the phone tighter. 'Where is she, Sullivan?'

'Somewhere.' Sullivan paused, and then asked matter-of-factly, 'Did you know she doesn't like confined spaces? I told her screaming would only reduce her oxygen supply, but—'

'You *fucking* animal!' Matthew's fury exploded. 'Where the *hell* is she?!'

Silence was Sullivan's answer. Then, 'I told you you'd find out when you'd called your pet dog off and delivered certain items, didn't I?' he reminded him evenly. 'I also told you to stop with the name-calling.'

This was utter insanity. The psycho had lost it, completely. Matthew swiped at the sweat on his forehead and tried to think straight, to somehow keep up with the gibberish Sullivan was spouting.

'*Didn't I?*' Sullivan barked.

*Christ!* 'Yes!'

'Well?' Sullivan asked. Again. And again. And *again*. It was like a rerun of Matthew's youth. But this time if he didn't supply the right answers, his punishment wouldn't be a sharp jab to the ribs, a vicious kick to the stomach ... *Dear God* ... What might he do to Becky?

Slamming his head back against the headrest, Matthew steeled himself and forced the words out. 'I apologise,' he said hoarsely.

Sullivan went quiet again, obviously considering: had his victim learned his lesson or did he need to reinforce it?

'Better,' he said, at length. 'But if you want your wife's pretty face to stay that way, watch the mouth, hey, Adams?'

*Don't.* Clenching his jaw so hard his teeth hurt, Matthew cautioned himself not to retaliate.

'So did you do as I asked?' Sullivan paused and waited, then, 'That was a question, Adams,' he said, a warning edge to his voice.

Matthew worked to keep the contempt from his own. 'I spoke to my DS, yes. He's putting a lid on it.'

'The file?'

'He's pulling it.'

'Good. And what about our little cash transaction, Adams. How's that going?'

Matthew closed his eyes, wishing it was possible to withdraw it in actual cash. Wishing to God he could hold Sullivan down and stuff every last pound coin down his throat.

'The money will be in my account by close of business tomorrow. I can do the transfer online. I'll need details, obviously.'

'Very organised, aren't we?' Sullivan drawled facetiously. 'I'll provide details when I'm ready to. For your wife's sake, when I do you'd better make sure it goes smoothly, Adams. No money, no goods. Got it? Share any of this with your friends at the station meanwhile, and you'll never see her again. She'll die, Adams, a slow painful death, wondering why her heroic husband didn't save her. *Comprendre?*'

Matthew pulled in a tight breath. 'If you touch her, Sullivan. If you harm her in any way, I'll—'

'What?' Sullivan cut in. 'What will you do, Detective Inspector? Kill me?'

'It's a promise,' Matthew assured him.

'Hah! That, Adams, would require you to grow a pair and fight back. You don't have the bottle, mate. Never did have. The inclination, yes, I'll give you that. You never could hide it very well, Detective, all that repressed anger. The bottle to do anything with it, though, no way.'

Matthew didn't answer, the terrifying thought occurring that the twisted freak might see anything he did say as a challenge.

'She has nice breasts, your wife,' Sullivan commented casually. 'Full and ripe. I like them like that, don't you?'

Matthew felt as if the air had been sucked from his lungs. 'You bastard.'

'Tut, tut, you've gone and done it again, haven't you?' Sullivan sighed despairingly. 'I'm not sure how impressed the lovely Rebecca's going to be that you're choosing to ignore my warnings, Matthew.

'Bastard!' Clenching his fist, Matthew punched the steering wheel hard.

*****

Showered and dressed in the tee Melanie had given her, Ashley wandered towards the kitchen and then hesitated at the door. Melanie was feeding the baby and Ashley wasn't sure her presence would be welcome. Trying not to be too obvious, she watched a while, the baby's little arms flailing as he suckled, Melanie gazing lovingly down at him. *Like mums should*, Ashley thought, a pang of jealousy, mixed with something else ... longing ... tugging at her chest.

'Had enough, little man, hey?' Melanie asked the baby after a while, lifting him higher in her arms. 'You can come in, you know?' she said, noticing Ashley hovering. 'We don't bite.'

Ashley's mouth curved into a small smile. 'He doesn't have any teeth,' she pointed out, doing as bid, and still feeling a bit spare, even though Melanie said she didn't mind her being there. She would though, if she was there for long.

It was a nice kitchen, bright and modern. Not like Matthew's and Becky's, which was warm and farmhousey, but still it was cosy. Like family kitchens should be. Would Becky really want her to stay, Ashley worried afresh, when she had a baby of her own, who would keep her awake at night and need loads of attention?

*No*, the insistent voice in her head said. *She'll be tired and snappy, and if you try to help, you'll only get it all wrong.*

Uncertainly, Ashley wondered across the room, as Melanie got to her feet, the baby still nestled in the crook of her arm.

'Does he have a name?' Ashley gazed at him, taking in his tiny rosebud lips, his huge blue eyes, wide and innocent. As Emily's had once been. They'd soon grown wary though. Ashley recalled how Emily had learned to read the signs even before she could talk, crying whenever their mum had picked her up, rather than gurgling contentedly.

'Lucas,' Melanie supplied, scanning his face adoringly and then looked at Ashley. 'We wanted something strong-sounding, you know, manly. What do you think?'

Ashley nodded. 'Yeah, it's cool.'

'Do you want to hold him?' Melanie offered, easing Lucas towards her.

Ashley stepped back a little. 'Uh, uh, better not.'

'It's all right,' Melanie assured her. 'They're not made of glass.'

'I know,' Ashley said, defensively. She did know how to hold babies. She just didn't want him ending up crying and her getting the blame.

'Go on,' Melanie urged her. 'You'd be doing me a huge favour. I could really use a quick break.'

'Okay.' Reluctantly, Ashley relented, as Melanie blinked beguilingly at her.

'Brilliant. Here you go then. Just pop one arm underneath him,' Melanie said, giving Ashley instructions as she handed him over carefully. 'And support his head with your other ... Oh, well, there you go.' She looked on, amazed, as Ashley took the baby expertly into her arms. 'You're a natural. You've got the job. I was gasping for a cuppa. It's a wonder I don't die of dehydration when my husband is working away. Want one?'

'Please.' Ashley nodded, turning to walk to the table and sit down with her charge.

'Do you have any sisters or brothers, Ashley?' Melanie asked conversationally, as she flicked on the kettle.

Ashley hesitated before answering. 'A little sister,' she said, after a pause.

'Oh?' Melanie eyed her curiously over her shoulder. 'Is she at the care home, or has she been—'

'She went away,' Ashley supplied quickly, her hair falling over her face as she looked down at the baby.

'Oh,' Melanie said again, awkwardly this time. She rattled the cups noisily as she turned back to the tea. 'So, how're you getting on with Becky and Matthew?'

'Yeah, good,' Ashley supplied, studying the baby, who was smiling up at her. It was probably just wind, Ashley suspected, but still he looked cute.

'Are you going to stay with them, do you think?' Melanie asked, popping teabags in cups and topping them up with water.

Ashley kept her gaze averted. 'Dunno.' She shrugged. 'I'd like to. Depends on what happens when they have their baby, I suppose.'

'*Baby?*' Melanie crashed the milk down so hard little Lucas jumped in his Babygro. 'She's pregnant?! You're joking! Why on *earth* didn't she tell me? Why didn't Matthew say anything? Oh God, is that why she's gone to her mother's? I bet it is. I bet there's something wrong. She'll be devastated. I'd better ring her.' Melanie furrowed her brow worriedly and turned for the hall.

*Shit.* Ashley couldn't let her do that. 'It's past midnight,' she reminded her urgently. 'She'll probably be in bed,'

Melanie checked her watch. 'You're right.' She sighed and turned back. 'Oh, I so wish she'd told me. That's what friends are supposed to be for.'

'She probably didn't want to jinx things,' Ashley suggested, easing the baby against her shoulder, as he was now getting a bit fractious.

'No wonder Matthew seemed so preoccupied. Poor man, he'll be devastated too, if things don't work out this time. He loves that woman to bits,' Melanie pondered out loud, as Lucas let out an ear-piercing wail. 'He's probably beside himself,' she said, tsking and shaking her head as she walked across to Ashley.

'It wasn't me,' Ashley said, as Melanie distractedly plucked the baby from her arms. 'I was trying to make him stop. I—'

'Well, good luck with that. I haven't found his off button yet.' Rolling her eyes, Melanie nestled Lucas against her own shoulder. 'Don't look so terrified, Ashley.' She looked back at her, surprised. 'It's not your fault he's crying. It's what babies do.'

****

Matthew realised his hands were shaking as he waited for the owner to come back to the front of the shop. Rage and frustration vying with absolute terror, he was shaking pretty much all over. Attempting to still his nerves and focus on what he was doing there, he paced a few steps, taking in the customer-facing wares. Bars at the windows, he noted, stuffed birds, feathers full of dust, perched beyond them. They were posed. Matthew smiled sardonically: two pelicans feeding, faux green grass under their feet. They wouldn't be pecking at that any time soon. Turning back, Matthew scanned the vast array of firearms he generally didn't study so interestedly. Everything from air rifles to big game rifles, and shotguns from .410" single barrel to 12 bore. Gun cabinets displaying sporting rifles, target rifles, military rifles, all lined up like soldiers. Matthew wasn't after any of those.

'Detective Adams,' Danny Caswell finally reappeared from his flat upstairs, dressed in something he obviously felt offered him more protection than his boxers when greeting the law in the small hours, 'to what do I owe the pleasure?'

He looked Matthew dubiously over as he attempted to smooth down hair that looked as if it had last seen water about the same time the pelicans had.

The whole place was dusty, dark corners and dodgy dealings going on under the counter, Matthew knew it.

'Not pleasure, Danny,' he informed him, 'business.'

Danny groaned. 'Aw, come on, Mr Adams. I'm legit. You know I am. Registered and all licenses in place.'

Matthew smiled wryly. 'On the surface, Danny.'

'Nah, that's not right. I keep my nose clean, Mr. Adams. Sportsman's Association membership and everything. You ain't got nothing on me.'

'Yet,' Matthew said.

Danny raised an eyebrow warily. 'Meaning?'

'Meaning there are at least two unlicensed guns at the station I reckon might be traced back to here.' Matthew shrugged casually.

'Uh, uh, no way.' Danny looked flustered. 'I ain't—'

'Plus the ammo.'

'That's bullshit.' Danny was now definitely ruffled. 'You know it is.' He eyed Matthew defiantly.

Matthew coolly held the man's gaze, though he could feel perspiration wetting the back of his shirt. 'Then there's the drugs.'

Danny dragged a hand under his nose. 'What drugs?' he asked, underlying fear now belying the challenge in his eyes, which was exactly what Matthew had hoped for. Any kind of conviction could mess up his so-called legit career. Danny knew it.

Reaching into his jacket pocket, Matthew walked calmly across to the counter the man was standing behind.

'These.' He placed the suspect plastic bag he'd extracted in front of him.

Eyeing the contents, Grade A cocaine, Danny's shoulders sagged. 'Aw, for fuck's …'

'Allowing the premises you occupy or manage to be used for the supply or production of controlled substances is illegal, Danny. Do you want to keep your license?' Matthew waited.

'Bollocks,' Danny muttered, looking away. 'I didn't have you down as dirty, Adams. Coppers, all the bloody same ...'

Matthew slid the bag closer.

Danny sighed and met his eyes. 'What do you want?' He didn't bother to hide his disgust.

'A gun,' Matthew said simply, as if he went shopping for one every day.

'Oh, right.' Danny's expression was now curious. 'For personal use, I take it?'

'Just the gun, Danny. Save the questions.'

Danny looked him over, seemingly debating, then shrugged and turned to his cabinets. 'Well, you've come to the right place,' he said, unlocking one and opening it with a flourish. 'I've got everything here: full range of sporting calibres, pump-action and semi-automatic shotguns ...'

The semi-automatic was a nice idea, but, 'None of those.' Matthew shook his head.

'Side-by-sides, over and unders?'

'Handgun,' Matthew supplied.

Danny furrowed his brow, puzzled. 'But why not get one from the police—' he started.

'Small, compact, nothing less than a .22,' Matthew said over him, no inclination to share why he couldn't go to the police armoury.

Danny's wary look was back. 'You mean business then?' He studied Matthew enquiringly for a second. Getting no reaction, he shrugged indifferently and turned to head back upstairs, where, no doubt, his under-the-counter stock was kept.

'That I most definitely do,' Matthew said quietly behind him.

# CHAPTER SEVENTEEN

His hands firmly under his chin, Matthew sat on his sofa surveying the items on the coffee table: his phone, the leftover half-empty bottle of whisky, which he badly wanted to finish, the gun. A gun, purchased with murder in mind, first degree murder, carrying a mandatory life sentence.

Taking a breath, he glanced around at the open-plan lounge he and Becky had worked on together. They'd wanted clean, white lines, but also comfortable and homely. With her flair for interior design—natural wood floors throughout, cream leather lounge furniture, white walls and an open fire—Becky had managed to achieve it. She'd even chosen the lighting to create mood and ambience, subtle up-lighting and side-lighting downstairs. Ditto the bedroom, which he'd jokingly christened their French Boudoir when he'd noted the white satin and frills, and voile canopy above the bed. The bed they'd lain in together such a short while ago. Made slow, sweet love in, as if touching each other for the first time after so long apart. Swallowing a lump in his throat, Matthew reached for his glass.

All this, he could live without, would if he had to. Becky though ... He took a slug of his whisky. Losing his freedom against Becky losing her life, suffering at the hands of that sick animal, there was no contest in Matthew's mind. Taking another sip, he looked around again, at the home where everything had been so normal. Becky and Ashley tucked up on the sofa, watching TV. Watching TV without him, because he was late, again, taking things for granted. Taking Becky for granted, when he knew ... *He knew!* He should have shot the bastard long ago. He should have gone for the pump action before now and splatted the sub-human's intestines all over the wall.

Shakily, Matthew reached for the bottle, pouring another two fingers and gulping it in one. He got no comfort as the liquid burned the back of his throat, sliding down his oesophagus and doing nothing to warm him. Nothing to stop the incessant shaking, as his mind played over and over the images of Sullivan's hands on his wife's body, his sneering lips on hers, his tongue in her mouth. His hands all over her: touching, probing, tightening around her neck.

*Christ.* Choking back a sob, Matthew grabbed up the whisky, dragged an arm across his eyes, and then banged the bottle back down. Where *was* she? He'd called at the club, got nothing but hunched shoulders and closed looks for answers. He'd walked the streets, tried calling in favours, coerced, bullied, though it stuck in his craw. He'd got nothing. No information, no sign of Sullivan anywhere, not even at home. Sullivan's house had been deserted, no lights, no signs of life, the place was as still as the grave.

Clamping his eyes shut, Matthew tried to oust the image that thought conjured up: Rebecca, alone and petrified in some confined space, palming the roof of what she would imagine to be her coffin, clawing at it, desperate as the suffocating dark pressed in on her.

*Dear God!* He couldn't do this. *Couldn't!* 'Help me!' Raking his hands through his hair, Matthew got to his feet and glanced desperately at the ceiling. *As if there had ever been anyone there to answer my prayers*, he thought furiously. Snatching up the bottle again, he filled his glass, tipped the contents towards his mouth—and then stopped. *So, drink yourself into oblivion instead, why don't you? Render yourself more pathetically useless than you already are.*

'Bastard!' he raged, hurling the glass at the opposite wall.

'Ring, you fucking thing!' He glared at his phone, dragged a breath raggedly into his lungs, and then pressed the heels of his hands hard against his eyes. He wanted to get drunk, preferably paralytic. He needed to make the pain go away. He wanted to cry, to sob like a child, but he couldn't do either. All he could do was sit here, knowing Sullivan wasn't going to ring. He was going to play with him, prolong the pain and make him wait. And Matthew had no choice but to. He *had* to stay in control. Stay focussed. Taking another deep breath, he took his position back on the sofa, then resting his chin once again on his hands, he fixed his gaze on the gun—and waited.

****

'You see the trouble with your husband, sweetheart, is that he bears grudges. Well, everyone does to a degree, I suppose. Wouldn't be human if we didn't, would we?' Patrick paused, glancing up at her. Looks like she wasn't answering him either, but he'd have to forgive her that under the circumstances, he supposed.

'With him it's a personal vendetta, though,' he went on. 'He just refuses to let bygones be bygones. I mean, it's childish, isn't it, wanting to get your own back?' Shaking his head, still not able to comprehend Adams' obsession with him, Patrick walked across to check the contents of his holdall: water, plenty of that. He didn't want her to die of thirst while they waited. Various ropes. The slip lead, a sturdy rope version he'd purchased from the gundog shop for just this occasion and which he was going to get great pleasure from using. Cartridges. His trusty short-barrel shotgun wouldn't be a lot of use without those.

Satisfied he had everything he needed should Adams attempt to outwit him, he turned back to the woman. Ah, a flicker of life at last. Patrick noted a flutter of her eyelashes. About time, too. He'd barely touched her, one slap was all, and she's spark out. Wasn't going to be a lot of fun to play with unconscious, was she? Hmm, he didn't know though. Even caked in mud, those legs were *very* tasty.

Patrick walked back to where he'd trussed her to one of the crossbeams, crouched, and slid a hand appreciatively up the outside of her leg, from her calf to her thigh. Her eyes sprang open then. Huge they were. She looked like one of those cute little bug-eyed bush babies, Patrick thought, standing to eye her amusedly. He'd caught her by surprise, obviously. Didn't like being caught by surprise, women, always complained if you fancied an impromptu shag, which astonished Patrick every time. Why else did they think he'd keep them around, stuffing his bathroom full of their crap?

She didn't look very comfortable. Patrick's gaze strayed upwards, climbing her stretched arms, to her tied wrists and then on to the tops of her fingertips. Actually, she looked nice like that, he mused. Like a ballerina mid-pirouette, graceful and feminine, like women should look. And quiet, not gobbing off all over the place. Patrick dismissed a pang of guilt, as his mind drifted briefly to Chelsea, who'd rattled on like a train, most of it inconsequential drivel which grated seriously on his nerves.

Her wrists looked sore. Patrick started a downward perusal. Her own fault though. She'd left him no choice but to tie her up properly. And Patrick was a bugger for detail. Never leave anything to chance, his old man had drummed into him. Get emotionally involved with a woman, chances were she'd use his emotions against him, rob him of his dignity and his dosh and then bugger off and leave him. They were like that, tarts: manipulative little schemers, the lot of them. Chances were this one, with her wide ocean-blue eyes brimming with tears, would try to do just that. Hadn't she already? Blinking beguilingly at him over the tape he'd placed over her mouth out of necessity. And then making a bolt for the sodding door the second he'd relaxed a bit and decided to trust her.

Well, no more. Give them an inch and they'd take a mile. Patrick reached to undo his tie, leaving it loose around his neck. If she wanted to piss about, she should know she'd be kissing her old man goodbye. End of.

'He's determined to settle old scores, see, your husband,' rolling up his shirt cuffs, Patrick picked up where he'd left off. 'Always trying to fit me up in any way he can. You'd think he'd let it go, wouldn't you. I mean, as far as I'm concerned, it's history. I beat the crap out of him. My old man does the same to me. He's responsible for the death of my brother. I kill his kid. That didn't go entirely to plan, I have to admit. She wasn't supposed to be with you, see, but when you have to rely on idiots ...'

Knitting his brow, Patrick paused to ponder. He didn't hold with hurting kids, not normally, but ... 'Quid pro quo, I call it plain and simple.'

He shrugged and went on. 'But will Adams let it go? Oh, no. Relentless, he is. Unbalanced, if you ask me. Dangerous in a copper that, especially a high-ranking—'

Patrick trailed off as his mobile rang. He plucked it from his pocket and checked the number.

'Typical,' he muttered. 'Work, wouldn't you know it? Idiots, all of 'em. Leave 'em alone for one minute ... Sullivan?' He pressed the phone to his ear and waited.

And paced, and sighed irritably.

Rebecca watched him, terrified. He was out of his mind, utterly insane, every statement he made more ludicrous than the last. What was he going to do with her? Dear God, what was he planning to do to Matthew? Following his progress, Rebecca attempted to tug on the ropes binding her hands, only to wince as a searing pain ripped through her muscles, every sinew in her body seeming to burn simultaneously. Feeling the stress of her impossible position through her abdomen, a dull ache in her pelvis, Rebecca was almost glad of the tape on her face supressing the choking sob in her throat.

'So why are you ringing me? Just sling her arse out the door!' he bellowed into his phone, turning sharply back to stride towards her. 'What does she think she's doing at a lap-dancing club, debuting for *Strictly Come Dancing?* Silly cow. If she's too stuck-up to fuck, tough!'

Growing obviously more agitated, he span on his heel and marched away again.

'*Christ-Almighty*, are you completely mental, or what? We do *not* discuss drugs consignments on the phone. How many times do I have to tell—?'

Rebecca watched him as he stopped talking to listen. 'Tell Hayes I'll call him,' he said tightly and then eyed the ceiling. 'I said. Tell. Him. I'll. Call. Him!'

He turned back then, his face taut and white. 'Right. And what about the progress on my boat?'

Another agitated sigh, then, 'What do you mean *what* boat? My yacht, you thick twat! Have the marina called to say the service is done?' He massaged a temple with his free hand. 'Good.'

Jabbing at the phone to end the call, he ferretted in his inside jacket pocket and retrieved his cigarette box. 'Heavies? Huh. Like a bunch of bloody fairies,' he muttered, flipping open the top and dropping one of his vile smelling cigarettes into his mouth. 'I swear if they had a brain cell between them, it'd die of loneliness.'

Pausing long enough to light up and draw in deeply, he turned back towards her, clearly considering what his next unpredictable, petrifying move might be. Rebecca felt herself flinch as he took a step towards her, his soulless black eyes roving all over her.

'Course, none of this would be happening if it wasn't for your husband,' he said, blowing out a fat cloud of smoke and then plucking tobacco from the tip of his tongue. Rebecca inwardly recoiled, recalling how he'd slid that tongue wetly across her cheek and down the side of her neck.

'*You* wouldn't be here.' Patrick pointed the joint he held between his thumb and forefinger at her. '*I* wouldn't.'

He took another draw, narrowing his eyes as he looked her slowly over.

'I certainly wouldn't be owing money to dangerous bastards who never give up. Do you know how they collect, sweetheart, if you can't come up with the goods?' Cocking his head to one side, he watched her, scanning her face as if waiting for answers. 'They start with fingers. Then they move onto more delicate areas. I'll leave it to your imagination as to where. Then again,' his mouth twisted into a disgusting smirk, 'why leave things to the imagination...'

Rebecca gagged as his gaze travelled down her body.

'What was that, sweetheart?' He looked back to her face, his eyes full of mocking innuendo. 'You getting all excited, are you? Desperate for a real man to fuck you, I bet.'

Rebecca tried to look away, but there was nowhere to look, except down. Lowering her gaze, she breathed deeply, her chest heaving, and then, courage surfacing from somewhere deep inside, she snatched her eyes back to his. She would *not* let him subdue her. He could hurt her, bruise her. Rebecca felt hot tears roll down her swollen cheeks. But she would *not* let him break her spirit.

'Can't say I blame you,' he went on lewdly, enjoying himself. 'I quite like to do it standing up. What d'y'think, shall we give it a go? Or maybe you'd like to wait until hubby gets here? Might turn him on enough to give you a proper seeing to, you never know. Nah,' he said, taking another step towards her. 'We might as well get you warmed up while we're... *What the—?*'

He stopped, whirled around as a loud crack beyond the door

interrupted his vile monologue.

'Stay,' he said absurdly, moving swiftly across the room to grope in his bag.

Rebecca's eyes grew wide, as he straightened up. *Oh, dear God.* Her heart twisted inside her, as her gaze fell on the shotgun.

※※※※

Dropping flat amongst the house-building debris, Steve didn't dare move to take even a breath. Mud oozing beneath him, in his mouth, in his nostrils, rain slashing against his back, he stayed down. One arm outstretched before him, his mobile God knew where, he tried to stay calm, to remain detached, to not recoil from the stone-cold hand protruding from the earth, touching fingertips with his. Then, squeezing his eyes closed, he prayed.

Sullivan was yards away, the only thing obscuring Steve from his view: discarded beams and abandoned breeze block. His gun held high, Sullivan stepped closer. Steve ducked lower, pressing himself into the slush and slime underneath him.

He was merely feet away now. Steve could hear the man's shoes squelching as he walked towards him. His heart hammering like an express train, Steve froze and waited, sure he would soon hear the dull thud of the gun emptying into his back, and then breathed out as he heard Sullivan mutter, 'Fucking foxes.'

His body jolting as a single shot rang out, Steve stayed low, cautioning himself not to react. His own skin aside, that bastard had Rebecca in there. Steve had to stay alive. He had to get help.

'Vermin, the lot of 'em,' Sullivan growled, his footsteps sucking into the mud as he moved away, back towards the house.

Overwhelming relief flooded through him; Steve stayed prone, praying hard. He let two minutes pass after he heard the front door open and close, and then eased his head up a fraction. He saw the coast was clear and slithered backwards, away from the lifeless grey limb, washed from the mud as if trying to claw itself free. A woman's hand, Steve had registered, wearing a gold wedding band.

Elbows for leverage, the contents of his stomach threatening to rear up and choke him, Steve shuffled around, swiped rain from his eyes and squinted in the vague direction he'd come. He had to get back to the lane. His car was a fair distance away, but without his phone which had flown from his grasp when he hit the ground, that was the only way he'd get help. And Rebecca needed it. Now.

He silently cursed Matthew for not confiding in him, leaving him to put two and two together. Wasn't hard, admittedly, once he'd realised Rebecca was on the missing list and who the apartment in Mayfair belonged to.

His heart breaking for the man, Steve took his chance. Glancing over his shoulder, he eased himself to his knees, checked again, and then pulled himself to standing. Keeping low, stumbling here and there over the deep tyre tracks left by digging equipment, he eventually straightened up and ran.

He'd almost reached the lane when he felt the impact, like a sledge-hammer slamming into his chest. The use of his legs gone in an instant, he seemed to fall in slow motion this time. His first sensation was an odd tingling, surging throughout his entire body. Seconds later, his left lung began to squeeze, making his breaths short and agonizingly painful. The warm sensation, he supposed, as his vision began to fade, was his blood flowing from the wound in his torso. His last thought, as he instinctively sought to protect his head from the assailant looming over him, was that if he didn't turn up for his wedding, his fiancée would probably kill him.

He didn't move as Patrick gave him another nudge with his foot. No reaction at all. *My, my,* Patrick thought, *we are an obedient little lapdog, aren't we? Jumping at your master's command, ready to die to protect him.* Had to admire that in a way, Patrick supposed. He only wished any of the cretins that worked for him were half as dedicated.

So, now what did he do with him? It occurred to Patrick, gazing around for signs of anyone in the vicinity, that whatever it was, he'd better do it quick. He was banking on anyone who might have heard the shots assuming it was a farmer going about his business. He'd heard shots himself, famers culling this or killing that, he'd guessed, so that wasn't a problem. A dead body out in the open, however, just might be. There was no way he could leave him here, ready for some nosy-parker early morning walker to fall over. The filth would be crawling all over the show in no time.

He'd have to move him, he supposed. Him and his sodding car, inconsiderate bastard, he might have parked it closer. Supressing his irritation in favour of getting the job done, Patrick propped his gun on his shoulder and squatted to go through the copper's pockets for his car keys.

*Well now, what have we here?* A smile crept across Patrick's face as he extracted an evidence bag containing certain personal items: his. Every cloud has a silver lining, he thought, holding the bag high.

'Job well done, DS Ingram. Take a promotion,' he said. Patrick's smile faded, though, as he noticed the blood staining his pristine white shirt.

# CHAPTER EIGHTEEN

He was taking a chance, breaking in. The likelihood of finding anything that might lead him to Becky here was slim, but Matthew had hoped to find something. What he'd found, up until now, was nothing. The house was pristine. Knowing Sullivan's meticulousness, the madman got irked if even fresh air dared settle on his clothes, the cleaner was no doubt made to earn her money. Removing bloodstains from grouting, though, obviously wasn't part of her job description. Whoever had attempted to scrub these stains out clearly hadn't had the right tools.

Crouching by the side of the pool, Matthew examined the stains more closely, and then, noticing several strands of hair, felt himself reeling. Nausea grinding inside him, he immediately registered the colour, blonde, not Becky's. *Thank God.* Relief flooding through him, Matthew carefully bagged the evidence and held it up to the light. Sullivan's wife's, he wondered? If not hers, then who's? And where was his wife? His daughter? A cold-blooded sadistic bastard the man might be, but Sullivan doted on his daughter. Matthew doubted any harm had come to her. Chelsea, however ... In Sullivan's eyes she'd be just a woman, ergo an object to be used for his pleasure and then disposed of when he felt inclined to move onto the next.

Matthew should call it in. Taking her obvious absence into account, the definite signs of injury to someone, evidently a female, he really had no choice, but how could he? Glancing out across the pool as he got to his feet, Matthew tried to think, and then almost had heart failure as his mobile echoed shrilly around the annexe.

*Dammit.* Matthew scrambled the phone from his pocket.

'Adams?' he answered curiously, having noted the caller was DCI Davies.

'Brace yourself, DI Adams,' Davies said stiffly, 'I have some bad news.'

Mathew heard the words, but what Davies was saying refused to register straightaway. When it did, Matthew's heart lurched violently.

'When and where?' He squeezed the words out, his stomach clenching, as Davies gave him the details. 'I'm on my way,' he said, cutting the call.

*How?* It made no sense. *Steve? What the hell were you doing?* Matthew tried to get his head around it as he yanked open his car door and threw himself inside. What in God's name had possessed him to wander through woodland in the dead of night? He'd been found by the river. Lying there for hours, apparently, losing Christ knew how many litres of blood?

Matthew tightened his grip on the wheel. Shaking his head, physically trying to oust the image of Lily, her lifeblood seeping into the road, of Becky screaming in terror, he groped frantically in his pockets for his inhaler. Taking two sharp puffs, his lights and sirens going and volubly cursing any other road user who got in his way, Matthew headed erratically to the hospital.

This was Sullivan. It had to be. Matthew rammed his foot down hard. The man was losing it, becoming more and more unpredictable, yet predictable: detached from reality, cold and calculatingly violent, caring nothing for his victims. *Bastard!* Rage, compounded by guilt, wedged itself like a stone in Matthew's chest. He could have stopped him, stopped this happening. If only he'd called it in when he'd taken Becky, called his bluff, he might have... signed his wife's death warrant. His other victims aside, if Sullivan had done this, if the blood on the grouting meant what Matthew suspected it did, then he would have no hesitation inflicting the same sort of punishment, as the twisted psycho saw it, on Rebecca. Punishment that was meant for him, Matthew had no doubt about that.

He'd given him no evidence, no sign at all that she was still alive. Nothing.

Matthew dragged a hand over his face, and then hit the brakes as his phone rang, causing a cacophony of car horns to blast around him. Careering the car to the side of the road, he stared at his handsfree. Another new number, unregistered obviously. Trepidation snaking its way down his spine, Matthew picked up the call.

'Mia,' Sullivan immediately supplied the baby's name Matthew had asked for. 'Make sure you have the funds ready to transfer. I'll call back. Oh, and, Adams, I'm guessing you know I mean business now, yes?'

****

It had never really bothered Matthew that much before: the antiseptic smell of the hospital wards, the sterile surroundings. Interviewing victims of crime, he coped with, generally; his jaw tightened as his mind leapt to Natalie, to Brianna. It was bothering him now, though. Approaching the resuscitation room doors, Matthew stopped, as DCI Davies stepped through them into the corridor, his expression grim.

'Any ideas what he was up to?' he asked, nodding behind him.

Feeling sick to his soul, Matthew glanced down. 'I think I might have an idea, yes,' he admitted. The force would be all over it once he told the whole story. Matthew knew they needed to be for the sake of their colleague, and for the sake of their sanity. He had nothing to go on, other than instinct, but that instinct was screaming at him that Steve had been doing what any good copper would do, covering a fellow-officer's back.

DCI Davies arched an eyebrow. 'I think you'd better share.'

He looked him over warily, and then scowled as his phone commanded his attention. 'Davies?' he snapped into it. 'Right. Right.'

Ending the call, he looked gravely back at Matthew. 'I need to get back to the station, try to calm a few tempers. They're baying for blood on this one. My office, DI Adams, pronto,' he instructed and headed past him towards the exit.

Wrestling with his emotions, Matthew braced himself and went on through the swing doors. Eyeing the doctor in attendance questioningly, he nodded towards Steve, who was immobilised and hooked up to every conceivable monitor available.

The doctor nodded back, offering him a smile of commiseration.

'How is he?' Matthew asked, gulping back a hard lump in his throat as he noted his sergeant's pallid complexion, the livid bruising to his forehead and heavy dressing on his chest.

Her expression concerned, the doctor walked across to him.

'Not good,' she said. 'His ribs are broken. The pleural lining of the left lung is damaged. We've relieved the pneumothorax with a cannula.' She indicated the chest drain. 'The good news is the debris missed his major blood vessels by a centimeter. The bad news is the thoracic spine may have been damaged.'

'*Fuck.*' Matthew felt his heart shift in his chest.

'We'll know more once a detailed examination has been carried out.'

'Which involves?'

'Well, he's drifting in and out of consciousness. Once he's fully conscious we'll be able to do an initial neurological evaluation, including testing reflexes, muscle function, sensitivity to touch ...'

Trying to take it in, Matthew nodded. 'The spinal cord?' he asked, his voice catching in his throat.

'Possibly compromised. We're not sure at this juncture.'

'Right.' Matthew tugged in a breath and focussed his gaze on the overhead lighting.

'Once we've assessed spontaneous motion of the extremities, we'll have a clearer picture,' she offered sympathetically, then turned away to give Matthew some space.

Matthew had only ever cried once in public, when he'd knelt by his daughter's side and a part of him had died with her. He felt like crying now, though. The man was about to get married. *Christ, where was the justice?* Bowing his head, Matthew pressed his thumb and forefinger hard against his eyes, then looked up sharply, as Steve groaned.

'Doctor!' Panic-struck Matthew stepped towards him, catching hold of Steve's arm as he attempted to pull the mask from his face. '*Shit.* Steve, don't ...'

Steve was trying to say something, mouthing something. 'Home,' he finally rasped.

'You can go home soon, Mr. Ingram.' The doctor glanced worriedly at Matthew, as she struggled to reattach the mask to his face.

Steve, though, continued to fight her. 'Becky,' he croaked, her name barely a whisper as his eyes fluttered closed.

\*\*\*\*

'Start talking, DI Adams,' DCI Davies demanded, on his feet immediately when Matthew came into his office. 'What the *hell* was your detective sergeant doing wandering around muddy riverbanks in the middle of the night?'

'I'm not a hundred percent certain.' Matthew ran a hand over his neck, feeling jaded to his very bones.

'Well, get certain!' DCI Davies eyed him furiously, as he stormed past him to close his office door. 'Did you know he'd withdrawn evidence from forensics?'

Matthew nodded. 'Yes.' He sighed heavily.

'Well?' Walking back, DCI Davies urged him on. 'Evidence appertaining to what, Matthew? What in God's name is this all about?'

Apprehensively, Matthew searched the man's face. Would he believe him, or would he go off on some high-profile attempt to corroborate his story, alerting Sullivan and driving him to do God only knew what? Whatever his reaction Matthew knew he had no choice. A police officer had been shot, and that was down to him. Steeling himself, he took another breath, then, 'Sullivan,' he said, his heart constricting as he realised that now he'd started there could be no turning back, possibly no hope of getting Becky back.

'Sullivan?' DCI Davies eyeballed him incredulously. 'I don't bloody believe this. You mean to say you roped Steve into …' He stopped, his gaze moving past Matthew, as his office door flew open.

'Oh, for Pete's sake, what?' he snapped, as DS Collins hovered uncertainly.

'Good news.' DS Collins glance was non-too-friendly as it fell on Matthew. 'We've found Steve's car, partial finger-print too, not Steve's.'

'Well, don't just stand there! Get on it, for pity's sake!' Davies barked.

'We are. Right now, sir. There's something else though.' DS Collins paused indecisively.

'Well?' Davies asked tersely.

'I, er, have the information on my desk, sir.' DS Collins glanced guardedly at Matthew again and then nodded towards the outer office.

'Right,' DCI Davies got the gist, as did Matthew. His presence clearly wasn't required. 'Show me,' Davies said. 'And you,' he turned back to Matthew, wearing his *don't-test-me* expression, 'wait right there.'

Sighing agitatedly, Matthew did as ordered. He should be in on this, for Steve's sake. Tugging his shirt collar loose, he checked his watch, agonisingly aware of the passing of time. Sullivan had supplied the information Matthew had needed, information that could only have come from Becky. But when had she given him that information? Matthew still couldn't be sure she was unharmed. Ergo, he wasn't about to stand around here, doing nothing.

Determinedly, Matthew walked to the door. He needed to be out there, ready to make the transaction, to do whatever Sullivan instructed him to. While there was even the slightest chance she might still be … Matthew's thoughts trailed off, as yet another flashback of Lily, lying still and cold on the mortuary slab, flashed through his mind. He clamped his eyes closed, yet the graphic images still assailed him. He couldn't do this, couldn't cope.

Couldn't breathe.

Scrambling through his pockets for his inhaler, Matthew turned back to the desk. Dropping heavily onto the edge of it, he inhaled sharply, air rattling into his lungs, as he did. He could actually hear it. *Christ,* he was so *fucking* useless.

Burying his head in his hands, Matthew tried to compose himself, to stay in control. *Control?* He laughed scornfully. Who did he think he was kidding? Sullivan was holding the cards here, all of them. He knew it. Knew that Matthew knew it. He'd done everything

Sullivan had asked him, and more. He'd been a coward, dancing to the madman's tune instead of taking him out in the only way he realistically could have before now. He'd screwed up, big time, risked Becky's life, risked Steve's.

Guilt and anger clawing at his insides, Matthew continued to wait, his breathing steadying, mercifully, as his DCI swung back into the office, DS Collins close behind him.

Matthew got to his feet immediately.

'I need to go,' he started, and then stopped as Davies held up a quieting hand, his expression grim.

'Michael Sullivan,' he said, as Matthew glanced questioningly between him and Collins, 'his body's been found on the river bank.'

Sullivan's father? Trying to assimilate, Matthew stared at him askance, then, 'Dead?' he asked, disbelieving.

'As the proverbial dodo,' DCI Davies replied dourly.

Goosebumps ran the length of Matthew's spine. 'How?'

'Natural causes, it appears, if you can call choking on your liver natural causes; with one small incongruity.'

'Which is?' Panic knotted Matthew's stomach as his mind processed the information. Two people found by the river, one dead, one close to? Clearly, they were linked. Clearly also, that link was Sullivan.

'No mud on his shoes,' DCI Davies supplied.

Which meant the body had been moved? Matthew's blood ran cold at the implications of what that might mean. Michael Sullivan had been chauffer driven wherever he went. He probably was this time, by his loving son, whose adulation of his father was nil. Patrick Sullivan had been walking a fine line between outward normality and complete insanity all his life. Matthew had seen it first hand, for years. Something had tipped him over the edge. He'd come down on the side of the latter, possibly precipitated by the demise of his father and, God help her, the animal had Becky in his filthy clutches.

'This case you had Steve working on,' Davies asked, as Matthew's thoughts raced through all sorts of scenarios, 'could this be why Patrick Sullivan decided on some sort of retribution? I assume it was something to do with your attack on the man and the subsequent accusations you—'

'He has my wife,' Matthew cut in quietly.

Davies stared at him, uncomprehending for a second, then. 'Becky?' he asked, now looking as if he'd been struck by a thunderbolt.

'He's ... taken her.' Matthew was struggling to hold it together, to contain his fury as he recalled Sullivan's gilded threats. Threats which Matthew had reported, only to be told he was being paranoid.

145

'You're joking,' DS Collins gasped incredulously to his side.

Feeling very close to losing it now, Matthew swept furious eyes over her. 'Do I look like I'm joking?' he snapped, and then turned back to Davies. 'He ... has ... my ... *wife!*

Galvanised into action DCI Davies took a step towards him, placing a hand on Matthew's shoulder. 'Okay, calm down, Matthew. Just try to remain rational. What does he want?' He nodded towards DS Collins as he spoke, indicating she should go through to the main office.

To get the ball rolling and mobilise all available bodies, Matthew assumed. A ball that could career out of control and lose him the woman he loved more than his life. No way. *No* way! 'Calm down?' he repeated, his anger mounting dangerously inside him. 'Remain rational!?' He pushed the man's hand away from him. 'The fucking maniac has Becky! He's a murdering psychopath and you tell me to *keep calm?*'

DCI Davies exchanged wary glances with DS Collins, as once again she hesitated uncertainly. 'I presume he's offered some trade-off?' he asked, clearly determined to remain rational where Matthew couldn't hope to be.

'Yes, he's offered a *trade-off*,' he spat satirically. 'He wanted evidence pulled. Steve pulled it. Because *I* ordered him to, by the way, no questions asked. He wanted Steve off a case he was working on, a case that has links with the murder of Brianna Phillips, ergo gives us a serial killer. Guess who the prime suspect is? He wants money. Of course he wants money, every penny I have and he'll get it, but do you *honestly* think he's going to let Becky go?'

'Right.' Nodding slowly DCI Davies walked around to his desk. 'He's called you with his demands then, obviously?'

'Yes. Unregistered phones, *obviously*,' Matthew stated flatly, as if he needed to.

Sitting down, DCI Davies nodded again, clasping his hands tightly in front of him.

'We can still pinpoint the phone using call triangulation,' DS Collins suggested, her expression now sympathetic as she looked at Matthew. 'If you keep him—'

'No.' Matthew cut in categorically.

DS Collins stopped, glancing concerned from Matthew to Davies.

'If he gets even a sniff of uniforms crawling all over this he *will* kill her,' Matthew stated, as if he needed to do that either, given what they now knew. What he'd *always* known. Assuming he hadn't already killed her that was. Matthew gulped back a sick taste in his throat.

DCI Davies took in a deep breath. 'Matthew,' he started carefully, 'I know how you feel, but—'

'You have no fucking idea how I feel! None!'

'No,' Davies conceded, his look a mixture of contrition and concern. 'No I don't, but ...' he glanced again at DS Collins '... you can't do this on your own, Matthew. I can't let you. We have to—'

'He killed my daughter!' Matthew took a step towards him, slammed his hands hard on the desk. 'He killed her, John. I know it. *You* know it.' He locked eyes with the man, his meaning, he hoped, implicit, and then turned for the door. 'I have to go.'

Pulling the door open, he walked out without looking back. The silence in the outer office was palpable this time, heavy, guilt-ridden. Matthew walked on, guilt weighing heavy in his own chest. Every single one of the officers here would go out on a limb to help him. Matthew also knew that. As Steve had, and got shot down like a dog for it. As Davies would, if only following protocol didn't get in the way of bringing animals like Sullivan to justice.

Matthew was on his own on this, though. Had to be. There was no other way.

Swinging into the corridor, he reached for his ringing phone, assuming it was Sullivan with account details to facilitate the transfer of the funds. And once he had what he wanted? Had Matthew really thought there was any chance he'd release Becky unharmed? Release her at all? He'd shot Steve, at close range. Killed his own *father*. Matthew had no doubt Sullivan had had a hand in that. No, he wasn't going to let Becky go. Money wasn't what he was after. Retrieving evidence that wouldn't stand wasn't his aim. Sullivan's motive in all of this, the motive of a madman derailed, was to prove he was the better man, the bigger man. Whatever had driven Sullivan as a kid to viciously attack his victims careless of the consequences was driving him now. Matthew *should have* stopped him.

Melanie's voice in his ear surprised him. He struggled to understand what she was saying initially, something about Ashley, but she was talking fast, the baby was crying in the background; and then the penny dropped, driving another knife into Matthew's heart. 'Gone?' he repeated, disbelieving. 'Gone where? When?'

'I don't know,' Melanie sounded distraught. 'We were getting along fine. At least I thought we were. I had to take Lucas for his check-up this morning. Ashley was still in bed when I left, or I thought she was. When I got back I found a note. Her bed didn't look as if it had been slept in. I have no idea what time she left. Oh God, Matthew, I'm so sorry. I didn't know what to do. I was going to ring Becky, but then Ashley had said she was at her mum's. I didn't want to worry Becky, or you, but—'

'Whoa, slow down.' Matthew tried to get his own chaotic thoughts in some sort of order. 'What did it say, the note?'

'Well, that's just it. It doesn't make any sense. Hold on, I'll fetch it.' Matthew waited again, every second he did seemed like sand slipping through a timer on Becky's life. *Come on, Melanie,* he willed her, hearing her shushing the baby as she moved around in the background.

'It's addressed to you,' she said, finally coming back on. 'She says something about none of it would have happened if she hadn't been there and … Hang on, I'll read it.' Melanie paused, while Matthew supressed a sigh of frustration.

'Here we go: *If I hadn't been there none of this would have happened. You were right. I've decided to go back.*' Melanie went on, reading from the note. '*I have some stuff to do first though, so please don't worry.* Don't worry? Honestly, you'd think she'd realise you'd be worried to death. Poor Becky will be out of her mind. Is Becky all right, Matthew? Only I was really concerned when Ashley told me—'

'I'll ring the care home,' Matthew said quickly. 'Thanks, Melanie. I'll get back in touch as soon as I can.'

Avoiding the inevitable questions out of necessity, Matthew ended the call and immediately redialled. No Ashley at the care home, he learned. No sign of. *Dammit!* He dragged his collar loose, sucked air deep into his lungs, then cursed out loud and raced for his car.

# CHAPTER NINETEEN

Ashley wriggled through the downstairs loo window she'd prised open, manoeuvred herself down to the cistern and waited, and listened. It was as quiet as a grave. Shuddering, as though someone had tiptoed lightly over hers, she dropped to the floor, squeaked open the loo door, and then shot across the lounge area, one eye on the wide patio windows, as she went. She didn't like those windows. She hadn't slept a wink the night the bird had splattered itself against them. If it was a bird. Becky had said it was, but Ashley hadn't been convinced, imagining it was zombies or something. She'd had nightmares about them ever since some of the kids at the care home had downloaded a zombie film, thinking they were being really cool. They weren't cool. Nothing there was cool. Ashley wasn't going back. Uh-uh, no way. She'd only told Matthew she was in hopes he wouldn't get an attack of the guilts. She wasn't sure where she was going, but definitely not back there. She'd just keep going, she supposed. She could steal enough to eat, she was good at that. She'd had to be, with no food in the cupboards and her mum passed out half the time.

She wasn't going anywhere without her locket though, she'd decided. Heading for the stairs, she tried to ignore Emily chuntering on in her head, something about hiding under the bed, like *that* was a really intelligent idea. Ashley wasn't going to sell the locket. Even if she needed the money, she'd made up her mind she wasn't going to do that. She was going to keep it, her one keepsake of the only nice time she'd ever had in her life. She was going to take a photo, too. The one on Becky's dressing table, of Matthew and Becky at their wedding. It was a nice photo. They were kissing, their lips lightly touching. Matthew's mouth curved up at the corners in a smile. It suited him. He looked much more handsome and happy when he smiled, which he hadn't done much of since Becky had gone, not surprisingly.

Ashley had heard him crying. She'd pretended she hadn't, and Matthew hadn't let on, but he had been. That time his policeman-friend Steve had called. Ashley recalled how Matthew had lied to him about where Becky was. He'd lied badly. Ashley had reckoned even his mate hadn't really believed him. Matthew had looked choked when Steve had left. Really choked. Ashley hadn't known what to do. She'd wanted to put her arms around him. Make things right for him, but she couldn't, of course.

She'd watched him worriedly instead, wondered whether she should make tea or something, as if that could help. Matthew had looked desperate, like a caged animal, walking relentlessly round and around, back and forth, checking his mobile. He was breathing really heavily, Ashley remembered, when he'd gone upstairs. To shower he'd said, making sure to tell her to keep the front door locked. He had run the shower. Ashley had crept up and listened, and that was when she'd heard him catch a sob in his throat, and another, because his heart was breaking, Ashley knew. Matthew loved Becky. That much was obvious. They were right for each other. That was pretty obvious too. Ashley was pissed, yes, that suddenly what she'd hoped might be, that she might finally have a proper family, wouldn't be, but she didn't want Becky not to come home.

Pausing on the landing, Ashley felt like crying too, something she'd rarely done. She'd made up her mind there wasn't any point a long time ago, knowing there was no one around who cared. Becky would have cared, she conceded. Ashley felt that funny sinking feeling in her chest again, the same feeling she'd had watching her mum leave for the last time.

She'd take the photo. Running her sleeve under her nose, Ashley nodded determinedly. And the locket. She'd grab some bottled water from the fridge and maybe a few biscuits, but that was all. Deciding an extra couple of jumpers might also be practical, Ashley was stuffing her rucksack when she heard it, a shuffling, snuffling sound down below, right outside the window. *Shit!* Ashley's heart flipped in her chest. It couldn't be Matthew. She made her way cautiously across the bedroom. She would have heard his car.

Visions of grey-faced, flesh-eating zombies or beady-eyed birds splatting against the window, Ashley crept warily towards it and peeked quickly out. Nothing, then, '*Crap*,' she ducked as she heard it again. Her heart beating a steady drumbeat in her chest, Ashley risked another look after a second, and then almost wilted with relief, as her eyes lighted on the little stray dog she'd seen once before. It wasn't much more than a puppy. *Oh, no.* Ashley squinted harder as it foraged around. The poor thing was limping.

'Here boy,' she called him. Then, realising he hadn't heard, she reached for the latch, pushed the window open and called him again. 'Hey, doggy, up here!'

'Duh.' Ashley rolled her eyes, as the dog gazed around, clearly too stupid to look up, then turned to grab up her rucksack, as it turned tail to go in the other direction.

She'd have to come back for the water and stuff, she decided, using the front door to exit faster than she'd entered. She'd have to give the dog some water, too, if she could catch up with the flipping thing. Obviously spooked by someone he couldn't see calling him, he'd moved pretty fast, even with his dodgy paw.

*Uh, oh.* Reaching the spot where the dog had been foraging, Ashley ground to a halt. Blood, she noticed, crouching to examine the rich red droplets, which had fallen on discarded plasterboard debris. Fresh blood, which meant he could be badly injured. *Brilliant.* This was going to hinder her progress a bit. She didn't want Matthew to catch her here. He'd be sure to take her straight to the flipping care home. Ashley chewed on her lip, debating whether to just take off. If she hadn't come here today, she would never have known the dog was hurt, after all. In her heart, though, despite her nothing-can-touch-me image, Ashley knew she couldn't just abandon him. Leave him to starve like she'd been left. She'd have to take him to a police station, she thought, setting off after the dog. *Yeth, brilliant idea,* Emily said in her head. *And what are you going to do when they ask you where you live, hmm?*

Good point. Ashley had to give her little sister that one. She'd tie him up outside a shop then. Someone would surely take him to a vet or a rescue centre.

'Here boy!' she called as she ran, feeling a bit panicky now. *God, where is the dumb animal?* Out of breath, Ashley stopped and took stock. She'd done the length and breadth of the field, flitted in and out of half-renovated properties, swinging barn doors and creaking hinges giving her the serious willies. No dog on site or in sight. Ashley glanced down, hoping against hope, given the sloshy mud, for signs of blood and realised her boots were caked in the stuff.

'Wonderful,' she muttered. Then, hearing her mobile beeping in her rucksack, she reached for it and scrolled warily through her messages.

Matthew. She'd guessed it might be.

*Hell.* So what did she tell him? Where she was, she supposed. He'd only worry otherwise. He'd already got enough to worry about without worrying about her. She'd tell him she was here collecting her stuff and that she was going to see a friend. That's what she'd do. That way, at least he'd know she was okay and she'd buy herself a little time.

Feeling a fat drop of rain plop on her head, Ashley glanced up at the gunmetal grey skies. God, it was desolate around here. And spooky. Not somewhere Ashley would fancy being out on her own when it got dark. *At home*, she quickly started keying her message, and then instinctively ducked, her heart skipping a beat, as a great fat crow cawed raucously above her.

'*Oooh*, bloody thing,' she muttered, scowling upwards, as she straightened up. She was about to resume texting when she found herself flailing forwards, physically winded, as something the weight of a WWE wrestler thudded into her back.

****

'Small puncture, right arm,' Nicky confirmed what Matthew had suspected.

'A syringe, do you reckon?'

'Almost definitely,' Nicky supplied, 'off the record, though, Matthew,' she added, obviously not happy disclosing information over the phone before she'd completed her report.

'The toxicology report?' Matthew asked, though he didn't need it. Michael Sullivan had been a supplier, a boozer, verging on an alcoholic eventually, but not a drug user. Small chance then he'd suddenly be injecting. The information Matthew already had was enough to carve another piece out of his soul. Patrick Sullivan had murdered his own father, at least two women to Matthew's certain knowledge. The man's wife was on the missing list. He had Becky, and Matthew had one aim in mind. Whatever the outcome for him, he was going to kill Sullivan. He'd wondered how he was going to find him, how he would find Becky. He'd thrown up until his stomach was raw, wondering where it would end. But, of course, it wouldn't end, he'd realised, until Sullivan had proven whatever he had to. To do that, he needed Matthew's full attention, ergo, he would need to keep Becky alive. Matthew tried to hold onto that hope. When Sullivan was ready, he would know where he was, Matthew had no doubt about that. He wouldn't have the element of surprise, but what he would most definitely have, something Sullivan had sneeringly pointed out he'd lacked over the years, was the killer instinct. God willing, that might be surprise enough.

'Tox report is being rushed through as we speak,' Nicky assured him. 'You must have friends in the right places.'

Davies, Matthew realised. It might have been better if he'd been there before now though, he couldn't help thinking. 'Cheers, Nicky.' Finishing his call, Matthew turned his attention to his incoming texts: one from Davies, calling him back to the station, where he was presumably supposed to wait calmly while Sullivan tortured his wife. Matthew swallowed hard on that thought. There was another text from Melanie and ... one from Ashley. *Thank God.*

*At home,* Matthew read, and furrowed his brow. He'd rung the care home again, prior to calling Nicky. Ashley certainly wasn't there then.

xxxx

The bitch had bit him! Left actual teeth marks! Examining the delicate flesh between his thumb and forefinger the little slut had almost bitten through, Patrick tightened his other arm around the writhing girl's torso, and then winced as the sharp heel of her boot found its aim, landing him a vicious kick to his shin.

That was it. Now he was pissed. Using his damaged hand to clutch hold of her hair, he yanked her head back, cutting her screams short.

'Keep still and shut the fuck up!' he growled furiously in her ear. 'Better,' he said, as she relaxed some in his grasp. 'Now, unless you want to end up decomposing flesh for the crows to pick over, you do exactly as I say, when I say, *comprendre?*'

She nodded, a slow gulp sliding down her exposed throat. Patrick felt a stirring of excitement, curiously heightened by the fact that the silly bint had practically disabled him.

'The phone,' he demanded.

Loosening her ineffectual grip on the arm he had wrapped around her, she fished her mobile from where she'd stuffed it down the front of her leggings, like Patrick wouldn't have found it. Clearly she wasn't the brain of Britain, this one.

'Take the card out,' he instructed. Allowing her enough movement of her head to see what she was doing, Patrick waited. Patiently, given they were out in the middle of a freaking field in the freezing cold.

Considerably patiently. He sighed and rolled his eyes, as she fiddled with the phone, finally managing to prise the SIM card free with a nail. She didn't chew on them then, Patrick noticed approvingly. He couldn't abide birds who gnawed on their fingernails, fidgeting and scratching while they did and usually needing their next fix. Doing it for effect half the time, thinking Patrick was a soft-touch and was going to provide it. Manipulators, the lot of them, he thought contemptuously.

'Throw it,' he said, as she held the card up, like he wanted to bloody well inspect it. 'Then chuck the phone on the ground.'

'Do it!' he barked when she hesitated.

Jumping as if he'd poked her with a cattle-prod, she lobbed it. Not far, but far enough.

'The phone,' Patrick repeated tersely. Forced to expose his cashmere coat to the lashing rain, his patience was now wearing very thin.

Reluctantly, she dropped the phone.

Obviously, she was intelligent enough to realise it might be her best option then.

'Obey instructions first time next time,' he warned her. Then, weaving her hair tighter around his hand, he whirled around to face the phone.

'Stamp on it,' he said, giving her a shove forwards.

Again, she hesitated.

'*That* was an instruction,' Patrick growled.

'*Fuck,*' she muttered, not very ladylike, Patrick thought, then lifted her boot and trod on it.

'Harder.' Patrick gave her another shove.

She pulled in a breath—Patrick felt the brace through her shoulders, and then smashed her heel down hard on it, and then again. And again, grunting with the effort of it, as if she was taking her own frustration out on it. Feisty little thing, Patrick thought. *Interesting.*

'That'll do. I think you've killed it,' he said, whirling her around again to go back in the direction he'd come from.

'Walk,' he said shortly.

Reaching up behind her, she attempted to loosen his grip on her hair.

'Where're you taking me?'

Patrick gave it another twist, for no particular reason, other than he didn't like being questioned.

'Don't speak unless you're spoken to,' he told her, 'and only when I've given you permission. Keep moving.'

She was dragging her feet, deliberately trying his patience now. If she wasn't careful, he'd drag her by her lovely silken hair through the mud and cow shit and be done with.

\*\*\*\*

Matthew tried Ashley's phone for a third time and got number unobtainable again. *Dammit.* He really didn't need this. What had she been thinking, taking off from Melanie's, pretending she was going back to the care home, when she would know he'd check up on her? Frustrated, he pulled over to the side of the road and tried a text. Seconds later, receiving a 'message not delivered' alert, Matthew closed his eyes, his heart plummeting further, if that were possible. What the bloody hell had happened? Had she had some kind of accident, which might explain why her phone had gone dead? But then, if she had arrived back at the home, surely someone would know something, have seen something? It just didn't add up. Dragging his hands through his hair, Matthew realised he absolutely had to call it in. There was no way he could risk leaving Ashley out there, wandering about on her own.

Matthew half-dialled the station, then stopped, his thoughts jolting back to what Steve had been trying to say at the hospital. What Steve *had* said: 'Home.' He'd been desperate to try to communicate something to him. He'd also said ... *Oh, Christ* ... Matthew dropped his phone on the dash and pulled out fast. *Becky.*

# CHAPTER TWENTY

'Inside.' The girl's hair still twisted tightly around one hand Patrick unlocked the door with his other, heaved it open and shoved the girl inside. *Ouch,* he thought, as she lurched forwards and then fell heavily, grunting as she made contact with the ground. Served her right. Patrick had no particular axe to grind with her. He doubted Adams had formed any kind of deep emotional relationship with her in the time she'd been with him. Probably just fancied shagging her. She wasn't bad looking.

Leaving the girl to spit straw and dust from her mouth, Patrick turned to lock the door. She really ought to learn some manners though, he mused, turning back. Effing and blinding all over the show and seemingly incapable of obeying a simple instruction, she was well out of hand. She should also realise that snooping around, poking her nose in where it wasn't invited, could land her in serious trouble. No, Patrick had no particular use for her, other than maybe to remind the copper that he really shouldn't allow minors in his charge to wander around on their own. Pretty, slim minors. He looked her leisurely over, as she rolled onto her back to scowl up at him, taking in her small, firm breasts, her long, sleek hair, the colour of rich ebony, and her eyes, like a frightened little fawn's. *Very interesting.* He might just find a use for her after all.

'It's you!' The girl's scowl deepened, as she scraped her hair from her face, the fear in her eyes giving way to fury as she recognised him.

Patrick smiled, mildly amused. She looked as if she wanted to tear his eyes out. He'd like to see her try. He'd snap her wrists like two brittle twigs.

'You don't say,' he drawled, glancing down at himself and then back to her livid little face.

'What do you want?' She shuffled backwards, as he took a step towards her. 'Where's Becky?'

'For me to know and you to find out.' Patrick smiled. Stroppy little thing, wasn't she? A feisty little fawn, bound to put up a fight. He quite liked a challenge. He also knew one or two other people who might be interested in knocking the fight out of her: Hayes, for one, who would view her as profitable merchandise. She wouldn't clear Patrick's debt, but she'd fetch a few quid towards it. Along with the money Adams owed him, that should go some way to squaring things. Maybe he'd revise his plan to get rid of her a.s.a.p., keep her around awhile instead. Warming to the idea of amusing himself with her, Patrick considered his options, and then felt his anger rising afresh when he remembered he didn't actually have that many options now he'd shot the copper's little lapdog sidekick. Knowing now how serious he was, he doubted Adams had offered up any information to help with the formal investigation of the shooting, but not all coppers were as spineless as Adams. Patrick had covered his tracks the best he could, but the law would be all over this like rats down a sewer anyway. No, he didn't have time for negotiations with Hayes. Patrick needed to finish up here and set sail for safe harbour pronto.

'Stand up,' he instructed the girl, who was now staring at him like something she'd stepped in, infuriating Patrick further.

'Fuck off!' She snatched her arm away, as Patrick reached for it.

Patrick eyeballed her, enraged, for a second, then, 'You really are trying my patience,' he seethed, clutching a fistful of her hair again instead.

She wriggled and squirmed, reached up to stop it parting company with her scalp, but she didn't cry out. Brave, as well as feisty, Patrick deduced, as he heaved her to her feet. Good. She'd need to be.

'Now,' he twisted her around to face him, 'you do as I say, when I say.' Forcing her head back, he fixed his gaze hard on hers.

'Do *not* let me have to repeat myself again.'

The flash of fear was back. Better, Patrick thought, mollified ... but not for long. 'I sent the text,' she said brazenly. 'Matthew will find us.'

My, my, this one certainly had got some bottle, unlike her imagined hero, Patrick thought bemusedly. 'Right, and you really think it's *you* he's going to come riding to the rescue of, do you?' He laughed derisorily. '*If* he comes, which I seriously doubt he'll have the balls to do, it will be his wife's and sprog's lives he'll be bargaining for, not yours. Do you really think he gives a toss about you?'

The girl's brow creased into an uncertain frown. 'He does care,' she said belligerently.

'Yes, course he does. Yet, here you are ... with me.' Patrick let it hang. 'Tell me, if the oh, so, caring DI Adams really gave a shit, what were you doing wandering around out there on your own, hey, with a gunman on the loose?'

A flicker of doubt clouded the girl's eyes.

'Let me guess,' Patrick studied her, 'he tried to get shot of you, didn't he?'

Tried to ship her back off to the care home, he guessed. Probably thinking of her safety, like a good little copper, but Patrick reckoned he might just be able to use the fact to his advantage. Yanking her head back further still, he examined her smooth, unblemished face. Luckily for her, he was disinclined to mark it, unless she forced him to. His gaze strayed to her naked lips. Tempting, he thought. Extremely. But no, he debated, not yet. He wanted to take his time, toy with her awhile. He wanted Adams here, straining at the leash, realising it was payback time for all the grief he'd caused him and that he could do fuck all about it.

'That was a question,' he growled, as the girl blinked reproachfully up at him. 'It requires an answer.'

'Yes,' her windpipe somewhat restricted by the angle of her neck, she squeezed out a reply.

'Thought as much.' Patrick smirked. 'Which means you're on your own, darling, so you'd better be a good little girl and do as I say, hadn't you?'

Relaxing his hold on her hair, he steered her around to face away from him. She was too close, too distracting. He needed to think.

'Over there. Sit down.' He nodded her towards the box under the cross-beams, which was placed just so, ready for when Adams did come charging in, which actually Patrick was thinking he would, given the enticement.

She glanced at the box when he released her, then to the door, all that fiery feistiness fading in her pretty fawn's eyes, he noted, with a mixture of regret and satisfaction. She looked at him then: a look so beseeching Patrick was taken aback, largely by the recognition of that same look he'd seen in his daughter's eyes. Lately, it was when she wanted something, a horse, a new gadget or phone. He always gave in. How could he not? The first time he'd seen it, though, and it had gutted him, was when Taylor had wondered why her bitch of a mother had abandoned her. She hadn't in actuality, but in abandoning Patrick for some pretty boy—bodybuilder sort—whom she'd imagined was sensitive, the woman had effectively sealed her own fate. The bloke was probably gay anyway. Patrick doubted he'd have kept her happy for long.

'Can I ask you something?' the girl said, as Patrick looked at her— unseeing for a second as his mind drifted.

Patrick nodded, as his vocal chords felt temporarily compromised.

'Becky, is she ...' she hesitated, glanced down and back, '... is she all right?'

'She's alive.' Patrick decided it wouldn't hurt to tell her that much.

She nodded in turn, apparently placated, and obviously working it. Patrick had clocked the demureness. No female went from wanting to scratch your eyes out to demure, unless they were working their charms. She was bound to be considering her options, he supposed, now he'd given her cause to wonder about the happy little family scenario they'd tried to sell her. 'And if you want her to stay that way ...' He indicated the box again.

※※※

Matthew left his car in the lane and walked, surveying the farmland around his own property, bleak and desolate under unforgiving grey skies, as he went. His assumption was that Sullivan wouldn't be reckless enough to be in the immediate vicinity of the barn conversions, but he was close, Matthew knew it. In an isolated building, he guessed. A farm outbuilding? He had no idea, no choice but to wait for the call. It would come. Of that much he was certain. Negotiating the perimeter of the field, he noted at least three barns. Two some way off, across adjoining fields, one closer, dilapidated and with good views of the surrounding area. Matthew was aware he was visible. He could probably be seen from some distance away. If it was Sullivan's aim to take him out now, he'd have a clear target.

But that, Matthew was aware, wasn't Sullivan's intention. His preference had always been to torture his victims slowly, make them beg, watch them suffer. Swallowing back his fury, Matthew made his way back across the field and headed towards his house. She was here, somewhere. He could feel it.

Why he'd chosen here, Matthew couldn't fathom. Possibly because it was the last place he'd think of, but more likely because he was desperate, making him more dangerous. Sullivan would know Matthew would make investigations, question people he had business dealings with, staff and clientele at *Seventh Heaven*, check out his local haunts. He'd banked on Matthew not calling it in, but secluded himself out here just in case, probably getting a kick out of Matthew finally realising. Had he called it in, Sullivan would also know coppers going door-to-door would question the usual suspects. The last place they'd look was right here, under Matthew's nose. But *where?*

Dragging his collar loose, he looked to the horseshoe arrangement of properties around his own, most half renovated, some barely started. Their house, his and Becky's house, had been the only one near completion. They'd debated whether to sink funds into

159

it, paying the workmen money in hand to get the place finished, wondered if there would come a day they might rue their decision. It was supposed to have been their dream house, their family home. They'd just finished decorating the nursery when ...

Pausing at the front door, Matthew gulped back the tightness in his throat and prayed silently, hopelessly. He had no idea what his next move was. What Sullivan's might be. He would use Becky. That much he did know. A pawn in his perverted game, he would use her to hurt him, hurt her to hurt him. How could any kind of God let that happen, knowing what she'd already suffered, knowing that Matthew would sacrifice his life in an instant to keep her safe? She'd done nothing to deserve any of this. *Nothing.* And Ashley? *She's just a child, for Christ's sake!*

Pushing his key angrily into the lock, Matthew rammed the front door open.

'Ashley?' he called, though he knew she wasn't there. She had been. Matthew didn't need the open toilet window to tell him that. Her text had been cut short. Matthew prayed again. Despite his biting cynicism, he begged that her life wouldn't be cut cruelly short too.

*****

Ashley watched quietly, as the twisted freak prised a wooden plank from the window, making a gap just wide enough to peer through with his binoculars. He was wrong. Matthew did care about her. He'd wanted to take her back to keep her safe, not to get shot of her. She tried to quash the insistent nagging voice in her head.

*But he wouldn't save you, would he?* Emily chuntered on, just like she always did, always there, always haunting her. *If he could only save one of you, it makes sense he would save Becky. She's having his baby.*

Shut up! Ashley mentally tuned out, turning her attention back to the freak.

'Why are you doing this?' she plucked up courage to ask him, as he took up his position at the window.

His back still to her, he shrugged. 'Because ...'

Ashley took the opportunity to survey her surroundings, a chill running down her spine as she noted the twisted rope hanging from the beam above her head. There were two windows, one each side of the front door, both boarded. A canvas bag was stashed against the left-hand side wall, bottled water standing next to it. A door behind her, she noticed, shut and bolted. Was Becky in there?

'Is it because Matthew punched you?' She turned back to him, noting the shotgun now leaning against the wall next to him. He'd checked it, before he'd turned his attention to the window. When he'd finished checking it, he'd aimed it at her.

'Pop,' he'd said, a sadistic smirk on his face. He was mad, madder than she could ever be, even with Emma whispering away in her head. He was going to shoot Matthew, Ashley felt sure. The thought filled her with panic. The thought that Matthew might be forced to make a choice, made her feel sick. She wouldn't throw up though, she wouldn't give that maniac the satisfaction, unless she was close enough to throw up over the fancy shoes he'd attempted to scrape the mud from, cursing as he did, muttering on about them being designer, and that it was all Adams' fault. He was loco, that's what he was, a complete psycho.

Still looking out of the window, he answered her, finally. 'Let's just say it's payback time, sweetheart, and leave it at that.'

'Is Becky all right?' she ventured again.

Lowering his binoculars, he sighed audibly.

'Did I say you could speak?' He glanced briefly over his shoulder.

Assessing his tone not to be quite so aggressive, Ashley decided to push it a bit further. 'Sorry,' she said, and then coughed, demonstrably, and then coughed again hard.

Ashley watched him as he shot her another glance over his shoulder, clearly irritated, then she pressed her hand to her mouth and emitted another throaty cough.

'For fuck's sake!' He whirled around, glaring at her, his flat grey eyes as hard as flint. 'Have you got a death wish, or what?'

'No!' Ashley spluttered. 'I've got a cough.' Proving which, she coughed heartily again.

'*You*,' he growled, stepping towards her, 'are seriously trying my patience.'

'I'm sorry. I can't help it,' Ashley said, a hand now pressed to her chest.

'Cough one more time and you will be sorry,' he warned her, his eyes now drilling pointedly into hers. 'Very.'

'A drink of water might help,' Ashley croaked, her gaze gliding towards the bottles.

'*Christ Al-bloody-mighty.*' He drew in an affronted breath and snorted it out through his nostrils. 'She'll be asking for room service next.'

Looking her over derisorily, he shook his head, and then grudgingly turned to fetch one of the bottles of water—and Ashley took her chance. Needing no bidding from Emily, who was urging her, *Now, now,* Ashley launched herself from the box, as he bent to pick up the bottle. She seized the gun, curled her fingers around the cold steel barrel of it, picked it up, and felt his loathsome hands on her, clutching at the back of her top, pulling it tight around her neck, his arm sliding around her, pressing hard against her throat.

Ashley's head reeled, her heart thrummed wildly against her chest. She kicked out, ineffectually. His other hand snaked around her, closed around the gun.

'Let it go,' he rasped, so near to her ear, she could feel his breath on her face, smell it, smell him, a cloying musky aftershave masking underlying body odour.

'Let. It. Go,' he repeated, increasing the pressure around her neck, forcing her head upwards, backwards into his shoulder.

'When I snap your spine, you'll hear it, sweetheart; gristle, bone and sinew grinding and then, *crrrrack.*' He gave her head another jerk upwards, lifted her until her toes scraped the floor.

'Not a pleasant way to go. Have you ever seen a bird with its neck wrung?'

Ashley clawed against his restricting hold, one hand, hopelessly trying to pull his arm away. Two hands. She let go. She let go of the gun, but still he wouldn't let go of her.

'Their eyes are vacant,' he said, and paused as if reminiscing. 'Wide open. In surprise, I used to think. My old man kept pigeons. Racing pigeons. I hated the fucking things, cooing and clucking and shitting all over the place. He loved 'em though. Told 'em he loved them. Kissed the bloody things, I swear to God he did. And then, if they didn't fly right ... click, clack, crack, dead pigeon. He made me do it once. Said it would toughen me up. I puked up afterwards, but the old bastard was right. I have no problem now breaking scrawny little birds' *necks.*'

The last was sneered in her ear as he dropped her, and then shoved her away from him.

She landed hard, on all fours, heaving her little guts up and gagging for breath. Served her right. Patrick ran the back of his hand across his face, his fury escalating as he realised there was a gob of spittle at his mouth. He ought to do it, break her back and hear it crack. Trying to pull a fast one on him, lying to him, testing his patience to the limit, who did she think she was? Defiant little cow.

Wiping his mouth again, Patrick left her where she was and fetched the bottle. She wanted water, she could have water. Removing the cap, Patrick poured, watched it trickle and splosh into her pretty, silken hair, and felt his temper cool to a slow simmer. He hadn't finished with her yet, but ... later, he decided. Right now, he had more important things to attend to.

'Get up,' he instructed, turning away, confident that she wouldn't try anything else just then. 'Go over there, sit on your box like a good little girl and don't utter a word. If you do, I'll bite your fucking tongue off, I swear.'

So said, Patrick took out his phone and watched, reasonably satisfied, as the girl stifled a whimper, pulled herself up from the floor, dragged her damp hair from her face, and did as she was told. *That's more like it*, he thought, placing his call. He didn't mind demure, much preferred them that way, as long as it wasn't contrived to manipulate him, as if he was so stupid he couldn't see right through it. Did any of them ever stop to think how hurtful that was? You give them everything they want, treat them with respect, and still they can't offer a bit of honest affection. Yes, he was a hard bastard. He had to be. But it didn't mean he didn't have feelings.

'Ah, Detective Adams,' he said into his phone, smiling at the girl, whose eyes grew wide when she heard mention of her supposed superhero.

'I bet you were wondering where I was. I've been a bit busy. Feisty little thing, isn't she, your niece?' He stopped and listened, quite enjoying the copper's valiant attempt not to react.

****

Closing his eyes, Matthew called on every ounce of his willpower to stay calm, to not feed the animal the ammunition he wanted.

'Do you have the account details?' he asked him, trying to sound neutral, unaffected, desperately struggling for detachment.

Silence on the other end, Matthew waited, his heart-rate ratcheting up as he did.

'All in good time,' Sullivan spoke, eventually. 'I see you managed to work out where we are. Brilliant detective work, Adams. Congratulations. Pity the girl had to suffer for helping you with your enquiries, isn't it? Not very caring, is it, allowing her to wander around, getting herself into dangerous situations? Do you care about her, Adams? Or do you just want to fuck her?'

Matthew clenched his jaw hard.

'She's worth it,' Sullivan went on, having his own perverse brand of fun. 'Put's up a bit of a fight, but then, that always makes it more interesting, don't y'think?'

*Bastard.* Matthew's gut twisted inside him.

'Did you realise you were looking right at me?' Sullivan asked him, and paused. 'That was a question, Detective Inspector.'

Matthew swallowed back his burning fury. 'I guessed I might be,' he answered tightly.

'So let's cut the crap, hey, Matthew? You know where I am. I know where you are. Come on over and we'll make sure the transaction goes through smoothly together. I'll have a nice little reception waiting for you. What d'y'say?'

Matthew dragged in a breath. 'You're a sick animal, Sullivan,' he seethed throatily. 'You need help.'

'Your police chums are not invited, by the way,' Sullivan ignored him. 'It's a private party, so don't make any calls, beforehand, or your little family will be life extinct, *comprendre?*'

'If you've touched either one of them, Sullivan,' Matthew could barely get the words out, 'I swear to God—'

'Bear in mind I have nothing to lose now I've put your little lapdog down, hey, Adams?' Sullivan said over him. 'So don't try anything else clever either, will you? Be here in half an hour. Precisely. Make sure you're on time and visible.'

Matthew's heart plummeted, as he heard Ashley in the background.

'He has a gun!' she shouted. The following shrill scream, cut short as the call ended, pierced Matthew's very soul.

# CHAPTER TWENTY-ONE

'You just had to go and make me do that, didn't you?' Patrick dragged his gun-free hand across his mouth, as the girl recoiled. He was spitting with fury, he really was. What was it with these women? Could none of them follow a basic instruction?

'What did you expect me to do!?' She glared at him, a hand pressed to her flaming cheek and her eyes burning with hatred. 'I wasn't just gonna sit here, was I!? Would you have done?'

No, Patrick thought, his fury dissipating a little as he conceded that fact. She'd want to warn him about the gun, he supposed, though Patrick was buggered if he knew why, considering Adams' motives regarding her were suspect, to say the least. *Oh, great.* Now she was going to cry. Patrick noted the tears brimming in her eyes and felt disconcertingly guilty. He wouldn't normally turn a hair, women only ever cried crocodile tears to tug at men's heartstrings, his father had reminded him of that often, but this one ... Did she have to look quite so much like his daughter?

'You know, you baffle me, you really do.' He cocked his head to one side, looking her over. 'Haven't you stopped to wonder why a thirty-odd year old bloke would be interested in having you around?'

She looked at him, clueless, obviously, for a second, before the penny dropped, then, 'He's not like that.' The scowl was back. 'He cares about me. He said—'

'Sweetheart, all he cares about is getting into your knickers,' Patrick cut her short. 'He likes 'em young. Trust me, I know,' he went on, figuring if he didn't have anything else to gain, her uncertainty might mean she was more compliant.

The furrow in her pretty little brow deepened. 'How do you know?' She scanned his eyes. The look in hers was curious, but alarmed, Patrick detected. *Interesting.*

He studied her carefully, noting the lowered eyes, the coy blush to her cheeks. 'Why? Fancy him, do you?'

'No!' she refuted, way too quickly.

Patrick hid a smile. 'Well, if you were fancying your chances, just so you know, he has far choicer cuts than you to choose from, sweetheart.'

Her look was perturbed now, very.

'He's paid for services rendered with at least three of my girls.'

Patrick casually examined his nails. 'Sex-workers,' he said, when she looked confused, then, 'they sell sex,' he spelled it out. 'They're a bit older than you, but still young enough to be his daughter, dirty sod.'

'You're lying,' she said. She believed him all right though. Patrick could see the little-girl-crushed look in her eyes.

'I say *paid for*,' he continued blithely, 'but, knowing him, he probably abused his police authority, gave them a load of bullshit about protecting their interests. You know what these coppers can be like.'

Got her. Patrick noted disappointment as the girl's gaze fluttered downwards. He was enjoying himself here, trashing the detective's goody-two-shoes reputation. No less than Adams deserved, mind, given his own reputation was totally destroyed, something Adams seemed to get some perverse kick out of doing. Patrick felt a rush of humiliation as he recalled the first time he'd embarrassed him. Years it had taken him to live down being hauled up at school, branded a coward in front of everyone, including that cocky little runt, Adams. He'd denied squealing, of course, pretended his oh, so, important father turning up at the school had nothing to do with him running home telling tales.

Patrick had given him a good kicking that time. It couldn't undo the damage done though. Yes, it would be most gratifying, seeing the copper's face when his little niece called him out on his predilection for younger flesh, preferably in front of his darling wife. Served the bastard right.

Aware of the ticking clock, Patrick considered. Should he leave it there, or drive the seed a little deeper? The latter, he decided. Might as well. Couldn't hurt.

'Look, I have a daughter not much older than you,' he said, trying for sympathetic as he crouched down in front of her.

'I know kids get crushes. It doesn't mean the emotions aren't real, though, that they don't hurt like hell. My daughter was besotted with her science teacher, broke her little heart when he left the school.' Patrick thought it better not to mention why the man had chosen to leave, losing his tackle being his other option.

'I understand, really I do. Your first love is always the most painful, especially when it's unrequited.' Patrick gave himself a mental pat on the back and wondered whether he'd missed his vocation. He ought to have been a bleeding poet.

She didn't answer, just studied her thumbnail. Upset obviously, Patrick deduced.

'I understand more than you think I do,' he pushed on. 'We're a lot alike, you and I.'

She blinked at him then. Patrick felt a bristle of indignation at the stunned look on her face, but valiantly supressed it.

'Both neglected by those who should have loved us, our innocent childhood trust abused. Just because Adams chose to do the same, abuse your trust to fill some empty void in his life and then toss you aside, doesn't mean there's anything wrong with you. It's him that's got the problem. I told the last girl he dumped the same.'

Noting he now had her full-on, fascinated attention, Patrick got to his feet. There was another lady who needed attending to. He hoped she hadn't expired prematurely out there.

'Natalie her name is, beautiful girl. In bits she was, until I put her right. Get good and angry with him, I told her. Seize that anger and use it. She was about to dob him in to the police when she ended up in hospital. Strange that.'

Shaking his head bemusedly, Patrick turned away, and then sharply back, as she promptly burst into tears behind him.

'Oh, for crying out loud, don't start blarting all over the show. You're giving me a headache.' He glanced to his side, the intensity of a naked light bulb definitely dancing in his peripheral vision. Wonderful, now he was getting a migraine, just what he needed. He could hardly shoot the copper's legs from under him, if he couldn't sodding well see him, could he?

'Emily, stop,' she blubbered, as Patrick closed his eyelids, testing to see how bright the flashing white light was, ergo what kind of a whopping headache he might be in for.

Patrick's gaze snapped back to hers. 'What?'

'Nothing.' She dragged a hand quickly under her nose. 'I was just willing myself to stop. You told me to.'

He looked her over narrowly. Was she taking the piss? No, he decided. Her expression was back to hostile though. Probably hated his guts now he'd revealed the detective in his true light. Whatever. As long as she didn't think the sun shone out of Adams' backside, Patrick didn't give a stuff.

Kneading his temples, quietly cursing himself for bringing everything in his bag except the Paracetamol, he glanced down and then almost shot out of his alligator leather loafers.

'What the fuck was that?' he gasped, stepping smartly back as something scurried between his feet, something he most definitely didn't want to come in contact with, not even through the leather on the soles of his shoes.

'What?' She stared at him, and then at it, as it bolted towards her like

a marathon runner. A huge, hairy, eight-legged marathon runner. His mouth running dry, his chest palpitating, Patrick stumbled back another two steps as it suddenly stopped, its disgusting legs hunched, poised to shoot off in God knew what direction.
'It's only a spider.' She looked back at him, incredulous.
The mother of all spiders, fucking ugly thing, Patrick thought, and then very nearly had apoplexy as she reached out and flicked it. 'What're you *doing?*' he croaked, his own legs distinctly wobbly as it took off full pelt, mercifully in the same direction it had been going.
'Sending it home,' she said, watching it as it scurried past her to the side of the box. 'It probably has babies.'
*Babies?* Patrick's eyes boggled, looking this way and that, searching for spiders crawling up walls and across ceilings, ready to drop on him. 'Yeah, well, they'll starve if the ugly fucker comes out again.' He pulled himself up, hurriedly wiping his sweaty palms against his sides. 'Vermin, the lot of them.'
'They're not.' She laughed. 'Spiders are good. They catch flies.'
'And what are you?' Patrick glanced derisorily at her. 'The resident sodding expert?'
'No,' she said, now looking at him bemusedly. 'It's just they don't do any harm. They're—'
'Shut it,' Patrick said quickly, guessing she might be about to tell him they were more scared than he was, which would be another reminder of his daughter he didn't want. Giving her a warning glance, he walked across to her and caught hold of her arm.
'Where're we going?' she demanded, as he pulled her to her feet, his gaze surreptitiously sweeping the floor for tarantulas as he did.
'Two words,' he said, suspecting he might have gone OTT with the big brother routine. She might be a bit more malleable now, but Patrick wasn't taking any chances. 'Shut the fuck up.'
He glanced at her, as he marched her across to the right hand wall. He was half-expecting her to retort that's four words, as Taylor would have done. Always ready with the smart retorts were teenage girls, Patrick thought, then stopped and caught himself short. Bloody hell, what *was* the matter with him, constantly comparing a homeless little tart, who probably wasn't even a virgin, to his own daughter? *Was he* going soft in the head? *Crap*, had he got a brain tumour? Is that why his migraines were so persistent lately? Forcing her down to sit on the floor, Patrick slid his eyes worriedly to the side. The aura was still there, flickering as nauseatingly intensely as ever.
'Stay.' He cocked the gun in her direction and backed towards his

bag of tricks. He'd better make a doctor's appointment, he thought, trying not to linger on the fact that the only doctor he might be seeing if this went belly up was the sort who laid out dead bodies. Nah, he reassured himself, extracted two lengths of rope from the bag and threw one at her. It wouldn't be him on a slab. A copper Adams might be, but if it came to a stand-off, the cowardly little wimp would back off. Always had. Always would.

'Wrap it around your ankles twice,' he ordered the girl. 'And then tie it, nice and tight.'

'But why?' She looked at him perplexed, as if it wasn't a perfectly clear instruction.

'Don't ask, just do it!' he snapped, irritated now by her cross-questioning him. Women, they were all the bloody same. Be nice to them for five minutes and they think they've got you wrapped around their little fingers.

Patrick had a quick perusal of the floor around him again, lest anything hairy might be sneaking up on him, then, keeping one eye on her, he pulled another item from the bag. Handy things, slip leads, he thought, testing the choke factor on it. Adams should have thought about getting one for his sidekick lapdog. Then maybe the man wouldn't have been trespassing on farmland and ended up getting himself shot.

Noting the girl had done as instructed, without any mouthing off this time, Patrick walked across to her, placing the slip lead to the side of the front door, as he went.

She watched him, her big Bambi eyes full of trepidation now. And well they might be, sweetheart. Patrick smiled, walking around her.

'Hands behind you,' he said. Waiting while she obliged, he parked his gun and then bent to tie her wrists nice and tight too. Didn't want to stop her circulation, but nor did he want her thinking he was anything but serious, which he most definitely was, given Adams had left him no choice. The girl he wasn't entirely sure what to do with yet. For the first time since he'd had nightmares about surprised pigeon's eyes, Patrick was feeling something akin to conscience. Moving her on to someone who might make use of her, he might be able to live with. Leaving her lying wide-eyed and cold in the ground would definitely keep him awake at night.

Job done, he straightened up and picked up his gun.

'Shuffle back against the wall,' he ordered her. He walked back around her while she did as instructed and he cocked the gun at her again, locking eyes with hers. 'Do *not* move a muscle or the lovely Becky gets it, *comprendre?*'

'Becky?' she said, her little face hopeful.

Really couldn't keep the lip buttoned, could she? Reaching into his pocket for his cigarettes, Patrick sighed with despair.

'Yes, *Becky*,' he replied patiently, flipped the lid on the box and dropped a pre-rolled spliff into his mouth. 'Now, stay.'

Giving her a last warning glance, Patrick walked back to his bag, dropped the packet in and ferretted for his lighter. Lighting his spliff, he dropped the lighter back in the bag too, and then, the gun under his arm, he headed for the door at the back of the room, drawing deeply, as he went.

\*\*\*\*

Rebecca had tried to keep calm, to keep her terror at bay and take only shallow breaths. Common sense told her she couldn't suffocate, but the air was thick, dark, and cloying. She'd lost all sense of time, even though, ironically, her only company had been the quiet tick of her watch. She had no idea whether it was night or day. She needed the toilet and a drink in equal measures. Her throat was parched and raw, made worse by her muffled, useless cries. Her hands were numb behind her; she'd long ago lost the sensation of pins and needles tingling down to her fingertips. Worse, though, was the pain in the small of her back. Please God it wasn't the familiar pain she suspected it might be. To miscarry her child here, in the clutches of a madman, would be more than she could bear.

Stifling a sob, Rebecca squeezed her eyes closed. They were already swollen from too many cried tears. Pointless tears. There was no one to hear her, and tears would be lost on the animal who'd taken her. His heart was as black as his soul. He had no feelings. None.

Attempting to curl herself tighter, wishing she could protect the little foetus inside her, Rebecca's knees jarred once again against a jut of hard metal. The pain shot through her, jagged and raw, a tender bruise further bruised. The pain was nothing, though, to the rawness in her chest when she thought of Matthew, imagined not seeing the smile in his eyes ever again; imagined what that monster might do to him.

Staring into the darkness, Rebecca wished she could sleep, that death might steal her away if she did. Better that than ... Her thoughts screeched to a halt as she heard something in the stillness, she wasn't sure what. A dull thud, doors opening and closing. Movement outside. Definitely movement. Rebecca held her breath.

She strained her ears, hoping, praying, as her heart fluttered like a helpless bird against her ribcage, that it wouldn't be him.

*Please don't let it be. Please let it be someone to help me.* Rebecca clamped her eyes shut again as metal scraped against metal and the car boot was flung open, light flooding the confined space and temporarily blinding her.

Hope faded as the odour of him assaulted her senses, immediately making her nauseous all over again.

'How are we, sweetheart, hey?' he asked pleasantly. Rebecca felt the hairs rise on her body, a thousand tiny spiders crawl over her skin, as he touched her, trailing the knuckles of his hand across her swollen cheek.

'Sorry I didn't come back sooner. I got delayed ...' he paused, stroking her hair softly from her face '... by your niece.'

Rebecca's eyes shot wide. *Ashley!*

'Pretty little thing,' he went on. 'Bit mouthy, though. Needed teaching a lesson. And you know me, always one to oblige. Come on, up we come.' He tucked his hands under her armpits, heaved her up, as Rebecca blinked at him, disoriented.

'But you don't know me, do you?' Hitching her out and planting her on her feet, he chatted on, his conversation growing evermore inane.

'Never mind, we'll change all that when hubby gets here. Whoops, careful, you'll be feeling a bit wobbly, I expect.' He steadied her, as she reeled. 'Now, where's your other shoe?'

Rebecca studied him, horrified, as he fished back into the boot of the car, searching for the one red stiletto that had become detached from her foot. He was completely insane. Stunned and terrified in turn she watched him, tutting and tsking as he searched, a furrow deepening his brow, as if he was troubled, genuinely troubled ... by a missing shoe?

Dear God! Had her hands not been tied, Rebecca would have slammed the boot shut on him, snatched up the gun that he surely intended to use, and shot him. And shot him again, and again, watched the blood spurt from his vile body, enjoyed seeing him squirm and beg, and die. She couldn't do this. She *couldn't*. Where was Ashley? What had he done, the deranged, sick ... There was no word. He was pure evil. Rebecca forced back the tears now threatening to spill over.

'Got it!' He emerged triumphant, holding the shoe aloft, as if he'd seized on the crown jewels. He turned then, smiling ridiculously as he took hold of her arm.

'Come on. You might as well lose the other one until we get you steady on the old pins.'

He paused and waited.

Rebecca scanned his face, confused.

'The shoe, sweetheart.' He glanced down at her feet.

Gathering he wanted her to remove the one she was wearing, Rebecca hesitated, but only briefly. The flash of irritation in his eyes meant his mood was swinging. Almost stumbling but for his grip on her arm, she kicked the shoe off. She fervently wished she could gouge his eyes out with the spindly heel of it, as he bent to retrieve it, taking his time, perusing her legs, smirking up at her.

'Right. Move it,' he said, standing so abruptly Rebecca flinched. 'Don't want to not be ready for when our hero arrives, do we?'

Matthew, Rebecca realised, any last vestige of hope she'd had failing fast. In height they were a good match. Matthew was fit and toned. But this thing by her side, holding her arm, leading her along like a child, his shoulders were broad. He had a shotgun. Matthew couldn't defend himself against that.

# CHAPTER TWENTY-TWO

'Becky?' Rebecca heard Ashley, her voice small and tremulous, as he bundled her through the door. *Thank God.* Rebecca offered up a small prayer of gratitude, relief flooding through her that Ashley seemed physically unharmed, repulsion for the unfeeling creature at her side following in its wake. She might seem physically unharmed, but psychologically ... ? Rebecca noted the look in her eyes. Sitting on the damp floor, wearing only her leggings and cropped sweater, she was shaking with shock, tearful, petrified.

Meeting her eyes, Rebecca tried to reassure her, to communicate with her that she was all right, but what good could that do? With her arms trussed behind her, no shoes on her feet, tape on her swollen face, she must look anything but. Did she have blood on her face too? She worried, for Ashley's sake. She'd tasted it after the last blow, felt it trickle warmly down her cheek, congeal in her hair, as she'd lain curled in the dark, praying for unconsciousness to claim her. It didn't come. There was no mercy here. Steeling herself, Rebecca twisted to face the monster who would show them none. Silently, she beseeched him. Would he not allow her to at least talk to Ashley, console her in some way, whatever was to come?

He cocked his head to one side, noticed the tears Rebecca now allowed to fall freely, and reached to wipe one roughly away with his thumb.

'Thirsty?' he asked her, sounding almost concerned.

A flicker of lost hope resurfacing, Rebecca nodded fervently.

He nodded in turn, assessing her, and then glanced suspiciously at Ashley. As if there was anything either of them could do to overpower him when he had them tied up like animals while he paraded around with his gun. 'Good job I thought to bring enough water, isn't it?' His gaze roved over Rebecca again, and then he turned to walk away.

Morbidly fascinated, Rebecca watched him, as he bent to place the shoes neatly next to the box. Standing back, he cocked his head to one side again, as if appraising them as one would an ornament or art form. Then, obviously dissatisfied with his arrangement, he bent again, re-aligning the shoes just so.

He was mad, utterly deranged. Rebecca felt icy fingers run the length of her spine, as he swaggered on towards his bag, his gun now

173

propped on his shoulder, and apparently not a care in the world.

'Left up to your little stray over there, we'd have no water left. Needs taking in hand, that one.' Glowering disdainfully towards Ashley, he retrieved a bottle of water and walked back towards Rebecca. 'Make it last. It's all we have left.'

If Rebecca wondered how she was supposed to drink it, she didn't wonder for long. Parking the bottle at her feet, he straightened up and then, with no forewarning, reached to rip the tape sharply from her face.

'Don't try anything,' he warned her, going around behind her. 'I'm untying you only long enough to drink and make sure she has one. Do anything stupid and the girl suffers. Understand?'

He worked quietly on the ropes for a moment, then, 'You didn't answer me.'

He spoke without emotion, but Rebecca sensed the underlying threat in his voice.

'I understand.' She swallowed back her revulsion, as his fingers brushed her flesh. Ignoring the red hot pokers shooting the length of her arms, she turned once the rope went slack. Her movements measured and slow, rather than risk riling him, she forced a smile, tried to offer Ashley some sort of comfort.

'I'm all right, Ashley,' she said, moving towards her.

Ashley just stared at her, her eyes wide and disbelieving.

Kneeling beside her, Rebecca pulled her gently into her arms.

'We'll be fine, sweetie, I promise.' It was a hollow promise, but she had to try.

'We won't!' Ashley choked back a sob. 'He's going to kill us, and it's all my fault!'

'Shhhhh.' Rebecca stroked her hair. 'He's not. He wants money, that's all. Once he has it, he'll let us go.' She faltered, not daring to look towards the monster, for fear of what she might read in his eyes.

'It's nothing to do with you, sweetie.' She wanted to say more, point out to her that evil existed, manifested in this madman, but to do that would definitely invite his wrath. She wanted to fight. While she had breath in her body, she'd sworn she would, but to make any rash moves now would be to turn that wrath on Ashley. Rebecca had to stay calm. Panic clawed at her insides even as she thought it.

'It *is*.' Ashley sobbed in earnest now, pitiful sobs. Rebecca could feel the shudders running through her. 'If I hadn't been here, none of this would be happening. I know Matthew doesn't care about me, but you do. I know you do. I'm so sorry, Becky.'

Rebecca shook her head, trying to decipher what Ashley had said. 'Ashley, Matthew cares about you,' she tried to reassure her, as another shudder racked Ashley's frail frame.

'Why on earth would you think—'

'Aw, for fuck's sake, stop with the grizzling, can't you?' Patrick interjected. 'You're giving me a headache. For information,' he said, glancing at Ashley as he passed Rebecca the bottle she hadn't yet drunk from, 'it's *not* your fault. You should listen to the lovely Becky. It's *Matthew's* fault, taking advantage of you like that. He deserves everything that's coming to him.'

*Taking advantage?* Rebecca felt an uneasy chill of trepidation creep over her. Tentatively she reached for the water, easing away from Ashley a fraction to offer it to her first.

'Why?' she asked calmly.

Patrick gawked at her. 'Why? *Why?* What is this, fifty questions? I've told you why. He's obsessed. Not right in the head.' Patrick gave himself a demonstrative jab in the head, and then wished he hadn't. The aura was back, bright and strong, and literally blindsiding him. 'Don't tell me you had no idea how he secures his convictions? He fits people up, sweetheart. Didn't I tell you that? To say nothing of messing with girls half his age. He's a paedo, darling. A bent copper and a perv. *Comprendre?*'

Obviously, she didn't comprehend. Patrick despaired as the woman just stared at him, a gormless look on her face, as if she had no clue what he was talking about. Hadn't he told her, gone to great lengths to explain Adams' obsession with him, his constant baiting him, attempting to fit him up, beating him up, to say little of the trifling fact that his brother was dead because of him? Patrick had lost a consignment because of Adams' constant interference. More importantly, he'd lost his good reputation. If Hayes caught up with him, he'd very likely lose his kneecaps, followed by his balls, and the stupid bint asks why? OK, so the paedophile bit was laying it on a bit thick, but true, more than likely. Adams obviously did like them young. Knowing what the consequences would be, why else would Brianna and Natalie have coughed their guts up to him, a copper? Not because he could offer them around-the-clock protection, that was for sure. Nah, Adams was sweet-talking them, along with a good few of Patrick's other toms, offering them a shoulder, and a bit more.

'That's not true,' the woman said. Her expression was composed, but Patrick saw the swallow slide down her pretty pale throat. Yeah, she was wondering all right. And so she should be.

'You don't think so?' He held her gaze. 'Ask your little stray what she thinks, why don't you? Someone who's been used and abused half her life, and then Adams comes along and uses and abuses her all over again. Disgusting I call it.'

Patrick stopped, watching with interest as the woman's gaze shot to the girl's.

'Ashley?' she said, her eyes questioning, her face ashen. It was heart-breaking really: the woman's obvious pain at realising her safe little world was crumbling around her.

Interesting, though, watching those insidious little seeds of doubt take root. At this rate, one of these pair might pull the trigger for him. Patrick's mouth curved into a slow smile. His face dropped though, as the woman seemed to pull herself up, taking a breath and straightening her shoulders. He was perplexed he had to admit, when she reached again to wrap an arm around the girl. She was obviously in denial, soppy cow.

'Enough with the lovey-dovey stuff,' growling, Patrick gestured her up. He'd had it with this happy family crap.

The woman didn't move, annoyingly. 'Can't you at least untie her?' she asked.

Patrick looked her over contemptuously. 'Do I look stupid?' Clearly, she must think he was. Did she really expect him to untie both of them, together? And then what, stand still while they leapt on him and scratched his eyes out?

'Up.' He gestured the woman again, and then grabbed hold of her arm to hoist the stubborn bitch up. 'She'll be untied when *you're* re-tied,' he informed her. 'Now, go over there, put your shoes on and stand on the box.'

****

Matthew walked purposefully, his breath freezing and flying into the crisp air like a soft white djinn. He'd debated hard whether to make the call. One call and air surveillance could be hovering overhead in minutes, armed officers despatched and honing in on their target, ready to shoot Sullivan down if they caught so much as a glimpse of him. And where might that leave Becky and Ashley? His thumb hovering over his mobile, he'd factored in that Sullivan would use them as a human shield.

Matthew hadn't made the call. Those were exactly the tactics the coward would resort to, and Matthew had no idea whether Becky was in there. Depending on the soundness of the roof, thermal imaging might have indicated how many people there were and pinpointed their location, but it couldn't have identified who was who. Ashley he'd heard. Matthew's heart sank afresh as he recalled her soul-crushing scream. Becky though ... The thought of her imprisoned in some dank, confined space ... an underground sewer, a box buried somewhere ... and the only man who knew where, shot down and killed before he'd disclosed her location? That was the unbearable scenario that had decided him.

The gun, bought with one specific aim in mind, to destroy Sullivan like the vermin he was, was now useless. Matthew had it with him. Biting rain now slashing down, obscuring his vision and soaking him through to the skin, he checked his jacket pocket for the lump of cold metal. He'd abandoned the shoulder holster, thought about trying to secrete the gun, but then abandoned that idea too. Sullivan would search him. He'd find it in seconds. Ditto any other weapon Matthew had considered. He had no plan. His only hope, he knew, as did Sullivan, was to do as instructed. Turn up at the designated time. Wiping a hand over his eyes, Matthew squinted at his watch. Thereafter, offer himself in exchange for Becky and Ashley, beg Sullivan to release them, take whatever crap the sick bastard dished out. Nothing could be worse than the pain tearing Matthew apart now, except to lose the woman he loved. To know that she and Ashley had suffered and he'd been able to do nothing about it.

Rage smouldering steadily inside him, Matthew stopped directly in front of the property making sure he was in full view. One clear shot and Sullivan could take him out in an instant. But Sullivan wasn't about to do that. He needed to satiate his depraved appetites, play his perverted little game, and in the nightmare this game had become, Sullivan was winning hands down.

Five minutes ticked by, excruciatingly slowly. Matthew didn't move, other than to blink away the rain falling from his eyelashes like icy tears from a frond. Trying not to imagine what might greet him inside, he scanned the outside of the building, mentally noting all available exits. Close up, it was more dilapidated than he'd thought: slates off the roof, the framework skeletal in places, upstairs: empty sockets for windows, dark, like blind eyes watching him. There was a hayloft-door hanging off, rotting supporting beams interlacing the brickwork. Two windows downstairs, both boarded, bar a gap in one, through which Matthew had no doubt he was being watched. A sturdy front door, cast iron hinges ... Matthew fixed his gaze on it and waited.

Eventually, he heard a bolt being drawn. Bracing himself, Matthew drew in a long breath as the door slowly opened, jarring on the uneven floor as it went.

'Ashley?' seeing her upright, unharmed, he blew out a sigh of relief. Relief turned fast to despair, though, as he looked her over. She was chalk-white, visibly shaking, petrified.

'I'm right behind her, Adams,' Sullivan's voice, arrogant, threatening.

'Keeping a very firm eye on her, aren't I, sweetheart? Wouldn't want her falling into bad company, would we, hey, Adams?'

Fury welled in Matthew's chest. His hand itched to reach for the gun, to pull back the trigger and watch Sullivan's guts spill out. More likely he'd watch his wife and Ashley die, lying crippled by a well-aimed shot while they did. Sullivan would do it. Someone mentally deranged enough to do what he'd done to Brianna, to who knew how many others, to his own wife; someone who shot a man at point blank range, someone who, as a boy, took pleasure in snapping the necks of birds and cats. Sullivan would do it without hesitation.

Sullivan appeared then, a shotgun in one hand, his free arm sliding around Ashley from behind, across her chest, coming to rest under her chin.

'Do invite our guest in, *Ashley*,' He took a step backwards, forcing Ashley to step with him.

Ashley looked to Matthew, beseeching, quietly pleading. Her hands went to the arm around her throat. *Don't.* Matthew took a step forward, knowing that would only make Sullivan tighten his grip.

'It's okay, Ashley,' he said, working to keep his voice calm. 'Don't struggle.'

'That's right, sweetheart,' Sullivan cooed in her ear, 'don't struggle. Didn't do you much good last time, did it?' He looked back to Matthew, his eyes goading, willing him to lose it. And, God help him, Matthew felt he just might.

'Don't be shy, Detective. Do come in,' Sullivan suggested. Even knowing this could only end hopelessly, still he was smiling. Matthew dropped his gaze to the shotgun. The same gun he'd used to blast a man's chest open from five paces away. He looked back to his face, trying to read what might be going on in his mind. What it was that might drive a person to end someone else's life without conscience.

'I'm waiting, Adams.' The smile slid from Sullivan's face as Matthew studied him. 'You really don't want to try my patience.'

Glancing again at Ashley, Matthew hesitated. He'd made a wrong decision. He should have made the damn call, trusted Davies to hold back and maintain covert surveillance. At least then, if the psychopath shot him, Becky and Ashley might have stood a chance. Hot and clammy under his jacket, Matthew felt his head swim. 'Where's Becky?' he asked, attempting to establish whether she was in there before he himself was trapped.

'For me to know and you to find out, Detective Inspector,' Sullivan drawled sardonically. 'Come on. Come see.' He gestured behind him.

'Let her go, Sullivan. You have me. I'll do whatever you want. You don't need them,' Matthew tried, knowing it was useless. He had him exactly where he wanted him, but he wasn't about to let hostages go. And Matthew could do nothing about it. Reaching into his pocket, whether for gun or phone, would be certain suicide. Going in there would also probably be. He'd weighed those odds, come to the conclusion that Sullivan's aim was to see him beg and crawl before killing him. Matthew would beg, would crawl. If he had to die, so be it. But, please God, only once Becky and Ashley were safe.

Sullivan appraised him as he debated. 'What, this one not enough to entice you inside, hey Adams? God, you're a heartless bastard. Told you, he was, didn't I, sweetheart?' He leaned down to Ashley, his mouth brushing her cheek, causing Matthew's chest to tighten.

'She was imagining a happy future with you, Adams. Not sure she realised she'd be sharing you, but ...' His meaning implicit, Sullivan trailed off.

Repugnance broiling inside him, Matthew stopped deliberating and started walking.

'She's feeling a bit spurned, aren't you, darling?' Sullivan continued with his disgusting drivel. 'A bit used.'

'No!' Ashley refuted desperately. 'I'm not. He's—'

Yanking her head back, Sullivan cut her short.

'Did I tell you to speak?' he growled.

Matthew was directly in front of him now, his jaw clenched, the urge to sink his fist into Sullivan's face overwhelming.

Sullivan met his gaze, his mouth twisting into its usual triumphant smirk. 'Perverts like you really should be locked up, you know, Adams, preying on innocent young kids, and you a policeman, and all.'

Matthew willed himself not to do exactly what Sullivan wanted him to. Instead, he tried to eradicate emotion from his own eyes as he looked into Sullivan's: cold, hard, uncompromising, simmering pools of pure hatred.

Sullivan sneered openly. Then, leaning again towards Ashley, he demonstratively breathed in the smell of her.

'I did try to console her.' He glanced tauntingly back at Matthew. 'I think I managed to take her mind off you, but I had to work at ... Whoa!' Sullivan jerked up, jerking Ashley's head further back, as Matthew moved towards him.

'Careful, Detective. We don't want to do anything rash now, do we?'

Sullivan's eyes were now full of intent, malevolence oozing from the man, and Matthew was powerless. Wishing with every fibre of his being he could reach past Ashley and throttle the piece of scum where he stood, he lowered his gaze to hers instead. Her eyes were wild, uncertain, guarded. *God, no.* Matthew's gut twisted. Did she really think there was any truth in whatever rubbish this sick bastard had been feeding her?

'Ashley?' he said quietly, willing her to meet his gaze.

'Don't tear yourself up over it, Adams,' Sullivan's tone was amused. 'I doubt she was much of a prize anyhow. Not exactly as pure as the driven snow, is she?'

Hatred searing through him, Matthew locked furious eyes on his.

'You evil son of a bitch.' He caught a wheeze in his chest, swallowed it, prayed hard that if there was a god in heaven he would give him five minutes alone with this *thing* without his gun. So help him, he *would* kill him.

'I thought I warned you about the name-calling, Adams.' Sullivan lost the smile.

'Inside. Now.' He stepped back, turning sideways and manoeuvring Ashley with him.

'Move it!'

His eyes never leaving Sullivan's, Matthew took a step only to find his progress barred by the barrel of the gun.

'A word of warning,' Sullivan said, 'if you're wired, if you've alerted anyone, your wife and Snow White here, they're both dead. Got it?'

*She was still alive.* Matthew closed his eyes, this time offering up a silent prayer of gratitude. '*Oh, Jesus ...*' Matthew's legs almost gave way as Sullivan allowed him further into the property.

# CHAPTER TWENTY-THREE

'Not very gentlemanly, keeping ladies hanging around, Adams, is it?' Patrick watched with interest, as the copper turned a pale shade of white. Reeling on his feet, he was, poor sod. He actually looked as if he might pass out. Didn't take him long to recover himself, though. Patrick watched on as Adams pulled himself up, bracing his shoulders in that bloody annoying Bruce Willis *nothing-gets-to-me* way he had. It obviously did though. He might be trying to keep a grip, but the little tic going in his cheek was a dead giveaway. Patrick had noticed it when Adams had paid him a visit in the nick. Seen it many times, when the pathetic little runt had tried to stand up to him as a kid. Most recently, before the bastard had kicked him to the floor like a dog, for which the copper was about to get payback. Oh, yes, his fuse was lit all right. The man was a ticking time-bomb, far too reactive to be on the force, in Patrick's humble opinion.

Patrick barely had time to free himself of the girl before the copper exploded.

'You *fucking* animal!' he seethed, lunging towards him.

But Patrick was ready. 'Down!' He levelled the shotgun, ready to blast Adams to kingdom come if he didn't back off.

Clearly realising he might be at a disadvantage, Adams stopped, his expression pure thunder, his chest heaving. Oh, dear. Was that a little wheeze Patrick could hear in there? Quietly amused, he noted how Adams was struggling to control his breathing, another giveaway as to the copper's high state of anxiety. Patrick probably knew the signs better than Adams did.

'I said, down, Adams.' Lowering the gun, Patrick indicated the floor, which is where he wanted Adams. No one, but no one, constantly refers to *Patrick Sullivan* as an animal and gets away with it.

'Unless you want your wife and Snow White to see your blood splattered all over the walls, that is?'

Adams didn't budge. Taking slow breaths, he stayed exactly where he was, his fist clenched at his side and in his eyes ... pure murder. Patrick felt the tiniest flicker of apprehension run through him.

'We can play the waiting game if you like, Adams,' he made sure to hold his gaze, 'but I'm not sure your good lady will be very keen on the idea. Are you?'

Patrick's gaze flicked in the direction of the man's wife.

'Do it,' he ordered. 'Face front and get down on your knees, copper, if you value her life.'

'You *bastard*.' Adams took another laboured breath and ran his hands over his face. Then, glancing heavenward, finally, he did as instructed.

Got him, Patrick thought, hugely satisfied that the copper seemed to be getting the message. Patrick had the upper hand now. This time, it would be Adams, defenceless on the floor, while *he* broke his fucking jaw. *Quid pro quo*, as far as Patrick was concerned.

'Right, you,' he swung the gun in the girl's direction, and then quickly back to Adams, 'get over here. And bring the dog leash with you.'

'What dog leash?' she asked, after a second glancing around stupidly.

Patrick felt a stab of irritation. Was she being deliberately insolent? No, he decided. Her tone had been one of undiluted fear. Unlike the copper, obviously she wasn't too dense to realise what the consequences of deliberately provoking him might be.

'On the floor by the door, and hurry it up.' Patrick kept his eyes on Adams, who was gulping back deep breaths now, considerably shaken, Patrick imagined, as he took in the carefully planned scene before him. Patrick actually thought his little wife looked quite nice, perched up there in her red stilettos. She really did have good legs. Shame not to show them off. She was wobbling a bit, though, he noticed. He did hope she didn't fall off them and do herself a mischief. Clearly, she wasn't used to wearing high heels to titillate hubs. Or maybe she couldn't be arsed, since Adams was no doubt into younger flesh.

'Loop it around his neck.' Patrick motioned the girl, who was taking her own sweet time. 'Move it!' he barked, as she dilly-dallied. They were all at it, trying his patience, as if he had all the time in the world, which he hadn't. He needed to be on his yacht, heading for sunny climes a.s.a.p., before the law did get wind of who'd shot Adams' little lapdog. The lovely Mrs Adams didn't want to hang about much longer either, from the looks of her. Shaking from head to foot, she was now. One slip and *click, clack, crack:* dead bird, swinging from the rafters.

'Pull it tight,' he instructed the girl, as she continued to fanny about, looking piningly at Adams. As if he gave a toss how she looked.

'For crying out loud ... Give it here!' Patrick snatched the end of the slip lead she'd draped ineffectually over the copper's head.

'Over there.' He nodded her over to the far wall. 'Sit down on the floor, like a good little girl and do *not* utter a word. Got it?'

Patrick waited while she complied and then turned his attention back to Adams, who'd clearly managed to put his dubious detecting skills to good use and realised he was in deep shit.

'Comfortable?' Patrick smiled.

Adams didn't answer, but Patrick forgave him that on the basis he was pretty choked.

'So, tell me again, what is it you think I am, Detective?' he asked pleasantly.

Adams hesitated before answering. 'Nothing,' he said, without conviction, in Patrick's mind, and certainly not with a whole lot of respect.

He yanked the lead tighter. 'What was that?'

'Nothing,' Adams repeated, and then gagged as Patrick gave the lead another yank.

'Telling me you think I'm nothing isn't the right answer, *is it,* you insolent bastard!?'

'Anything... *Christ.*' The copper spluttered and coughed.

'I'm waiting, Adams.'

'I don't... think you're anything,' Adams rasped, his hands going to his throat.

Patrick held the tension. 'Not an animal then?'

'No.' A little more conviction this time, Patrick thought, but probably not a lot of honesty. Still, on the basis he didn't want the copper actually choking to death just yet, he relented and slackened the lead off a little.

Adams pulled air into his lungs.

'Let her down,' he asked, obviously struggling to breathe now. Patrick wasn't slow to notice the rattle in his chest. Poor bastard looked well on the way to an asthma attack. Such a shame.

'You forgot the magic word,' he reminded him.

'*Please,*' Adams obliged immediately. 'I'll do anything. Whatever you want, you've got it. Just... *please* let her go.'

'Anything I want?' Patrick enquired, cocking his head interestedly on one side.

The copper closed his eyes and nodded, humiliated, Patrick hoped, but not enough. Not by far.

'What? Like bring my brother back?' Patrick paused to let the man ponder the impossibility of this task.

Adams' answer to which was to look defeated. He would really, wouldn't he? Patrick felt a knot of anger unfurl in his chest.

'Restore my good reputation with Hayes, will you, Adams? Tell him what a great guy I am and return his consignment?'

Adams had nothing to say there either, surprise, surprise.

'And what about my daughter, hey, Adams? She's training to be a veterinary nurse. I was looking forward to seeing her graduate. And now you've gone and fucked that up, too, *haven't you?*'

Patrick was so furious about that, he was tempted to shoot his brains out right here, right now. Still no answer from Adams, ignorant sod.

'*That* was a question, Detective,' Patrick reminded him of his manners. Again.

Adams gulped hard. And well he might. In his position, the man should be scared. Very scared.

'I'm sorry,' he finally offered, at least attempting something near contrite.

'Too little too fucking late, Adams,' Patrick snarled and tensed the lead. 'Will *sorry* bring Chelsea back? Well, will it? If *you* hadn't turned up, poking around in *my* business, she wouldn't be lying out there now stone-cold-fucking dead!'

'*Jesus Christ!* What do you *want?*' Adams looked up at him.

Terror in his eyes, Patrick saw, with some satisfaction. Wasn't so high and mighty now, was he? Towering over him, putting the boot in, his little lapdog standing by and watching him. Bastard.

'For starters: you to grovel, Adams. To crawl on your hands and knees and beg.'

'I'll do it! Whatever you need, I'll do it. Please ...' Adams glanced towards his wife and back '... let them go.'

Patrick looked him over. 'And where would the fun be in that?' he asked leisurely. 'I want them to see, Adams. I want your adoring little family to *know* what a snivelling little coward you are under all that police bravado. How, when push comes to shove, you would gladly sacrifice them to save your own worthless skin.'

The copper ran the back of his hand over his forehead.

Patrick wasn't too happy with him moving without permission, but he gave him that, given his current position.

'You see, Adams,' he went on coolly, 'in my mind, people who intimidate and bully other people, calling them names, like *bastard* and *animal*, when they're obviously neither of those things, need to be taught a lesson, don't y'think?'

He paused to let that sink in. 'You've humiliated me once too often, Adams. Even way back when we were kids you just couldn't resist, could you?'

Matthew looked desperately at him, no idea where the hell this was going.

'Don't look as if you don't know what I'm talking about,' Sullivan fumed, 'getting me hauled up, in front of everyone, taken the piss out of. I bet you just loved that, didn't you, Adams?'

The school assembly? Matthew's heart lurched in his chest. This was utterly insane.

'That requires an answer, Detective.'

Panic clutching at his insides, Matthew scrambled for the right one. 'No. I ...'

'Louder, Adams.' Sullivan gave the lead another tug.

'Yes! Whatever! Just ...' Matthew's voice cracked. 'For pity's sake, let them go!'

'Pockets, Adams, empty them,' Sullivan instructed. 'Everything on the floor. Now. And if you're thinking of using the gun you no doubt have secreted about your dubious person,' he aimed the shotgun at Rebecca, 'she just might fall off her shoes. Get my drift?'

Hopelessly, Matthew nodded and looked back to Becky.

The fear constricting his throat threatened to choke him as he met her eyes. Her eyes were haunted, desperately pleading above the ugly tape on her face. Her limbs were shaking. Her feet pushed into stilettos. Blood-red stilettos. Matthew felt his own blood run cold. The kind of heels she'd often said she couldn't walk in to save her life. And now her life depended on her staying upright in them, perched on a box, her hands tied behind her, a rope around her neck which would pull tight and hang her in an instant if ...

God, no. Perspiration running in rivulets down his back, Matthew hurriedly fumbled to retrieve the contents of his pockets. Finding his wallet, he laid that on the ground, followed by his phone. His hand closed around the cold metal of the gun in his other pocket. It might as well be a water pistol. There was no way to use it. No way to risk trying. Pulling in a ragged breath, which stopped painfully short of his chest, he lifted the gun out, laid that on the ground, and then waited.

'Push it away.' Sullivan nodded towards it.

Matthew noted the bastard's finger brushing the trigger of his shotgun and did as instructed.

'The cuffs, Adams,' Sullivan reminded him.

His gut twisting as he guessed what use Sullivan would put those to, Matthew reached around under his jacket and retrieved his handcuffs. His mind raced as he placed those down, frantically searching for a way to try to persuade a psychopath from doing what he was intent on, dread settling like a hard stone in his stomach as he came up with nothing.

'You've forgotten something else, Adams,' Sullivan commented, glancing down at the items.

Confused, Matthew shook his head.

'Your little puff tube, Adams. Where is it?'

*Shit.* Matthew blinked away the sweat tickling his eyelashes. Without that, if he had a full blown attack, he'd be worse than useless. Sullivan would reach for it anyway, if he didn't give it up. Matthew knew him well enough to know that. Gulping back his mounting terror, he pulled the inhaler from his inside pocket, praying that the preventer he'd taken earlier might help ward off an attack, which felt more imminent by the second.

He fully expected Sullivan to crush it under his heel. Perplexed when he didn't, Matthew concluded that Sullivan needed him alive and functioning, for now, until he'd completed the transfer of money. Thereafter … For himself, Matthew was past caring. For Becky, though … He looked back to her, his heart cracking inside him. For Ashley. Matthew glanced towards her. Ashley's eyes, where he'd glimpsed a glimmer of happiness, of hope, were back to those of a guilty, frightened child's.

'Oi, Snow White,' Sullivan gestured her, 'bring me some water. And be *very* careful if you don't want to end up in more trouble than you already are for shagging the copper. She didn't rate you much, by the way. Did you, sweetheart?' Sullivan went on, revelling in his pathetic power. 'Prefers it rough. I must say, she gives good—'

He stopped, panic flooding his eyes, as Ashley shouted behind him, 'Stop! Stop now, or I'll shoot!'

*Oh, Christ.* Matthew's gaze shot past Sullivan, to where Ashley stood, the gun—his gun, which somehow she'd managed to pick up—held in both hands—and pointed at Sullivan. Pointed very shakily at Sullivan.

She was ashen-faced, unfocussed. She hadn't got a cat in hell's chance of hitting him. 'Ashley, don't,' Matthew attempted to inject some kind of calmness into his voice.

'It's not worth the risk.' He glanced towards Becky, praying Ashley would understand.

'You'd better fucking not, *Ashley.*' Sullivan turned his gun towards Matthew, 'unless you want to splatter the copper's brains all over the show. Then again, maybe you do. Hey? What do you think, sweetheart? Would you like to take a pot-shot at him? Shoot him in the leg or the arm for using you so cruelly and then casting you aside?'

Ashley's eyes at last found Matthew's; he saw palpable fear in hers.

Matthew's insides flipped over as she tightened her grip. 'Don't listen to him, Ashley. We'll get out of this, I promise. Just put the gun down safely.'

'Yeah, right. Course you will, sweetheart, if you do as I say and don't listen to anymore of the copper's bullshit. You really are full of it, aren't you, Adams?'

'Ashley?' Matthew tried to concentrate on her, watching helplessly as a tear cascaded down her cheek, then another.

'Ashley,' he tried again, but Ashley appeared not to be hearing him. Catching a sob in her throat, she lifted the gun higher.

'I'll do it!' she cried, shaking so badly now she could barely support the weight of it, let alone aim it. 'I will.'

'You do, and *click, clack, crack*, sweetheart, the lovely Becky swings.' Sullivan's aim swung back to Becky. 'Put it down! Now! Over there, by my bag.'

'Do it, Ashley,' Matthew implored her, his heart almost imploding. 'Ashley, *please ...*' he begged.

'Better do as the copper says, sweetheart,' Sullivan warned her. 'It's her funeral if you don't.'

Matthew felt the cloying atmosphere close in on him, as Ashley deliberated. She glanced at him, back to Sullivan. Then, choking out another sob, she lowered the gun.

'Over there.' Calmly, Sullivan nodded towards the bag. 'And then, sit.' He waited while she placed the gun where he'd instructed and then made her way falteringly to the far wall, where she slid, looking shell-shocked, to her haunches.

Sullivan moved then, pointing his shotgun towards Matthew.

'Stay,' he said and backed away, to pick up the gun and secure it at the back of his waistband.

He didn't look at Ashley, didn't acknowledge her at all, but strolled back to Matthew instead. 'You have some online banking to do.' Pausing in front of him, he pulled his mobile from his pocket and thumbed something into it. 'You have an incoming text. Make the transaction. Make it smoothly. Make it now, and no funny business. Do I need to add threats?'

Matthew glanced incredulously at him, as Sullivan picked up his phone and handed it to him. Did he really think he'd try anything? That he gave a stuff about money compared to the life of his wife? Dragging a hand quickly across his eyes, Matthew pulled up the message, as Sullivan walked around him. Calling up his bank details, ignoring Sullivan's slow whistle of appreciation as he obviously noted the balance, Matthew selected *Make a Payment*, pasted Sullivan's details in and hit *Send*.

It didn't go. *Fuck!* Matthew's heart stopped.

'What are you pissing about at, Adams?' Sullivan asked warily behind him.

Matthew felt the hairs rise on his neck. His mouth went dry.

'No signal,' he said tightly.

Sullivan didn't speak for a second, and then, 'You prat!' he fumed. 'Do you really expect me to believe that? You've just been online. I sent you a—'

'It died!' Matthew shouted desperately. 'There's no coverage!'

'Gimme the fucking phone.' Sullivan reached over him and snatched it.

Fear permeated every pore in Matthew's body. The money had been his only hope, his aim to try to persuade Sullivan to take it and run, to convince him that fleeing the country leaving three dead bodies behind him wouldn't be his smartest move. Matthew's only hope now was that he wouldn't do what the fear gripping the pit of his stomach was telling him he might.

Walking agitatedly back and forth, Sullivan jabbed at the phone, cursing as he did. He checked his own phone, then, 'The handcuffs,' he said, turning back to Matthew, his tone flat, his expression inscrutable. 'You know what to do.'

Wiping at a bead of sweat dripping from his face, Matthew swallowed back his nausea and reached for them.

'One wrist and then arms behind you.' Walking back around him, Sullivan nudged him in the back with a knee.

*Classic execution position.* Matthew's stomach churned, as he clicked a bracelet in place.

'Behind you, Adams,' Sullivan repeated coldly.

Not even enough saliva to wet his dry lips, Matthew did as instructed. The sound of Sullivan clicking the cuffs into place was like a thunderclap, deafening, final. Matthew dragged air raggedly into his lungs and waited.

'I think it's payback time, Matthew,' Sullivan said, quietly in his ear.

'Don't!' Ashley screamed, scrambling to her feet. '*Please* don't.'

'Sit!' Sullivan barked. 'Or you're next!'

*Sit down, Ashley. Please sit down.* Matthew willed her. Then, mentally reciting a useless prayer as he felt the nozzle of the gun come to rest at the base of his skull, he closed his eyes and braced himself. He heard the blow before he felt it, the dull thud, before the searing pain ran the length of his spine.

'Sweet dreams, sunshine,' Sullivan snarled, as Matthew went down.

'Oh, dear ...' Matthew heard him again as his vision swam in and out, finally turning to white. 'She really is a sloppy cow, your wife. She's gone and lost one of her shoes.'

# CHAPTER TWENTY-FOUR

Her sobs catching raw in her throat, the toes of her bare foot scrambling desperately for hard surface, Rebecca fought to stay upright. She *had* to. *Please God! Make him stop!* She clamped her eyes closed as the animal plunged the butt of the gun down again against Matthew's back, and again, so brutally Rebecca was sure she heard bones crack.

Hearing the foul obscenities spilling from his torturer's mouth, Ashley's sobs, as she rocked to and fro where she sat on the floor, Rebecca snapped her eyes back open, to see him pulling back his foot and landing another vicious blow to her husband's side.

'Payback, Adams,' he snarled, bending to clutch hold of his hair, forcing his head back at an impossible angle. Blood trickled from Matthew's mouth, he didn't move, which only seemed to inflame Sullivan's temper further.

Uttering, '*Bastard*,' he slammed Matthew's head back down to the ground, and then kicked him again, hard.

'Stop!' Ashley screamed, her voice high-pitched and hysterical. 'You'll kill him!'

'Be quiet!' Sullivan yelled. 'Shut the fuck up, unless *I* tell you to talk!' He jabbed the gun in her direction, dragged an arm over his mouth and then looked down at Matthew, his breath heavy from his exertions, his face twisted with hatred.

'Scum,' he spat and pointed the gun downwards, pressing it against Matthew's temple.

*No!* Struggling to keep her balance, her legs trembling violently beneath her, Rebecca felt the rope jerk tautly at her throat as her foot slipped, nothing but fresh air beneath it. *Please don't. Please don't let him do this. Please ...* Time seemed to slow down as she prayed hopelessly to a god who couldn't hear her, her head swimming, her senses dulling.

'Fetch the knife!' She heard him shout over her heartbeat, now a sluggish thrum in the base of her neck. 'In my bag, silly cow! Fetch it. Now!'

Rebecca felt him catch her, an arm around her thighs, then higher, around her waist. Her ankle bone scraped against the edge of the box, sharp pain shooting through her, as he yanked her towards him, his odious body supporting hers.

Was he going to cut her, or cut her down? Vaguely, Rebecca wondered. She didn't care. She didn't want to be here without Matthew. Didn't want to be. She'd rather be with her babies. But then, she *would* be with Matthew, too, wouldn't she? Rebecca's thoughts made no sense in her head as her vision turned blood-red.

'Silly bitch.' She heard him again, close to her ear. 'More trouble than you're worth, the lot of you. Stand up!' he shouted urgently. 'I said, stand up!'

His torso was pressed close to hers, hers close to his. She didn't want this. Didn't want to be here. With him. Touching him. Feeling him, touching her. Rebecca's cry was muffled. Her face wet with hot tears and snot. She couldn't find the floor. Couldn't...

'Stand the fuck up!' He jolted her upwards, his hands roughly under her armpits. 'Stay on your feet, can't you!?'

Rebecca's eyes fluttered open. Her face: an inch from his. His eyes: cold, unyielding, evil. Did he ever have parents, she wondered obliquely? A mother's love? Or was he spawned from the Devil himself?

'Fetch the water!' His voice: back to commanding. 'Move it!'

Loosening one hand from her, as she stood woozily under her own steam, he reached to rip the tape from her face. Rebecca involuntarily squeezed her eyes closed, but rebellion, pure unadulterated anger, surging from somewhere deep within her, she snatched them immediately open again. She *would* see him. He would see her. Her! Not a piece of meat, someone to play with and then slaughter.

'Stop bloody eyeballing me,' he growled, groping for the water Ashley handed him, then tipping it towards Rebecca's mouth.

Rebecca sipped, and gagged. He offered her more. She drank, feeling the comforting coolness of the water slide down her throat, dribble from her mouth and trickle down her neck. Glad of the sensation jolting her senses awake, she continued to stare at him, trying to find any spark of humanity within.

'Stop with the icy glares, sweetheart. They're wasted on me,' he sneered contemptuously. 'Turn around,' he commanded and took hold of her arm, his fingers digging deep into her flesh. He was taking her back. Rebecca felt a new kind of panic rise in her chest.

'No!' she resisted as he steered her around. She *wouldn't!*

'Move!' He clutched hold of her hair, pushing her, shoving her in the direction of the door that led to the kitchen where there was no kitchen, to the garage that housed the car that might well be her tomb.

'No!' Rebecca refused to budge. He shoved her again, but Rebecca kicked back. He wove an arm around her chest, gripping her tight, and Rebecca fought harder. Jabbing backwards with the heel of her one disgusting shoe, she made contact, felt a small wave a triumph as he winced, and then winced in turn as he squeezed his arm still tighter around her.

'*You are really...*' His growl cut short, Rebecca felt his grip slacken, felt herself flailing forwards. Landing heavily, the breath forced from her body, she rolled over, ready to kick, bite and gouge, to see Ashley had beaten her to it, her fingernails clawing deep scores in his cheek.

Momentarily stunned, he pressed a hand to his wound. Drawing it away, he examined the blood on his fingers, and then, as Rebecca tried to scramble up, he lashed out, landing a blow to Ashley's face that sent her sprawling.

'You disgusting *animal!*' Becky screamed, as he turned back towards her, his nostrils flaring, his face rabid. 'Keep away!' Rebecca kicked out.

'You really do ... *not* ... want ... to do *that*,' he snarled, catching hold of her foot, twisting it, sharply, dragging her along until her kicks became useless flails.

'Finished?' he asked, as she tried futilely again to reach him.

Abhorred, repulsed by the very nearness of him, Rebecca just looked at him.

At which his mouth curved into a slow, sadistic smile. 'Corpses don't need shoes, sweetheart,' he said, and calmly removed the shoe from her foot.

****

Vaguely compos mentis, Steve focussed his eyes on his fiancée, his overriding feeling, apart from feeling as high as a kite, one of immense relief. She wasn't going to kill him then, judging by the expression on her face.

'Steve!' Her tone was a mixture of delight and incredulity. 'I thought you were going to die, you bloody idiot.' With which she jumped up to plant a fat kiss on his cheek. Fair enough. Steve could live with that. He was alive. He offered up a silent prayer of gratitude. Either that or he'd gone to heaven. God, she was beautiful, even when she was having a go at him.

'What were you *doing?*' She jabbed at the call button, 'Typical bravado,' and fussed with his pillows, 'Typical Steve,' and straightened his sheets, 'Typical...' Trailing off, she stopped fussing and promptly burst into tears.

Steve reached to pull the mask from his face. '*Shhhh,*' he said hoarsely, extending an arm stuffed full of tubes towards her. Lindsey grabbed his hand, squashing the needle still in the back of it. Steve winced but tried not to mind. 'I'm okay,' he rasped, his throat feeling like sandpaper.

'Oh, right yes, of course you are.' She rolled her pretty eyes, clearly not convinced. 'You'll be back to putting your life on the line in no time, I expect.'

Now she looked annoyed again, understandably.

'I am, I promise. Or I will be as soon as I'm out of this flipping contraption.' Steve glanced down at the brace; he wasn't thrilled he was going to be stuck in it for five weeks or more.

'You'd better be,' Lindsey huffed. 'You don't get away from me that easily, Steve Ingram. We're getting married if I have to push you down the aisle in your hospital bed.'

'That'll be one for the album.' Steve tried a little levity.

Nope, that didn't work. Lindsey swiped at a tear on her cheek.

'We could still have the honeymoon,' Steve suggested, patting the bed to his side.

'You're awful.' It was a bit of a wobbly one, but she managed a smile.

'I know.' Steve smiled cheekily back. 'But you love me?'

'Just as well for you.' Lindsey gave his hand another squeeze.

Steve reciprocated, relieved that he could. His injuries, to the front of the spinal cord, meant there might be some loss of motor function, pain or temperature sensation, but his limbs, thank God, should retain their normal movement and equilibrium. Evidence of which, if he wasn't mistaken, there was definitely something going on down below. *Thank you, Lord.* Apart from weddings and funerals, Steve had never been much of one for church, but he just might be visiting more often in the future, he decided.

'Couldn't do us a favour, could you, Linds?' He gestured to the water on the bedside locker with his thumb. 'My throat's like the bottom of a budgie's cage, I swear. I could use a drink.'

'Several, I should think,' DCI Davies quipped, from the door. 'Better wait until you're back on your feet, though, Ingram.'

'As long as you're buying,' Steve risked a flippant retort, perversely pleased to see him too. 'Matthew?' he asked when Davies reached his bedside.

Davies shook his head, his expression dour.

'Gone to ground. We've got every available body on it.' He paused, looking Steve thoughtfully over. 'You were aware that ... ?' Again he hesitated, glancing towards Lindsey, who, clearly assuming this was police work, attempted to extract her hand from Steve's. Steve held on to it. She should know. It might go some way to explaining why he had felt compelled to act like a bloody idiot and put their future together at risk.

'That his wife has been taken? Yes,' he said, and felt Lindsey's hand tighten around his. 'Have you done a sweep of the area?'

Davies eyed him curiously. 'Area?'

Steve knitted his brow, realising he'd been more or less out of it since Sullivan had shot him. He hadn't had the chance to talk to anyone yet. It hadn't even occurred to him he might have been found anywhere but in the field where ... *Shit!* 'Where was I?' he asked urgently. 'Where did you find me?'

'The riverbank,' Davies supplied. 'There are other details you should know about. We'll discuss it later, when you're—'

'Matthew's and Becky's house,' Steve cut in grimly. 'The field adjoining it. That's where the bastard is holding her. Or at least, he was.'

\*\*\*\*

*'Incy wincy spider climbed up the waterspout. Down came the rain and washed the spider out. Incy wincy spider...'* Ashley sang softly to herself as she chased the spider up the side of the box and across the top of it.

*That's four!* Emily said gleefully in her ear.

'Five,' Ashley corrected her. 'You can't count.'

*Yeth, I can.*

'Can't.' Ashley fed the spider carefully from the palm of her hand into the cigarette box.

*Do you think they'll eat each other?*

'I don't think so.' Ashley peered in after it, to see spiders' legs flailing as their owners frantically scurried over the knotty bodies of their mates. 'They might get a bit high though.' She watched as one settled between the ends of two joints. She hoped they didn't. She didn't want them chilled. She wanted them scared, hunched legs scurrying and running, preferably into his mouth.

Carefully closing the packet, she stood up, dusting her knees free of the dust and crap from the floor, then walked across to position the packet back in the bag, exactly where she'd found it. It wasn't much of a plan, but it was better than none. Her task complete, she looked worriedly back to Matthew, who was still lying still and cold on the floor. He was breathing though. She could hear him. She didn't like the wheeze. She wished he'd wake up. She wished the freak hadn't put all those fucked up pictures of him in her head.

Glancing back to the windows, she decided to have another go at the boards. Sullivan could come back in at any minute, but she had to try to do something.

*You'll only get more splinters.* Her mithering sister warned her.

'I wish I could get a big splinter,' Ashley told her. 'A long, sharp splinter and stick it right in his jugular.'

*And watch him gag as the blood spurts, and then ...*

'*Shush!* Hearing movement behind her, Ashley whirled around.

'Ashley,' Matthew croaked, attempting to lever his head from the floor.

He was moving!

'Matthew!' Ashley skidded towards him, and then back-stepped to grab up the water.

'Ashley?' he said hoarsely again. 'Where's ...' Trailing off, he tried to draw a rasping breath into his lungs, only to end up coughing his heart out.

Ashley dropped quickly to her knees beside him. '*Shush,*' she said, planted the water down and helped him roll over.

'Drink,' she ordered him, easing her arm under his head, picking up the bottle, and pressing it to his lips.

Matthew tried. He took a sip and then coughed again, a cough that seemed to rack his whole body. Then he drew in a breath that rattled his chest and only made him cough harder.

Oh God, what should she do? Wiping the blood and sweat from his face, Ashley tried frantically to think. The wheeze was worse, louder. There when he breathed in, there when he breathed out.

'Matthew!' she whispered urgently. 'Matthew, *please* ... I don't know what to do!'

'Inhaler.' Matthew struggled to get the word out. Then, closing his eyes, he inclined his head to the floor somewhere beyond her.

'Don't close your eyes. Please, don't close your eyes,' Ashley begged him. Desperately, she looked around, overwhelming relief sweeping through her as her gaze fell on the little blue tube that still lay on the floor. 'I see it!'

Easing her arm from under him, she scrambled across to it. 'What do I do with it?' she asked, coming back to his side. 'Matthew!' Glancing panic-filled at the door behind her, she shook him. He didn't respond. His breathing was awful, laboured. 'Matthew!' She shook him hard. 'What do I *do* with it?'

Mathew dragged heavy-lidded eyes open, the look in them:

absolute desperation.

'I need ...' he tried, and stopped. It was barely a whisper, accompanied by another rattling wheeze.

'What?' *What* did he need? 'Matthew!'

Matthew swallowed, and coughed, his whole chest and shoulders seeming to heave as he did.

*He needs to breathe. He'll die if he doesn't.*

'I know!' Quashing down her rapidly rising panic, Ashley looked at the inhaler clutched in her hand. Seeing how the shape fitted between her thumb and forefinger, she pressed the little canister inside it down, saw the medication spurt into the air, then, 'Got it!' she cried, triumphant.

Swiping her hair from her face, she pressed it between his lips. 'Breathe, Matthew,' she pleaded quietly. '*Please* breathe.'

Praying in earnest, Ashley waited until he pulled another shallow breath in and then pressed it sharply, simultaneously. Would it work? Would that teensy puff of stuff help? Holding her own breath, she waited again, watching him carefully, as he sucked air into his lungs, short breaths in, sharp pants out, then, 'Again,' he said.

Immediately doing as he asked, Ashley repeated the procedure and then sat back on her haunches, studying him intently. Hearing his breaths slow, become deeper, quieter, normal, she couldn't quite believe it.

'Did it work?' She stared at him incredulously, as his eyes at last focussed on hers.

'It worked,' Matthew assured her, relief swiftly followed by undisguised terror flooding his features.

'Where's Becky?' he asked, immediately attempting the impossible task of sitting up with his arms still cuffed behind him.

'She's okay,' Ashley assured him quickly, as she reached to assist him. 'He cut her down. She's ... not hurt.'

Matthew nodded and gulped back hard, 'Where has he taken her?' he asked her, his words strangulated, as if he was struggling to contain his emotion.

'Out there.' She nodded towards the door, where the freak had dragged Becky screaming and kicking, fighting him with every fibre of her being. That's when Ashley had decided she would keep fighting too, whatever Matthew had done.

Matthew looked at her as she turned her gaze back to him.

'Ashley,' he said, holding her gaze, now clearly working to keep his voice calm, 'he's lying. You know that, don't you?'

Ashley looked uncertainly back at him, searching his eyes. He had nice eyes, dark eyes, but not dark evil, like the freak's. Matthew's eyes were kind. They had a little twinkle in them when he smiled. Or they had, before. Now all she could see was deep-rooted fear. There was determination there too, though, Ashley could see, as he continued to study her. She nodded slowly. 'Trying to mess with my head, you mean?'

'Exactly that.' Again, Matthew's relief was obvious. 'He's trying to divide us, psychologically. Turn us against each other. Do you understand?'

Ashley nodded more assuredly. 'He's a freak,' she said, firmly wishing there was a way to loop that leash around his neck, as he had Matthew's, and yank it until his eyes bulged.

'That he is.' Matthew nodded weakly and attempted to move, wincing with pain as he did. 'So do we let him?'

# CHAPTER TWENTY-FIVE

'Take me with you,' the woman said, as Patrick checked the rope around her ankles.

Surprised, but only briefly, Patrick glanced up to where she was perched on the bumper of the car he'd paid cash for. She wouldn't get in quietly, he guessed. She could try the patience of a saint, this one. Patrick didn't consider himself a saint exactly, but she'd be enough to test any man. He'd be glad to get shot of her, drive her off to some secluded spot and dump her. Once he'd gone back and knocked the fight out of the other little bitch, that was. And checked the copper hadn't snuffed it. He still needed him, for now. No doubt Adams' bank would have auto-logged him out. Should have made him write his online banking details down. That was short-sighted. Careless. It wasn't like Patrick to be careless. Mind you, with these two silly tarts messing with his head, acting coy one minute and trying to claw his eyes out the next, it was no wonder.

'Take me with you,' she repeated. 'On your boat.'

Patrick laughed derisorily. 'You really do think I'm stupid, don't you?' Shaking his head, he stood up, now looking down at her bemusedly. She was taking the piss, as bold as brass. She definitely had some bottle though. He had to hand it to her.

'On the contrary, I think you're very clever,' she said, meeting his eyes, a determined look in her own.

Which was supposed to mean what? Mind games, he thought. She was playing with him. Well, he had news for her. He was cleverer than she knew, by far. And he'd had more practice than her. His old man had been *the* world expert at building people up and then knocking them down, in particular Joe and him. She was wasting her breath, which she really ought to be saving. She was probably going to be in that boot an awful long time before anybody stumbled across her.

'Zip it,' he said. 'And stand up, or it'll be worse for hubby.'

'Hah!' she spat, as he assisted her non-too-gently to standing. 'Do you think I *care*?'

Feigning interest, Patrick looked at her curiously. 'Well, do you?'

Boldly, she notched up her chin.

Patrick cocked his head to one side, quietly amused, wondering how far she was going to go with this little charade.

'It's his fault! All of this! The selfish bastard! Always thinking about work, work, work. Even after Lily...' She stopped, a swallow sliding down her neck. Pretty neck, Patrick thought, slender, white, tempting. Shame about the rope marks.

'He killed her! Him and his bloody job. Do you really think I give a flying fuck what you do to *him?*'

Patrick watched on, as she acted her little heart out. She was good. He'd give her that.

'All I ever wanted... after Lily...' She stopped again, choking back a sob. *Very good.* Patrick almost felt like applauding '... was a warm body up close. Someone to hold me, comfort me. He couldn't even do that.' The last was said with bitter-edged contempt.

Oscar material, definitely. Patrick's mouth curved into a smirk.

'What? Not so hot in the sack, then, our super-hero detective?'

'He ...' she paused, glancing up at him, her huge saucer eyes all teary and distraught '... has other needs.'

Patrick knew it! None of the girls had ever coughed up to it, but he bloody well knew it. The copper had been taking advantage, taking liberties, with *his* girls. And *he'd* had the balls to take the moral high-ground? Call *him* a sick bastard? Patrick wasn't best pleased. Not pleased at all. That piece of information would earn Adams a more painful death.

'Right.' Patrick propped his gun on his shoulder. He wasn't overly pleased with her either, taking him for a complete moron. 'Yet, here you are, with child,' he pointed out the obvious flaw in her cunning little scheme.

Blimey. He looked her over as she dropped her gaze. *She blushes like she's the bleeding Virgin Mary or something.* 'Immaculate conception then, was it, sweetheart?' He smirked sarcastically.

'Fertility Clinic conception, actually.' She looked back at him, a hint of embarrassment in her eyes. 'He doesn't even know yet.' Cue more teary eyes. 'Probably won't even care.'

Patrick guffawed at that. He couldn't help himself.

'You mean the not-so-great detective can't even get it up?' Oh, dear, dear, that was an interesting turn of events. *Poor Adams.* Obviously, he had one or two problems in the bedroom department, which might explain why he was paying for it. Or rather, not paying. Patrick's humour evaporated. *Helping himself is what Adams had been doing.* Abusing his position and hiding his dirty little secrets from his wife. *Payback time, most definitely.*

'I hate him,' she sniffled.

'Stand in line, darling,' Patrick drawled. 'Come on, time to tuck you up.'

She glared defiantly at him. 'I hate *you!*'

'I'm broken-hearted.' Patrick reached for her arm and pulled her up.

'Bastard!'

'You're overstepping the mark, sweetheart,' he warned her, close to losing his rag.

'And I suppose you're going to keep me in line, are you, great big man that you are?' she challenged him, which intrigued Patrick, given her current predicament.

He studied her, noting all that untamed hostility and fire in her eyes. He'd have tamed her, all right. She wouldn't be bad-mouthing him all over the show, if she was his wife.

'Actually, you'd be surprised.' He looked her over languidly. 'I wouldn't have had to fuck you twice to get you pregnant, let's put it that way.'

She looked a bit flustered then, lowering her gaze again, pretending coy. She should go to acting school. She really should. Or, should he say, *should have*. It was entertaining, though. Patrick was beginning to wonder if he shouldn't play along. *He'd* pay to see the copper's face if she spouted that lot in front of him. Adams also didn't know she was pregnant, it seemed. So why had he come? If relationships were this bad between them, why had the copper come to her rescue? Could it be that it *was* the girl he was after? *Interesting. Very.*

'Would you like me to prove it?' he asked, nudging her chin up with the barrel of his gun and searching her eyes, a definite 'come on' therein, he noted.

Why not? Patrick thought, testing the water and leaning in to taste her. Definitely game, he realised, feeling a rush of excitement as she panted out a soft breath.

*Quid pro quo*, copper, he thought, pressing his mouth harder against hers, lingering awhile, tempted, almost, to push his tongue in her mouth. But, no. The bitch might just bite it off. 'So, what do you say, sweetheart?' He smirked as he pulled away. 'Would you like me to show you how it should be done? Or how about we show hubby how, hey?'

That had called her bluff. She looked flummoxed for a second, then, 'Why not?' she said, her huge ocean-blue eyes full of innuendo, causing Patrick to feel a bit flummoxed himself. 'But why don't you pass me his phone first, so we can get this banking transaction done?'

Patrick looked her over narrowly. Now what was she up to? 'Are you telling me you have his password?'

'*Our* password,' she said, with a smug smile. 'I'm not as stupid as I look either, Mr Sullivan.'

Obviously she wasn't. Patrick's interest was piqued afresh, considerably. Well, well, looked as if fate was on his side, after all.

'Sit,' he said, decisively. 'The hands stay tied, until I need you to use them. Any smart moves you'll be saying goodbye to your baby. *Comprendre?*'

# CHAPTER TWENTY-SIX

Sullivan's gaze swept the room as he came back in. Seeing Becky behind him, relief surged through Matthew's entire body. Her eyes were downcast. Her face deathly pale. Dear God, what must be going through her mind? She'd been dragged into this screaming insanity because of *him*. He should have got off the force. He should have killed that *bastard* and done time for it.

What if Becky died, here, now? Panic gripped at Matthew's insides and wouldn't let go. What if Sullivan chose her instead of him to punish further, humiliate murder in cold blood, getting his perverse kicks from doing it in front of him? *Christ,* this could not be happening. Matthew blinked away the sweat from his eyes and tried to focus his thinking. He looked Becky over, attempting to make some kind of contact. Her hands were tied in front of her, Sullivan holding firmly onto her arm. Noting again the blue-black bruise to her cheek, Matthew swallowed back the hatred that was urging him to somehow make a dash for Sullivan. It would do no good. Even if he waited for him to turn his back, with his hands cuffed behind him, Matthew couldn't hope to bring him down, and that gun would be swinging free. No, no way to do it.

'Becky?' he said throatily.

She didn't look up; didn't look at him. Probably too petrified by the thought of what Sullivan might do, what he'd already done, the disgusting piece of scum.

'I see your breathing's less inhibited. Feeling better, are we?' Sullivan's gaze flicked from Ashley, who was sitting quietly against the opposite wall, to Matthew.

Matthew looked him over contemptuously and looked away.

'That was a question, Adams,' Sullivan warned him.

Matthew tugged in a breath. 'Yes,' he answered tightly, knowing that not to would incite more violence and that this time it might not be aimed at him.

'Your little niece been looking after you, has she, Detective? Tending to your every need?' Sullivan's tone was full of its usual nauseating innuendo.

'I'll bet she has, hey, Becky?' he went on, when Matthew didn't respond.

Not demanding answers this time, then, Matthew noted.

Obviously he'd decided to put beating him to a pulp on hold in favour of amusing himself. Matthew waited to see where this was leading. Biding his time until an opportunity presented itself was the only realistic option he had.

'Becky's come to a decision, haven't you, sweetheart?' Sullivan asked then, causing Matthew's gaze to snap back to her.

'She thinks it's time to cough up, don't you, darling? Come on then, Becky. Don't be shy.' Sullivan urged her forwards. 'Tell Matthew the good news.'

*Becky?* Realising he was using her Christian name, rather than the choice derogatory names by which he normally referred to women, Matthew looked narrowly back to Sullivan, whose expression was highly amused.

'Confused?' Sullivan cocked his head to one side. 'I'll enlighten you then, shall I, Adams, since your detecting skills are obviously not as sharp as they should be? She's on to you. Knows you've been dipping your wick where you shouldn't be. So she's doing something about it, aren't you, sweetheart?'

Becky looked at Matthew. Her head high, she looked right at him, her expression ... Matthew couldn't read it. A new kind of panic clutched at his stomach. She seemed to have eradicated all emotion from her eyes. What had he done to her, the sick bastard?

'Well?' Sullivan looked back at her, a self-satisfied smirk on his face. 'Are you going to tell him, or am I?'

Becky kept looking at Matthew, looking almost through him, then, 'I'm leaving you,' she announced—causing Matthew's emotions to collide violently inside him.

'And?' Sullivan prompted her. 'Go on. Don't leave poor hubs on tenterhooks.' He gazed languidly from Becky to Matthew. 'The poor bloke looks as if he's going to have heart failure.'

'I'm going with Patrick.' Becky's gaze didn't falter.

*Patrick?* Matthew swallowed back hard. She was lying, playing for time. Obviously she wasn't going anywhere with him. Clearly the psychopath had coached her, threatened her with God only knew what. She was following instructions, repeating what he'd told her to. But why didn't she give him some sign, anything? She knew him well enough to know he'd read it. Trying to hold onto his own last shred of sanity, Matthew searched her face, desperate now for some way to touch base.

'You can't blame her, Adams, for wanting to protect her unborn baby, now can you?' Sullivan drawled, and let it hang.

'Baby?' She was *pregnant?* Oh, *Christ* ... Matthew's heart slammed against his ribcage. But how did...? Closing his eyes, he clamped his mind down hard on the ridiculous thoughts ricocheting around in his head. It didn't matter how Sullivan knew. All that mattered was getting her out of here, away from that sadistic animal.

'Baby,' Sullivan repeated, propping his gun on his shoulder and strolling casually towards Ashley.

'There's some debate as to whether it's yours, you being, shall we say, challenged in the bedroom department.' He glanced back at him, the gloating look on his face telling Matthew he intended to push his latest pathetic psychological game as far as he could.

'Becky confided in me, see. Told me you couldn't even offer her a little comfort after she lost her kid. Selfish that, Adams. Personally, with a good looking woman like her gagging for it, I'd have gone for sexual counselling, but I suppose you were too busy playing macho man, hey? Too preoccupied with your personal vendetta to give a fuck, no pun intended.'

Matthew's heart lurched painfully in his chest. He was baiting him, picking mercilessly at wide open wounds. Twisting information he'd somehow managed to get hold of. His gaze flicking back to Becky, who seemed to be looking at him but not seeing him, Matthew tried to keep his breathing steady, his thinking focussed away from the lies that were way too near the truth.

Sullivan stopped in front of Ashley, whose head was bent, her hair hiding her face, as she picked at the straw and dust on the floor.

'This one thought you were a bit of a disappointment, too,' he droned disgustingly on, causing revulsion to rise like rancid bile in Matthew's throat. 'Told me you couldn't stay the pace, didn't you, darling?'

Ashley didn't answer. Recoiling further into herself, she kept her gaze fixed downwards.

Crouching in front of her, clearly revelling in her humiliation, Sullivan attempted to nudge her chin up with his gun. The gun that Matthew was itching to relieve him of and shove barrel first down his throat.

'Not talking, hey? Can't say I blame you. Becky's not very happy with you shagging her husband. You're probably wise to keep schtum.'

Smirking, Sullivan got to his feet and strolled back towards Matthew.

'Now, the pressing dilemma is, what to do with you two?' Again he paused, standing over him, sliding the barrel of the gun this time slowly across his cheek. 'I don't need you, Adams, any more than she does. Careless of you to share your bank details with a wife you couldn't be bothered to keep happy, don't y'think?'

Feeling the cold metal brush his temple, Matthew dropped his gaze, his heart thundering inside him. He didn't dare look at Becky now, lest he draw the bastard's attention back to her.

'That ...' Sullivan lunged forward, grabbed a fistful of Matthew's hair and slammed his head back into the wall '... was a fucking question!' He lowered his face, snarling into Matthew's.

Matthew looked into his eyes, eyes swimming with undiluted hatred, those of a raving madman. *Don't react*, he cautioned himself. Play the game. Wait for the bastard to make a mistake.

'Extremely careless,' he confirmed, smiling sardonically as he gave Sullivan what he wanted.

'Correct. But not quick enough.' Sullivan straightened up, his intimidating expression telling Matthew what was coming next.

He didn't use his feet to deliver the blows to his abdomen, as was his wont. Matthew guessed he wouldn't, not when he had a heavier weapon, a sharper, more brutal weapon. The first blow, well-aimed at his solar plexus, knocked the air out of his lungs and winded him completely. Matthew doubled up, searing pain shooting through him, as the butt of the gun landed heavily again.

Wiping a hand across his salivating mouth, Sullivan loomed over him.

'Stand up,' he said calmly.

Gasping, Matthew couldn't even look up, let alone stand up. The bastard knew it.

'Are you deaf as well as pig-ignorant? I said stand up!' Leaning down, Sullivan hooked an arm under Matthew's and attempted to heave him up.

'Oh for ... Useless prat,' he muttered, as Matthew struggled to find any leverage in his legs.

'You,' Sullivan gave up and turned to Ashley, 'help him up. And you ... Becky, sweetheart,' he smiled flatly in her direction, 'take the weight off your pretty feet and sit on the box, yes?' Seeing Ashley was doing as instructed, Sullivan took a step back. Heading for his bag, he checked his mobile for coverage, leaving Ashley to it.

Glancing over her shoulder, making sure his attention was diverted, Ashley leaned quickly in towards Matthew. 'Be ready,' she whispered, close to his ear.

Matthew squinted at her as he managed to get to standing, trying to understand what she was saying, rather than the burning pain ripping through him.

Ashley swivelled her eyes in the direction of the bag, but then dropped her gaze quickly as Sullivan glanced in their direction.

'All right, sweetheart, enough. I said help him up, not kiss him.' Sighing, Sullivan turned his attention back to his phone. 'Go back over there and sit down.'

Shooting Matthew a meaningful look, Ashley backed away.

'Good girl,' Sullivan commented, distractedly watching her progress. 'Behave yourself and I might find a use for ... Ah, bingo, we have a signal.' A slow smile curving his mouth, he waved his mobile in Matthew's direction. 'Doesn't take a detective to work out what's happening next, does it, Adams?'

Pausing, Sullivan crouched to ferret in his bag. 'That's a question, Adams,' he reminded him, as he retrieved his cigarettes.

Matthew smiled derisorily. 'No, Sullivan,' he said, looking in his direction, 'where you're concerned, it doesn't take a detective to work out what's coming next.'

Sullivan nodded, satisfied, though his expression told Matthew he wasn't entirely sure he wasn't being disrespectful. 'Unlike some people, though, who abuse their position to intimidate and bully other people, I don't kick a dog when it's down, Adams. That's why I want you standing. So I can look you in the eye when I end your miserable little life, comprendre?'

Smirking up at him, Sullivan flipped open the lid of the packet— and Matthew did a double-take. He stared disbelieving for a second, as one long-legged spider fumbled its way over the top of the packet, and then his astonished gaze shot towards Ashley.

'I'm just trying to decide whether to let you kiss your wife goodbye,' seemingly oblivious, Sullivan went on, his taunting eyes on Matthew's, as he tipped the packet towards his mouth. 'But then, I don't suppose she wants you ...' Sullivan stopped, the look on his face one of shock, escalating to sheer terror, as the spider plopped neatly onto his face.

Instinctively sealing his mouth closed, he clawed at his cheeks, neck and torso, trying to pluck it off. Realising it had fallen into his lap, he flicked frantically at it, only to find another scurrying over his hand, heading fast for his shirtsleeve. Whimpering, as Matthew looked on, momentarily stunned, Sullivan lost his balance, falling backwards. He saved himself with his arms, but succeeded in jamming his fingers under his gun in the process.

'*Fuck!* He fell all the way then, landing heavily. 'Fuck! Ugly bastards. Get them off me!' Scrambling backwards, he yelped hysterically, as one determined spider ran the length of his lapel. Horror-struck, Sullivan sat up swiftly. Dementedly swatting at his clothes now, the bastard was clearly petrified.

Matthew felt hope rise in his chest. *The gun.* He prayed, moving towards him, his hope to stamp Sullivan, not the spider, into the ground. *Let go of the gun, you son of a bitch.*

But Sullivan was on his feet. The gun still in his hand, he continued to swipe frenziedly at his clothes, glancing down at his trousers—and Becky moved swiftly behind him, looping her tied hands over his head and around Sullivan's neck in one smooth movement.

'The key!' Matthew shouted desperately, propelling Ashley into action.

Ashley wasted no time. 'Top pocket,' Matthew told her where to find it, as Sullivan clawed at his throat with one hand, raising the gun with his other. 'Keep out of his aim, Ashley! Keep to his side!'

Still delving into his pocket, Ashley moved sideways. Two steps away, Matthew did too. Too late. He heard the shot, felt something graze his upper arm, a tingling sensation, pain: not too intense. Matthew didn't falter, but took another step, and then stopped. Sullivan's pain, he imagined, as Sullivan dropped to his knees, would be extremely intense. The kick Matthew had been intending to deliver to his gut wouldn't have been half as effective as the one Ashley had just delivered to the man's balls.

'Aim it straight, Ashley,' Matthew instructed her, as she bent to pluck up the shotgun while Sullivan's hands were otherwise engaged. 'And aim it low.'

'Becky?' Matthew turned his attention to his wife, whose tied hands were still pulling tight under Sullivan's neck. 'You need to let go, Becky,' he said quietly. 'You need to get the key to the cuffs from Ashley.'

Becky wasn't hearing him. She wasn't looking at him. Her gaze was focussed intently on Sullivan. She pulled tighter.

'Becky,' aware that once Sullivan's pain subsided, his first instinct would be to reach up and grab her, Matthew moved carefully towards her, 'Ashley needs our help,' he tried to connect with her. 'Undo the cuffs, Becky, please?'

Could she even hear him? Could his words penetrate the shock and unbearable pain she must be in, override her understandable urge to squeeze the life out of the animal who'd caused it? 'Becky?' he repeated urgently.

She blinked, bewildered, at last looked at him, and the anguish Matthew saw in her beautiful aquamarine eyes cracked his heart wide open.

'The key, Becky,' he urged her softly.

Disoriented, clearly, Becky nodded slowly. Then, relaxing her grip, she slid her hands from under Sullivan's neck and haltingly up over his face. She looked down at him, as Sullivan looked towards Ashley, her expression once again worryingly devoid of emotion. Sullivan's expression Matthew could read. He could almost see the cogs going around in his fetid little mind. He was contemplating making a grab for the gun. Apparently, Ashley was wise to him too, stepping further away from him, as Matthew shouted, 'Becky! The key!'

Becky nodded again, more certainly this time, and moved towards Ashley.

Releasing a hand from the gun, Ashley pressed the key between the thumb and forefingers of Becky's right hand, and then clamped her hold determinedly around the gun again.

'Rest your finger on the trigger, Ashley,' Matthew instructed her quietly. 'Squeeze it—'

'No! Don't!' Sullivan's gaze snapped to Ashley's face. 'Don't tell her to squeeze it, you mad fucker!' Sullivan looked bewildered back to Matthew. 'Are you mental, or what?'

'Squeeze gently, Ashley, just enough to feel the tension.' Matthew ignored him, his attention on Ashley. 'Hold the gun firmly. If he moves even a hair, shoot the bastard.'

'What?' Sullivan gawked. 'You want her done for manslaughter?' He looked frantically between them. 'You'll go to prison, sweetheart. Don't listen to him. He doesn't give a stuff about anyone. Look what happened to you, to her, to his colleague. He—'

'Or his mouth,' Matthew grated. 'One more word, you fucking freak and you're dog-meat. *Comprendre?*'

Though he was willing Becky to hurry, he could feel her shaking as she fumbled with the key. 'Take a breath, Becky, and focus. You can do this.' He kept his tone quiet, his eyes locked on Sullivan's.

Feeling one cuff slacken, Matthew moved fast, one stride and he was clutching hold of the bastard's designer lapels and hauling him to his feet.

'I wasn't going to hurt her!' Sullivan shouted, his voice high-pitched, his expression petrified, as Matthew pulled his face up close to his.

'Either of them, I was going to let them go.'

He was pallid, visibly shaking, Matthew noted. Pathetic piece of scum.

'I didn't touch her,' Sullivan insisted, blinking rapidly. 'I swear, I didn't. It was all bullshit. Ask her, your wife. She'll tell you. I didn't.

I ...' Sullivan trailed off, swallowing hard, as Matthew fixed his furious gaze unflinchingly on his.

Desperately, Sullivan searched Matthew's eyes, in his own palpable terror.

'I didn't,' he repeated faintly, his gaze now darting wildly past Matthew in hopes of rescue. 'Please don't ...' Sullivan swallowed again and glanced down. 'Please ... don't hurt me.'

That was the spark that escalated the fast-burning fuse. His fury building dangerously inside him, Matthew clutched Sullivan's collar tight.

'How many times?' he seethed, twisting the collar still tighter. "How many times did you make people beg, grovel and crawl? You *fucking animal?*'

Sullivan gagged and clawed desperately at the hands at his craw.

Matthew heaved him up, ramming him backwards into the wall. 'How does it feel, *Sullivan?*'

'*Please.*' Sullivan pleaded through a bubble of snot.

'Please what? Stop?' Matthew yanked him forwards. 'Isn't that what they asked you to do, Sullivan? Your victims? Did they beg you to stop? The people you punched and kicked to the floor? Did my *wife?*' He glanced quickly towards Becky, who was sitting with her knees hugged to her chest, rocking silently, shaking; driven half out of her mind.

Matthew tightened his grip. 'Did *she* ask you to stop, you *bastard?*'

Sullivan gagged again, his Adam's apple bobbing in his throat.

'And *did* you stop, Sullivan?'

Sullivan nodded and then shook his head, dazed, confused. Terrified, Matthew thought, with some small satisfaction.

'Which makes you what, Sullivan?' he seethed, so close he could smell the man's fear.

No answer from Sullivan, Matthew shouted, 'That was a *question!*'

'A bully!' Sullivan blurted.

'And?' Matthew waited.

Sullivan's eyes flew wide, scanning Matthew's, uncertain.

Matthew kept his gaze locked firmly on his.

'A coward,' Sullivan finally rasped.

'Louder!' Matthew lifted the man from his feet and slammed him back hard.

'A coward!' Sullivan screamed it.

Matthew sucked in a tight breath, the jagged pieces of his heart twisting painfully in his chest. *He* had the power now. He could kick this excuse of a human being until he *couldn't* crawl, until *he* didn't have breath enough to beg anymore.

'Matthew?' Ashley said uncertainly to his side.

Closing his eyes, Matthew exhaled long and hard, attempting to hold on to the values that separated men from animals. Every part of him wanted to give in to his base instincts and kill this thing parading as a human being with his bare hands. All that had sustained him was the thought of finally being able to crush him, yet, somehow, he couldn't. Slowly, reluctantly, relaxing his grip, he watched as Sullivan crumpled and slid to his haunches, cowering at his feet now, like the weakling he was.

Sullivan blinked up at him, as Matthew struggled to bring his rage down to a controllable level.

'Not so different, are we, Adams?' he said after a second, dragging a hand across his mouth and then looking at him full on.

'You and me, when the chips are down, we do what we have ...' Sullivan trailed off as Matthew reached to take the gun from Ashley, his eyes never leaving Sullivan's.

Aiming it squarely at Sullivan's chest, Matthew looked him over disgustedly. What use were the kind of values that would allow vermin to crawl the streets, he wondered, murderers, child abusers. The punishment would *never* be enough to fit the crime.

'Probably not a lot different, no.' Venom lodged like acid in his windpipe, he dropped the gun pointedly lower.

Noting its target, Sullivan paled. 'Don't,' he croaked, now looking considerably panicked.

'The chips are down, Sullivan.' Matthew gave him a *c'est la vie* shrug.

'You're losing it, Adams,' Sullivan said shakily.

'Yep,' Matthew said simply.

'You won't get away with it,' Sullivan tried, his eyes now fixed on the steady trickle of blood snaking its way down Matthew's arm to plop onto the floor.

'Oh, I think I just might,' Matthew assured him, 'me being a copper and you being a lowlife piece of scum. The thing is, Sullivan, I do have the balls. What I also have, something you haven't had since the day your mother had the misfortune of giving birth to you, is a shred of decency. Compassion, Sullivan. A conscience. Now though, I'm beginning to think that ending your miserable existence is worth losing sleep over. I mean, an eye for an eye and all that. No one could blame me. So, *what d'y'think*, Sullivan? Shall I do the world a favour?'

Sullivan gulped. 'Don't,' he repeated, his voice cracking.

'You didn't answer the question, Sullivan,' Matthew pointed out quietly.

'No!' Sullivan said quickly. 'Don't do this, Adams,' he begged. 'Think of your family.'

'Oh, trust me, I am.' Matthew's jaw tightened. 'Maximum pain, Sullivan,' he promised him.

'For fuck's sake, you're supposed to uphold the law! You can't just shoot me.' Sullivan now looked extremely worried.

But not worried enough, Matthew decided. No contrition, no feelings that were remotely human. 'How sorry are you for killing my daughter, Sullivan?' he asked him, keeping his tone calm.

Sullivan appeared to be struggling for an answer.

'That was a question! You snivelling little *shit!*'

Sullivan jumped, visibly. 'Very!' he answered, sweat popping out on his forehead he didn't dare move to wipe away. 'I didn't mean for your daughter to die. I ...'

Matthew felt the ground shift beneath him. Even the thought of Sullivan thinking about her, made his stomach turn over. Closing one eye, he tensed his finger on the trigger.

'I didn't!' Sullivan shouted. 'It was meant to be a warning. That was all. I swear to God it was. I told the guy to scare your wife, to warn you off. I told him ... *Oh, sweet fucking Jesus.*' Glancing upwards, Sullivan trailed off, relief flooding his features as he obviously noted the distinct sound of rotor blades going round outside.

Evil. Matthew gulped back the sour taste in his throat. The man was pure evil.

'I'm sorry!' Sullivan looked desperately back at him. 'I swear I am. Don't do this, Matthew.'

Matthew cocked his head to one side and considered. 'You forgot the magic word,' he said, at length.

'*Please,*' Sullivan obliged immediately, steepling his hands in front of him. 'I'm not a well man, Matthew. I ...'

'You know, you can be dead irritating sometimes, don't you, Sullivan?' Matthew said evenly.

'I'm not well,' Sullivan repeated desperately. 'I ... I have a brain tumour!'

Matthew's mouth curved into a slow smile. 'Must be your lucky day. I have just the cure.' He levelled the gun.

'I do! I get these headaches!' Sullivan swiped a hand under his nose. 'Really bad. They affect my eyesight, my judgement. It wasn't my fault, Matthew. For pity's sake, show some mercy.'

Mercy? The man who destroyed people's lives, prostituted young girls, pumped them full of drugs, murdered people without compunction was expecting mercy because he had a headache?

Matthew might have laughed, had it not been so sickeningly absurd. 'Shut ... the ... *fuck* ... up, Sullivan,' he grated slowly.

'I have a daughter.' Sullivan clearly didn't *comprehend*. 'I know ... I can imagine how you must have felt, but it wasn't my doing. You *have* to believe me.'

Hearing the whirr of the copter growing louder, Matthew tuned it out. He didn't bother trying to still the images playing staccato through his mind, his daughter's eyes, silently pleading, her blood staining the road crimson, the tiny white coffin; too small, too precious a cargo to let go. He'd carried her in his arms.

'Are you deaf, Sullivan, or just stupid?' he asked, swallowing back the too familiar tightness in his chest.

Sullivan blinked at him, uncertain. 'What?'

'Clearly you're not capable of obeying a simple instruction, are you?'

'I ...' Sullivan looked frantically past him towards the front door.

'Question, Sullivan,' Matthew reminded him.

'Oh God.' Sullivan attempted to wet his lips with is tongue.

'He's not home,' Matthew growled. 'Now answer the fucking question!'

'I ... Yes,' Sullivan answered unsteadily. 'No,' he added quickly. 'I don't know! *Which* question?'

'Stupid, obviously,' Matthew answered it for him. 'You appear to be struggling, so I'll give you another, easier question, shall I?'

Matthew waited, his heartrate escalating, his throat dry and his hands visibly shaking, he waited, and debated. *Had* he got the balls? Was he really going to shoot a defenceless man down on his knees? The man who'd killed his daughter, his unborn child, tormented and tortured his wife? Tugging in a ragged breath, Matthew asked his question.

'I think it's payback time, Sullivan, don't you?'

'*No!* Sullivan yelled, reaching behind him as he attempted to scramble to his feet.

*Shit! The handgun.* 'Say your prayers, you bastard.' Matthew focussed his aim.

And then stopped.

Stunned, he lowered the gun and looked towards Ashley and then back to Sullivan. He would most definitely not be feeling too well now, if the ugly red stiletto heel lodged in his neck was any indication. Matthew guessed from the fountain of blood it had severed a main artery and prevaricated for a split-second longer.

Sullivan's look was one of surprise when Matthew finally shot.

# CHAPTER TWENTY-SEVEN

'He fell awkwardly.' Seated reluctantly in the back of a patrol car, Matthew answered questions around the circumstances of Sullivan's demise vaguely. He needed to be with Becky. *Now.* Swiping agitatedly at the blood and crap on the side of his face, he watched as she and Ashley were helped into the waiting ambulance. His focus was on her. It should always have been. He hoped never to have to think about or hear about Sullivan ever again. He would have to, of course. There would be an enquiry. Mathew's aim, though, was to try to keep Ashley out of it. She needed help. That much was clear. She needed the right help though, and being cross-questioned wasn't it.

'Right.' DCI Davies frowned pensively. 'And this was after you shot him?'

'That's right.' Matthew looked back to where Davies stood outside the car, obviously contemplating the spurious details of his story. He didn't believe him, but the look in the man's eyes told Matthew he wasn't about to dig too deep.

'John, I need to go,' he said, growing more anxious by the second. Once the cavalry had arrived, too late to save Sullivan, fortunately, pandemonium seemed to break out, blue lights and uniforms everywhere. Matthew hadn't had the chance to hold Becky more than briefly, and she'd been frighteningly unresponsive in his arms.

'I need to be with them, John. Surely this can wait?'

Clearly hearing the desperation in his tone, Davies nodded soberly. 'I think you probably do,' he conceded, glancing down at the blood oozing through the wad of gauze wrapped around Matthew's arm.

Nodding, relieved, Matthew immediately heaved himself out of the car.

'Do you need any help?' Davies asked him, stepping aside to allow him to pass.

Pausing, Matthew turned back. 'No, sir, I don't,' he said, eyeing him levelly. 'Not anymore.'

DCI Davies lowered his gaze, at least having the decency to look contrite.

'We'll need statements, Matthew,' he called after him, as Matthew headed for the ambulance. 'As soon as you're able.'

'You'll get them,' Matthew assured him. They would go in together, as a family. Once they'd given all the information that was needed, he was taking a sabbatical, rather than enforced gardening leave. A long one. His wife needed him. God willing, she still wanted him. Matthew prayed that Becky and he could get through this intact.

He glanced worriedly at her as he climbed into the ambulance. Still she was quiet, subdued, not looking at him. Ashley was knotting and unknotting her fingers, her head bent, her hair hiding her face.

The paramedic offered him a sympathetic smile.

'It's a bit of a squeeze, but I thought you'd all want to travel together,' she said jovially. Attempting some kind of normality, Matthew guessed, as if anything could ever be normal again.

'Thanks.' Glancing again at Becky, whose gaze was fixed on the ligature marks on her wrists, her mind no doubt playing over the horrific scenario she'd just endured, the horrific details of the "accident", Matthew lowered himself carefully onto the bunk next to her. Every bone in his body ached now, every muscle. How much must Becky be hurting?

Would she ever forgive him for not telling her the whole story around Lily's death? How could she? Matthew doubted he'd ever forgive himself. It had been a monumental mistake, one that had almost cost Becky her life. If she'd known about Sullivan, if Matthew hadn't decided to keep the information to himself, she would have been on her guard. He'd thought he'd been protecting her. He'd actually put her directly in the line of fire. He should have trusted her. Instead he'd shut her out.

Looking down at her hands resting listlessly in her lap, Matthew wanted to reach out, but didn't know how. Selfishly, he had no idea how he'd cope if she recoiled from his touch. And she had every right to. He waited instead, hoping that some space was all she needed. *Yeah, right.* He laughed inwardly at his damn, stupid naïvety. That and a whole new life with someone who cared enough to let her in.

Ashley glanced at him, as the ambulance pulled off, dipping in and out of the deep divots in the mud, as it went. 'Okay, Ashley?' he asked her softly.

She nodded uncertainly. 'Emily told me to,' she said, her voice an urgent whisper.

Not sure he'd heard her right, Matthew looked at her curiously. 'Told you to what, Ashley?'

Ashley shrank further into herself.

'The shoe,' she said, her gaze flicking fearfully between Becky and him.

'Right.' Matthew nodded slowly. 'Ashley, who is Emily?' he probed gently.

Ashley shrugged and looked away. 'My sister,' she said, glancing warily back at him. 'You're still bleeding.' She immediately changed the subject, her gaze drifting to the gauze on his arm.

'I know. It's only a flesh wound. It'll mend. We all will, given time.' Matthew smiled reassuringly, though he was reeling inside. She had a sister? Which meant Kristen had had another child? *Christ.* He really had been emotionally missing, hadn't he? Too wrapped up in himself to see anyone else.

Growing more aware of his failings, on all fronts, Matthew glanced back to Becky. She didn't return his glance, didn't speak. Swallowing back the pieces of his heart, which seemed to be wedged like a thousand shards of glass in his windpipe, Matthew dropped his gaze, mentally playing over each and every one of his failures. He *should* have been there. *Dammit.* Dragging a hand across his eyes, he prayed hard, hoping if there was any kind of god up there, he would make sure Becky, a woman who'd given so much of herself, would survive this, with or without him. He'd been labouring under the illusion he was being strong. He'd been wrong. There was no strength in silence, shutting his emotions away, allowing his anger to fester.

He should have *been* there, building a new life together with the woman he would gladly have died for rather than live without. Becky was the strong one. Stronger than he'd ever been. She'd tried to understand his self-centred preoccupation with his work. She'd been there, for him, always. Now it was his turn to help her. To make sure she got through this, somehow. To make sure he was there. If he'd lost her, then so be it. He would still be there, wherever and whenever she might need him. That much Matthew promised himself.

'Is he dead?' Finally, Becky spoke, her tone so quiet she was barely audible.

Overwhelmingly relieved, Matthew snapped his gaze to her. 'Yes,' he said, uncertain, even after all she'd been through, how she would emotionally process the fact.

Becky fell silent again. 'The gunshot?' she asked, after a minute.

Matthew glanced at Ashley. 'The gunshot,' he confirmed, holding her gaze briefly before turning back to Becky.

Slowly, Becky nodded. Matthew watched her intently, as she drew in a long breath and held it. Hesitantly, he reached to wrap his good arm around her as she dropped her gaze to her lap. Easing her gently to him as her shoulders sagged, he waited, hope surging through him as she leaned into him. He felt the shudders run through her, heard the sob catch in her throat, saw the tears, hot and wet on her cheeks, as she looked at him.

Seeing the myriad of emotions in her eyes, shock, deep-rooted sorrow, relief, Matthew caught a lump in his own throat.

'Did I ever tell you how much I love you?' he asked her hoarsely, uncertainly. He scanned her face, bruised and swollen, but still she was beautiful, the same beautiful woman he'd fallen in love with and never dared hope might love him back. Could she now, still? He wished he could kiss her tears away, were it so easy, that he could hold her and keep her safe forever. That he had, instead of being blind, insensitive to anybody's pain but his own.

Becky searched his eyes, then, 'Ditto.' She swallowed, turned to bury her face in his shoulder and cried harder.

# CHAPTER TWENTY-EIGHT

It didn't take long for Matthew to piece things together. Ashley had been as adamant about the day her sister had disappeared from her life as she was that she'd had a sister. It had been Ashley's birthday, apparently, when Kristen had walked out on her.

The child, Emily, had finally been identified as a girl, now in long-term foster care, abandoned as a toddler in a hospital A&E. Ashley, it seemed, had simply refused to let go of her. He'd yet to broach the subject of ongoing counselling with Ashley, whose symptoms—trouble discerning dreams from reality, seeing things and hearing voices—pointed to childhood schizophrenia. It wasn't going to be easy to convince her about counselling and ongoing psychiatric care. Not only was Ashley strong-willed, but she simply refused to believe that admitting to having problems wouldn't mean she'd end up back in care. Matthew, somehow, had to first convince her it was manageable. That she was wanted, her, for who she was, that being different wasn't something she should be ashamed of.

Finding Kristen took a little longer than he'd expected. Then he'd had to tail her, making sure to pick his moment to confront her. Thereafter the rest was up to her. She had a trust fund waiting for her, a daughter who might possibly want something to do with her, another she might not see again, but who was healthy and happy. Watching her from where he sat, freezing cold, on yet another windy canal embankment, Matthew waited. She was alive, still breathing, stirring occasionally as dawn broke. He doubted she'd be sober when she eventually woke, but she wouldn't be totally inebriated either. He might get through to her. He might not. Knowing he had been emotionally missing when she needed him though, Matthew had to give it one last try.

Kristen stirred again, wriggling, like a caterpillar in her sleeping bag, as a gust of wind sharp enough to strip the bark from the trees whistled through the tunnel. Blowing into his hands to warm them, Matthew let her be. He needed her to be fully awake, under her own steam, and paying attention.

Finally, a narrowboat chugging past lurched her to consciousness.

'Bloody thing,' she muttered, burying herself deeper in her bag and tugging it over her head.

Matthew waited a little longer.

'Kristen,' he said then, loud enough for her to hear. He didn't stand, but waited patiently again.

The top of her head appeared first, followed by her furrowed forehead and heavy-lidded eyes. 'Matthew?' she muffled, blinking blearily at him.

'One word,' Matthew got to his feet, 'Emily.' He let it hang, assessing her reaction carefully.

Kristen just stared at him, her eyes rounded and filled with guilt, swiftly followed by the belligerence Matthew had seen too many times before.

'You have an appointment,' he said, holding his temper and placing a card on the ground next to her. 'Alcohol recovery and mental health services. Be there, Kristen, or I won't be ever again.' With which Matthew turned away.

'I knew she'd be safe!' Kristen blurted behind him.

Matthew conceded that much. In leaving her at the hospital, Kristen had done her best, given her addiction, ergo lack of caring skills, to make sure she was. That had been the deciding factor when Becky and he had discussed whether to try again to seek her out.

'I thought she'd be better off,' Kristen added, as he slowed. 'I mean she'd have to be wouldn't she, anywhere but with me.'

Matthew hesitated, then turned around. Whatever she said next would be the crucial comment, the one that would persuade him to keep caring, to keep tearing himself up over her.

Kristen looked at him, looked down under his unflinching gaze, dragged a hand under her nose.

'Is she all right?' she asked hesitantly, looking back at him after a second. Her expression told Matthew all he needed to know, the beseeching look in her eyes. She cared. In there somewhere she did actually care what had happened to her kids.

'She's safe,' he assured her. 'You did that much for her. Get your act together, Kristen. There's help out there. Here, too. But you have to want it.'

Kristen glanced away again, her face resolute and uncertain in turn, her willpower already doing battle with her demons, Matthew guessed. He watched while she chewed doggedly on a fingernail. 'Well?' he asked her.

No answer. No surprise. Matthew sighed and turned away, this time for the last time. He'd done his best. He wasn't going to force march her there. Not again.

'Wait!' Kristen stopped him. 'Walk with me,' she asked him, 'to the centre.'

Matthew debated, checking his watch, as if that could tell him when the baby might come. *Hell,* now what did he do?

'Please?' Kristen said, scrambling out of the sleeping bag behind him. 'It's only a short walk.' She grabbed up her meagre belongings and stumbled towards him. 'You've come this far ...'

That he had. Matthew ran a hand over his neck.

'Okay.' He relented, with a sigh. 'Just as far as the centre, though, Kristen. After that, it's up to you. I have to get back.'

'Why?' Kristen asked, struggling to keep step with him as Matthew set a brisk pace, checking his mobile for messages as he walked.

'Ashley has a psychiatric appointment,' he said, deciding that much information couldn't hurt, given Kristen was interested.

Kristen's step faltered. 'How is she?' she asked, no hint of indifference this time.

'Good,' Matthew said, and turned to reach for the rucksack she was struggling with.

'Is she in school?' Kristen was now almost running to keep up with him, as Matthew resumed walking.

'Yep.' He checked his watch again. 'But not today. She's standing in in lieu of the expectant father, which is why I can't hang about.'

'Do you think she'll ever want to see me again?' Kristen almost blurted that question out.

Matthew thought about it. 'Honestly, I don't know. Maybe, in time. Like I say, it's up to you, Kristen. You need to get sober. I'll make an effort to be around, but only if you ...' Matthew stopped, realising he was talking to himself.

Glancing back he gathered Kristen had also stopped. 'You're having a baby?' she asked, her expression now stunned, her sleeping bag clutched to her chest.

'Imminently.' Mathew reached for his mobile, checking that again too.

Kristen blinked at him in wonder, as he looked back at her.

'Oh, Matthew, that's fantastic news.' She smiled. The first time Mathew had seen her smile properly in a very long time, reminding him of the girl she once was. A scrawny little thing in her teens, she'd been amazingly pretty. Still was, even with the crew cut, when she was sober.

'I'm so proud of you, you know. I know I slag you off and give you grief,' she shrugged embarrassedly, 'but just so you know.'

'Ditto,' Matthew said, nodding meaningfully towards the location of the drop-in centre.

****

'Are you sure you're not about to go into labour?' Matthew asked, noting the size of Becky's considerable and low bump, as he pulled on a fresh shirt.

Rebecca paused in her attempts to tie her hair up in a topknot. Matthew wished she wouldn't. He loved it tumbling down her back in all its fiery auburn glory.

'Um, hold on, I'll just check.' She glanced at him through the bedroom mirror, a wry smile on her face and then bent to address her tummy. 'Hullo, little bump. Daddy wants to know when we're expecting you.'

'You're taking the pee, Mrs Adams.' Matthew smiled, walking across to wrap his arms around her, as she straightened up.

'And you're worrying too much.' Becky gave him a mock-scowl. Be gone,' she said, 'before I have you arrested for ogling naked, pregnant women.'

'It'd be worth it.' Dropping his hands to her tummy, Matthew planted a soft kiss on the nape of her neck. 'You sure you're going to be OK?'

Becky twizzled in his arms. 'Fine,' she assured him. 'I'm pregnant, not made of porcelain. I think I can manage to waddle as far as the phone if I need you.'

'Not too much waddling. You're supposed to be resting,' Matthew reminded her, his gaze straying to her succulent lips, also naked, fresh out of the shower and begging to be kissed. 'Did I ever tell you you're beautiful?' He gave in to temptation and pressed his mouth lightly against hers.

'Often,' Rebecca assured him. 'You're an excellent liar.'

Matthew was about to say, would I ever, but mindful that he hadn't been wholly truthful in the past, caught himself. But for Ashley, he might have lost her. Why Becky had stayed with him, still loved him—and she did, it was right there in her beautiful aquamarine eyes, Matthew couldn't fathom. One thing he was sure about, though, was his absolute love for this woman: his wife, his friend, his lover, the mother of his children. Never again, would he lose sight of the fact that she was the most important thing in his life, the one constant, his anchor. If there was anything good to take away from that godforsaken day, it was that it had made Matthew more determined to be the best husband and father he could be, to make sure every decision that was made was made jointly, to be there, one hundred percent, emotionally, physically. His family was his priority. It should always have been.

'You'd better go,' Becky murmured, as his lips involuntarily found their way to the soft curve of her neck.

'I know, just ...' Matthew strayed lower. Tempted by her far-too-enticing bare breasts, he took one inviting nipple into his mouth, sucking gently, circling with his tongue, until a low moan escaped her.

'I could do unspeakable things to you, right now,' he whispered huskily, finding her lips again with his own, his need growing, considerably, as she dipped the pink tip of her succulent tongue into his mouth.

God, if only she knew how much he wanted to sweep her up in his arms, lay her down on the bed and make tender sweet love to her. She was so desirable like this, he couldn't keep his hands off her. Sensual lovemaking, however, possibly wasn't on the agenda, given his wife was now past her due date. Aware he might be a little over-demanding, Matthew eased reluctantly away.

'Now *that*, DI Adams,' Becky breathed, blinking hazily up at him, 'is just plain unfair.'

'I know,' Matthew smiled, tempted now to throw caution to the wind and kiss every delectable inch of her, 'but you love it.'

'I do, frequently,' Becky assured him, grazing a thumb lightly across his mouth. 'However,' Her gaze flicked to the bedside cabinet, on which sat the alarm clock.

'*Crap.*' Matthew squeezed his eyes closed, realising he was about to make Ashley late for her first appointment. 'Sorry,' he said, turning to grab up his watch. 'Reluctant though I am, I have to go.'

'As I pointed out to you before you took advantage of me.' Becky gave him her best admonishing look.

Matthew smiled. 'I didn't,' he said, slipped on the watch and then reached to finish buttoning his shirt. 'Did I?' He looked worriedly back up.

Becky laughed, that gorgeous sexy laugh, deep in her throat.

'No,' she assured him, with a roll of her eyes.

'Go.' Flapping him towards the door, she reached for her dressing gown from the bed.

'I'm gone.' Matthew collected his jacket and headed for the door.

'Got your inhaler?' Becky reminded him.

Matthew patted around his pockets. 'Yep. Catch you later.' He glanced at her over his shoulder, not quite able to believe he was about to leave unfinished business in the bedroom with his wife invitingly, gorgeously naked.

'Love you,' Becky said, as he disappeared onto the landing.

'Ditto,' Matthew called behind him, then, 'Ashley,' he shouted down to where she was watching TV. 'We have to go. Are you ready?'

Becky was slipping into her dressing gown when he peered back in. *Gorgeous.* Matthew watched her for a second.

'I love you. More than my life,' he amended softly, walking across to her to give her a parting kiss.

'You too, bump.' He bent to place another kiss on her tummy. 'Behave yourself,' he said, addressing it firmly, then turned again for the door.

'We'll do our best, but we can't promise,' Becky called after him. 'Drive carefully, Matthew.'

※※※

Matthew sighed and glanced back to the windscreen. No amount of persuading seemed to convince Ashley that psychiatric care didn't mean she would end up back in care.

'Ashley, you're staying with us, okay?' he tried again, vying for her attention with whatever she was plugged into on her phone.

'Given it's what you want, your home will always be with us, you know that. Or you should.'

He decided not to go over old ground. Guilt over *the freak* as she'd labelled him, he'd managed to persuade her was wasted emotion. That bastard had pushed her to the limit, he'd told her that. Convinced her that no one would have blamed her. At least, he hoped he had. Matthew certainly hadn't wasted too much time worrying over Sullivan. The forensics on the nail file coming up with no incriminating DNA had shaken him to the core, making Matthew wonder if he really was as much a cold, sadistic killer as Sullivan had been. He would have taken the shot. Knowing no other way of ensuring his family wouldn't live in constant fear of their lives, whether Sullivan was banged up or not, he would have shot to kill, making it definitely murder in Matthew's mind. Since that day, though, when he'd agonised about whether he'd made the right decision regarding Ashley's part in it, seeing their baby grow, seeing Ashley grow emotionally, despite this latest blip, he'd called it *quid pro quo* and tried to relegate it to history.

The dreams would always haunt him. Becky too, who still cried in her sleep. Ashley he wasn't sure about. *Christ,* he hoped he'd made a right decision that day.

'Ashley?' He glanced sideways at her.

Concentrating on scraping the black polish from her thumbnail, Ashley only dropped her gaze further.

'The condition is manageable, Ashley,' Matthew tried to alleviate her fears, but wasn't quite sure how. She'd gone quiet on hearing the diagnosis, which meant the psychiatric assessment hadn't gone as well as it might.

'With counselling and the right medication, we can do this; together, as we discussed. You will need to go to your follow-up appointments, though. Do you think you can do that?'

So far, so good. Matthew sighed again, despairingly, as Ashley turned her attention away from him to glance out of the side window. He wasn't doing such a great job on the parenting front if he couldn't even communicate with her, was he?

'Ashley?'

Still, Ashley didn't look at him. 'I don't want to.' She shrugged moodily.

That much Matthew had gathered.

'Okay, so,' he ran a hand over his neck, 'talk to me, Ashley. Tell me why. I promise I'll do my best to understand.'

Ashley said nothing for a while, then, 'You can't. You don't.'

Matthew wasn't quite sure what to say to that.

'No, I probably don't,' he conceded, 'but I want to. Talk to me ...' Matthew stopped, his eyes shooting worriedly to his hands-free as his mobile rang. Seeing it wasn't Becky, he hesitated, but then *being there* meant being there for Steve too. He owed the man, big time. 'One minute,' he said apologetically to Ashley and took the call.

'All right, boss?' Steve said, sounding chipper. Matthew truly was in awe of how he always did. Even when Matthew had first seen him at the hospital, flat on his back, in a brace for at least five weeks, still Steve's droll sense of humour had been intact.

'Yep, good,' Matthew assured him. 'Still expecting.' He gave him an update on his imminent fatherhood.

'Blimey, she's determined to hang on to that one, isn't she?'

'Definitely.' Matthew smiled, recalling how Becky had clawed her way back from the brink, determined to be there, for Ashley, for him, to stay healthy for the sake of their baby. He was in awe of her, too. Always would be.

'Sorry, Steve, can I call you back?' he asked. 'I'm just in the middle of something with Ashley.'

'Oh, right, no problem. It was just to let you know we got it: the dog kennels and rescue centre out in Worcestershire. It's pretty spot on for what we want. The living accommodation is the pits, though, so if you fancy a little DIY sometime? Assuming you have the time, that is?'

'I'm your man,' Matthew assured him, although he wasn't entirely sure he was into viewing dilapidated properties.

'Excellent.' Steve, who still struggled with some pain, but was determined not to give into it, sounded well-pleased.

'I'll catch you later. Good luck with the sleepless nights.'

'Cheers, Steve.' Reminded of the downside to new parenthood, Matthew smiled and rang off. 'So,' he turned his attention back to Ashley, 'are we talking?'

Still nothing but mute silence.

'Ashley? You need to help me out here. I can't help you unless you talk to me. Can't you at least tell me why you're so adamant you won't go to the appointments?'

Ashley drew in a breath, physically drawing up her shoulders. 'Because they'll think I'm loopy,' she said, immediately deflating again.

Matthew wasn't sure what to say there either. 'You have mental health issues,' he opted for. 'It's not a crime. Most of the population does at some time or...'

'Do you really want someone with mental health issues around your new baby?' Ashley said then, flooring him completely.

Matthew considered: how the hell was he supposed to respond to that? Truthfully, he supposed.

'Okay, I'm going to be blunt here, Ashley, because I think you're mature enough to realise why. I've seen too many runaways your age, too many broken spirits, broken bodies, to allow that to happen to you. Yes, I do want you around. *We* want you around and not out of some misguided sense of duty or moral obligation. You're family. We're related by blood and, while I might not be your father, I am your uncle, and I love you. Becky and I—'

'Matthew, stop!!' Ashley cut in determinedly.

Right. Matthew shook his head. That worked. So where did he go from here?

'Ashley... You have to trust us. I know it's not easy but—'

'Matthew! *Stop!* Ashley screamed it this time.

Mathew couldn't quite believe it when the dashboard died, causing someone to plough into the back of them as the car rolled to a stop. He was less able to comprehend the juggernaut jumping the traffic lights directly in front of him. If he'd gone on, he realised, his heart flipping over in his chest, there would have been nothing left of his car but scrap metal.

THE END